REVIVE ME

PART ONE: THE ACT

J.L. SEEGARS

❀ Created with Vellum

To the survivors who hid their wounds and built something beautiful
out of the destruction

"In all the world, there is no heart for me like yours. In all the world, there is no love for you like mine."

— MAYA ANGELOU

AUTHOR NOTE

Please be aware that this story involves sensitive topics such as rape (off-page, no graphic description and not between the couple), maternal mortality, grief, nightmares, emotional and reproductive abuse (not between the couple) and a brief mention of suicide ideation. Although many of these situations are referenced in the work, and happen off-page, I still advise you to consider your own health and well-being before diving into the first part of Mallory and Chris' story.

I also want to take a moment to remind you that this is only the beginning of Mallory and Chris. There won't be a happy ending for them in this book, but I promise you it's coming.

THE PLAYLIST

01./ Bleeding Love by Leona Lewis
02./ When I See U by Fantasia
03./ Diary by Alicia Keys
04./ Make You Feel My Love by Adele
05./ Complicated by Nivea
06./ Smash into You by Beyoncé
07./ There Goes My Baby by Usher
08./ And I by Ciara
09./ teachme by Musiq Soulchild
10./ Impossible by Shontelle
11./ Take a Bow by Rihanna

1

MALLORY

I t was supposed to be a simple kiss.

A brief, awkward pressing of lips together in front of a crowd of people—which unfortunately included my twin brother—that wouldn't last for more than ten seconds. Ten seconds. That was it. Ten seconds of holding my mouth to a mouth that I've thought about more than I should have over the last year. A mouth I happened to be staring at when Sloane, my brother Eric's girlfriend and my *former* best friend as of sixty seconds ago, called my name and asked me the most juvenile question known to man. She was a drunk and giggling mess, perched on Eric's lap with his arm wrapped around her waist and our best friend since diaper days, Nic, frowning in her direction as she hiccuped between every word.

Truth. Hiccup. *Or.* Hiccup. *Dare.* Hiccup. *Malllll?*

I chose dare because....well, I don't exactly know why I chose dare. It was out of character for me, which is probably why every eyebrow in the room lifted in surprise when I made my choice, voice laced with confidence I wasn't used to feeling anymore. The only person who didn't look surprised was Sloane. She had a mixture of pride and mischief etched into her features, and the moment I saw her eyes flick over to the same face I'd just dragged my gaze away from, I knew I was in trouble.

Her dare was a simple one—*Kiss Chris, on the lips, for at least ten seconds*—but from the way my heart sank into my stomach, you'd have thought she dared me to dive head first off of the apartment building we were currently partying in. It wasn't even the worst dare that'd been issued tonight, just a few rounds ago, someone was dared to strip naked and run a lap around the building in the bitter January air, but it felt like the worst thing that I could have been asked to do, especially in front of Eric and Nic, whose groans of displeasure could be heard over the sound of my blood rushing through my skull as I watched Chris cross the room over to me.

I was sitting on a barstool at the island in his kitchen. A chair I watched him and Eric put together just a few days ago when we helped him move into The Emerson—one of the more expensive apartment buildings close to campus. The ones that all the trust fund babies move into when they're no longer required to live in the dorms. It's a nice building, all glass and metal, and modern finishes that make it clear not everyone can afford to live here. Despite his patented lighthearted demeanor, Chris looks like he belongs here. Among the marble tile, stainless steel appliances, and immaculate hardwood floors that bespeak solemnity and wealth. Something about the aesthetic here brings out a warm air of sophistication that swirls around him, and it fits him better than the halls of any of the dorms on campus ever have.

That's what I was thinking of when he stopped in front of me. Chestnut eyes with flecks of honey and bourbon in them tracing my features as he placed his hand on the side of the barstool and turned me completely around to face him. Treating me to an up-close view of that classic Chris smile that reminded me that I've never seen him take anything seriously. He's always smiling, laughing, and joking his way through life, completely oblivious to the reality the rest of the world just has to deal with, so it shouldn't have surprised me he would approach a literal child's game the same way.

My knees brushed his hard thighs, and I felt every eye in the living room on us as he leaned in close, resting his palms on the edge of the island. His body stretched over mine, blocking out my view of the crowd behind me. Not that I cared that I couldn't see them. I was too focused on the way his smile was fading, shifting into a complex mask devoid of humor and mirth. I'm shocked at how quickly he does it. Goes from being the capricious guy I've known him to be to...*this.*

"Make it good for her, Chris!" Someone behind him shouted, laughing loudly, and I half expected him to turn around and say something stupid and cocky and completely on brand for a guy who, as far as I can tell, has never met a woman he doesn't want to take to bed, but his eyes stayed on me. Soft. Serious for once in his life.

"Nervous?" He asked, eyes on my teeth digging into my bottom lip.

"Nope. Why would I be nervous?"

His brows lifted, amusement slipping over whatever conflicted emotion was shining in his irises just moments ago. "Because you don't really do this kind of thing."

"What kind of thing?" I tried to sound casual, but my voice wavered a little. "Play truth or dare?"

"Get roped into kissing random people at parties."

He wasn't wrong even though it felt like he was sugarcoating it a little. The truth of the matter was, I didn't kiss anyone. Not at parties. Not anywhere. Because the worst decisions I've made in my life have been sealed with a kiss.

Get ready to add this one to the list. The snarky voice in my head quipped as Chris waited for my response, completely unbothered by the restless crowd behind him begging us to get on with it already. "Are you a random person?" I arched a brow, sass coating each word.

"No, I guess not," he answered, letting me sidestep the point he was attempting to make.

"Then I guess we should kiss before they start to riot."

"Yeah, I guess we should."

I watched his face move closer, and his breath skated across my skin as I fought the very real urge to let my eyes fall shut. My lungs burned, demanding air that was laced with his earthy scent and protesting when they were denied.

I knew I needed to breathe. I didn't want to run the risk of passing out and giving everyone here another reason to think I was weird. It was bad enough that I didn't date, didn't even engage in the most casual of hookups. Crumbling into a breathless heap the moment the most coveted pair of lips on campus met mine would only make it worse.

Chris lifted one of his hands, bringing it up to my chin and cupping it between his index finger and thumb. With a barely discernible movement, he applied the lightest bit of pressure, forcing me to focus all of my attention on him.

"Breathe," he whispered, the quiet command pulling the trapped air from my lungs and giving me a glimpse of a side of him I'd never seen before.

Dark. Dangerous. *Lethal.*

My eyes went wide, shock winding its way through my chest to mix with the mild panic being held in his gaze sent through me. All at once, I started to doubt the wisdom of going through with this dare, of breaking one of my personal rules to appease a room full of drunk college students playing middle school games to distract them from the spring semester starting in a week, but before I could say or do anything to take it back, Chris' lips crashed down on mine.

Taking me by surprise that was equal parts delight and terror as his tongue slid over my bottom lip asking for more. My chin was still in his grip, which meant I couldn't move if I wanted to, so I gave myself over to it. Over to him.

It was supposed to be a simple kiss, but it's not.

It's an awakening.

It's a million bolts of electricity reviving a stalled heart.

It's a montage of a thousand lifetimes spent in a million reckless, beautiful ways.

It's the best thing that's ever happened to me, and, though I have no way of knowing this for sure, my biggest mistake.

2

MALLORY

"When are you going to forgive me?"

Sloane whines from behind me, her voice a playful, but frantic, plea as she runs to catch up with me. A mass of black curls whip around her face, covering her hazel eyes and light-brown skin for a second. She lets out a low growl of frustration and pushes her hair back behind her ears as she weaves through the crowd behind me. It's the first Friday of the spring semester, and I'm still not completely over the mess she pulled last weekend at Chris' party. I probably would have already forgiven her for exploiting her knowledge of my crush on him so publicly if I wasn't so distracted reliving the damn thing. Reminiscing over the feel of his lips. The way his fingertips dug into my flesh as his tongue swept over mine in slow strokes that demanded things I shouldn't want to give him. Or anyone for that matter.

"Never." I toss the word over my shoulder and speed up, hoping she'll give up and let me continue to make my way to my Principles of Finance course in peace. Due to a last minute change regarding the instructor of the course, I've been nervous about this class all day. Every business major I know signed up for it because they were looking forward to taking it with Dr. Brennan, but now that she's decided to take a sabbatical, we don't know who we'll be dealing with this semester. Jasmine, my suite mate from freshman year, texted me this morning and said she heard Dr. Richardson—an old, frumpy white guy who's research and clothing choices haven't made it past the seventies—took over the course, and I nearly cried because the man hates me. Well, he hates almost every female student who dares to study business. He thinks we're all too emotional and irrational for the field, which is hilarious considering how he's the one constantly throwing tantrums about classroom designations, course offerings and teaching assistant assignments.

"Mal!" Sloane grabs my arm, forcing me to stop and talk to her. "How many times do I have to say I'm sorry?"

"As many as it takes to make me forget the humiliation of kissing someone with a hundred greedy little eyes watching." I glance at my watch, noting that I have less than five minutes to make it across campus and up two flights of stairs. "Maybe even more than that if you make me late for class."

"How about I buy you iced coffee every day for the rest of the semester?"

I purse my lips to hide the smile threatening to break free. She knows how much I love my iced coffees and how much I hate being mad at her. "Throw in a pastry and you've got yourself a deal."

"Done!" She opens her arms and pulls me into a quick hug. "*Now* get to class before I have to get down on my knees and beg your forgiveness for making you late."

Slipping out of her hug, I start to back away, heading in the direction of the lecture hall I'll be in for the next hour. Sloane waves at me through the crowd of people moving around her to make it to their classes, looking relieved that she's finally managed to harass me into forgiving her. Even though I could never truly be mad at her, I'm glad we're good again too, but it doesn't stop me from taking the opportunity to get back at her.

"For future reference," I call out loudly, making sure everyone on the sidewalk can hear me. "You can always stand while you beg me for forgiveness. Save that whole getting on your knees thing for Eric."

Her mouth dropping open and her face turning red is the last thing I see before I turn and rush towards my building, hitting what can only be called a desperate run that thankfully gets me to the classroom before all the good seats are taken. The lectern at the front of the room is still empty, which means the professor hasn't arrived yet, and I breathe a sigh of relief as I settle into a seat on the second row, pulling out a pen and a notebook to look prepared even though I don't necessarily feel it.

Starting off the semester on uncertain footing for one of my major courses has me on edge, and I don't like it. For the last few years, school has been a source of calm consistency for me. A place where I decide the variables and control the outcome. And not only have I appreciated that control, I've *craved* it. I've used it to soothe old wounds and memories of a time when my ability to choose, to decide was ripped from my grasp.

I push the thought away and roll my shoulders back, putting all of my energy into slowing my heart rate only for it to kick right back up when the door to the classroom swings open again and two men walk in. A collective sigh moves through the room, starting at the back and weaving its way through the rows of desks until it reaches the ears of Dr. Richardson who turns his steely gaze on us. Blue-gray eyes, watery with age and hidden behind dirty glasses he's famous for cleaning multiple times over the course of a single lecture, slide over each face in the crowd, and there's no missing the disappointment when they land on me. The frown lines on either side of his thin lips become even more prominent, and I would be upset about it if I wasn't so distracted by the person standing behind him. A familiar six-foot frame, golden brown skin, angular features I've memorized, and jet black hair with curls that are only a few inches off of his scalp.

Chris Johnson.

I haven't seen him since the night of the party almost a week ago, and his presence in this room right now is threatening to send this runaway train completely off the rails. Familiar chestnut eyes sweep over the room, and I'm caught between the desire to disappear altogether and the desperate need to ask him what the hell he's doing *here* in my business course dressed like a fucking banker and standing beside the one professor I prayed wouldn't walk into this room. It takes him all of two seconds to find me, and when our eyes meet I immediately want to look away because there's no way I can hold his gaze without thinking about that kiss, but actually bringing myself to do it feels impossible.

We stare at each other for a second that feels like a minute, and it's Chris that finally looks away, giving me a sheepish smile before turning to make his way over to the desk in the corner that's usually reserved for teaching assistants.

Oh. It dawns on me then. The professional clothes. The sudden appearance in a course that he's already taken as a biology and business double major. He must have traded his resident assistant job for something that would be less demanding than supervising a bunch of eighteen-year-olds living away from their parents for the first time.

Dr. Richardson clears his throat and sets his briefcase down beside the lectern. A hush falls over the crowd, but I can feel the dread in the air. No one in the department likes this guy, and he's about to remind us all why.

"We'll start this first meeting off by stating the obvious. You all enrolled in this course hoping for Dr. Brennan and an easy A, but you got me. As you might already know, I'm Dr. Keith Richardson, and I don't tolerate mediocrity or suffer fools. If you fit into either of those categories then I'm happy to tell you that you have until the end of the day to drop this class and enroll in another, less rigorous, course that will meet your degree requirements."

Somewhere behind me, I hear paper shuffling, the tell-tale sign of some scared student letting the old man's words send them scrambling for the course catalog. A glimpse of perverse satisfaction flickers across Dr. Richardson's face, and I cringe. Professors who take pleasure in scaring students away from their courses have no place in the classroom.

"Those of you who feel brave enough to stick it out—" he continues, leaning down to pull a stack of papers out of his briefcase and handing them over to Chris, "—should prepare yourselves now for a challenging semester."

Tuning him out isn't a conscious decision, but when I realize that I am doing exactly that, I don't make any effort to correct it. Instead, I focus my attention on Chris moving in between the desks on the front row. His long legs and smooth gait reminding me of the easy strides he took when he crossed his living room to come over to me. I wonder if he smells the same way he did that night. If his skin is still that mix of clean sweat and earthy tones I can't quite name. Without even looking around the room, I know that I'm not the only person staring, watching his every move, and maybe even thinking about what it was like to kiss him.

Some of the women around me might even know what it's like to do more than kiss him.

The thought sends heat rushing to my cheeks. I don't know why my brain even went there or why the thought of someone in this room knowing what it's like to have more than ten seconds of physical contact with him makes me feel positively violent. Since last year, when Chris made a point of taking Eric and Nic under his proverbial wing, I've seen him with lots of girls. Girls who have happily climbed into his bed in hopes of becoming a part of his life. A fixture in the small inner circle I was inducted into on my first day here because of my brother.

All of that to say, I've been aware for quite some time now that Chris makes a habit of sleeping around, but before our kiss, I never gave it much thought, and I don't see why that should change now.

It shouldn't.

It doesn't.

It doesn't change a single thing because he's the campus fuck boy. A handsome, charismatic golden boy who's lived a charmed life that's never left him wanting for anything including sexual partners. And I'm….well, I'm the girl who doesn't fuck with fuck boys even, no *especially*, when their kisses are electric and their mere presence makes me forget where I am and how to avoid getting caught staring.

"*Ms. Kent,*" Dr. Richardson's sharp tone slices through the air, causing me to jump so hard I knock the pen and notebook from my desk. Eyes from every side of the room bore into me as I lean over and pick my things up. Once I have everything back in order, I sit up and plaster on a fake smile. The room is quiet, so the tremble in my voice is evident when I finally answer.

"Yes, Professor?"

"Your obvious infatuation with Mr. Johnson brings me to my next point. Perhaps, I should thank your hormones for the smooth transition." Shock and embarrassment slam into me, pushing all the breath from my lungs as I struggle for a response. Before I can say anything though, he waves a dismissive hand at me. "As you might have already guessed, Mr. Johnson is the teaching assistant assigned to this course. He'll mostly be assisting me with administrative duties as it relates to this class along with covering select lectures. He is not a formal instructor for this course."

Out of the corner of my eye, I see Chris moving again. He must have paused when Dr. Richardson called my name, but now he's just a few desks down.

"However," the old troll continues. "I expect you to treat him with utmost respect which includes, but is not limited to, keeping the ogling to a minimum and sparing him the uncomfortable experience of being propositioned in exchange for power he does not have over your grades." Another curt glance at me as Chris breezes by, dropping the syllabus on my desk. I don't dare to look at him, choosing instead to keep all of my attention on the professor, which makes my stomach turn. I can't believe the university lets someone as vile and rude as he is continue to teach.

"While there are no university policies against fraternization between teaching assistants and students in the courses they assist with, it is my personal belief that engaging in such a relationship is a moral and professional failure for everyone involved. Please consider that before you decide to waste the valuable time you'll need to make it through this course trying to cozy up to him. Now that you all have the syllabus, open it up so we can review."

The rest of the hour-long class drags by with Dr. Richardson droning on and on about how he likes to use his courses to weed weak students out and send them crying to other, less rigorous, majors. By the time he dismisses everyone—with three chapters to read and a problem set on present value to do by our next class meeting on Monday—I'm certain he's managed to make a least five students drop the class. Some of them are muttering about taking it when Dr. Brennan returns next semester as they head towards the door. Eager to get out of the room, I throw all of my things into my bag and start to head for the exit with the last crowd of students.

"Not so fast, Ms. Kent," Dr. Richardson calls from behind me, forcing me to stop in my tracks and turn around to face him. "I'd like to have a quick word with you."

He's leaning against the lectern like he doesn't need to be clearing out as well to make room for the class starting in the next few minutes. I take a few steps closer, painfully aware of Chris is still in the room. He's standing off to the side, packing his bag with a slowness that feels deliberate and tension lining his shoulders.

Don't stare, Mal.

"What can I do for you, Dr. Richardson?"

"Are you sure you're in the correct course?"

My brows pinch together, and a flare of annoyance runs through me. It's bad enough the man called me a horny teenager in front of a room of my peers, but now he's questioning whether I'm competent enough to take this class?

"Yes, I received permission to take the course. Were the requisite signatures not included in Dr. Brennan's notes when you took over for her?"

Getting clearance to expedite my coursework had been relatively easy with Dr. B on my side. She did most of the leg work for me last year, talking to Dr. Wilson, the only other woman in the department who also happened to be everyone's boss, with the transcripts from the dual enrollment program I participated in during high school in hand. By the time I graduated high school, I had the equivalent of an associate's degree in business, and she didn't want me wasting any more of my time in introductory level courses when I could be jumping into the meat of a major I clearly already loved.

She was so excited about getting me approved to expedite my degree work, I didn't have the heart to tell her that it wasn't my love for business that got me through those classes. It was the need for distraction, for the ability to sink my teeth into something that wasn't trauma and secrets.

"Yes, it was noted on the course roster," he says, clearly agitated. "I was trying to be diplomatic with my phrasing, but perhaps I should be more direct."

"*Please.*" All of the agitation I'm feeling at the moment is wrapped up in the one word.

"Do you honestly believe you're prepared to take this course?"

"Yes, and your colleagues obviously agreed with me, or else I wouldn't be here."

A faint cough rings out, and even though I can't allow myself to look at him, I know who it came from. Richardson glances over his shoulder at Chris and then back at me, and I can tell that he's pissed. He doesn't like to be challenged.

"Even after struggling in my Data Science course last semester?"

Resisting the urge to roll my eyes takes every ounce of strength I have. "I made a B in that class."

It had been hard to pull it out though. I practically lived in the library all semester, but I did it. And getting a B in one of his courses is the equivalent to an A+ for anyone else. He presses his lips together, the thin line of his mouth practically disappearing into the wrinkles on his face as he considers me.

"This course will be significantly harder. There's no shame in dropping it now and returning to the course plan professors such as myself spent years developing for students like you."

My fingers tighten around the strap of my bag as my throat constricts around words I can't say if I don't want to be roped into an argument that will inevitably end with me punching his old ass in the face.

"I appreciate the warning, professor, but I think I'm fine where I'm at." *On track to graduate from one of the most respected business programs in the state a year and a half early.* "Did you need anything else from me? I was on my way to the library to get a head start on the chapters you just assigned."

"As a matter of fact—"

"Dr. Richardson."

The terse response I was about to receive is cut off by a deep voice with a precise syllable enunciation that spells trouble with every vibration of his vocal cords. Both of the professor's eyes go wide as he processes the interruption and turns toward its source. Only when his eyes are no longer on me, do I allow myself to look in Chris' direction. He's striding towards us, looking cool as a cucumber in clothes that would make any other guy his age look like a kid playing dress-up in his dad's clothes. On him, the designer ensemble—navy slacks, a freshly pressed white button-up, and tan oxfords—looks like *him*. Like a uniform he was born to wear.

When he stops in front of us, I take an unconscious step back, and something passes behind his eyes as he tracks my retreat, but I don't bother trying to decipher what it is.

"I'd love to have a word with you." Chris is saying now, angling his body so he's standing between Richardson and me. "Is now a good time?"

The older man glances at me and then back at Chris whose commanding presence isn't at all in alignment with where he falls in the pecking order of this classroom.

"Of course, Christopher. I was just finishing up with Ms. Kent."

"I heard." The note of disapproval is a far cry from his usual, laid-back, approach to things, and I find myself once again caught off guard by the glimpse at the other side of him. He turns to look at me. "Sorry for interrupting. Did you have anything else you needed to discuss with the professor?"

I'm already backing towards the exit when he finishes his question. "No. Nothing at all."

Neither of them gets a chance to acknowledge my answer before I'm out the door. Once I make it back to the sidewalk I left Sloane standing on an hour ago, I breathe a sigh of relief, happy to have survived what has proven to be the worst first class of the semester known to man. Chilly wind whips around me, and I pull my jacket a little closer to my body as I start to make my way towards the library.

It's a Friday afternoon, and campus is relatively empty. Most people are probably in their dorms getting ready for whatever craziness they're going to get into this weekend. I'm honestly surprised that Sloane hasn't called me already, trying to wrap me up in whatever plans she and Eric have made. As if on cue, my phone starts to vibrate. Sighing, I pull it out of my back pocket and laugh to myself when I see Sloane's name flashing on the screen.

"What can I do for you Sloane Elise?"

"You can start by never calling me that again, Mallory Pearl," she mutters, sounding snarky as ever. "And then you can tell me you're on your way to my room, so we can figure out what we're going to wear tonight."

"Oh no, ma'am." I shake my head even though she can't see me. "I'm not going to any more parties with you."

"Come on! I thought we were past the whole truth or dare thing."

"We are."

"Then why won't you come out with us?" The rustling of fabric bleeds through the speaker, and I imagine her standing in her closet looking through clothing options. "Scared you're going to end up kissing Chris again?"

"*No!*" I answer a little too quickly.

"It's okay if you enjoyed it, Mal," she teases. "He looked like he knew what he was doing."

Unbidden images from the kiss flash through my mind, and I try to force them out because I know what will follow if I don't. Memories of how soft his lips were. Questions about how they would feel gliding down my neck, skating over my breasts, and going lower and lower until finally….

"Mal!" For the second time today, I nearly jump out of my skin at the sound of my name.

"Stop yelling, girl," I hiss into the phone, scolding Sloane in hopes of scaring her away from this topic. "I'm right here."

"Yeah, but you're not listening."

"Because you're not saying anything worth hearing."

"Whatever. I would think that you'd be ready to thank me by now."

"Thank you?" I ask in an incredulous tone as I bypass a group of freshmen moving at a snail's pace and discussing their first class meetings. "For what exactly?"

"Opening the door for you to finally explore the crush you've had on Chris since last year."

I roll my eyes. "I don't want to explore it. I don't have time for relationships."

"Mal," she scoffs. "*You* have more time than anyone. You're literally graduating next year. I wish you would use your last few semesters in college doing something other than studying."

This isn't the first time we've had this conversation, especially not as it relates to my lack of romantic entanglements, but it's gotten even worse since Christmas break when I made the mistake of coming clean about my crush on Chris. Sloane has always suspected that I liked him, and I, admittedly, haven't done a great job of hiding it, but before then I hadn't said the words out loud to anyone. And I definitely hadn't acknowledged how long it had been there, simmering underneath my skin, soaking into my bones, making it hard to remember all the things that went wrong the last time I let myself feel like this for someone so magnetic.

"All the time I spend studying *is* the reason I'll be graduating next year."

"And that would be all fine and dandy if the only guy I've ever seen you show interest in wasn't graduating *this* year."

I groan loudly, which makes her laugh. "I should have never told you about that."

"But you did, which suggests you wanted someone to push you to do something about it before it's too late."

"It is too late." *Was already too late when I laid eyes on Chris on move-in day and a foreign mix of attraction and desire slammed into my body, laying waste to the carefully constructed wall I built around my shredded heart.*

"Hardly. The semester just started."

I'm halfway to the library now, but the growling in my stomach causes me to change directions at the last minute. If I'm going to be in the library for the next few hours, I might as well stop by The Grill to get some sustenance to see me through.

"That's not what I mean," I say, raising my voice a bit to adjust for the chattering in the crowded dining area. Most people are in line for hot food, but I want something quick so I make my way over to the cooler with sandwiches, chips, and bottled drinks.

"Elaborate whenever you're ready," she pauses. "Where are you?"

Walking over to the checkout station, I hand the cashier my stuff and swipe my student ID once she rings it up. "The Grill, grabbing food before I head to the library."

"Mal, you can't seriously be spending the first Friday of the semester at the library."

"Probably the whole weekend since Dr. Richardson assigned reading and a problem set that I have to have done by Monday." I grab my stuff and walk towards the door, moving back into the cold so suddenly makes me shiver. "Knowing him, we'll probably have a quiz on it at the start of class."

"Richardson? I thought you weren't taking any of his classes."

"I wasn't planning on it, but apparently Dr. Brennan decided to take a sabbatical and we got stuck with him."

"Oh, no." There's a dread in her tone that matches what I felt when he walked into the room. "That sucks Mal."

"Yeah," I sigh. "And that's not even the worst part."

"No?" Sloane sounds distracted now, and the absence of hangers clinking around tells me she's finally found an outfit for where ever she's going tonight. "What could be worse than that?"

"Chris being his TA."

3

MALLORY

Getting Sloane off the phone proved to be difficult once I told her about Chris TAing for my class, mainly because she wanted a second-by-second description of the entire ordeal so she could hold all the details she pried from me up as proof that the universe was bringing me and Chris together. While I didn't agree with her, not even a little bit, I pretended her theory had merit, so I could get her off the phone and dive into my work. Thankfully, she was so caught up in the new development on the Chris and Mallory 4Eva front that she forgot to harass me about coming out with her tonight, so I've been working in the library in relative peace for the last few hours, trudging through paragraph after paragraph of dense finance terms before switching over to the problem set that has twenty questions in it altogether.

I'm in the process of calculating the present value of a 12-year annuity with payments of fifty-thousand dollars a year when someone sits down at my table. I'm in the middle of the first floor of the library, nestled between two of the dustier sets of bookshelves, so I'm more than shocked to hear the sound of a chair dragging across the carpet. Even more shocking is the set of chestnut eyes that bore into mine the second I look away from my paper. At first, I think I'm hallucinating him—and it wouldn't be that far-fetched since his handsome face has taken up a quarter of my brain since the kiss—but then his mouth turns up into one of his signature smiles, and I know I'm not.

"*Ms. Kent.*" His eyes flash with humor as he does his best impression of Dr. Richardson, and heat creeps up my neck at the reminder of being called out for staring at him. "I would say it's fancy meeting you here but—"

"You knew this is where I'd be." I finish for him, lifting a brow.

"Exactly." He leans forward, resting his arms on the table and drawing my attention to the oatmeal-colored sweater he's wearing now, the sleeves pulled up to expose his corded forearms. The table is blocking my view of the lower half of his body, but I assume it matches the top. Chris is always well put together, making it look easy to be so ruthlessly coordinated. "I heard you mention it to Richardson before you left class."

"Right." I clear my throat, hating the way my heart is thundering in my chest just because he remembers something I said hours ago. "What are you doing on campus so late?"

"Going to a party."

Eye contact isn't usually a thing that makes me uncomfortable, but something about the way Chris is holding my gaze makes me want to get up and run. To put as much space between him and me as possible.

"You do know this is a library right?" I make a show of glancing around the quiet space, acting like I'm confirming that we're actually in a library to avoid acknowledging what being the sole object of his attention is doing to me. "Not the typical spot for a party."

Tilting his head back, he releases a deep, throaty laugh that makes his Adam's apple bob up and down. By some small miracle, I manage to pry my eyes away from the oddly arousing sight by the time he's done.

"No shit, Mal," he chuckles. "I came here to talk to you."

My heart sinks. I don't know what he wants to talk to me about, but given the embarrassing incidents I've experienced in his presence in the last week, I don't think it could be anything good. Needing something to do with my hands, I start to shuffle through the pages of hand-written notes I took while I was reading.

"About what?"

"Just wanted to know if you were okay after the whole thing with The Dick."

My breath gets stuck in my throat and I cough, loudly, as all of the papers in my hand fall back onto the table in a messy heap. "The *what*?"

"The Dick," he says again, like repeating the words will make them make sense to me. "That's what all the business majors call Richardson because of his glowing personality and, you know, cause men named Richard are usually called Dick for short."

"No," I shake my head vehemently, still coughing. "I don't... honestly that makes no sense. His first name is Keith."

"Jesus, Mal. It's just a joke." Chris pushes out of his chair and rounds the table, dropping down on his haunches beside me and patting my back. "Don't die on me."

I know I should be concerned that I'm literally choking off of nothing more than air, and probably my own saliva, but all I can focus on is the steady rhythm of Chris' palm colliding with my back and the warmth of his skin bleeding through the fabric of my shirt. When I finally get it under control, my face is on fire, burning up from embarrassment. I don't look at Chris as he stands and goes back to his seat.

"You good?"

"Yeah." I nod, rubbing at my now aching throat. "You just caught me off guard with that one." A smirk lifts one corner of his mouth as he reaches across the table and grabs my papers, straightening the pile back up and setting it down in front of me.

"You've seriously never heard anyone call him that before?"

"No. Never."

"Damn, you really *haven't* been in the department long."

On instinct, my eyes narrow, turning into slits as irritation slides down my spine. Somewhere in the back of my mind, I know he's not trying to be malicious—Chris doesn't play that way—but his words still strike the wrong chord. One that Dr. Richardson has been dancing on top of since last year when I had my first class with him.

"I've been in the department long enough to know it's a tired boys club full of assholes who think women, especially Black women, aren't fit to study or conduct business. I also know that every year the same people they work to keep out of the field are running circles around them in every way that matters. Having *that* information feels a lot more pertinent than knowing what you and your friends call a man whose ass you kiss publicly behind his back."

Venom coats each word, and I watch Chris' expression change, intrigue mingling with surprise. Warmth spreads through my chest at the idea of being able to surprise him, to turn whatever he used to feel or think about me into something new. Something different. Something that more closely reflects the reactions guys like him gave the girl I used to be. A girl he's never met because she died before I knew him. Chris raises his hands, palms facing me in a gesture of playful surrender that only lasts for a second and makes me want to smile at him for no reason at all.

"Shit." His tongue comes out, swiping over his full lips and sending a tremor through a part of me that's lain dormant for years. "Where have you been hiding all that attitude?"

The question takes the wind out of my sails, so to speak. Well, it's not the question as much as it is what it reminds me of. The loss of my fire. The dimming of my light. The death of the sassy, fun, spontaneous Mal who believed in people's inherent goodness. All the best parts of me that I left lying broken and bruised in a place I should have been smart enough never to go.

I shrug and reach for the stack of papers on the table between us, shuffling through them again. "I don't know. Guess you don't really need it when you spend all your time studying."

Studying? More like using books to hide from life.

Chris stares at me, looking more thoughtful than I've ever seen him. Silence stretches between us, blanketing the small corner of the world where only he and I seem to exist, and I squirm in my chair.

Uncomfortable with being held in his gaze, with feeling like he's seeing me in ways I'm not used to being seen.

He must sense my discomfort because his eyes drop to my hands, watching me flip through the pages to find a good place to tuck my notes. Even though I just got the book earlier this week, it's already starting to look well used. Streaks of brightly colored fluorescent ink from my highlighters marking passages I deemed important, a few sticky tabs flagging things I needed to review for better understanding.

Eric and Nic pick on me for how anal I am about note-taking when I read, but it helps me keep my mind on the text and away from things I'd rather not think about.

Chris purses his lips, letting out a low, semi-impressed, whistle as he takes it all in. "You really do take studying seriously, huh?"

"Yeah, unlike *some* people, I take most things seriously."

Both of his brows lift, and he places a hand on his chest, feigning hurt. "You wound me."

"And you prove my point every time you open your mouth."

Don't talk about his mouth, Mallory! It'll only make you think about kissing it.

The snarky voice in my head—who has decided to be helpful for once—is right to warn me because the instant the words pass my lips all I can think about is the kiss. About Chris' hand cupping my jaw. About every urgent, incendiary swipe of his tongue against mine. I didn't know kissing him would be like that. Hell, I didn't know kissing anyone could be like that.

A burst of energy.

The first satisfying crackle of kindling catching fire.

The sweet, heavy scent of rain clinging to the air after a storm.

"Contrary to what you might think," Chris says, pulling me out of my thoughts and looking at me with eyes so intent they make me wish I could disappear inside them again. "I do take *some* things seriously."

I swallow, sending the stupid question his words and suggestive tone inspired back where it came from. Nothing good can come from asking him for the list of things he takes seriously. Especially when I've seen firsthand just how serious he can be about a kiss.

"Sure you do." My voice sounds small, shrinking under the pressure of my constricting throat.

Chris leans forward, resting his arms on the table. "You don't believe me?"

"I don't need to. You believe you and that's good enough for me."

"So you just think everything with me is all fun and games?"

He tries to make the question sound light-hearted, but something in his tone is all wrong. For a second, it sounds like he's upset by the idea of me accepting his playful, jokey persona at face value, but that can't be right. No one puts so much work into being seen one way just to be upset when people buy into their act. In fact, and I'm speaking from experience here, it's usually the other way around.

Pressing my lips together, I try to think of a way to answer his question that won't make this moment any more awkward than it already is. "Maybe a little."

The dissatisfied puff of air that comes from his flared nostrils is the only sound around us, and I sit there horrified and steeping in the cold silence as a bubble of anxiety starts to expand in my chest. Every second that ticks by with Chris staring at me like I've accused him of being an ax murderer contributes to its growth, and just when I think it's about to pop, Chris' lips twitch.

It's a small movement, but I catch it, see it turn into a full-blown smile that's only there for a second before his lips part and a dark, smooth chuckle hits the air. It starts out low, with a slow rumble I can feel deep in the pit of my stomach, and it builds until his broad shoulders are shaking from the force of it.

My jaw drops. "You're such an ass."

"You should have seen your face," he wheezes, wrapping one of his arms around his torso in a futile effort to stifle the laughter. "God, I wish I had a camera. I've never seen your eyes that wide before."

Another wave of heat floods my cheeks, and I shake my head, trying to look exasperated when what I really am is embarrassed. *Again.* It seems to be my constant state of being at this point, and I hate it. The way it makes me feel like I've lost my grip on the mask I'm too used to wearing now. Even though it doesn't fit right anymore, with its fused edges that leave no room for the kind of self-assuredness you need to be able to laugh at yourself chafing against my skin, I'm reluctant to part with it.

I flip my textbook back open, avoiding his gaze. "Don't you have a party to get to?"

"Yeah." All the humor has left his voice, and I don't know how to feel about him reading my shifting mood so accurately. The table shakes a little as he prepares to rise from his seat, and I expect to see his retreating form fading from my peripheral vision in the next few seconds, but a full minute goes by and it doesn't happen. I don't need to lift my head to know that he's still at the table. I can feel his eyes on me. "Do you want to come with me?"

My head snaps up, shock coursing through my veins. "No, thanks. Not really in the mood to spend the next few hours in a crowded room breathing smoke-filled air and watching drunk twenty-year-olds bump and grind on the dance floor. I can think of a million different ways to spend my night."

Actually, I can only think of one, and he's standing smack dab in the middle of it.

"Funny, I don't think I heard you complain once when we were at my place last week."

I shrug, willing myself not to stumble over my words even though the mention of his party last week has my heart pounding against my rib cage. "That was different, the crowd was smaller."

"True." Chris nods, a teasing glint in his eyes as they skate across my features. Tracing every line of my face before landing on my mouth. "And I guess the game made a difference too."

Air leaves my lungs in a small whoosh. "Right, the game…" I mutter, eyes bouncing between his face and the dusty bookshelves. "Yeah, that could have been it."

"Why'd you choose dare anyway?"

"What?"

"Dare," he repeats. "When Sloane called your name, why'd you choose dare?"

That was a question I'd been asking myself since the moment the word left my mouth, but I've yet to come up with an answer, and it bothers me that Chris looks like he has it. "Oh, I don't know. Guess I didn't want to be the only person choosing truth when everyone else went with dare."

He looks thoughtful for a moment. "Yeah, but that's not like you."

This is the second time he's said something like this. A summarizing statement, a finite declaration, a resolute testament that speaks to the truth of who I am even though I don't feel like that's something *I* know anymore.

"What's not like me?"

"Going along to get along." I raise a brow, unsure about what he means, and he continues. "You don't let other people's choices influence yours, Mal. You might not want to admit it to yourself, but you chose dare because *you* wanted to, not because every other drunk idiot before you did."

The absolute certainty in his voice renders me speechless, and I watch as a self-satisfied grin takes over Chris' entire face, making him look even more handsome as he taps the table twice with his large fist and finally stands.

"I guess I'll let you get back to studying. See you in class on Monday."

4

CHRIS

They always start the same. The nightmares. With the echo of the slamming front door and the heels of my mother's shoes sliding over the threshold. The last time I saw her. From there it switches to flashes of her in the hospital, her strained cries filling the room, her body bowed with pain, her blood soaking the sheets and spilling onto the floor as faceless doctors rip her apart with scalpels and ruthless fingers to pull my sister into this world.

Trading one life for another.

The last half, the bit about the dimly lit hospital room with cruel surgeons and evil nurses, is pure conjecture, of course. I wasn't in the room when my mother died, but I've seen it. Years after she took her last breath, when I'd all but forgotten her face and the smell of her hair, I visited it—a large and luxurious birthing suite on the private floor of Johnson Memorial Hospital because the Chief of Surgery's wife and the daughter-in-law of the CEO of the hospital couldn't possibly give birth anywhere else—and waited to feel her. To sense some part of her spirit in the sterile white tiles and multiple thread count linens on the oversized hospital bed.

I never felt her there.

Just like I never felt her in the home my father moved her into after they married, and continued to raise us in after she was gone, or at the spot at the edge of our property in the country where he spread her ashes. I don't feel her anywhere. She is, and has always been, missing from me. A hole in my heart where nothing else can grow. A dark cloud over my head that nothing can pierce through. A glaring emptiness in my life that nothing will ever eclipse.

And the nightmares ensure it stays that way.

They started when I was four, just after my dad came home with the fluffy bundle of pink that was Teresa and no mom. I would wake up screaming, tears and snot running down my face, sobs wracking my body so hard I threw up. My father woke up with me the first time. His thick, dark brows pinched in disapproval and frustration as he barked orders at Margaret—the live-in nanny who'd been with us since my older brother, RJ, was born—to clean me up and get me back to bed. After that, he didn't get up anymore, so it was just me, Margaret, and baby Teresa.

Margaret would always try to get me to go back to sleep, but the taste of vomit and the metallic tang of invisible blood filling my nostrils clung to me, making it impossible to rest. It took months of her trying every sleep remedy under the sun to get her to accept that once a nightmare woke me, sleep was no longer an option, but once she did we developed a routine. She'd fix me a cup of warm milk while she prepped a bottle for Teresa's next feeding, tuck me into the twin-sized bed she had in the corner of the nursery, and let me read to her softly while she went back to sleep. Eventually, when I was tired of reading and Margaret was giving off too much body heat, I would trade my spot in her bed for the rocking chair next to the crib and watch my baby sister sleep.

It was a nice routine. One that evolved as I got older and the nightmares progressed. Margaret hasn't been with our family for some time now, but we still keep in touch, and I still value the role she played in helping me realize the ways stability and routine can help you live with the monsters you can't slay.

She'd be scandalized by my routine now, though.

It's all about mind-numbing sex, followed by long runs and a hot shower before starting my day at a time when most people my age are just going to bed. *Not a drop of warm milk or a freshly laundered footed pajama in sight.*

At least that was my routine before I knew what it was like to kiss Mallory Kent.

"Put it out of your head," I mutter to myself, letting the cold February air carry the words away. I might as well have not spoken them at all for all the good the order does me. In an instant, my mind is back on our kiss. A ten-second joining of lips and tongues that happened almost a month ago and has turned my entire world upside down.

I should have known she would be a problem for me when she wasn't the least bit phased by the idea of kissing me. I strode over there to her, a shit-eating grin on my face to hide that my heart was pounding in my chest like I was back on the stage of Margaret's church stumbling over an Easter speech, and she just looked ready to get it over with.

Talk about a blow to the ego.

I don't know what I expected from her—the most focused, goal-oriented person I've met since I moved to New Haven—but it wasn't indifference. Beautiful, but stoic features that only moved, only showed a glimmer of emotion when I touched her. That small point of connection had short-circuited my entire system, and the taste of her had done the rest. Ruined me. Made it so no matter what I did all I could think about was the way she responded when our mouths collided. Nothing has been able to touch that moment, and I guess that would be bearable if it didn't fuck with my carefully curated nightmare recovery routine.

Of course, I didn't know that it had until tonight. As soon as I opened my eyes the familiar sensation of restlessness started in on me. The urge to *move* until every muscle in my body, including my brain, is too wrung out to do anything let alone replay the scene of my mother's death until I'm nauseous and angry and wondering if I ever woke up at all, had me picking up my phone and sending out a few texts to see who was up.

Alisha—a senior Biology major who has even less time for relationships than I do—got back to me first, so I rolled out of bed, got
dressed, and braved the storm to head over to her on-campus apartment, ready to hunt down carnal satisfaction and force it to take the
place of the bone-crushing guilt and grief constantly brewing inside
of me.

Instead, I ended up walking out ten minutes later, more agitated
than when I went in. Not because I was still being haunted by thoughts
of my mother, but because even the sight of another woman on her
knees wasn't enough to free me from thoughts of Mal.

As if I needed another ghost haunting me.

And I do feel haunted. When I see her in class every Monday,
Wednesday, and Friday, especially when she's listening so intently
that she starts chewing on the end of her pen, or random times over
the weekend when Eric or Sloane manage to drag her out of the
library long enough to go to a party or catch a movie with the rest of
us. Every moment that I'm around her is filled with me obsessing
over the taste of her lips. The faint scent of jasmine wafting off of
her skin. The way she doesn't look at me unless she absolutely
has to.

All of it, *every single thing about her*, is distracting as hell, and I
don't have time for distractions. There's no space for them on the long
list of things I need to do in order to become the man I want to be. One
who stands on his own two feet and doesn't depend on the benefits of a
legacy and name he was born into.

When I left Alisha's, the only reasonable thing left to do was work
off my frustration with a run. I started off at a breakneck pace, the
sound of my sneakers pounding the half-dry wet pavement echoing
around me and disrupting the quiet of the night. Because of the rain, I
was only planning to run for thirty minutes or so, just enough to
appease the raw, primal emotion that seems to be hardwired into my
being, but I'm closing in on an hour and it still hasn't let up.

It's forcing me forward, pushing my body past the brink of exhaustion and into something else. Some realm of being where it doesn't
seem to matter that sweat is spilling down the lines of my chest and

back in steady rivulets because my aching muscles are begging for more.

Of what, I don't know.

Slowing down feels unnatural, but I know I need to do it anyway. If I keep going at this pace, I'll be dead to the world for the rest of the day, and the only thing that would be worse than this clawing urge to be in constant motion, searching for answers to questions I don't even know how to ask, is not being able to move at all. Stillness has never agreed with me.

I eye the dimly lit path in front of me, noting the deep curve in the sidewalk that leads to the lot where I parked my car and deciding to downshift once I round it. The music in my headphones blasts loudly in my ears, and the edges of my hoodie cling to my face, making the darkness enveloping me all the more poignant.

Maybe that's why I don't notice the small, curvy figure coming up the path towards me until it's too late. Until I'm colliding with her, knocking her to the ground and sending the things she's holding in her hands flying into the air before one of them lands somewhere on the pavement with a loud, wet splat.

"*Fuck.*" I take a few steps toward her, my shadow stretching over her prone form as I reach out to help her up. "I'm so sorry."

She scrambles to her feet and although there isn't much light, I can see the tension lining her shoulders. Her posture is rigid and defensive as she gets her bearings. Head swiveling from the left to the right like she's trying to find the best way to move around me. Light skates across her features, and it's then that I recognize her. The smooth mahogany of her skin, the soft slope of her nose and line of her jaw. Full curves that are covered in a hoodie and leggings that accentuate her thick thighs. Hints of amber glittering in wild eyes that are seeing but not. Subtle notes of jasmine and citrus waft through the air towards me, washing away the stench of antiseptic and blood from my nightmares.

"Mallory." I expected her to relax a bit when I said her name, but it has the exact opposite effect. She takes a few staggered steps back and to the left of me, everything about her stance suggesting that she's about to cut and run, and I tense, anticipation flooding my veins as I shift on my feet, ready to follow her. I tell myself it's because I can't let Eric's sister run off in the middle of the night for God knows what to happen to her, but the part of me that's been craving something more since my feet first hit the pavement, knows that's not the truth.

Before I have the chance to admit why the idea of chasing her makes every nerve ending in my body light up, I realize she probably can't see me that well. What little light there is on the path is drawn to the lines of her face and neglecting me altogether. I hold my hands out and push my hood back, taking a step forward into the light.

"It's just me." Then, because she probably has no idea who 'me' is, I add, "Chris. Chris Johnson."

Her posture relaxes, and she moves toward me instead of away from me, but only by an inch or so. "Chris?" *My name on her lips.* I pull in a deep breath and force myself to focus on her mouth curving into a wan smile instead of what the sound of her voice is doing to me.

"Yeah." I take a step towards her, moving slowly so as not to alarm her. "Are you okay? I didn't see you."

"I'm good."

But her hands are shaking. I can see that clearly even though she's hiding them inside the sleeves of the hoodie she's wearing. "You sure? You hit the ground pretty hard."

Both of her brows pull together, and I see a flicker of amused annoyance pass over her features, which makes me smile. Maybe I read her wrong. "That's kind of what happens when someone runs into you at full speed."

"Right," I say slowly, tilting my head to the side and conducting a not-so-subtle scan of her body to make sure she's not hurt. The lack of light makes it hard to see, but from what I can tell, she's okay. I can't say the same for the bag laying at her feet with what looks like french fries spilling out of the top, or the plastic cup that's currently oozing its contents all over the sidewalk. "Damn, is that a cookies and cream milkshake?"

Her eyes, which have a weird wariness to them, leave my face long enough to take in the mess. When she looks back at me, there's something close to bashfulness playing across her features. It's adorable.

"Yeah," she sighs. "It was."

"I'm sorry."

The words pop out of my mouth again, and I marvel at the way they make her shoulders relax a little. Suddenly, I want to say more words, utter more apologies. Anything to get rid of the last bit of discomfort passing between us and let her know that she's safe with me.

Safe. The word echoes around my brain, making me think of my mother. Did she feel safe in that room where she died? Did she think giving birth in a hospital with the name she married into emblazoned on the walls would stop her from meeting the same premature end as so many Black mothers that came before, and after, her?

"It's okay." Mal's incredibly soft cadence sounds like a lullaby, but it's strong enough to pierce my dark thoughts, pulling me back to her questioning gaze. "Are *you* okay?"

Amber eyes assess me, skating over my body like she's checking me for injuries even though she's the one that fell. "Oh, yeah, I'm good, just thinking about how much I hate seeing a good milkshake go to waste."

It's a lame response. I know it. She knows it. We both know it. But for some reason, it's the only thing I can think to say with her examining me with the kind of precision lionesses reserve for their prey. A heavy weight settles in my chest as the thought of going from being haunted by her to being hunted by her takes over my mind. Just a second ago, I was thrilled by the idea of chasing her in the literal sense, and now I'm wondering what it would be like to be on the receiving end of any part of her desire.

To be pursued by someone that I....

I swallow that thought, letting it go back down the depths of my loins where it surely sprouted from. Thinking with my dick isn't something I have the luxury of doing, especially not now when the stopwatch attached to my freedom is rapidly winding down. I can practically feel my father's well-insured, perfectly manicured fingers wrapping around my ankles, preparing to yank me back to Boston and plop me into the life he's already planned out for me.

"Right? And it was so perfectly blended, I think I might be jealous of the sidewalk right now."

I don't mean to laugh, especially when she looks so serious, but that's what makes her off-hand comment so funny: she's not trying to be. Not many people can pull off the kind of dry humor Mallory specializes in. She's witty, clever, with sharp barbs that strike you before you even know that you've been hit. My laughter echoes between us, and an odd warmth takes over her expression, like she's surprised and thrilled by my laughter. That catches me off guard because she's usually annoyed by my sense of humor.

When I sought her out in the library a few weeks ago, she accused me of never taking anything seriously, and for the first time in my life hearing that bothered me. I wasn't angry when she said it because it wasn't a lie. I've been aware of my tendency to use humor to shield the people in my life from the shadows lurking in the corners of my mind for a long time. Mal was just the first person to say it like it was a bad thing.

I glance down at the mess spreading between her sneakers and mine. "Well, at least the ants will be well fed."

"The raccoons too," she muses, tentative humor lighting the honeyed butter of her irises as she bends at the waist to scoop up the bag of ruined fries on the ground.

At the same time, I lean down to pick up the plastic cup, and the sudden move nearly causes us to collide again. Mal glances up at me, her round eyes stretched wide, and our faces inches apart, reminding me of the sliver of space that was between us before my lips touched hers for the very first time. That moment plays on a constant loop in my mind, suspended in a slow, viscous syrup of delight that doesn't come close to the sweet perfection that was us.

Melted ice cream coats my fingertips as I finally grab the cup and stand up quickly. The muscles in my back and legs scream their protest as I stroll over to the closest trash can and throw the cup away, reminding me I never did an actual cool down. Mal sidles up next to me, tossing the fries into the trash too.

"Fries and a shake at almost two in the morning," I muse, turning towards her. "Another late-night study session?"

"More like early morning, but yeah." She runs her hands over her hair, which is in a loose ponytail made up of box braids that I know for a fact cascade down her back and brush the top of her tailbone. "The last few questions on the latest problem set are kicking my ass."

It's a fight to keep my brows from climbing up my forehead because I don't think I've ever heard Mallory "I'm Graduating Early So Fuck You and the Patriarchy" Kent admit she doesn't have a handle on something. Shock mixes with a dangerous kind of intrigue—the kind that's got my mouth forming words my brain knows it shouldn't.

"We could talk through them," I say the words slowly, like I'm not sure I want them to come out, and what little humor was in Malory's eyes a second ago dissolves. I wonder if she thinks I'm trying to be funny and find myself rushing to finish my thought. "If you want, I mean. I took the class last year and made an A, so I could probably be helpful. Plus, I kind of owe you for feeding all your brain food to the sidewalk."

She presses her lips together, considering my words for a second and, thankfully, deciding I'm not trying to make a joke out of her struggling with coursework that kicked my ass.

"Oh, no, you don't—" Her head moves from side to side, denying my offer. "—It's fine, honestly. I think it's probably for the best since the sugar would have kept me up all night anyway."

"Wasn't being up all night the plan?" I ask, the words tumbling out of my mouth silky smooth while inappropriate images of the million different ways I could keep her up flash through my mind.

Mallory rolls her eyes. "You never miss a chance to do that, do you?"

"Do what?"

"Make everything sound inappropriate."

"All I'm offering is milkshakes, fries, and a little private tutoring session. If that sounds inappropriate to you, maybe you should get your mind out of the gutter."

She bites her lip, hiding a small smile I want more of. "Private tutoring isn't a part of your teaching assistant duties, Christopher."

"How would you know? You haven't seen the fine print in my TA contract."

"Pretty sure the speech Richardson gave about how you're basically his secretary made it clear he wouldn't trust you with teaching course material."

"Oof. That might be an insult to secretaries everywhere." I grin at her, hoping to tease the rest of her incomplete smile out. "Their jobs are much more comprehensive than what I do for The Dick."

"God, I hate that nickname," she mutters under her breath. Then, even lower, so low I almost can't hear, she says, "It's starting to ruin dicks for me as a whole."

There's no stopping my eyebrows from shooting towards my hairline. Late Night Mallory is much more candid than Daytime Mallory, and I think I might like her a little too much. "Spend a lot of time thinking about the general dick population, do you?"

I can't see it happen because of how dark it is, but I swear she's blushing.

"No," she scoffs. "That's not how I meant it!"

I hold my hands up, fighting to keep the laugh building in my chest from breaking free. "Hey, you don't have to explain yourself to me. If you want to think about dicks, think about them, I'm not going to judge you."

She stares at me, trying to convey some level of severity but struggling to get a hold of the composure she usually has such a tight grip on. "I should hope not, judging a woman for thinking about dick would probably make the whole hoeing around thing kind of difficult."

"Quite." I incline my head, conceding to her point even though I feel quite certain that my hoeing days, as she put it, have come to an end. "Now, are you going to take me up on my offer or are we going to stand here all night waiting for the raccoons to come collect the sacrifice we've left at their trash altar?"

5

MALLORY

Stupid, stupid girl. The words filter through my head on repeat, flitting through with the same kind of speed and precision Chris is using to move us through the empty streets surrounding New Haven University's campus. It's close to three in the morning, but I'm not the least bit tired. I guess being knocked on your ass by someone running through campus like they're trying out for the lead role in a werewolf movie will do that to you.

Not just someone.

Right. Because of all the people in the world and all the students on campus that I could have been trampled by, it *had* to be Chris. The one person I've been diverting an obscene amount of brain power to not thinking about and the last person I expected to run into on campus during prime-time booty call hours. I mean, it wasn't strange for him to be on campus, it was just strange that he was on that path, heading back to his car instead of fucking the brains out of whatever girl answered his 'you up?' text first.

Once I got over the initial fear of finding myself on a dark path with a hooded figure in the middle of the night, my body went straight into shock.

Shock that he was there in front of me.

Shock at his careful, and not at all subtle, visual examination of my body.

Shock at his ability to toe that line between joking and being totally serious, and, what's worse, making me want to walk it with him.

He made me like his laugh, made me want to say stupid, embarrassing things just for the sake of hearing it again, and that in and of itself should have made me turn down his offer to replace my shake and fries, but I didn't.

So here I am: sitting in the passenger seat of Chris' midnight blue Mercedes, sleep-deprived with a sore ass and a stomach full of butterflies.

I'm choosing to blame the sleep deprivation for my bad decision-making tonight, well, this morning. Otherwise, I'd have to own up to not using my brain at all when I agreed to this impromptu trip to….

Fuck, I don't even know where we're going.

Chris seems content to just drive around, and for whatever reason, I'm happy to let him. For the first time in a long time, I feel comfortable. It's an odd sensation, this willingness to let someone else hold the reigns, and I know it's only temporary.

Eventually, the knot that's lived in the pit of my stomach will return. And so will the intense, unshakable fear that if I'm not the one driving the bus then it'll run right off the road. But for now, I'm choosing to focus on their absence while not delving too deeply into why they seemed to have disappeared the moment Chris called my name.

I glance out the window into a dark sky that's ugly and gray, clouds heavy and burdened with another bevy of raindrops they'll set free without a moment's notice. It's been storming on and off all night. Most people hate when it storms this time of year. They bundle up in their beds, dreading the wrath of the rain and praying it won't mix with the bitter cold to turn into something else. But I love storms, especially the moments after, when the world is still, caught between beginning the process of recovering from the sudden onslaught and bracing for the possibility of another.

I can relate to that feeling, to wanting to move on and heal from damage you never deserved in the first place and being afraid to because you know a second wave of destruction can sweep you away at any moment.

"Are you okay with a little ride?" His voice, a deep, husky timbre with all the crisp sophistication you'd expect from someone raised up north, pulls me out of my head and back into the car. There's music playing, some old-school R&B tune, and it's the only thing that's been filling the silence around us since we climbed inside. Now the music is drowned out by Chris' question hanging in the air and the weight of his gaze on the side of my face. When I turn to look at him, his eyes are back on the road.

"Longer than the one we're currently on?"

"Yeah." He chances another glance at me, chestnut eyes moving over my features as he switches lanes. "There's a twenty-four-hour diner about forty-five minutes from here. It's right on the edge of the Georgia state line and real popular with truckers, but they have the best shakes."

I should say no because leaving the state, even just barely since New Haven is so far on the edge of South Carolina it might as well be Georgia, isn't a good idea. But there's something endearing about the small smile tilting up the corner of his mouth, that makes me feel reckless, daring, more like me than I have in months.

"Yes. I'm cool with a longer ride."

Hopefully, by the time we get there, the butterflies will have cleared out and I'll be able to properly investigate his claim about these milkshakes.

* * *

"Good right?" Chris asks me, gesturing towards the old school milkshake glass nestled in between my hands. A dark teasing expression plays across his features as he watches my lips wrap around the thick red straw protruding proudly from the creamiest cookies and cream milkshake I've ever had the pleasure of tasting.

This is my second pull, which, if I'm being honest, began before

I'd even swallowed the contents of the first. Something about the silky smooth texture of the base ice cream had caught my attention and refused to let go, prompting me to moan and dive in for another taste, not caring that the sound I made had made Chris' eyes glow danger-ously for a second, all sorts of emotions I couldn't name, and didn't care to, flitting around in a warm gaze that threatened to melt me and the best damn milkshake I've ever had.

Not that I'd ever tell him.

Reluctantly, I release the straw and sit back a little. My back brushes against the electric blue vinyl of the booth we're sitting in. It's identical to all the other booths that run along the walls of Curly's—a Black-owned and family-run diner that, according to the burly, gray-haired gentleman that showed me and Chris to our table, has been keeping children in the Blackmon clan fed for close to fifty years now.

What the older gentleman, Al, left out of the diner's history, Chris filled in for me, telling me how Charles 'Curly' Blackmon built the building with his bare hands and put his entire family to work. They started simple, with burgers, hand-cut fries, and sweet tea. A few months into business, his wife, Alberta, introduced milkshakes—that she whipped up with nothing but a whisk and elbow grease—to the menu and the rest was history. A history, Chris knew like the back of his hand.

I wasn't able to hide my surprise when he finished reciting it or when Al sent our server, a young girl named Jalisa, out to our table and she greeted Chris by name. Only then did he admit that he came here a lot, on late-night drives when he needed to clear his mind. Everything in me wanted to ask what he, a young man from an affluent family and the world at his feet, could need to clear his mind of, but I didn't.

His demons are his business.

"It's okay," I say finally, lying with the same tongue that was already longing for another taste. "I think I've had better."

"Mallory." Both of his brows come down, knitting together to form a disappointed line. A shiver of awareness tickles my spine and warmth spreads through my lower belly at the stern timbre of his voice. And it's such a foreign sensation, such a shock to my system, that I try to cross my legs underneath the table to suppress it.

Unfortunately, that results in my knees brushing against the inside of Chris' hard thighs, which are bracketing mine. The contact jolts me further, but somehow I manage to keep the shock off my face. "We both know that's a lie."

Suddenly, I'm not sure if we're talking about milkshakes or….

Or what? What else would we be talking about?

Pushing the ridiculous thought away, I shrug. "No, we don't. I mean it is good, but I just don't know if it's everything you made it out to be. You might have overhyped it a bit."

I hold my index finger and thumb up, pinching them close together to indicate the amount of over-selling I'm wrongly accusing Chris of doing. His eyes narrow, chestnut dancing with mischief and danger as he looks from my hand back to me. He crosses his arms. I watch him sit back in his seat and foolishly wish he wasn't wearing that hoodie so I could see the muscles in his arms contract with the action.

"You moaned."

"*What?*"

"You. Moaned."

Chris waits patiently for me to respond, and while he waits everything about him is tuned into me. His eyes locked on mine, his body inclined towards me. Hell, even his breathing seems to match mine, and it's weirdly comforting to be so in sync with him. To be held in his imploring gaze makes me feel like I've been dipped in a warm bath of whiskey and honey.

"No—"

Thankfully, my lie is cut off by the sudden appearance of Jalisa. She's holding a plate of curly fries in one hand and one with a double cheeseburger and home fries in the other. I watch her set the plates down, eyes focused on her hands, the table, and the same shade of blue lining the edges of the plates. Anything but the man across from me who has managed to send jolts of shocked arousal through me with just two words.

"Thank you, Jalisa," Chris says. There's a smile in his voice that I refuse to look up to see even though I desperately want to know if it's as mind-melding as it sounds.

"You're welcome. Can I get you guys anything else?"

"Mallory?" I can still hear the smile and somehow it sounds even more decadent wrapped around the syllables of my name. Unable to stand it any longer, I steel myself and meet his eyes.

"Yes, Christopher?"

He tilts his head to the side, one thick brow lifted in amusement. "Do you need anything else from Jalisa?"

I turn to look at the young girl, who can't be any more than seventeen years old, and smile. "No, Jalisa. I'm good."

"Okayyyy," she says, slowly backing away from the table and looking at the two of us like we've lost it. "Just holler if that changes."

In the blink of an eye, she's gone, leaving me with an irritatingly handsome, and frustratingly smug, Chris. I make a show of rolling my eyes at him as I pick up a fry from my plate and pop it into my mouth. Then, because I'm a little embarrassed but not foolish enough to miss out on another milkshake today, I take another pull from my straw and let out a happy sigh.

"It wasn't a moan."

"Oh?" He laughs, taking the top bun off of his burger and rearranging the order of the fixings so there's lettuce and tomato between each patty instead of just on top. "What would you call it then?"

"A satisfied exhalation."

"That's a moan, Mallory."

"It isn't," I insist, heat flooding my cheeks at the idea of anyone hearing this ridiculous debate. Everything we've discussed since he ran into me has been ridiculous. Secretary job descriptions, my supposed dick-filled thoughts, the formal definition of a moan.

I can't remember the last time I felt comfortable enough around anyone that wasn't my top three to joke around like this. It feels nice. Familiar yet foreign enough to have warning bells ringing in my mind.

Reminding me that once upon a time, I learned a lesson about trusting charismatic guys who use jokes to make you comfortable around them. They laugh and kid around with you until your guard is down and then….and then it's too late.

Chris is still smiling when I finally manage to claw myself out of my own dark thoughts.

"I know what a moan sounds like, Mal."

I do my best to ignore the way the words seem to hit me right in my gut and take another long pull of my milkshake before I finally say, "Another perk of being the resident man whore, I bet. Doesn't mean you know what *my* moans sound like."

He takes my comment like he takes everything: in stride. He doesn't flinch even though somewhere deep down inside I'm cringing at the cattiness of my first statement and the pure awkwardness of the one I chose to follow it up with.

"You're right," he replies simply. "I don't."

Then he picks up his burger and takes a big bite out of it. His eyes fall closed as he chews, and at first, I don't know how to identify the sound he makes in the back of his throat. It's a low, rumbling sound that's almost animalistic in its refined intensity.

Every person within earshot of our booth turns to see where the sound is coming from. Some of them even look frightened, like they're trying to calculate the possibility of a starved tiger wandering into the diner, drawn in by the delicious, greasy fumes seeping out of every crevice in the old building.

The sound, which is totally not the right word for what's happening in Chris' chest, strikes a chord deep inside me. It winds its way through me, slipping under my skin and weaving through my bloodstream, curling up along every nerve ending that's linked to my system, and I freeze.

Literally.

With my mouth halfway open, hovering over the straw in my cup. Even my eyeballs don't move, which means I have no idea if or when the other patrons stop looking at us. It also means that when Chris opens his eyes again, with that same soft severity I saw before he kissed me all those weeks ago shining in their depths, I'm staring right at him.

"Something wrong?" He asks, no, *purrs*, innocently, sending more heat to flood my cheeks and other places I won't mention.

The question sets me in motion again, and I shake my head. "Nope."

"Good."

He flashes me a cocky grin, one that lets me know he did all of *that* on purpose, and goes back to eating his food. We eat in relative silence —well, he eats and I do this weird thing where I pretend I'm not watching him as I sip on my shake—and it doesn't take him long to clear his plate. When he's done, he leans back in the booth and takes a long sip of his chocolate shake with his eyes on me.

I push my empty glass aside and pop a fry in my mouth. "Are you just going to stare at me until I finish eating?"

A flash of pink, his tongue, swipes over his bottom lip, and I'm hit with the image of him eating me alive. Those perfect white teeth sinking into my skin and his tongue, wet and hot, soothing the carnal wounds with long strokes. It should be disturbing, but the only thing that bothers me about it is that I like it.

"Maybe."

"Please don't." I miss the weight of his gaze as soon as it leaves my face, and a few awkward moments pass where he's looking around the room at the patrons who were just staring at him before I sigh heavily. "I didn't say you couldn't look at me at all."

"Make up your mind, Mallory," he mutters, happily moving his eyes back to me. "Either you want me to look at you or you don't."

Something about his phrasing—probably the suggestion that having his eyes on or off of me is a desire I hold, which he's obliged to meet—makes my heart beat a bit faster. "You can look, just don't stare."

He lifts his brows, amusement making his gaze turn warm. "How else am I supposed to figure out the logic behind eating all of your french fries after your milkshake is gone?"

My brows pull together. "It's not exactly a mystery. I just always need something salty after I've eaten something sweet."

It's an old habit, one I no doubt picked up from my mom who

always grabs a handful of chips after she eats dessert. When Eric and I were little, we would always beg her to give us some too, and then it just became this thing we all do without even thinking about it. Chris pulls a face, and until now it never really occurred to me that other people might find it strange. "You think I'm weird, huh?"

He holds his hand up, pinching his index finger and thumb close together like I did earlier. "Just a little."

My mouth drops open. "You're not supposed to actually say yes! Didn't your mama ever tell you if you don't have anything nice to say, not to say anything at all?"

The smile that was in the process of taking over his entire face starts to fall, turning his expression from amused to closed off in a matter of seconds. I watch the sudden change with equal parts interest and dread, wondering what I said to make his mood shift so quickly.

"Probably. I'd like to think that's exactly the kind of thing she would have taught me, but I don't—" His gaze drops to his hands and stays there while his mouth works to form words I get the sense he has trouble saying. "I couldn't tell you if she did or not. I don't really remember her."

Oh. The solid, heavy weight of his words makes me feel so stupid for saying something so careless even though I had no way of knowing I was stumbling onto a land mine.

"I'm sorry," I whisper. "I didn't know you lost your mom."

When he looks back at me, there's a darkness creeping into the corners of his eyes, threatening to replace the swirls of rich chestnut. "It's okay. No one out here really knows. I don't talk about it a lot."

"I'm still sorry though."

And I am because I know what it feels like to walk around with such an important person missing from your life. My dad died when Eric and I were babies, so I don't remember anything about him. Never got to hear his voice or feel the comfort of his arms wrapped around me, holding me close and telling me that I'm safe.

"Don't be. It's been a long time."

"What does that have to do with anything? She was still your mom, and I'm sure you still miss her, which means I'm allowed to be sorry."

I'm not sure why I'm pushing this. I should have just accepted the out he gave me and moved on, but something about the way he dismissed his own grief, and minimized the impact the loss of his mom had on him, bothers me. His wooden tone, the hollow resolve in his words when he suggested that the length of time had anything to do with the compassion he deserves—like he was repeating someone else's words instead of his own—none of it sits right with me.

"Yeah," he laughs softly, but the darkness is still there, in his eyes, and it makes my heart hurt for him. "I guess you're right."

"I am." I keep my tone light, adding in a hint of sass in hopes of making him smile again, and after a full minute he gives in, gifting me with a rueful grin while he spins his empty glass around on the table.

6

MALLORY

"I don't understand why you can't miss *one* lab," my mother sighs heavily in my ear. The slight pout in her voice evident even over the wind whipping around my face as I speed walk to the biology building.

"Are you seriously encouraging your daughter to skip school, Ma?" I ask incredulously. "That kind of seems like the opposite of what you should be doing as a parent."

"Now you're missing my birthday party and calling my parenting abilities into question? Is that what they're teaching you in those fancy business classes, Mallory Pearl?"

One thing I've always appreciated about Mama is that she's not a small-time guilt tripper. She doesn't just make you feel bad for a moment, something quick you can shake off the second you're out of her presence and the disapproving tisk she makes after every word fades from your mind.

No, she has a way of making it last, of making you feel like whatever thing you've done is just as bad, or maybe even worse, as telling everyone in the family the secret ingredient in her red velvet cake or taking the Lord's name in vain in the middle of the church on Easter Sunday.

And unlike most parents, who raise their voices and berate you while they guilt trip you, she speaks softly so you have to focus on every word and absorb her disappointment into your very being.

It's effective, even when she's only half serious.

"Ma!" I shake my head. "I'm not missing your birthday party. I'll just be getting there at the same time as every other guest."

Honestly, I'll probably make it there before most of them. Our family members are perpetually late, always showing up on their own time with nothing but their hands out and mouths open. It's Mama's birthday, but she's still doing the majority of the work—taking the day off to cook food and decorate the small recreational center she rented out because it's too cold to do it in the backyard. Fortunately, Eric and Nic were able to head over to help her after they finished classes this afternoon, or else she would have run herself ragged before the shindig even started. *Unfortunately*, their availability has resulted in this lovely conversation.

"Hmmph. I guess that's fine."

"It's going to have to be, lady," I laugh, nestling my phone between my shoulder and ear as I reach for the door to the biology building. The halls are nearly empty, mainly because no one takes labs on Fridays. No one but me that is. "I'll see you in just a few hours, birthday girl. Okay?"

"Okay. How are you getting to the rec center again?"

I adjust the strap of my bag, groaning softly under my breath as I think about the answer to that question. My plan was to make the hour drive across town in the car Eric and I share since he was going to ride down with Sloane, but that plan went to crap when Sloane's mom called, ordering her to come home immediately to try on dresses for some charity gala.

I never really liked Lauren Carson. She's an overgrown mean girl who takes an odd pleasure in bullying her daughter, and today she moved up a few spaces on my shit list because her power move left me with only one option for a ride home.

Chris.

When Eric told me that he'd asked Chris to bring me down, I

immediately became anxious. Not because I have qualms about his driving abilities —obviously, that's not the case. I mean, our little trek to Curly's on Monday, and the nap I took on the way back to campus, is more than enough proof that I feel safe with him behind the wheel— but because the idea of spending more time alone with him made me more excited than it should have.

Plus, there was the ever-present issue of showing up to a family function with a handsome guy. Everyone would take one look at us arriving together and assume there was something more to our flirta-tious, but completely platonic, relationship, and I'm loathe to spend the entire night fending off my nosey aunts and cousins who refuse to accept that my perpetual singledom is a choice and not a character flaw.

Mama usually doesn't play the whole 'when is Mallory going to fall in love' game, but I already know that her eyes will be shining with unspoken questions when we show up together.

I push out a hard breath, pausing outside the door of my lab. "Chris. You remember him, right? Eric and Nic's friend?"

They met once last semester when Mama came up to campus for a homecoming game, and we all took her out to dinner. As someone who's worked in hospitals her entire life, she'd taken a shine to Chris as soon as he said he wanted to be a doctor. By the end of the meal, she'd declared him one of her bonus children and given him one of those bone-crushing hugs and a kiss on the cheek that left him blushing like a school boy.

I didn't understand his reaction then, but now, knowing that he lost his mom so young he can't even remember her, it makes sense. The warm hugs and that unique brand of motherly love Eric and I grew up with were glaringly absent from his life. Mama scoffs like I just accused her of forgetting one of her actual children.

"Of course! My future doctor," she muses, while I pray she doesn't ask the question most mothers would ask their daughters in this situa-tion. "Well, I can't wait to see you, sweetheart, but tell Chris not to break any laws to get you here."

"Okay, Ma." Relieved, I take another step towards the door. There are only three people in the room, which means I'm not late. *Yet.*

"Oh, and Mal?" She sounds distracted, probably because she's preparing to move on to her next task.

I turn away from the door, pressing my back against the wall. "Yes, ma'am?"

"Could you please text Tasha and tell her we'll be starting at eight instead of seven?"

"Tasha? Tasha Davis?"

"Yes, child," she says impatiently, probably because she doesn't understand why I sound like I don't remember the girl I called my best friend for close to a decade. We met on the first day of second grade and stayed joined at the hip until one weekend during our junior year of high school changed my life and, by extension, our friendship. "I ran into her at the store yesterday and invited the whole family. She and Trent are really looking forward to seeing you."

All of my thoughts come grinding to a halt and then, within the span of a second, kick into high gear. My stomach rolls violently, and the ball of anxiety I've been carrying around all day in regard to showing up to a family function with Chris is shoved out of the way by the sudden and intense wave of nausea.

It's been years since I've heard that name, longer since I've let it pass my lips or laid eyes on the face it belongs to. No part of me was prepared to hear it from Mama or for the dreadful memories it would inspire. My stomach twists, images of a night I've worked hard to forget flitting through my mind in rapid-fire flashes that take my breath away.

*Rough hands holding my wrists. Alcohol laced breath on my neck. Weight I couldn't possibly move on my own pressing me into the mattress...*I bend at the waist and force the air from my lungs out through my mouth. Slow and steady until my heartbeat is no longer pounding in my ears.

"Hello? Mallory! Are you still there?" Mama calls. "I know this child didn't hang up on me."

"I'm still here, Ma," I say, my voice just above a whisper. I hate that. That the mere mention of him has taken me back to a time when I was too weak to speak up for myself. A time when I smiled and laughed even though I was uncomfortable. A time when I said nothing at all when I should have said no—when I should have *screamed* it. "But I don't know if I still have Tasha's number. I'll check and see."

"Okay, thank you."

"You're welcome. I've gotta go, Ma."

"Of course, sweetie. I'll see you soon."

The line goes dead, and I close my eyes, pulling more deep breaths in through my nose and pushing them out the same way because if I open my mouth the only thing that will come out is the hollow, gut-wrenching scream that's building in my throat. It probably wouldn't be loud. Might not have the chance to reach its full potential because of the icy, skeletal fingertips of panic wrapping around my windpipe, but I can't risk it anyway. Not when I'm in public.

In public, Mallory Kent is strong, focused, capable. She doesn't break down. She doesn't let the ghosts of her past creep into her present and wipe away all the progress she's made. She doesn't give her power to anyone.

That's right. The voice in my head assures me, and I'm bolstered by it being on my side for once. If my brain is on board that means the rest of my body can fall into line.

All I have to do is stand up. My body obeys, my once bowed back straightening until I'm standing at my full height. *And look in my phone for Tasha's number.* My hands lift the phone up, fingers flying over the keyboard to scroll through my contacts. It doesn't take me long to find her name and before I can stop myself, I click on it and type out the shortest possible text.

> Mallory: Hey, it's Mal. Mama says the party is starting at 8.

And then, just because I can't go another second without knowing.

> Mallory: Is Trent coming with you?

I stare at the screen for a few seconds, hoping she'll text back immediately, but the thread stays quiet and eventually I give up, stashing the phone in my back pocket and pulling the door to the lab open.

With every step I take into the room, I feel more grounded. More like the Mallory I've worked so hard to become and less like the naive little girl who let herself get trapped in a web of lies with a venomous spider disguised as a harmless fly.

7

CHRIS

"**Y**our sister was disappointed to hear you weren't coming home for her debutante ball." My dad's gruff tone spills out of the speakers of my computer, filling up the quiet space in my apartment with its perfect diction and commanding timbre.

I sigh, exhausted already because I know that his irritation will bleed into the rest of our conversation. Since the start of my last semester at NHU, all of our weekly check-ins have started this way, with him bringing up a topic that will inevitably lead us back to his real issue with me: my refusal to come to heel.

Sometimes I wished he'd have the balls to start there because we both know he doesn't give a damn about Teresa's debutante ball. *She* doesn't even care about it. When I was home for Christmas break, she told me she'd much rather be spending her time in the art studio she rented without Dad knowing.

"I sent Ter a gift to congratulate her for making it through those classes without stabbing someone in the eye. It should get there tomorrow morning." The necklace is a custom-made piece from one of her favorite designers. It's artsy and colorful and nothing like the string of pearls all the other debutantes will have on; she's going to love it.

"And that would be fine if anyone actually gave a damn about presents," he mutters, finally looking up from the files spread out across his cherry wood desk.

The russet brown matches the expansive bookshelves lining the wall behind him, which means he's in his home office. I study the shelves behind him, noting how they're full of medical books, awards he's received over the years, and copies of journals he's been published in. There aren't any pictures of us there though, and none of the wife he's spent the last couple of decades grieving.

"This weekend is extremely important for our family. Teresa will be presenting herself to society on Saturday night, and we'll be breaking ground on the new surgical wing *named after your grandfather* that morning. You should be here, in Boston, with your family, not in the middle of nowhere at that godforsaken school. I had an entire speech prepared for you to give, but now I guess I'll have to let RJ do it."

"RJ is an actual doctor, Dad. I would think a speech from him at the opening of a wing he'll be running in a few years would be a bit more appropriate than one from me."

There are a million other things I want to say in response to his little tangent, but I learned the importance of choosing my battles a long time ago. It's been four years since I moved to New Haven for college, and he still hasn't accepted that I chose my own school instead of honoring his legacy and attending his alma mater, which means he never will.

It, along with the million other things I've done to assert my independence from him, will be a point of contingency between us for the rest of my life.

RJ, on the other hand, has done everything my dad has ever asked him to do, including forget his own mother. You would think a control freak like Reese Johnson Sr., would be elated that his oldest son—and his namesake no less—is so eager to please him, but it seems like no matter what he does, he can't get a sliver of the light Dad seems intent to shine on me.

I'd give it all to him if I could. All the expectations. All the pressure.

The derisive scoff he makes in response to my words filters through the speakers, filling the room with the evidence of his disdain for his own son, which I've never understood.

"We both know your brother isn't cut out for medicine."

"No, we don't know that. I think he'll make an excellent doctor and an even better surgeon."

He scoffs, annoyed that I possess the belief in his child he seems to lack. "It'll be a cold day in hell before he holds a scalpel in one of my operating rooms."

Irritation trickles down my spine, causing my nostrils to flare. Something about being next in line for the CEO title of the Johnson Hospital Group—one of the largest, minority-owned medical conglomerates in the country—makes Dad feel like he holds the careers of every emerging surgeon in his unfaltering hands. It's annoying, but what's even more problematic is that after nearly thirty years of practicing medicine and rising to the elite level of a world-renowned heart surgeon, everyone around him allows him to do just that. The board members of the hospitals he operates in, the surgeons he works with, even the nurses, they all default to him. Bend over backward to get his approval. Take his word as law. Allow him to make or break careers with one look.

Which means he could very well keep RJ from becoming a surgeon, but I don't understand why he ever would. Out of the three of us, RJ is the most eager to please Dad. Desperate for his approval. Happy to follow in his footsteps without a single opposing word. None of that matters to Dad though, because everything RJ is dying to give him, he wants from me.

"Good thing your operating rooms aren't the only ones he'll be licensed to work in."

I watch his mouth turn into a flat, disapproving line as he snatches his glasses off and tosses them on the desk. The black and gold frames land on the stack of papers with a quiet thump as he scrubs a hand over the bottom half of his face.

"I'm not in the mood to argue with you, Christopher."

"We're not arguing, Dad." But under my table, my hands are balled into fists, like I'm prepared for a fight.

"Good," he says lightly, but his eyes have gone cold like they do when he's decided the best strategy for winning the argument at hand is to concede for the moment and come back harder in the next round. "Tell me what's new. How are your classes going?"

"Classes are going really well." My shoulders relax a bit, and my eyes flick to the clock, making sure I have enough time to finish up this conversation and make it to campus to pick up Mallory. The thought of seeing her makes my chest ache a bit but in the best way. "Just working hard and waiting for May."

A fond smile stretches across his face, making him look like the man who taught me to drive and never missed one of my awards days growing up. Suddenly, I feel guilty about being so angry with him for wanting the best for me.

"You might not believe it, but I'm just as eager for you to be done as you are, having you back in Boston full-time will be a great relief."

I do believe it actually, because the sooner I come back to Boston, the sooner he can go back to dictating every aspect of my life. "Dad—"

One of his hands comes up, effectively cutting me off. "I don't want to hear it, son. We made a deal. I allowed you to finish your degree down there, but you *will* go to medical school in Cambridge."

"There are other medical schools."

"Not for you."

"Dad."

He shakes his head and the light from the wall of windows on the opposite side of his desk, which allows him to see the courtyard in the center of our estate, bounces off of the wrinkles in his forehead.

"We're not discussing it anymore, Christopher. You will come home after you graduate and finally begin living the life I've worked so hard to give you."My stomach twists, knowing exactly what the life he's worked to give me entails.

Obligation over choice.

Purpose over passion.

Legacy over love.

"And what if I don't want it?"

"Want?" A boisterous laugh fills my ears, mocking my, admittedly, pointless question. "The kind of life you were born to live isn't about want, son. It's about duty, to your family, to the legacy of Johnson men that came before you, to the patients who will trust you and their family members who will depend on you to stand between their loved ones and certain death. There's no room for *want* in that."

Leaning back in my desk chair, I stare at him, completely unmoved by the speech I've been getting since I was ten years old. "I don't believe that. Grandpa Joe let you live the life you wanted. You chose medicine, you chose cardiothoracics as your specialty, you chose to break family tradition and date Mom even though you didn't have his approval at first."

His eyes go wide at the mention of my mother and the antiquated Johnson family tradition of fathers choosing their son's wives, picking them from high-class families to breed generations of children steeped in excellence. He's probably shocked I brought it and her up in the same sentence since we never talk about either of them. I press my lips together to keep anything else from spilling out and hope he doesn't notice that I've just spouted off a piece of information I shouldn't even have.

All of the details I have about how my parents ended up together came from the stories Margaret told me when I was a child, and more of them were filled in when I asked my grandfather about her when I was home over Christmas break. He was reluctant to share, not wanting to anger my dad or upset my brother, but when I told him about the nightmares and the hole in my life shaped like her, he took pity on me.

He said at first he was against them dating, adamant that my father not waste time with someone he would never allow him to marry. Mom was a poor, damn near homeless, ward of the state who only met his son because she was smart enough to win a scholarship to the elite private school he attended.

Funnily enough, the scholarship, which covered the entirety of her tuition for the year and provided a small stipend for transportation, was funded by Grandpa. I guess he never expected his prince of a son to fall in love with the recipient—a lifelong foster kid with a smart mouth and wild ideas—but eventually, she grew on both of them.

Her and dad became attached at the hip, companions and then competitors who vied for the top spot in their class for years. Tears, accompanied by a sad smile, shone in the old man's eyes when he revealed that she ended up being valedictorian. When I asked him how Dad—a man as competitive as they come—took that, something dark passed over his features before he changed the topic.

The urge to double back, or try to come up with some quick excuse to explain away what I just said is strong, and it only grows stronger as his eyes bore into me through the screen. I send up a quick prayer of thanks that he's not here, not physically in the room with me, because otherwise I'd be spilling my guts by now, compelled by the power of his presence to give up my source.

"Your grandfather may have led you to believe that he let me make my own choices, but he only allowed me to marry Celeste because he thought she was a good match for me. She met all of his criteria: smart, even-tempered, willing to challenge me when necessary."

Something dark passes over his face. I read it as grief or regret even though it looks remarkably similar to anger. "And by some miracle, we both agreed that it was a good fit."

There's a distinct lack of warmth in his voice as he talks about how his union with Mom came to be. Grandpa Joe wasn't all that warm in his recounting, but there aren't a lot of things that get the old man riled up. I would have expected more from Dad though, especially when he's talking about his late wife.

"It sounds more like a business deal than a romantic relationship." The words pop out of my mouth, unbidden, and Dad's eyes harden. I know he's about to take me to task for being so disillusioned about how marriage works for people like us. We were raised to believe in logistics not love.

"It wasn't far from it, but I did what needed to be done to ensure the arrival of another generation of Johnson men." It all sounds so clinical. A business deal masquerading as a marriage. Dad laughs, but the sound is bordering on humorless. "I can see that you don't approve, Chris, but this is how our family has worked for years. Fathers choosing for their sons, using all the wisdom they've earned over the years to ensure the continuation of our bloodline. I accepted it, and one day soon, you will too."

"I'm only twenty-two, Dad, I think I have some time. Plus, you have another son you should be worried about choosing for." RJ is eight years older than me, which means that Dad is, once again, misplacing his energy.

He waves his hand. "RJ is not my concern. You are, and you don't have as much time as you think. Not if you want to find a woman of substance and worth. Half of the young ladies you graduated with are already engaged. Snatched up by your former classmates and friends who had the foresight you lack."

I let out a long sigh, knowing exactly where this speech is going. Giselle DuPont. The only girl I received his permission to date. All of my other relationships happened under his radar, but with Giselle, it was different from the start.

I can still remember the pride shining in his eyes when he gave me his formal blessing, which I had refused to ask for because even then I was determined not to adhere to some dusty ass rules made by men in my family that died long before I was born. We dated for a few years in high school, and our coupling was more about proximity than it was about attraction.

We grew up together, attending all the same schools, camps and extra-curricular activities, so being together just made sense. My dad and her parents—Oscar and Ramona— were thrilled about the relationship, envisioning a merging of our medical empire with their pharmaceutical kingdom. And, much to my father's dismay, that vision shattered into pieces when I broke up with Giselle a few weeks before leaving for New Haven.

I think he has always seen the ending of our relationship as the catalyst for my departure and hopes that pushing us back together will be the thing to finally make me come home. He's wrong though. If anything, his constant nagging about us reviving the long-dead relationship so he can officially choose her for me, makes me want to stay away even more.

"Giselle is still single though. In fact, she was Teresa's mentor this year, and she asks about you quite regularly. She will also be disappointed to hear you won't be home for the ball. Don't suppose you put her a gift in the mail too?"

"No," I bite out. "I didn't have any reason to."

He shakes his head as if the dissolution of an ill-conceived high school relationship is the most tragic thing he's heard. "Once upon a time, not so long ago, you loved Giselle. You used to look at her like she hung the moon and the stars. I knew then, just like I know now, that you two had a bright future ahead of you. A bright, happy life here in Boston with both of your families there to support you."

"It was a high school sweetheart situation, Dad. No one was talking about marriage or buying rings. We were just kids."

"Well you're plenty damn grown now, son," he snaps, his voice going low and impatient before it evens back out. "And I'm sure you two could grow together again if you'd just try. Start today, send her a gift to let her know you appreciate her showing your sister how to be a woman of worth. I'll even deposit a few thousand in your bank account, so you can make it nice."

"Dad—" I'm shaking my head no, but he's already got his phone out, no doubt transferring the funds.

He clicks a few buttons before turning his eyes back on me. "There. It's sent. I expect the purchase to be made within the hour. Arrange for it to be gift wrapped and delivered to the DuPont's home, Giselle is staying there while her townhouse is being renovated."

Before I get a chance to respond, a knock sounds on his side of the call, drawing his attention to some point in the office beyond what I can see. It's probably his personal assistant coming to tell him that something or someone needs his attention more than me. There was a time when I would have been frustrated by that, but today I'm thankful for the interruption.

Let him go off and save a life or meet with his fellow board members to discuss the acquisition of another hospital or medical group, anything to add another gem to the crown he's hellbent on passing down to me.

"Dr. Johnson, you'll need to leave for your dinner with the DuPonts in the next few minutes if you want to make it to the restaurant on time." Lyla, the latest in the long line of personal assistants, says in a sweet, syrupy voice that lets me know why she's lasted as long as she has. Dad likes women who will placate him, make him feel strong and powerful even when he can't manage to make it to a simple dinner with his oldest friends without her telling him what time to leave the house.

"Thank you, Lyla. I'll be out shortly." He turns his attention back to me and fixes me with a stern stare. "Send the gift, Christopher. It will be the first step toward securing the future of this family."

Tension builds in my shoulders and neck, overtaking my muscles as annoyance slips down my spine at his insistence. "I don't want to live like that, Dad. I don't want a business deal masquerading as a marriage. I want to choose a partner that's right for me at a time that's right for me, not for the family."

"And when exactly would that time be, son?" He asks, eyes turning cold with anger he's actively reigning in. "When you're done sleeping your way through New Haven? Or should I hold off until you get to Harvard and have the chance to fuck every female in your cohort?"

"Dad—"

"No." He shakes his head, clearly on a roll. "*No.* You've had four years, Christopher. Four years to make your own choices and as far as I can tell the only thing you've chosen to do is fuck everything that moves while I keep your best and only option open. And don't get me wrong, I've had my share of women, but every dog has to learn how to come home when called."

I clench my teeth. "I'm not a dog."

"No, you're my son," he says softly. "And I love you very much.

That's why I want to see you happy. Settled. Not wasting the energy you'll need to build your legacy fighting against it."

"And by building a legacy you mean…."

"Continuing the Johnson name. Fathering the next generation of doctors who will practice groundbreaking medicine in the hospitals my ancestors built for them."

The urge to roll my eyes is so strong, I almost lose the fight not to do so. He has two sons and a daughter. The continuation of the Johnson name doesn't have to depend solely on me.

"That can all happen, Dad, but it doesn't have to happen now and it doesn't have to happen with Giselle."

This is the part I can't wrap my head around. The Giselle of it all. If he wants to choose my wife so badly, why does it have to be her instead of, I don't know, anyone else? Dad wraps his fingers around the edge of the desk and pushes back.

"Giselle is a lovely young woman, Chris, and she's from our world. She understands what it takes to keep an empire running and never over-inflates her role in doing so. She knows when to step back and be quiet, and when she speaks she always says the right thing. In short, she is the perfect person for you."

I frown at his description of my so-called perfect partner. Once again, he's not wrong, Giselle is all of the things he described her to be and more. She's docile and submissive. Exceptionally smart but always playing the role of the ditsy damsel in distress because it makes the powerful men around her more comfortable. And she would make a good partner, for someone, but not for me.

I open my mouth to say just that, but Dad holds his hand up, his attention on the door where Lyla must be urging him to wrap up our call.

"I have to go now, Chris, but hear me when I say this: there's great-ness in you, untapped potential that's just waiting to be unleashed, generations of Johnson men waiting to be born into a world you have the power to shape with your hands. And I know how important it is to have the right woman beside you to do it."

I shift in my seat, hating the weight his words are placing on my shoulders. When he talks like this, like everything—the future of our family, the lives of hundreds of nameless, faceless patients and employees —hangs on the choices I make. The anxiety and doubt it induces, makes me wonder if I want to practice medicine at all.

Keeping my expression blank, I return his stare and deny him the pleasure of acknowledging his 'father knows best' speech.

"Have a good dinner, Dad. I'll talk to you later."

I watch him pick up his glasses and stand as he slides them back on, leaning over the desk with one hand on the laptop, prepared to close it once he's had the last word.

"Same time next week, son." The order moves through me, pushing my frustration to a dangerous boiling point.

"Yes, sir."

He ends the call without even saying goodbye, and I sit, barely containing the urge to swipe my arm across the table and send everything on it crashing to the ground.

After a few moments, I'm calm enough to see the wisdom in buying Giselle a gift though. Making the purchase will placate my father for a few weeks while I figure out an actual plan to get him off my back, and out of my personal life, once and for all.

Opening the computer again, I go to the website of my father's favorite jewelry store, purchase the first thing I see, and have it sent to Giselle's parent's house via overnight delivery. It should get there just before the ball starts, which means Dad will be extra pleased. Once I'm done with that, I push up from the table and grab my phone, keys, and the small overnight bag I was instructed to pack because for some reason everyone is planning on staying at the Kent family home for the night.

Sloane has already called dibs on the guest room while I am slated to ride what will be left of the night out on the pull-out couch in the living room. Sleepovers haven't been my thing for quite some time, but Eric insisted that I stay. He said his mom would be upset if she didn't get a chance to have all of us gathered around her table in the morning, eating a home-cooked meal before we went back to campus. Since I hate the food on campus, and spend most of my time ordering take-out or eating at Curly's, I didn't argue.

I'm pulling out of the garage underneath my building, with about twenty minutes to make it to campus before Mallory gets out of lab, when my phone starts to ring. Looking down, I see my brother's name flashing on the screen with a picture of us at his medical school graduation in the background. I seriously consider not answering, because sometimes talking to RJ is just like talking to my dad, but at the last moment I pick up, putting the phone on speaker and letting it rest on my lap.

"What's up, RJ?"

"*What's up?*" He drawls. The sound of him mocking me tap dancing on my last nerve. "Who answers their phone like that anymore?"

"I do," I say tightly. "So, like I said, what's up?"

RJ never calls me unless he wants to gloat about something. Here lately, all of his calls have been about Dad and me constantly bumping heads.

"Nothing. Just saw Dad leaving for dinner. He looked pretty annoyed, and I figured since it's Friday afternoon, it must be because of you."

My jaw clenches, and I find myself grinding my teeth to bite back the urge to ask him why Dad being mad at me makes him so happy. It's a dumb question though because I already know the answer. Dad's obsession with my life, with my future, has been a constant source of contention for RJ and me.

When we were growing up, the eight-year difference between us meant that I placed him on a pedestal. He was my hero, my big brother, the one person I looked up to and modeled myself after. That is until I realized that he resented me for getting the love our father refused to give him.

"Yeah, we had words, so what?"

A cruel laugh follows my question, and somewhere in the background, I hear the clinking of glass and the faint sound of liquid being poured. He must have taken up residence in Dad's office after he left for dinner and helped himself to the Scotch he keeps in there.

"You're being very vague, Christopher. Whatever did you and father argue about today?" He sighs heavily, and I imagine him plopping down in the seat behind the desk. Folding his lean frame and long legs into the plush leather. "I can only think of one subject that could make him so upset with his favorite son."

"Is that what you called for? Gossip?"

"Not gossip, little bro. Information."

I feel my own cruel laugh crawling up my throat as I think about the information I *could* give him. Information that would crush him, that would help him realize the man whose approval he works so hard for, will never give it to him.

"Just the same shit, RJ," I reply, woodenly. "Dad hates that I came to New Haven. Dad wants me to go to Cambridge for medical school. Dad wants me to come back to Boston and bend the fucking knee, so he can run my life the way he runs yours."

"See that's where you got it all wrong. Dad doesn't run my life. He'd have to give a fuck about my life to run it." Both of my brows pull together in shocked agreement as I switch lanes, but I don't get a chance to reply before RJ continues. "Don't worry about me though. I'm going to give him plenty of shit to care about pretty soon, starting with this cardiothoracic fellowship at JMH."

I wince at the mention of his fellowship, remembering how adamant Dad was about keeping RJ from operating in the hospitals we were raised to run. I should warn him, let him know that his fellowship won't impress Dad in the least because he has no intention of letting him learn a damn thing, but I swallow those words too. He won't listen to me anyway.

"Yeah, well, good luck with that, man."

"I don't need luck, Chris, I'm a Johnson. I was born to be a surgeon."

I don't know anything about my brother's surgical ability, but I hope for his sake it matches the arrogance coating his words. "Right. That's all you need to succeed, that good ole Johnson DNA."

"Damn, right," he says, a smile in his voice. "You're the only fool who acts like being born with greatness in your blood is some kind of curse."

"Blessings don't usually come with strings attached." Regret winds its way through my chest almost instantly. I know better than to play into RJ's hand. He always does this: ropes me into conversations I don't want to have about things neither of us can change.

His side of the line is quiet for a second, nothing but the sound of more expensive liquor being poured into an even more expensive glass echoing in my ears as I turn onto the two-lane road that will take me to the back side of campus where the Biology building is located.

"Shit, if Giselle DuPont was one of my strings, I'd die a happy man."

Turning into a parking spot, I cut the engine and let out a bitter laugh. "You know it's gross to refer to her that way right? She's a person, not a string or a pawn in whatever game you think I'm playing with Dad."

"You're right," RJ says, sounding contrite before he starts laughing snidely. "She's not any of those things. She's the fucking princess of pharmaceuticals and she wants to be your wife."

I roll my eyes. "I don't want a wife." Not yet, anyway. I want a life of my own, a legacy I carved out with my own hands. A name that I earned.

"That's 'cause you're an idiot."

"Is it really so crazy to want to live my own life, RJ? To want to make my own choices?"

"Fucking everything with legs isn't making your own choices, Chris. It's actually the exact opposite because you're not *choosing* anything, you're sampling everything."

Once again, my brother has shocked me. Mainly because he's managed to form a coherent thought while he's clearly getting wasted on expensive Scotch, but also because of his uncanny ability to echo our father's sentiments so accurately.

"What's the point of choosing?" I ask, exasperated. "Let's say I did get serious with someone, it's not like Dad's going to respect that choice. He's dead set on it being me and Giselle and nothing is going to change his mind."

"Normally, I'd agree with you, man."

"You've never agreed with me on anything, RJ."

"Yeah." He laughs. "You're right about that. Well, I guess I have to disagree with you yet again."

"About what?"

RJ sighs, and I wonder if all the liquor is catching up to him. "Grandpa Joe told me that you asked him about Mom."

The sudden change in conversation catches me off guard. "I did. What does that have to do with anything?"

"He told you about how Mom and Dad got together, how he didn't approve of her when they first started dating?"

"Yeah."

"Did he tell you how Dad got his approval?"

I flip back through my thoughts, searching for any mention of how they finally got Grandpa to agree to their relationship and coming up empty. "No, I don't think he did."

"Well, they'd been dating for years and Grandpa still refused to give his blessing, so when they were juniors in college, Dad just brought her to the house on the day of the annual charity gala and introduced her to everyone in the room as his future wife."

"He proposed without Grandpa's blessing?" There's no way to keep the shock out of my voice. I can't imagine my father like that. Young, in love, bucking against a system he's determined to make me abide by. It doesn't make sense. This version of events. Neither Grandpa nor Dad mentioned it to me. "But Grandpa and Dad said he approved in the end. That he wanted him to be with Mom."

"Oh, he did. Once he saw them together, he realized that Mom made his son better in every way. She made him brave, gave him the courage he needed to stand up to his own father. He respected the fuck out of her after that, maybe even more than Dad."

The look of pride and admiration on my grandfather's face when he spoke about my mother flashes through my mind, and once again, I'm left wondering how that made my dad feel. If the respect his father showed his future wife contributed to the bitter way he spoke about their union now, all these years later.

"That's a cool story, RJ, I'm still not sure what it has to do with me."

"For you to be so damn smart, Chris, you can be fucking dense sometimes, you know that?" The doors to the Biology building fling open and a student comes out. I watch them for a moment and sigh with relief when I realize it's not Mallory. I don't want her to hear any part of this conversation. My family's elitist bullshit isn't something I'm proud of.

"If you've got a point, make it."

"My point," he says, slurring slightly, "is that Dad might seem like a rigid bastard, but he wasn't always like that. He wants you with Giselle now, but given his history, it stands to reason that he could be convinced to back off and let you choose."

I scoff. "And how the hell am I supposed to do that?"

"Hmm." RJ hums thoughtfully, and I don't know whether to be scared or relieved that he's actually putting thought into this. "You could do the same thing he did."

"Get engaged without his permission and use his obsession with public perception to force him to accept her?" I frown. "Pretty sure that one won't work."

"I don't even think you need to go that far. Just stop fucking around so much and date someone. You haven't been in one serious relationship since Giselle, which is probably why he's so stuck on you two together. This whole detour to New Haven just looks like four years of sowing your wild oats before you come back to slide into the place in her life Dad has been encouraging her to keep open for you. Everybody, including her, thinks that's the case, and you sending her all those nice gifts while still being single after all this time keeps the hope alive."

"I'm not getting in a relationship just to get Dad off my back."

"Well, then you might as well come back to Boston with an engagement ring in your pocket because the only way men like Dad stop walking all over you is if you stand up and stop being a rug. It worked for Dad with Grandpa. I don't see why it wouldn't work for you."

I massage my temple with one hand, hating that his logic is sound. That his words have planted a seed in my brain my desire for freedom and independence will water until it blooms at the most inopportune time.

8

MALLORY

Chris was oddly quiet when I climbed into his car after lab. Normally, I wouldn't mind the silence, but today I do because it leaves too much room for me to think about the multitude of ways things at this party can go left. Tasha still hasn't texted me back, so I don't know if she's bringing him with her or not, and it's the not knowing that's killing me. Or so I'd like to think.

To be quite honest, I'm not sure that knowing would be any better. I mean, of course, I'd know, but knowledge isn't always power. Sometimes it's a life-sucking force. Sometimes it's a tornado that you can't avoid, a train wreck you can't look away from. A car crash you can't stop no matter how hard you hit the brakes.

My leg bounces, and I pick at the skin of my cuticles while toying around with the idea of skipping Mama's party altogether. It would be a plausible solution if I could be certain she wouldn't murder me herself for doing so. As it is, there's no way to know because missing the party would mean giving her a reason, and I can't do that. She doesn't know about that night with Trent, or the months of me and him sneaking around that led up to it, and I have every intention of keeping it that way.

Those ugly truths are mine and mine alone, which means I'm going to have to plaster on a fake smile and power through a party that will feel like my own personal hell. Long fingers land on my leg, resting right above my knee, making it impossible to keep moving, and pulling me out of my anxious reverie. I glance at Chris' hand, noting the way his fingertips are pressing into my thigh, and then up at him. He's still got the majority of his attention on the busy road, but I can tell he knows I'm looking at him.

He switches lanes and glances at me. "Tell me what's wrong."

I'm intrigued and annoyed that it's not a question. Most people would say 'what's wrong?' or 'are you okay?' but not Chris. He just jumps straight over pleasantries and personal boundaries and gets to the heart of the matter. Too bad I can't tell him the truth either.

"Nothing, I'm just worried about being late." It's a bad lie since the party started at 8:00 pm and it's only 8:45 p.m. Most of the guests probably haven't even arrived yet.

"We're not going to be that late. I bet we'll get there before the DJ plays the Electric Slide for the first time."

"Yeah," I agree reluctantly, my gaze dropping to his hand on my thigh again. "Maybe."

His fingers twitch slightly, like they aren't sure if they should still be where they are, and I watch with a kind of disembodied interest as he removes them one by one and then puts his hand back on the steering wheel. "Is that all?"

The way he asks the question, with a gentle prodding tone, makes it feel like he already knows the answer, and I force myself to continue looking out the window so he doesn't see the panic that has to be playing across my features right now. It's a slow-moving thing, slithering through my veins like molasses, and although I hate the feeling, I'm grateful for it because if it's moving slow that means I have a chance to stop it. To beat it back before it forces me to spill secrets I have no intention of ever sharing.

"Of course," I say. "What else would I have to be worried about?"

"I don't know, but I'm here when you're ready to talk about it."

When you're ready to talk about it. Not *if*. Because he already knows there's more to the story. A terrible mix of relief and dread spreads through my chest, curling around my breastbone and squeez-ing. I don't know why the relief is there. The prospect of sharing the ugliest, most broken, part of myself with him should be terrifying, but my brain refuses to code it that way. It's too busy reminding me that he shared a hard truth with me earlier this week, something no one else knows about him.

"Thank you." My throat is tight as I say the words, and I still don't look at Chris. Can't when I know thanking him for the offer means that for the first time in a long time, I'm admitting there is actually a prob-lem. Chris gives a quick bob of his head, just enough to let me know he heard me, and then it's done. We ride in silence the rest of the way.

* * *

IT'S ALMOST twelve in the morning when I take my first real breath. One that's not pinched by anxious misery I work too hard to hide behind big smiles that make my cheeks hurt and bright laughter that sounds overly chipper and all wrong to my own ears. When the release finally comes—courtesy of Tasha Davis waltzing into my mother's birthday party three hours late with a fire engine red dress hugging her petite frame and not another soul behind her— the relief is so swift and intense, I drop the knife I'm using the cut my Aunt Mary a slice of birthday cake.

"Whoa!" The word rolls out of Chris' mouth, smooth as silk, and I fight the urge to roll my eyes at him as he swoops down and picks the knife up off of the floor. Ever since we got here, he's been suspiciously underfoot. Whenever I make a move, he's right behind me. Following me to the kitchen to dig up some more spoons and forks. Helping me get more sodas to put in the coolers Mama has set up by the door. Escorting me to Aunt Mary's car to get the extra pack of cigarettes she keeps in her glove compartment.

At first, I was too preoccupied with thoughts of Trent showing up here with Tasha to care that he was following me around and giving unnecessary credence to the rumors that he's my new boyfriend, which sparked the moment we walked through the door. But now that she's here and he's not, I'm thinking clearly enough to address it.

"Are you okay?" he asks, his eyes gliding over my body the same way they did when he ran into me on that path the other night. "The blade didn't cut you, did it?"

"Relax, Dr. Johnson. I'm perfectly fine."

He sits the knife on the table, and I pick it up and start to move towards the kitchen doors. I don't even have to look back to know he's following me and just before I make it to the doors, I spin on my heels and hold the hand without the knife up. He doesn't stop walking in time though, and in a matter of seconds, my palm is resting flat on the rigid muscles of his pectorals. The heat radiating through the fabric of his shirt melts all of my nerve endings and for a second I forget what I was about to say.

Warmth spreads from the center of my palm down my arm and through the rest of me without warning, and just like I did earlier when his hand was on my thigh, I stare at the place where our bodies are touching. It's a small bit of contact, but it makes me think about what more would feel like.

Like that kiss but a million times better.

I snatch my hand away, hoping my unfounded desire isn't showing on my face.

"Not yet," Chris says softly.

My eyes stretch wide, panic rising in my chest at the thought of him somehow knowing what's going on in my brain. "What?"

"You called me Dr. Johnson, but I'm not a doctor yet."

"Oh. Right. I mean, duh, I know that. I was just being...." A flash of red moves somewhere behind Chris' head, and my eyes are immediately drawn to the sight of Eric giving Tasha a friendly hug and introducing her to Sloane. As glad as I am that Trent isn't with her, I'm still not over the moon about seeing her after all this time. What if she wants to know why I cut her out of my life? What if she wants to be friends again? What if she....

"*Mallory?!*"

Startled, I turn my attention back to Chris who is the picture of confusion. "Yeah?"

"Are you sure you're—"

"Oh my God! Please don't ask me if I'm okay again, Christopher. I'm fine. I just told you I was." Turning again, I storm through the kitchen doors and breathe a sigh of relief when I find the room empty.

Hopeful that Chris won't follow, I march over to the sink and rinse the knife off. Once I'm done, I grab the nearest dish towel and take too much time drying it off. My back is still to the door when it swings open. Music, laughter, and talking filter into the room, swirling in my ears until they close again. The person who just entered the room isn't Chris—I can tell because the air isn't vibrating with the currents of electricity that like to run between us these days, teasing my senses with possibility—so that means it must be a guest looking for something that's already out on the tables.

I heave a long sigh and start to use the towel in my hand to dry the sink. "All of the food has already been put out."

"I wasn't looking for food, Mal."

The soft, playful lilt of my former best friend's voice sends memories from a lifetime ago skittering through my brain like jarred marbles being spilled on the floor. Sleepovers and dance parties. Family dinners at each other's houses. Oaths made with bloody, wounded palms pressed together under the light of a full moon. Text messages sent from our very first cell phones back in the days when you had to use colons and parentheses to make emojis.

A bond.

A friendship.

A sisterhood.

For a second there, when Trent and I first started dating, we thought we would be the real deal one day. Sisters by law if not by blood. Tasha was the only one who knew about us, but she only found out because she caught us one night when I was sleeping over. I had snuck out of her room to meet Trent downstairs in their finished basement, and she found us making out.

I remember being impressed by that room. I'd never been in a house with a basement, let alone one that had a pool table, couch, and TV. Everyone in our class loved Tasha's house and every girl was infatuated with her handsome older brother who smiled at us when we came over for her birthday parties and cheered for all of us when he came to our games.

But I was the lucky one.

The one who got his extra attention. Who got his smiles and jokes and lingering glances that lasted longer when I was the only friend sleeping over. There were some nights, when we were freshmen and he was a senior, that Tasha would leave me downstairs in the living room with Trent while she went upstairs to talk on the phone with her boyfriend.

At first, I felt awkward around him, afraid that the way I felt about him was too obvious, but then he'd do or say something to put me at ease: make a joke or toss the remote in my lap and ask me to put on a show while he made popcorn. After a while it became our norm, Tasha going upstairs to talk her boyfriend's ear off, and Trent and I downstairs alone.

The first time he kissed me—on the night of my sixteenth birthday when I talked Mama into letting me sleep over because I was hoping for another one of our special nights—my heart soared, and everything changed.

Including me and Tasha.

I pull in a long, steadying breath before I turn to face her, and she doesn't look the least bit bothered that I made her wait. A brilliant smile takes over her face, turning her full lips, which are painted red to match her dress, up. Her light brown skin is smooth and clear and her hair is wild and sexy, flowing over her thin shoulders in auburn tresses that make her look older than she is.

"Tasha, hey."

"It's so good to see you, girl!" She moves in for a hug but stops short when she sees the knife in my hand. "Oh! I guess I better keep my distance."

Her laughter spills into the awkward space between us, and I force myself to laugh too just so she's not laughing on her own. "Oh, right, sorry. I was cutting cake before you arrived and dropped it."

"Yeah, Mama told me I should see you if I wanted a slice."

"Of course she did. I'd be happy to get you some." But my feet aren't moving. It's like vines have shot through the tile and wrapped around my ankles, rooting me to the spot.

"And I'd love to have some, but first I'd like to catch up without all that noise if that's okay."

It's not okay. Actually, it's the last I want to be doing at this moment. "Sure."

Her smile falls apart, cracks into pieces, and then slips off of her face. Suddenly, she looks so uncertain of herself, and I feel bad for doing that to her when she hasn't done anything to me.

"If you don't have time, I can just...." she trails off, hooking her thumb over her shoulder to indicate the door.

"No!" My feet finally regain their ability to move, and I take a step toward her. "I'd love to catch up. *Really.*"

Tasha smiles again, relief washing over her features. "Awesome. Tell me about NHU. I still can't believe you ended up there after all that talk about attending NC State with Trent."

A shudder rolls down my spine at the mention of his name and my foolish plan to follow him to college so we could be together forever. "NHU is good. I like it. Are you happy at...."

Now it's my turn to trail off because I actually have no idea where she ended up. After that weekend I just cut her off. Stopped talking to her at school. Stopped taking her calls. Stopped acknowledging that anyone with the last name Davis existed.

"The Dollar General on Camel Street?" She asks, half laughing. "Yeah, it's okay. I'm working there full time, hoping to make manager next month."

"That's good, Tash. I'm sure you'll be a great manager."

"Thanks." She raises her hand, tucking a lock of hair behind her ear. "So, um, I'm sorry I didn't text you back earlier. I was working and didn't see it until I was on my way home to change."

I wave a hand at her. "No worries. I'm glad you were able to make it. I'm sure it means a lot to Mama." It's not lost on either of us that I left myself out.

"Yeah, I was glad to get the invite. Trent was sorry he couldn't make it though."

My stomach begins to churn, but I still manage to smile politely. Like hearing his name doesn't feel like a punch in the throat. Like it doesn't send me back to a dorm room with condom wrappers in the trash can and dirty boxers on the floor.

"He was happy that you asked about him though." I stare at her blankly, unable to come up with a response to a statement that makes it sound like I'm curious about her brother's well-being. Tasha takes my silence for confusion, and she laughs and shakes her head.

"In your text. You asked if he was coming with me tonight, but he couldn't because he had already promised Jamar he would go to his basketball game. You remember our cousin Jamar, right? He got a full-ride scholarship to NHU. We're all so proud of him, and Trent goes to all of his games, especially the home ones. I'm surprised you haven't run into him yet."

Another wave of nausea rocks me as dread seeps into my bones. The thought of Trent on campus, *on my campus*, where I thought I was safe from him makes me angry and scared. Tasha's looking at me expectantly, an innocent smile on her face that makes me wonder, not for the first time, if she knows who her brother really is.

Or if I'm the only person who's ever seen his true face. The ugly, snarling monstrosity that hides under the easy smile and full lips that took my first kiss and slowly, and then all at once, talked me out of the rest of my firsts.

That's my secret shame. The silent surrender. The words that stayed caged behind my clenched teeth while he told me how much I wanted what he was giving to me. I never disagreed with him. I never said no. I never told him he was wrong, and when it was over, I let him hold me.

Stupid, stupid girl.

My hands are shaking, and the knife is coming dangerously close to hitting the ground again, so I tighten my grip on it. "Yeah, that's weird."

Tasha nods enthusiastically, and when she starts speaking again the words sound faraway, like she's in a bubble. Or maybe I'm in one. In a bubble that's running out of air. That's shrinking around me as my former best friend drones on and on about things I can't hear and don't want to listen to.

Just as black starts to creep into my vision, and I'm sure I'm going to pass out, the kitchen door swings open, and for the briefest of seconds I think, no, *I hope* it's Chris coming to my rescue, and relief courses through me. But the sensation is short-lived when I see Eric walking in instead.

"Yo, Mal, Mama wants to know what happened to the knife for the ca—" he pauses, looking between me and Tasha who's finally stopped talking. "Oh, sorry, Tash. I didn't know you were in here."

"It's fine, Eric." She's talking to him, but she's looking at me with a strange, confused expression. "I was just about to head out because I have to be at work early in the morning."

"Damn," Eric says, reaching out to give her a hug. "Well, I'm glad you were able to come through."

"Me too." She lets him go and casts a furtive glance across the room to me. "It was good to see you, Mal."

I don't trust myself to say anything, especially not in front of Eric, so I offer her a tight smile and a wave with the hand that's not holding a knife. She looks put off by that as well, but I can't find it in me to care because I'm just glad she's leaving and taking all the memories of her brother with her. The sooner I can get back to a life without the Davis family looming over my head like a dark cloud, the better.

Pushing out a harsh breath, I look at Eric. "Mama didn't really send you in here to harass me about a knife did she?"

He grins, shoving his hands in his pockets. "Nah, Chris said you were acting a little weird ever since Tasha got here and said I should check on you."

"Ugh." I move past him, heading back into the party, so I can finally finish cutting the slice of cake I know my Aunt Mary is waiting for. "Your friend should learn how to mind his business."

Eric follows closely, his brows knitted in confusion as he takes up residence on the opposite side of the long table that holds all the food Mama made for the party. "My friend? You're the one kissing him in the middle of house parties."

"Shut up!" I glare at him then look around to make sure no one else heard. "I kissed him as part of a game that your childish girlfriend insisted on playing."

"Oh, so now Sloane's *my childish girlfriend* instead of your best friend who you supposedly love more than I do?"

I'm still glaring at him as I cut a perfect line through the cake with the knife. "Yes, she's always your girlfriend when she does stuff like that. She's only my best friend when she acts like she has some sense."

"Got it." He nods like he really does have it, but I know he just wants to move on to the next topic of conversation. "And what about Chris? You really gonna be mad at the man for noticing how weird you were acting with Tasha?"

Shifting my attention back to the cake, I concentrate on cutting out six even servings, all perfect squares, some of which I'll wrap up and take home so Mama can have some later. "I'm not mad at him for noticing the *alleged* weirdness between me and Tasha. I'm annoyed with him for running to tell you and thus, subjecting me to this conversation."

"Alleged weirdness?" Eric arches a brow. "When I walked into the kitchen you were looking like you'd seen a ghost and she was looking like…well shit, I don't know what she was looking like, but it was definitely weird energy between y'all, so it wasn't alleged."

"It was alleged because Chris didn't even see me talking to Tasha."

"Okay, so he picked up on the energy change from across the room, but he wasn't wrong. You were being weird with her, just like you were all throughout senior year." He turns his head, eyes scanning the floor for Sloane, probably making sure her and Nic aren't somewhere bickering.

"She's on the dance floor with Mama, and Nic is over there with

Chris." Eric follows my fingers as I point out their respective locations and breathes a small sigh of relief before focusing on me again. "Listen, I'm fine, Eric. Why don't you go dance with Sloane and have fun, so I can take Aunt Mary this cake?"

"Because I want to make sure I'm not missing anything."

His answer, and the fierce protectiveness that tints it, gives me pause, and I have to take a moment to gather myself. It's been years since Eric has sounded this worried about me. In fact, the last time I heard him sound like this was the day I decided to tuck away all my hurt and anger and become this version of myself. The girl who always has such a tight grip on her life that no one bothers to look to see if she's falling apart on the inside.

That's who I am now. Not the naive girl Trent knew. Not the gullible friend Tasha had. Not the depressed sister who spent the two weeks following her rape in bed pretending to have the flu. It only took Eric one of those to figure out that something else was up, and he pressed me for answers. Pleaded with me to share my burden. To tell him what happened between me and Tasha at her house, which is where I lied and told him and Mama I was going to be. Only once did he ask if something happened with Trent, but I denied it so quickly, so vehemently, he let it go completely.

I lift my head, meeting his eyes. They're my eyes. Mama's eyes. And I know every swirl of amber and gold inside of them like I know my own name. I've spent my entire life looking in them, and that's how I can so easily picture how they'd look if I ever told Eric the truth. The confusion, the pity, the shame, the anger he'd use as fuel to burn the images of that night from his brain. The determination that would creep into the corners while his brain weaved a tale of revenge in the form of justice that will never come.

He won't understand that my revenge, the only version of it within my grasp, is *this*. This life where I craft the narrative and control the outcome, where I decide who knows what and when they find out. Where I am the force to be reckoned with and not a victim of the reckoning.

Sighing, I pick up a napkin and wipe the extra icing off of my fingers. "Eric, I'm only going to say this once, so make sure you relay this message to Christopher as well: I'm fine. Seeing Tasha was weird, yes, but I knew she was coming and now she's gone, and that's all there is to it. Nothing to see, nothing to discuss, nothing to miss."

Eric is quiet for a moment, but then his eyes soften and that fierce, big-brother-by-two-minutes protectiveness fades away. "If you say so."

"I do," I insist, nodding to emphasize my words.

"Okay." And without another word he walks away, leaving me to finally deliver the piece of cake Aunt Mary's been waiting ten years for. Once I make that delivery, I get called over by another family member to do something else, and the night continues like that. Everyone dancing and having a good time while I run around like a chicken with my head cut off until the wee hours of Saturday morning.

By the time the last guest leaves, I'm bone tired, but I still help the small crew Mama tasked with cleanup take down decorations, and put away food. Together, it only takes a few hours to set the rec center back to rights.

When we get back to the house, Mama is asleep, but there's a stack of pillows and blankets on the couch for Chris. I leave Eric to deal with getting his guest settled and head to the hallway bathroom for a quick shower. When I get out the house is quiet save for the hum of the TV in the living room and the low rumblings of male voices I can only assume belong to my brother and his friends.

I'm half tempted to go out and talk to them because there's nothing I love more than a post-event play-by-play with Nic who stands in the corner, sipping soda or water while everyone else is drinking, seeing and hearing everything, but just the thought of spending another hour upright makes my already tired brain even more exhausted, so I make a beeline for my room and climb into bed, falling asleep before my head even hits the pillow.

9

MALLORY

It's dark in here, and it stinks. That special blend of stale food and dirty laundry that's found in the dorm rooms of college boys who left their housekeeping skills and manners at home with their mamas. It clings to the air, fills my nostrils, suffocating me and saving me all at once.

Because focusing on the stench is the only thing keeping me from being inside my body. From feeling his unwanted movements and wondering, for the millionth time, why I'm not telling him to stop.

"You knew I'd make it good for you, didn't you, baby?" Trent croaks, slurred words passing through sloppy lips at my throat. "This is what you came here for."

"NO!" I jolt awake and tumble out of bed, scrambling for the door as the contents of my stomach rise up, threatening to paint the walls and floor of my room. With one hand clutched to my mouth, I half walk, half crawl across the hallway to the bathroom, and turn the light on. I don't even bother to close the door as I slither across the cold tile to the toilet and lift the seat. It's barely out of the way when the vomit forces its way past my lips and horrible retching sounds fill the room. Sobs rattle my bones as my body forces everything I've eaten in the last twenty-four hours out with agonizing heaves that continue until my knees hurt from the way the tile is digging into them.

It doesn't occur to me to be worried about someone hearing me until the sound of footsteps coming toward me from the front of the house fills my ears. I'm on my feet in an instant, wiping my mouth with the hem of my t-shirt and leaning into the mirror to make sure there are no dried tear tracks on my face.

"Mallory."

Chris' voice shocks and soothes me, and I whip around to face him, slightly off balance because of the nightmare and vomiting. He's standing just outside the door in low-slung basketball shorts and a white tank top. Despite the change of clothes and the late hour, he doesn't look like he's been asleep at all. His eyes are clear, alert, and not one of the short curls at the top of his head are crushed from being pressed against a pillow.

"Chris, what are you doing up?"

Something about my question catches him off guard, and I watch his answer pass over his features. I can tell it's complex, but when he finally opens his mouth the words are simple, direct, and not at all what I expect.

"I heard you scream."

"What?"

I heard him just fine. Of course, I did, but I just can't begin to process the unfair reality where Chris is around to hear the first nightmare I've had about that night in months. And the vomiting. He hasn't even mentioned the vomiting yet.

"You were screaming," he repeats himself, taking a step closer. "At first I wasn't sure that's what I was hearing but then, before you came out of the room, it was very clear."

My heart descends into my stomach. I usually don't talk in my nightmares, which adds to the eerie realness of them, and so I don't know what I said or, more specifically, what he heard. And try as I might, I don't have the energy to come up with or sell him a lie, so I decide to tell him the truth. Or at least the safest version of it.

"I had a bad dream."

He takes another step forward, his face a mask of emotion I can't decipher. "I figured as much. Do you have those a lot?"

I bite my lip, anxious to be done with this conversation that seems to be leading to more questions the longer I stand here giving him answers. And Chris looks like he wants those answers. His eyes rove over my features, searching for something more than the truth. Something like connection. But unfortunately, I have no plans to bond with him over this, especially when I can't trust him to keep anything I say to him between us. My stomach rolls, another wave of nausea snaking through my empty intestines at the thought of him mentioning this to Eric and tacking on yet another reason for him to worry about me.

"No," I say flatly, turning to the sink and snatching up the bottle of mouthwash on the counter. I can feel his eyes on me, watching me as I untwist the cap and flip it over to pour some of the blue liquid inside. And still when I toss the liquid back and swish it around my mouth before spitting it in the sink.

"Do you always throw up after?"

The question comes as I'm using my hand to spread water from the faucet around the sink to rinse it out, and it hits me right in my already sensitive gut. I turn the faucet off and spin on him. He's in the doorway now. His large frame filling the space and somehow, even from outside of it, managing to make the bathroom feel like it's shrunk to half its size.

Or maybe it's not his frame at all—although it *is* quite distracting because I can clearly see the outline of his abs through the thin fabric of his shirt—maybe it's the way he's leaning against the door jamb with his arms crossed and his eyes, serious and assessing, on me, drinking in the sight of my scowl and still creased at the corners with concern I can't convince him not to feel for me.

Or *maybe* it's the way having his eyes on me makes my heart beat a little faster, not in the panicked way it does when other guys look at me now but in a way that makes me feel like I'm being examined with the same precision and care given to the most precious gem.

I swallow and wipe my wet palms on my thighs, which are bare because I don't sleep in anything but a t-shirt and underwear. The motion draws Chris' attention, and his eyes drop from my face to my legs, lingering on them for a fraction of a second before coming back up and stretching wide to indicate that he's still waiting on my response.

"I don't have them often enough to keep track." That's only a partial lie because my nightmares have been pretty scarce lately. But the amount of time between them hasn't rid me of my memories about what follows the nausea and vomiting: sore ribs and a raw throat that keep me up just as much as the fear of falling asleep again.

Chris nods, and I'm too relieved to see that he believes me. "You should drink something before you lay back down. I could check in the kitchen and see if there's"—he stops, rubbing at the back of his neck and looking mildly embarrassed—"you don't need me to do that, this is your house."

"That it is, Dr. Johnson." I smirk, relief from the break in tension making my shoulders sag. I'm generally annoyed with Chris' unintentional ability to lighten even the darkest moods, but right now I'm grateful for it. For the joy his self-deprecating smile sparks in my soul, reminding me that I'm safe here, in my home with people who care about me, and not in that godforsaken dorm room. "But I appreciate the medical advice."

Moving towards him isn't something I realize I'm doing until I'm standing so close he has to tilt his head to look down at my face. "I'm not even sure I want to do it."

"Do what?" I blink up at him, surprised and a bit confused because of what the change in conversation has done to his expression. He's exchanged his self-deprecating, but still endearing, smile for an intense thoughtfulness I don't quite understand.

"The whole doctor thing."

Shadows of conflicted emotion move behind his eyes as he studies my face, trying to gauge what I think of his unprompted confession. I'm quiet for a moment, wondering if he's going to elaborate, but a full minute passes and he doesn't.

"You don't want to be a doctor?"

Surprise colors my words even though I try not to let it. I don't know him well enough to be shocked about him feeling trapped in his life. And if seeing Sloane interact with her witch of a mother over the past year has taught me anything, it's that kids who come from families with big bank accounts, and even bigger expectations, are born with life plans they are never consulted on.

He shrugs, and his gaze drops from mine for a split second. "It's the only thing I've ever wanted to be."

"And that's a bad thing?"

"Not necessarily."

I rest my hip against the sink and cross my arms, matching his pose. "Then I'm confused." Thoroughly. This conversation isn't going anything like I thought it would, but I'm thankful that we're having it because nothing gets my mind off of my own problems like discussing someone else's.

He pushes out a long breath and the warm air rushes over my already heated skin. "Everyone on my dad's side of the family, specifically the men, have gone into medicine. There are generations of Dr. Johnsons that have come before me, including my dad and my big brother, and if my dad has his way, there will be many more after me. Medicine is in our blood, coded into our DNA just like the perfect amber shade of your eyes is written into yours." My breath catches, shock coursing through me at him referring to any part of me as perfect. "All of that history, all of that pressure to honor our family's legacy, it makes it hard to know if the desire to practice medicine is really mine or just another thing they told me to want."

"But you just said you always wanted it."

"I have."

"Then does it really matter where the desire came from? I mean, if it's still in alignment with the vision you have for your life?"

"I don't know," he says softly, looking as tortured as I feel.

"Wanna know what I think?"

"Yes."

"I think desires can be born out of any circumstance, good, bad, or ugly, and still be valid representations of the things we want for ourselves. The source of the desire doesn't matter so much as what we do with the dream it sparks in us."

That night with Trent had sparked all sorts of desires in me, chief among them, the desire to break my world down into tiny, manageable parts. To sort everything into boxes marked black and white and do away with anything that didn't make the cut. That's why I like business so much. Everything is simple, broken down into questions and answers that can be found with formulas and numbers.

A small smile is playing on Chris' lips, and it makes me think that this change in conversation was more for me than it was for him. And we're standing so close it's almost impossible to take a breath that isn't laced with his scent. I know I should take a step back, should let the electricity charging the air between us dissipate, turn into something that isn't *this*. I don't even know what this is, but I'm not ready for it. Not so soon after a nightmare. And not with Chris, who looks too close and sees too much.

"You make a good point, Ms. Kent."

"Thank you, Dr. Johnson."

"You're welcome." A small yawn parts my lips. I slap my hand over my mouth to stifle it but Chris still sees it and frowns as he steps back from the door frame. "I should probably let you get back to bed, huh?"

Still yawning, I wave my hand at him. "No, I'm fine. You're not keeping me up." But I am tired all of a sudden. The dark, icy weight of the nightmare has subsided, leaving me with nothing but a bone-deep exhaustion.

His brows dip low in a movement I'm starting to associate with that bossy, demanding side of him that likes to tell me what to do. "Mallory, you're literally dead on your feet."

"Gee, thanks," I quip, moving out of the bathroom and into the hallway with him. We're still just a few inches apart and standing in front of my dark bedroom, and my exhausted brain hallucinates grabbing his hand and pulling him inside. Asking him to climb into bed and hold me. Falling asleep in his arms and feeling, for the first time in a long time, safe. Pushing the thought aside is harder than it should be, but I finally manage to do it and finish my sentence. "Because every girl wants to hear a man tell her that she looks like the walking dead."

He chuckles, turning his body slightly so the short path to my room is clear. "I didn't say you look like the walking dead."

"You might as well had," I mutter, walking across the hallway on leaden feet. Just before I cross my threshold, I turn to look at him. "I won't take it to heart though, since I know I must look terrible right now."

Braids falling out of my ponytail. Dried tears streaking my face. Breath smelling like a lovely mixture of vomit and mouthwash. Chris frowns again, his eyes turning dark as they skate over every inch of me. Then he takes a step forward, and then another, until he's in front of me. I stop breathing as he looks down and one of his hands comes up, tucking a haphazardly placed braid back into the band of elastic holding them together.

"You don't," he says thickly, shaking his head. A heated gaze moving from my parted lips to my eyes, and I wonder if he's thinking about the kiss because I am. Even with the inky darkness of my nightmare still clinging to me, I'm thinking of his kiss. And wondering if I'll ever feel like that again. Weightless and grounded all at the same time. "You look the exact opposite of terrible."

I'm too stunned to speak, to move, to breathe, and his words hang in the air between us. He doesn't look bothered by my silence, actually, he looks satisfied with himself, happy he could leave me speechless. I watch him step back, smiling to himself as he starts to walk down the hallway, back toward the living room.

"See you in the morning, Mal."

10

CHRIS

Mallory Kent is a liar.

And a good one at that. I almost bought the whole "I just had a bad dream" act. Almost wrote it off as a one-time thing, and accepted that she, unlike me, didn't have any demons lurking in her dreams on the regular. But then, a few hours after she went back into her bedroom, I heard her again.

The creak of her bed frame as she tossed and turned.

The subtle, tearful whimpering.

The mumbled words I couldn't make out no matter how hard I tried.

I sat on the couch, unable to sleep for fear of being woken by my own nightmares, with tension lacing all of my muscles and the urgent, desperate need to hold her washing over me like furious waves.

No one else could hear her. That much was clear from the way no one woke or peeked their heads out when she came rushing out of her room, crawling across the hallway like a wounded animal, and just barely making it to the bathroom in time to empty her stomach in the toilet.

All of those sounds were so familiar. Even in that unfamiliar setting, I'd know them anywhere. The underscore of agony. The sound-track of pain and horror too terrible to face in your waking hours.

Of all the things for us to have in common.

The nightmares and the adeptness at hiding them. The shadows we don't let anyone see. The ones she hides behind a serious facade that's all business, all the time. The ones I blot out with a routine that still isn't working for me. It's been nearly two months since I kissed Mallory, and in that time I haven't laid a finger on another woman. I'd probably be more upset by this unintentional bout of celibacy if it didn't leave me so much time to think. About how to maintain my freedom after graduation. About RJ's suggestion that a serious relationship might help my father let go some. And most of all, though I'm loathe to admit it, about Mallory, her lies, and the truths I want her to only give to me.

I'm in no position to ask for them, have no reason to believe I deserve them, but I want them all the same. I might have asked for them too, might have used the vulnerabilities I revealed to her in order to take her mind off of her dreams to get her to open up to me, but the morning after her nightmare she acted like it never happened.

Now, almost a week later, I haven't had a single opportunity to broach the subject, and I can't help but feel like she wants it that way because ever since our conversation in the hallway, she's made a point of not being alone with me. I don't even catch her glancing at me in class anymore, and that shit bothers me more than it should.

Actually, that's wrong, it bothers me the exact right amount because I don't think there's a rule about how upset you can be about someone icing you out after you've seen them at their most vulnerable. It almost feels like I'm being punished for seeing a side of her she hides from everyone else.

I wonder how she would feel if she knew I wanted to see more.

Sighing, I roll my neck from one side to the other, trying to release the ache that can only come from being crouched over a table all day grading papers. For all his talk about not trusting me to do anything in class, Dr. Richardson has made grading problem sets my sole responsibility. At times, I think he assigns them just to make sure I have something to do during the office hours he insists I hold in his office when he's off campus.

Today has been relatively quiet, which is surprising because there's a paper due that's worth forty percent of their grade, but you won't find me complaining. I hate doing office hours. Students coming in with all the frantic pleas and dramatics, in near tears because they're drowning under the weight of Richardson's insurmountable expectations and non-existent grading curve.

I slap a grade on the next to last paper in my stack and move it to the side, deciding to call it a day after I finish the last one because the home basketball game starting in a few hours pretty much guarantees that no one is coming by. Since Richardson left me with a grading key, it doesn't take me long to move through the problem set and determine what's right and what's wrong. I'm flipping to the last page to check the final problem when a frantic, and yet hesitant, knock comes from the closed office door.

"Come in," I say, working to keep the annoyed edge out of my voice.

The door opens, and I look up just in time to see Mallory's face—which is already pulled into a deep, desperate frown—fall even further. "Oh, you're here."

I lift a brow. "Were you expecting someone else?"

"Dr. Richardson," she responds, not missing a beat. "You know, since it's his office."

"Well," I glance around the room, pretending to look for someone. "Sorry to disappoint, but I'm here alone."

"Yeah," she mutters, sinking her teeth into her bottom lip. "I can see that."

With the door partially open, I can only see part of her frame, but it's still more than enough of her to appreciate the way the skin-tight jeans she's wearing and soft, oversized heather gray sweater that's hanging off one of her shoulders highlight the best parts of her. The shapely legs and thick thighs. The smooth mahogany of her skin. The slightly lighter color of the stretch marks that run underneath the strap of her bra.

She's an exquisite, perfect thing. With all her secrets and half-truths and anxious habits that make me want to make all her problems go away.

I rise from my seat, moving around the table next to Richardson's desk to the door. "Did you need something?"

She watches me approach, still biting her lip and now shifting her weight to one leg like she's preparing to leave. Once again, I'm hit with the thought of how thrilling it would be to give chase. My reaction is confusing. Watching anyone else prepare to walk away has almost no effect on me, but if I get even the slightest inkling that Mallory is about to walk away from me, I have this deep-seated need to follow.

It's only as I move towards the door, placing my hand on the handle to pull it open further and reveal all of her, that I notice the laptop in her hand and the frustrated wrinkles in her forehead.

"No, I—uh, I was just going to ask Dr. Richardson a question."

There she goes lying again. I smirk to myself, not because I find lying funny, it's actually a trait I despise, but because Mallory's lies, which are meant to push people away, only make me want to lean in closer. To chase the whispers of the truth across the planes of her perfect face, find them in the pools of her amber eyes, and claim them as my own.

"A question?"

"Yes." She nods. "But he's not here, so I'm just going to go."

She takes a step back, out of the office, and I immediately move forward. "What was it?"

"Huh?"

"The question. What was it? Maybe I can answer it for you."

Not maybe. I can definitely answer it. She knows it. I know it. Still, she shakes her head again. "Oh, I don't think you can. It's not that kind of question."

"What kind of question is it?" I look from her face to the computer she's clutching in her hands, remembering the paper that's due at three p.m. because Richardson is an asshole and refuses to make his deadlines a minute before midnight like every other professor in the world. "Is it about the paper?"

Her expression changes—panic causes her eyes to stretch—and I know I'm right. I glance at my watch, surprised to see that it's already a few minutes past three.

"Yes," she admits, a thread of despair wrapping around the word. "I was going to ask, *no beg*, Richardson for an extension."

I press my lips together, immediately understanding her mood. Everyone knows Richardson doesn't do extensions, he doesn't believe in them.

"Mal—" I start, but she cuts me off.

"I know!" She throws her hands up, walking back into the office and brushing past me so she can fall into a chair at the table where I was just working. I stand at the door, stunned by a cloud of jasmine and her while she opens up her computer. "He doesn't do extensions, but my fucking computer crashed when I was trying to submit it, and I just grabbed it and ran over here hoping to explain what was going on." She turns around, frustrated tears glimmering in her eyes. "Richardson hates me, but I thought that maybe if he saw the computer doing whatever the fuck it's doing, he'd take pity on me, but I ran all the way over here and—"

"And found me." I finish for her, walking over and taking a seat at the table beside her. "His glorified secretary with no power or respect." My self-deprecating joke makes her smile a little, and the sight of it, as well as knowing I caused it, has warmth spreading through my chest.

"Yes." She puts her head in her hands. "I'm going to fail this fucking class because of one damn paper. I can't believe it. Richardson is going to have a field day with this." She peeks at me through her fingers, and I act like I don't see the tears slipping down her cheeks because I know she'll appreciate it. "He'll say I never should have been allowed to take this class, and I'll fail. I won't be able to graduate early." Her voice cracks, and I feel something inside me break with it. "Fuck. Fuck! *Fuck!*"

"Hey." I don't know how or why I'm doing it, but suddenly I'm moving one of her hands away from her face and taking her chin between my thumb and index finger. Her eyes are wide as I turn her face towards mine. "Breathe, Mal. We'll figure this out. You're not going to fail, okay?"

Our faces are inches apart now, and the abrupt stream of air that moves through her lips and over my skin reminds me of the moments before the kiss. When she looked at me like she's looking at me now and followed my order without hesitation. I feel her head moving up and down, letting me know she heard me, and I release her chin.

"How?" she asks, quietly. "I can't pass if I'm missing forty percent of my grade."

The solution comes to me quickly, and my decision to go through with it, knowing full well that it will more than likely result in me getting fired, comes quicker. Reaching over, I grab my open computer from beside the stack of graded papers and pull it over to our side.

"You won't be."

Mal scoffs. "Unless you're about to work some kind of two-part miracle that involves turning back time and reviving my computer, yes I am."

Instead of responding, I continue to focus my attention on my computer screen, logging into the Blackboard website with the password and username I saw Richardson type into his desktop computer just a few days ago. I wasn't planning on memorizing his login information in the moment, but now I'm glad I did.

"*What are you doing?*" She hisses, peeking over at my screen. "Did you just log in to Blackboard using his credentials!"

The shrillness of her tone coupled with the bulging of her round, brown eyes would be funny if she didn't look so terrified. Strangely enough, I'm the calmest I've ever been. Completely chill about breaking some kind of teaching assistant honor code because it's for her.

"Lower your voice, Mal." Her eyes narrow, and I watch as indignation takes over her face. "All I'm doing is setting the deadline back to give you a chance to figure out what's going on with your computer."

"Chris, no, I don't want you to do that. I'll figure something else out. Take the zero." The desperation is back in her voice, and it makes me work faster. "I can retake the class."

"Or," I say, double checking that the settings have changed and hitting the save button. "You can turn in your paper and finally get the A that asshole's been keeping from you."

Again, her eyes stretch, but it's only surprise there and then a softness takes over her features. Something like appreciation dancing around the edges of her irises. It's not much, but I'll take it.

She bites her lip, looking conflicted for a moment before finally saying, "Thank you."

Those two little words resonate somewhere deep inside me. Sounding off like a grandfather clock in the dead silence of the midnight hour.

Loud. Jarring. Beautifully deafening.

"You're welcome." I force myself to look away from her face. "Now let me see your computer."

"No." She shakes her head, opening the laptop with hands that have a slight shake to them. I wonder if she's nervous. If *I* make her nervous. "I've got it. You've already done enough."

I shrug. "It's not a big deal."

"Yes, it is." I feel her glance at me, but I can't take my eyes off of her fingers. Long and elegant, they move with a swift efficiency over the keyboards, and an image of them wrapped around my dick and then fisted in my sheets, hits me so I look away. "You could get fired if Richardson finds out."

"Then he better not find out."

She turns back to the computer, which now appears to be functioning correctly. "I won't say anything but won't he know that the deadline was changed?"

"Mal, the man's password to Blackboard is 'Business123' I don't think technology is exactly his thing."

The laughter that erupts from her is hauntingly beautiful, and I soak it up. Take it into my being and resolve myself to never let it go. It's a dangerous thing, her laugh. Deep and sultry and perfect. A sound I don't hear often enough, especially not just for me.

"Business123?" She wheezes, shoulders shaking as she turns to face me, showing me her face crumpled with unguarded humor. It hits me then. The full power of her beauty. The might of her joy. "God, that man needs to retire."

I nod my agreement. "Yes, and I'd love to help you plot his demise, but maybe we can get your paper turned in first?"

"Right. Right."

Again, she turns back to the screen, and I watch her sign back into the computer which looks like it has completely reset itself. Mal groans softly under her breath as she logs in, and I hear her muttering something about stupidity and procrastinating.

"Procrastinating?" I ask, brows lifted in surprise. "You don't procrastinate."

In fact, she's always one step ahead of everyone. Including me. I know that she heard me, but she doesn't acknowledge my question, leaving me to wonder what could have happened over the last few days to throw her so far off of her game. The office is quiet, nothing but the sound of her hands flying across the keyboard filling the space as I study her profile. Admiring the wrinkle between her furrowed brows and the way her nose is scrunched in concentration as she hunts down the file she needs.

I linger on her skin, specifically the place around her eyes where the skin is darker and a little puffy from a lack of sleep. My heart sinks, free falling into my stomach as the memory of her strangled sobs moves through me. Nightmares. She's been having more of them.

"Have you been getting enough sleep?" I try to sound casual, but I fail because ever since that kiss nothing between us has been casual. Mallory goes still, whipping her head around to glare at me, and her furious hostility snapping at me from behind the careful mask of calm that is her face is all the answer I need.

"I'm really not in the mood to hear that you think I look like shit, Christopher. Once was more than enough."

"I've never said that you look like shit, Mallory. Stop deflecting and answer my question."

"Why?" She slaps her hand on the table. "I don't owe you answers."

Most people would see the flames burning in her eyes and back away, but I must be a damn fool because I'm watching them grow and the only thing I want to do is step closer.

"You're right. You don't owe me answers, but maybe you owe yourself the relief of telling someone the truth."

She rears back as if I've struck her, and I guess in a way I have. For months, I've watched Mallory operate in this space above everyone else. Looking down on the rest of us from an ivory tower heavily guarded by sarcasm and seriousness that all but shamed us for relishing in experiences she was too good to partake in.

Up until a few months ago, I bought the act. I believed that she truly was too focused on school and whatever else was going on in her brilliant mind to care about having regular college experiences. Growing up, I knew lots of people like that, so her behavior—the lack of interest in dating, the unbridled focus and dedication to her courses, and the plan to graduate early— didn't strike me as odd.

Then the kiss happened.

And I saw her desire for something else, *something more*. I tasted her fear. Identified it as the thing keeping her from being the woman who sighed with relief and gave herself over to me when I pressed my lips to hers.

The fear was the one thing I couldn't make sense of. I didn't spend enough one-on-one time with her to parse out where it came from, but that's changing. Slowly. Between the wild look she had in her eyes the night I ran into her on the path and scared her and hearing the haunting melody of her nightmares, I feel like I'm closer to the truth of her than anyone has been in years, and she doesn't like it.

Something shifts behind her eyes, and it's angrier and darker than anything I've ever seen from her. She pushes back from the table, snatching her computer up as she goes. "People always think they want the truth until you give it to them. Once you do that, they never look at you the same. It's all sad eyes, pitiful glances, and empty words that don't help. But you already know that, don't you, Chris? That's why no one here knows about your mom. That's why you hide the demons that keep you up at night behind a big smile and bury the rest of it inside whatever girl finds her way into your bed."

She's glorious. Standing above me, all curves and perfect skin and amber eyes that shine like melted gold as they burn into me, and all I want to do in this moment is kiss her. Even as she lays into me, lashing out with her words and striking all of my vulnerabilities with frightening precision, all I want is to feel those lips, the same ones spitting venom at me, against mine.

It's madness.

And it forces me out of my seat, propels me towards her. I only stop when my sudden advance makes her back up several steps and that fear appears again. Shimmering behind the fury and then slithering back where it came from when I go still. Mallory lifts her chin, a reckless challenge in her eyes, daring me to come closer and demanding me to stay away all at once. I tuck my hands into my pockets, trying to appear nonchalant even though, with her words ringing in my ears, I feel anything but.

"They never make it to my bed."

It's a stupid response, meant to unsettle her because everything about her, including not being able to touch her, is unsettling me.

She frowns. "What?"

"The girls," I say, a small, antagonistic smile on my lips. "They never make it to my bed." Disgust and then something like looks a lot like jealously laces her features, and I hate myself for liking the way it looks on her.

"Oh!" She slaps her hand across her mouth in mock surprise. "How silly of me to assume you treated your partners with common decency. You probably like to fuck them against walls or on the floor like a true animal. I'll be sure not to get that part wrong next time."

Like a true animal. The words echo around my brain, and I'm momentarily shocked by how close they are to the ones I'd use to describe the way I like to fuck. There's nothing gentle about it. The hair pulling, the biting and desperate clawing that punctuates the moans and slapping of skin. Mallory doesn't look as disgusted as she did a moment ago. Embarrassment and arousal coupling with her rage and making me wonder what it would be like between us.

If she'd like what I do. If she'd give in to me like she did with the kiss or fight me every step of the way, making me work for her submission. Making me earn it. The thought makes me hard, and I have to widen my stance to make room for the rapid swelling of my dick. She's staring at me, waiting for my response, and when it doesn't come quick enough she rolls her eyes and turns on her heels, heading for the door.

"That's not the only thing you got wrong."

She stops, turning her head to glance over her shoulder at me. "What else did I get wrong, Christopher?"

"You said no one here knows about my mom." I come up behind her, standing close enough to touch her but refraining from doing so because I don't know how either of us will react. "But that's not true."

"Oh, did you let it slip out in the middle of some drunken hook-up?"

"No, Mal, I was dead sober when I told you."

11

MALLORY

I keep letting him have the last word.

The night at Mama's in the hallway, and earlier today in Richardson's office. It's becoming a worrying pattern, one I can't let continue, or else the cocky bastard will think he's gotten the better of me.

Hasn't he? My subconscious asks, and I grimace, hating how right it is. The fact of the matter is, Chris Johnson is under my skin, in my thoughts, and, when my brain isn't torturing me with recurring nightmares about Trent, in my dreams. His eyes and smile. The way his mouth curled around each word when he told me I looked the exact opposite of terrible. The tingles that started in my face and spread throughout the rest of my body when he gripped my chin and told me to breathe before doing the single nicest thing anyone has ever done for me as far as school is related.

A thing I didn't actually get to thank him for because he had to start with his questions and compassion and stupid brown eyes that split open my skin and see right through to my soul.

It was hard to stay angry when I was leaving Richardson's office, especially with the reminder that I had a secret of his in my possession. A piece of information he trusted me with implicitly. One he wanted to exchange for access to mine. But I managed to do it, wrapping myself up tight in a blanket of logic that had never failed me before.

My secrets are mine and mine alone. Sharing them with anyone will only give Trent the power to hurt them, and that will hurt me.

After I got to my dorm and submitted the paper, I stood in the mirror and repeated that mantra to myself. Over and over and over again until it stuck. Until the crack in my resolve caused by Chris' persistence and gentle eyes was glued back together again. And then I grabbed my purse and keys and headed out to meet Nic, Eric, and Sloane at the basketball game.

When I finally get to the gym and find them way up in the bleachers, I'm glad I took the time to shore up my resolve. Because right beside them, next to the only open space on the entire row, is Chris.

I feel rather than see his eyes on me as I scoot past everyone and make my way toward him. The game is packed. The home side of the gym is full even though we're playing some small liberal arts college from the low country, so it takes me a while to maneuver through the tangle of legs and knees. But eventually, I make it to him and see that he's slid down the row some, vacating his spot to create a space for me between him and Nic.

"Thanks," I mutter, sounding anything but grateful, which makes him laugh.

"No problem."

With a swift roll of my neck, I turn my attention to Nic, who's enthralled in the game and will probably be annoyed with me for even trying to talk to him.

"Did you get your paper turned in, Ms. Kent?"

A shiver rolls down my spine. Chris' lips are so close to my ear I can practically feel them moving, shaping every word. I clench my teeth together, attempting to disguise the waver in my voice.

"Yes."

"Good. I emailed Richardson and told him Blackboard was undergoing maintenance this afternoon and multiple students had emailed me about having problems with their submissions."

I turn to face him, and that's a mistake. A huge one. Because now my lips are millimeters away from his, and his eyes are on them. "What did he say?"

Chris smiles, and I feel the faintest hint of the motion. His skin ghosting over my skin, inciting goose bumps and invisible sparks that light me up from the inside out. "Exactly what I thought he would. He told me to roll back the deadline, gave me his password to Blackboard and everything so I could send an email to the class about the change from his account."

Truthfully, I'd planned to deal with the potential fallout surrounding what Chris did for me if, and only if, it came up. Otherwise, I was going to tuck it into the little box in the back of my head marked 'Things I Should Never Let Chris Johnson Do Again'—next to calling my eyes the perfect shade of amber and hearing me vomit after a nightmare—and never think about it again. But now, he's bringing it up, letting me know that he's not only a willing accomplice to Mallory related crimes, he's a competent one as well. Allowing Richardson to think the due date change was his idea is brilliant, and it keeps him from looking too closely at the submission times.

A fresh surge of gratitude rolls through me, followed by the swiftest panic because this is how Trent used to make me feel. Grateful. For his time and attention. For the things he did that felt like a big deal to me but never really cost him anything because he was risking nothing. All the lies and sneaking around that kept our relationship afloat were told by me. All the risk was mine. And at the end, when I stumbled out of his dorm room in the wee hours of the morning clutching my shredded underwear in my hands, I was the one who paid the price.

It would be the same with Chris and this Richardson situation. The late paper was mine. The falsified conditions exist because of me. And if anyone finds out, I'll be the one to pay. No one will lay a finger on Chris. He'll graduate with his reputation in tack and a glowing recommendation from the very professor he tricked for me.

And why? So I'd feel indebted to him, so he could feel comfortable hanging this favor I never asked for over my head as some kind of reminder that I owe him my gratitude, my secrets…my body?

I've waited so long, Mal. You can't say no now.

The buzzer sounds for halftime, working with my frazzled thoughts to shatter whatever was just happening between me and Chris, and I shoot out of my seat. Taking advantage of the empty spaces in the rows below us created by the break in the game to make my escape. Behind me, I hear Sloane ask where I'm going, and I think Chris answers her, but I can't be sure. The crowd of people spilling out of the gym and into the concession area swallow me whole. Dazed, and slightly embarrassed for running off like that, I let them push me towards the front of the concession stand line. Even though I don't want anything, I get an order of nachos and a bottle of water, figuring I can give it to Nic or Eric and distract them from the weirdness surrounding my departure.

By the time I've paid and gathered everything in my hands, the crowd has thinned out a bit. Most of the people in the lobby now are waiting to use the bathroom or talking with their friends. There's a girl huddled in one of the corners with her laptop plugged into the wall, desperately pounding away at the keyboard. I'm so caught up in watching her, wondering if she's feeling the same stress Chris saved me from earlier, I don't bother to check my surroundings.

And I know, the instant my body collides with a rock-solid muscular form with arms that wrap around my waist to stop me from falling and hands that touch me like they know me, that not paying attention was a grave mistake.

Shock seizes me, making it so the only part of my body moving is my head, allowing my eyes to scan the body in front of me. Taking in the barreled chest, the light skin, the thick arms bulging with muscles that came from lifting weights religiously in order to stay fit for football season.

And then, even though I already know it's him, my gaze travels up his neck, noting the presence of the first Adam's apple I ever found attractive, the cleft in his chin I always adored, and smiling brown eyes that turned dark and cruel when I told him I changed my mind about losing my virginity.

The bony, ice-cold fingers of dread and fear slip around my throat, but still I manage to choke out one word as my nightmares slither out of the shadows of my mind and take shape in the harsh light of reality.

"Trent."

12

CHRIS

Sloane is out of her seat before I even process Mallory's departure, telling Eric and Nic she's going to go check on her. They all look mildly concerned, like they find her behavior weird enough to merit following up but not alarming enough to launch a full-blown search party, which is exactly how it always is.

They love her, and occasionally they'll find cause to worry about her, but then she'll do something spectacular like make an A in every class during a semester with a bloated course schedule, and they'll believe that she's fine.

It's not a lack of care on any of their parts; it's just damn good acting on hers.

And even though I have a million and one other things I should be concerned about, all I want is to go after her and find out why she's hellbent on playing this role.

"I got it," I tell Sloane, already up and heading down the bleachers.

She twists her lips to the side, looking skeptical. "*You* got it?"

"Yeah." I nod, fighting back a laugh because Sloane is so protective of Mallory. Sometimes I wonder if she loves her more than she does Eric. "I wanted to get something to drink anyway, I'll find her and make sure she's good."

Nic eyes me, and I wonder how much he heard of the conversation I was having with Mallory. He's quiet, but he's always listening, always watching, and paying attention even when he looks like he wishes he could tune out.

"Going to get something to drink is not the same thing as checking on her." This from Sloane whose arms are crossed over her chest, hazel eyes narrowed into slits.

"He didn't say it was," Nic mutters under his breath, and I find myself once again fighting back a laugh as she turns her glare on him.

"Don't start with me, Dominic."

"No one is starting with you, Sloane," Nic says, stretching his legs out on the bleacher in front of him and leaning his elbows back on the one behind him. "Chris says he's got it, so sit back down on Eric's lap and wait for the game to start. Maybe tonight will be the night you finally grasp the concept of a free throw."

"Yo, Nic." Eric cuts his eyes at his best friend, looking annoyed. "Cut it out, man."

They share a tense look, communicating silently in that way only brothers—or two people who grew up like them—can do. A pang of jealousy moves through me because I've never had that with my brother. But after our talk the other day, I'm hopeful that we might.

RJ has texted me, unprompted, several times, mainly to ask me if I've decided to take his advice about Dad and Giselle. To be honest, he seems more invested in me getting out from under Dad's thumb than ever before, and in the back of my mind I know I should be skeptical about his intentions, but I can't bring myself to care when I'm just glad to have something more than bitter exchanges with him.

While Eric and Nic do their weird silent communication thing, Sloane stares at me with her arms crossed over her chest. "Well if you're going…"

She trails off, motioning toward the exit with her hand, and I take the opportunity without hesitation, rushing down the bleachers and into the lobby where the sight of Mallory in someone else's arms immediately makes me wish I would have let Sloane come instead.

I stand by the door, lingering in the slight shadow created by the brick entryway, and watch them together. The guy is big, with muscles everywhere including his thick, veined neck and the arms he currently has wrapped around Mallory. I can't see her face, can't tell if she's happy to see him, but she's letting him hug her so I have no reason to believe she's not. Maybe he's the reason she shot out of her seat and ran into the lobby so quickly. Maybe he texted her and said he was here and wanted to see her. Maybe they're together.

The thought sends another pang of jealousy through my chest, and this time it's so sharp, so fucking painful, I have to take a moment to rub at the spot it seems to be radiating from. It feels like hours go by with Mal in his arms, her shorter frame swallowed whole by his much taller and larger one, and I'm just about to turn around and head back inside to let everyone know she's fine, when he finally lets her go.

That's when I see it. The panic and fear lacing her features, dancing just underneath a smile so brittle it threatens to shatter right there on her trembling lips. And this guy, whoever the fuck he is, is completely oblivious to her discomfort, to her pounding pulse, evident in the way it's throbbing beneath the thin skin at the base of her throat. He's still touching her, his big, meaty hands on her shoulders while she balances a plate of nachos in one hand and a bottle of water in the other. He's talking animatedly, clearly happy to see her, and she's looking at him, but her face is frozen, her eyes unseeing.

Like she's in a waking nightmare.

Moving towards her isn't a conscious decision. One second I'm standing there, watching her make faces I know with absolute certainty usually accompany the sounds I heard her making the other night, and the next I'm standing beside her. Sliding my arm around her shoulder and feeling the muscles in her body relax as she registers that the person touching her is me.

She turns to me quickly, her eyes pleading with me, asking me for things I won't hesitate to give her, things I think I might have been born to give her. I flash a reassuring smile, one that doesn't even hint at the riot of emotions happening inside me. The fierce swirl of protectiveness, the hot heat of rage that I don't let show in my eyes until they're burning into the face of the guy in front of me.

Mallory's curves bleed into the rigid lines of my side, and I'm momentarily distracted by the heat of her. The soft weight of her breast brushing against my ribs, the scent of jasmine filling the air around me. Tension spreads throughout the silence between the three of us, and I realize then that I need to fill it, so I say the first thing that comes to mind.

"There you are, baby," I murmur, my eyes still on the guy whose face is now shifting from confused to angry. His eyebrows fall together when the pet name leaves my mouth and his lip curls upwards in disgust. "I was looking for you everywhere."

I turn and look at Mallory, she's staring up at me, still struggling to speak. I've never seen her like this. Stricken with fear and dread, looking borderline nauseous while tears shine in her eyes. I know I have to get her out of here, away from this guy, but trying to leave with her when she's like this is risky. She might freak out on me, but I still have to try.

"Can you run out to my car with me real quick, Mal? I think I left my phone in there."

"Actually," the guy in front of me says, brown eyes bouncing between the two of us as rage creeps into the corners. He tries to hide it, pushing it down and plastering on a big smile that's supposed to convince me he's harmless even though Mallory's body language is telling me everything I need to know about him.

He hurt her.

I don't know when, where, or how, but I know he did, and the knowledge makes me want to murder him.

"We were just catching up." His eyes flick to Mal, and her spine stiffens. "Weren't we, Mal?"

"Yeah." Her voice trembles, and she drops her eyes to the ground. I can practically feel the shame slithering over her skin, and I grip her shoulder, pulling her closer to me.

"Right, so you might have to go look for your phone on your own....sorry I don't think I caught your name."

"I didn't give it."

His smile slips, revealing the depth of ugly emotion it was designed to hide for just a second. He holds his hand out to me. "Well, I'm Trent. Mallory's ex-boyfriend."

I feel a tremble run through her as I release her shoulder and grasp his hand. His palm is sweaty, and his shake is weak. "Chris. Her current boyfriend."

Mallory has a reaction to my lie. I know she does, but I can't look over at her to see it because if she looks shocked or horrified by it, then that'll send up red flags for Trent and prevent me from getting her out of here, which is all I care about doing right now.

Getting her out of here. Forcing her to breathe. Holding her in my arms and letting her know that no one, least of all this walking meat-head, will ever hurt her again.

Flashing another fake smile, Trent releases my hand, focusing his attention on Mallory. "I didn't know you were into pretty boys, M."

My hands clench, turning into fists I have every intention of intro-ducing to his face, but then Mallory lifts her chin and looks him dead in the eye. "I'm a lot different from the girl you used to know."

"Right," he mutters, looking between the two of us. "I guess you are."

Now that she's talking, I feel a little more confident in my ability to get her out of here. I step in close, wrapping my arm back around her shoulder. She leans into me for a fraction of a second, and I take the opportunity to really sell the lie, turning my head to graze my lips over her temple.

"Let's go, babe." I breathe against her skin, low enough for it to feel private but loud enough for Trent to hear over the chatter of the thinning crowd. "If we wait too long, we might miss the second half of the game."

She inhales deeply, like she's harnessing every bit of her strength. Like she needs it to get away from this guy, a grown-ass man wearing a high school letterman jacket at a college basketball game. I can't believe he ever touched her.

"Okay."

All it takes is that one word, and I'm moving us away from him. My hand slides down from her shoulders, over the soft folds of skin at the place where the band of her bra wraps around her torso, to the small of her back, guiding her towards the doors that will take us to the parking lot.

"I'll see you later, M." Trent calls from behind us, but I don't let her turn around to look at him. Don't want to give him the satisfaction of seeing the relief flooding her face now, smoothing her features as her chest rises and falls rapidly.

The heavy metal doors slam behind us, and Mallory lets me lead her away from the entrance and towards the parking lot. It's dark, and even though it's late spring, the air has a slight warmth to it. When we've put a good bit of distance between us and the gym, and I'm sure no one has followed us, I stop walking. Mallory slows down too, but her breathing is still erratic, and I send up a silent prayer that she's not having a panic attack.

Reluctantly, I drop my hand from her back and bring it to her waist, using it to turn her to face me. The plate of cold nachos in her hand shakes, and I slowly slide it and the bottle of water out of her grip. Her fingers tremble against mine, and I close my eyes briefly, wanting nothing more than to go back in that gym and snatch Trent up by his neck and make him regret ever knowing her. With her hands free, she covers her mouth, stifling a scream that's already silent.

"Mal."

She bends at her waist, braids spilling out of the neat bun she had pinned to the top of her head. They cover her face as her knees buckle, and I take one of her arms, moving her back towards the only bench on the path and lowering her onto it. Setting the plate and bottle on the ground by her feet, I drop down on my haunches in front of her.

"Mallory, look at me. You're okay." Gently, I wrap my fingers around her wrists, pulling her hands away from her face. "Do you hear me? You're okay."

I don't know what else to say, what else to do to help her. To convince her that she's safe. That I'll keep her safe. I run my thumbs over her pulse points, slow swipes in a steady rhythm that matches the cadence of my words. My reassurances to her.

"I'm right here, Mal. You're okay. Just breathe, sweetheart."

Something I said strikes a chord inside of her, making her come alive. She snatches away from me, shaking her head as she forces my hands off of her. "Don't call me that."

I stumble back then stand. "What?"

"Sweetheart." She shudders. "Don't call me that. He used to…."

"Oh." She peeks up at me, swiping her braids out of her face. "I'm sorry. I didn't mean to….I won't call you that again."

"It's okay." I watch her scrub her hands down her face, sighing heavily before beginning the quick work of putting her braids back into a bun. The simple task seems to be working wonders for calming her nerves, and by the time she's done, she looks more like herself than she did moments ago, and I'm staring at her. A thousand questions running through my mind. "Please don't ask."

My brows shoot up. "What?"

"The questions written all over your face," she says, securing the bun by looping the elastic ban around one last time. "Don't ask them because the only answer I'll give you is that it's none of your business."

"None of my business? I'm the one that got you out of there."

She pushes to her feet. "And I appreciate that."

"But you won't tell me why I had to rescue you in the first place." Mallory stares at me blankly. A silent confirmation. I laugh bitterly, tasting the frustration I'm becoming too used to experiencing when it comes to her and this confusing pattern we keep finding ourselves in. "Is that how it's always going to be with us? Me, giving you my help without question and you refusing to tell me why you needed it?"

"I didn't need—"

"The hell you didn't!" I snap, cutting her off. "You needed me, and I was there. Don't you think that I deserve to know what I stepped in back there? You can at least give me that, Mal. You owe me that much."

"*Owe you?*" Stubborn defiance flashes in her eyes as she raises her chin. "I don't owe you a God damn thing, Chris. I never told you I wanted your help just like I never told him…" Her voice cracks, breaks off, and then comes back. Stronger. Fiercer. Deadlier. "I don't owe you anything, and just so we're clear, you being a decent person doesn't put you in a position to demand anything—but especially answers to questions I told you not to ask—from me."

And just like that, she's back. In all her magnificent, scathing glory that's directed at me. Designed specifically to keep me from coming close enough to see the cracks in the facade she works so hard to keep up. I hate myself for saying that she owes me something because she's right, I'm not entitled to her secrets even though, for some reason I still can't explain, I want them.

13

MALLORY

It would be just my luck that the one time Chris lets me have the last word, I feel like shit for taking it. It would be significantly worse luck that mere hours after telling him I didn't need his help, I would be standing on his doorstep preparing to ask for it.

Again.

Okay, technically all the other times were a combination of me sending up the proverbial bat signal and him answering without hesitation so they didn't really count as asking, but this time does.

And it's a big ask.

A ridiculous ask.

An ask that I know I'll live to regret.

God damn Trent and his big mouth and his stupid face and his infuriatingly paralyzing presence on my campus making me go along with lies that made no actual sense. Lies that I took too much comfort in hearing. Lies I co-signed with my silence last night, and then, my voice early this afternoon when Tasha called me and asked if me and my boyfriend wanted to go out to dinner with her and the guy she was seeing.

I was half asleep when the phone rang, having stayed up all night obsessing over everything that happened after I ran into Trent.

Letting him hug me.

Standing there like a fool, listening to him talk about how he's missed me and never saying a word to make him think he didn't still have the right to touch me.

And then the relief that flooded me when Chris appeared, wrapping his arms around my shoulders, replacing the disgust and shame inspired by Trent's touch with the calming warmth caused by his.

Using all that brainpower recounting the night's events left me unprepared for the phone call with Tasha, and I found myself agreeing with whatever she was saying just so I could get off the phone. It wasn't until she squealed with excitement and started asking me where we'd like to eat, that I realized what I'd done.

Agreed to go on a double date with my former best friend, the guy she's currently dating, and the boyfriend I don't have.

Fuck.

I've just worked up the nerve to actually knock when the door flies open, and I'm hit with the sight of Chris' bare chest and arms as he slips a long sleeve shirt over his head. He's moving quickly, and I have to jump back to avoid colliding with the swell of his pectoral muscles and the rigid lines of his abs.

A small, surprised sound escapes me, drawing his attention to my face and making his fluid movements come to a grinding halt. It's almost comical to see him freeze so completely, to go from strong, certain motion to total stillness. Nothing but his eyes moving as he studies me with the kind of thoroughly efficient sweeps I'm starting to enjoy associating with him even though it reminds me of a predator going still just before it strikes, catching its prey completely off guard.

"Mallory," he says smoothly, like it's totally normal for me to be standing on his doorstep on a Saturday afternoon without my brother or Nic in tow. "Is everything okay?"

"I—" Words seem to fail me as I process his question and the feelings it inspires in me. Specifically low in my belly, where nothing has been happening for months now. "Yeah, everything's okay. I just had a favor to ask."

"Shoot." He finishes slipping his arm through his top, which now that I'm actually looking at *it* and not his body, looks like one of those moisture-wicking shirts Nic and Eric wear when they play basketball. Another quick scan of his body shows that he's wearing sweats and a pair of old, beat-up sneakers that look like they only get pulled out for exercise purposes.

"No, never mind. You're busy." I start to turn on my heel, prepared to deal with Tasha and her boyfriend on my own. Maybe I can cancel. That's what any normal person would do, except there's nothing normal about this situation. I'm here asking Chris to pretend to be my boyfriend, so I can....what? Send some subliminal message to Trent that I'm off limits?

Maybe.

Because up until Chris walked up calling me baby and touching me like I belonged to him, Trent was looking at me the way he used to. Like I was his. Like I would always be his and the years I spent cutting him out of my life, and my soul, meant nothing.

Intellectually, I know that time travel isn't a thing, but it had never felt more real than it did when I was standing there, wrapped in Trent's arms like we were back in his basement stealing kisses and hugs before his parents came down and asked what we were doing.

Warm fingers wrap around my elbow, stopping me from going any further.

"What do you need, Mallory?"

I glance down at his hand on my arm, waiting for that familiar wave of dizzying fear to hit me like it often has when a man who isn't Eric or Nic has touched me since that night, but it doesn't come. Still, I force myself to assess the situation, the way my self-defense instructor always tells me to, even if it's just to remind myself that I'm safe and in control.

Chris' grip is secure, firm, and tight with all five of his thick fingers cradling my elbow, but I could break it if I needed to. And that knowledge keeps my brain from switching into fight or flight mode.

His eyes drop from my face, following my gaze down my arm to where he's touching me, and comes back up again.

"Sorry," he says, releasing me from his hold and looking anything but apologetic. "Why are you trying to leave before you even asked for your favor?"

"Because you're clearly busy, and it was dumb."

With his eyes still on me, he pulls his door closed and leans against it. His biceps bulge underneath the black fabric as he crosses his arms over his chest. "I'm not busy. I was just about to go for a run. Tell me what you came here for."

I blink slowly, the silky purr that is his voice making my blood simmer in my veins. "Chris, it's fine. Really." My feet are moving me backward, back down the hall and away from the havoc he's wreaking on my body. He tracks my movement with his eyes, and there's something decidedly primal about the spark of amusement that starts to glitter within the pools of honeyed bourbon. It's subtle at first, but as I take a few more steps away from him and he pushes off the door to follow me, it catches fire. Burning bright with a hunger I don't understand but am weirdly enthralled by.

My heart is in my throat as I hook a thumb over my shoulder. "I'm just going to go."

"Not before you tell me what you wanted to ask me for." His long legs have eaten up the distance between us, and before I know it, he's standing in front of me. I glance up at him, seeing that he's reigned the hungry predator look all the way in. *Maybe I imagined it.*

"A date."

"A date?" He repeats the words slowly, like he's tasting each syllable. Savoring them.

I blush furiously and launch into my explanation so he can stop looking at me like I just asked him to give me one of his kidneys. "Yes. A date. Because apparently you're my boyfriend now, or did you forget about engaging in a dick measuring contest with my ex last night."

"No, I remember." A quiet storm of emotion darkens his features, and he looks like he's going to say more about what happened with Trent but at the last second he decides against it. "I don't know what that has to do with us going on a date, though."

"Well, Tasha called and invited me out on a double date. You remember her from Mama's party, right?"

"Yeah, your old best friend. She knows your ex?"

I cross my arms over my chest and press my lips together, hesitating on the one part I should be flying through in order to get it over with quickly. "He's her brother."

"Her brother."

"Her *older* brother."

A set of small wrinkles forms in between his eyebrows. "How much older?" he asks darkly.

I have to push down the urge to tell him it's none of his business, to say something harsh and biting to get him to back off, but it is his business now. Because I want his help, because I *need* his help with this.

"Three years, almost four."

Watching him do the mental calculation is excruciating and fascinating. I can see him doing the math, adding in the information I'm sure Eric gave him at Mama's party about when Tasha and I stopped hanging out to draw the correct conclusion that I was underage when Trent and I started dating.

"And you were...." he trails off, giving me the space to fill in the blank.

"Sixteen." I nod, barely hiding the cringe rippling through me. "I was sixteen when it started, and no one knew about us but Tasha."

Chris scoffs. "You sure about that? He seemed pretty damn proud to let me know he was your ex-boyfriend at the game last night."

"Yes, because he's a possessive asshole who likes to mark his territory."

A dangerous heat flashes in his eyes, charring the chestnut of his irises."You're not his to mark."

"No," I agree, a strange warmth spreading through my chest at the ferocity of his words. "I'm not."

He runs his hand over his head, mussing up the short, black curls there. "So you need me to what? Go on a double date with your secret ex-boyfriend's sister so you can prove that you've moved on or something?"

Never have I felt more grateful for the serious side of Chris I've been seeing here lately. Goofy, I'll-make-a-joke-out-of-everything Chris would have just made a stressful situation worse.

My head bobs up and down as I fumble around in my brain, searching for words that will encourage the flower of understanding slowly blooming between us to grow not shrivel up and die. "Or something."

His eyes narrow, suspicion lining his features. "Mallory, if you want my help, you're going to have to tell me everything. Not some Cliff Note's version of the truth."

For a second I allow myself to imagine what it would be like to tell him everything. To unburden myself. To place the weight of the truth in someone else's hands and let them carry it for a while, but then I imagine that same truth finding my brother, finding Nic and Mama and Sloane, ripping into the flesh of their outstretched hands as they attempt to help me carry it, and I know I can't do it. Not now. Not ever.

"You know everything you need to know, Chris."

A bitter laugh that sounds more like a bark escapes his lips. "You're unbelievable, you know that?"

"Yes, but I also wouldn't be here if it wasn't for you and the lies you told last night. All I'm doing is asking you to step back into the role you chose to play."

"A role I chose to play to help you."

"I didn't ask you to."

"I know you didn't." He throws his hands in the air. "But you didn't see your face, Mallory. You were terrified. I could see it clear as day from across the room, and he was standing right in front of you and it didn't even register. Do you know what that tells me about the relationship the two of you had?"

I shake my head because the last thing I want is to hear what Chris saw when he looked at me and Trent. He takes a step closer, moving slowly, carefully, like he knows that advancing too fast will scare me.

"It tells me that he never cared enough to see you, Mal, and when he did see you, he made you feel like your feelings weren't important. Like they didn't matter more than his. Is that what it was like between you two? His wants, needs, and feelings always overriding yours?"

"Stop." I plead, the one word hitting the air and making the entire hallway go still. Chris is still standing just a few inches away from me. His eyes are soft with concern. "The things you want to know. I can't tell you. All I can tell you is that I need your help, and it's not easy for me to ask for it, especially after last night. But I'm here doing it because as fucked up as it is, the only way guys like Trent back off is if there's another guy forcing them to do so, and for better or worse, you've positioned yourself as that guy. So either say you'll help me or tell me you won't so I can leave now and figure something else out."

He clenches his jaw, making the veins in his neck pop and throb in a way that shouldn't be attractive but is. "What time is dinner?"

Although I'm relieved to hear the question, I can't help but notice that he hasn't fully agreed to help me out, so when I finally answer him, the words come out shaky and unsure.

"Tasha said she gets off at seven, so she was thinking eight thirty."

A small bubble of hope tries to swell in my chest, but it's stifled by the hard look in Chris' eyes and the frustration etched into his features. He's angry with me because I won't give him the answers he wants, the answers that, truthfully, he deserves because I'm dragging him into a shit show, and what's worse, asking him to fly blind.

Without a map or a single direction to tell him how to navigate it all. I bite my lip, preparing to beg him for an answer, but before I can do that the sound of a phone ringing pierces the tense air between us.

Since I keep my phone on silent, I know it's not me, which means someone has to be calling Chris. He curses under his breath, dropping my gaze to search his pockets for his phone. When he finally finds it, he looks between me and the screen, which is lit up with text messages, finger hovering over the green icon that will connect the call.

"I have to take this."

"Oh." My desperation is palpable. I need his answer now, so I can spend the next few hours preparing for whatever version of this dinner is going to be happening, but I can hardly press him for it, not when I'm holding so much back myself. "Yeah, sure, go ahead and take it."

But he's already connecting the call, the phone cradled between his ear and shoulder as he turns back towards his apartment and unlocks the door. At the last second, he glances at me.

"I'll text you about dinner."

Then the door closes and he's gone, leaving me in the most agonizing suspense with no idea when or how it's going to end.

14

CHRIS

The door slams behind me, and I instantly want to turn back around. To go back into the hallway and tell Mallory of course I'll help her. Not just because the thought of her being sixteen years old and being groomed by a fucking grown man makes me furious, but because she's right, I inserted myself into this whole situation. Told a lie to protect her, to shield her, and ended up creating more problems than I solved.

That seems to be the theme of my day: problems, problems and more problems.

Some I can solve, like this situation with Mallory and her ex.

Some, I can't begin to wrap my brain around like the call I got from Vanessa, Margaret's niece and one of my closest friends, this morning where she told me, with tears clogging her throat, that the only mother either of us had ever known was diagnosed with stage four breast cancer and things weren't looking good.

I spent the entire day in that blurry space of anticipated grief, mourning a loss I hadn't even experienced yet, and when I finally emerged from it, that thrum of restless energy started to rush through my veins. Prompting me to move, demanding the kind of distraction only physical exertion can provide. I was heading out for a run, partially annoyed that I couldn't work through this feeling the way I used to, when I ran smack dab into the person stopping me from doing so.

I was shocked to see her, especially after the way she stormed off last night. Leaving me standing on the path, staring after her magnificent curves while a cloud of jasmine swirled around me in her wake. I wanted to go after her, had to force my feet to stay planted on the cement as she walked away from me, and once she was gone, I promised myself I was done. Chasing her. Helping her. Focusing on her problems when I have my own to deal with.

With graduation just a few months away, my dad is becoming even more giddy about my return to Boston and increasingly harder to reason with. Yesterday, on our weekly call before the game, I was talking to him about my choice to specialize in obstetrics and gynecology with a focus on maternal and fetal medicine that would prepare me for dealing with high-risk pregnancies like the one my mother had with Teresa—something I've always been very clear about doing. He acted like he'd never heard the idea before, and told me I'd be specializing in cardiothoracics before I even got the chance to tell him that one of the doctors leading the field in maternal and fetal medicine had just accepted a position at MUSC—the medical school I *actually* wanted to attend.

We got into a tiff about it, falling into the same redundant patterns as all of our calls here lately, and by the time we hung up, we were both seething. I expected to hear from RJ immediately after because even when we're getting along, he never misses a chance to gloat, but the call never came.

Not last night at least.

No, he chose this afternoon, when I was standing in front of Mallory in the rarest of forms, to send me five SOS texts back to back and then follow them up with a call I felt compelled to take because days that start shitty typically continue to go that way.

Problems, problems and more problems.

"What's wrong, RJ?" I pinch the bridge of my nose between my fingers, still leaning against my door. "Is Teresa okay? Dad? Grandpa?"

"Relax, man," he laughs. *Laughs.* Like he didn't just send up the type of smoke signal most people reserve for deaths and natural disasters. "Everyone is fine."

"Then why the fuck did you text me five different times and then call?"

"I only called because you didn't answer my texts, asshole."

I push out a harsh breath. "I was busy."

"That's code for 'balls deep in some pussy,' right? Damn, bro, it's dumb as hell, but I gotta say, I respect your determination to make the most out of your last days of freedom."

Completely ignoring his crass, and wrong, assumption, I push off the door and move into the living room, plopping down on the couch. "Tell me why you called."

"Dad sent me to get Mom's ring out of the safety deposit box at the bank."

"RJ, I don't give a fuck about the errands Dad makes you run."

He continues, not even pausing to acknowledge me. "Then he had me take it to the jeweler with specific instructions to resize the band and upgrade the stone."

"Is this supposed to mean anything to me?"

"You're the one he's determined to see wedded and bedded in the next few years, Chris. You tell me if him having a family heirloom upgraded to fit the finger of the woman he wants you to marry means anything to you."

A knot forms in my throat, and it matches the ones taking shape in my neck and shoulders. "How do you know it'll fit Giselle?"

"The new band will be a size six. Giselle's ring size is a six." He says it simply, like it makes perfect sense for him to know the ring size of a woman he's never bought jewelry for.

"But how do you kn—"

"It doesn't matter how I know, Chris." The line is quiet for a moment, and I imagine him in his high-rise apartment shaking his head at my pointless questions. "What matters is that you are running out of time. Giselle and Oscar were at the house for dinner last night. She asked about you, like she always does, and Dad invited her to your graduation, said it would be the perfect time for you two to reconnect since you'll be taking a break from your studies."

"Fuck."

"Yeah, that's what you are. *Fucked.*"

Breathing becomes hard, damn near impossible as the silver spoon that's been in my mouth since the day I was born tumbles down my throat. Lodging itself in my windpipe and refusing to move. I sit up, pulling air in through my nostrils and pushing it back out through my mouth as visions of the life I spent the last four years laying a foundation for slips through my fingers.

"Jesus," I mutter under my breath. "What the fuck am I going to do?" I'm not talking to RJ, but he still answers.

"I don't know, man, but if you've got a secret girlfriend in your pocket, now would be the perfect time to pull her out."

"I already told you—"

I pause, his words sparking a dangerous fuse that outlines a plan that just might solve two of the problems brought to my attention today. I won't be able to execute it alone, though, I'll need the help of two of the most stubborn people I know. But as luck would have it, one of them is already halfway on board and the other is on the phone right now unwittingly playing an integral role in the farce taking shape in my mind.

"Actually," I hedge, hoping like hell I'm making the right choice. "I have been seeing someone."

My brother is quiet for a second, probably digesting this new information, before the line explodes with his excitement. "I knew it! All that time out there pretending like you were playing the field. I knew you didn't have that shit in you."

"Yeah, I guess I didn't."

"Is it serious?" He asks, sounding hungry for information, interested in my life for once. "Is she the reason why you've been so adamant about not getting back with Giselle?"

"Yes, it's serious." I scrub a hand over my face, willing myself to answer these questions without letting the doubt winding its way through my gut show. "Mallory and I are very serious." My heart starts to beat faster at the words, at the way they don't sound wrong or feel like a lie at all.

"Mallory," RJ repeats her name. "Is that the girl you're always hanging with? Your friend's sister."

"Eric's sister, yeah." Surprise colors my response because I didn't expect RJ to remember any of my friends' names. A low, appreciative whistle filters through the speaker from RJ's side, and my fist clench instinctively. "Keep whatever it is you were about to say to yourself, RJ."

There's a dark severity to my tone, and he picks up on it immediately. "Damn," he laughs. "You really are serious about this girl."

"I am, which is why I need your help with this whole Dad and Giselle thing."

"I don't think you do, bro. Just talk to Dad, let him know that you're in love just like he was with Mom, and you're not going to give this Mallory girl up. Hell, if you use the same tone with him that you just used with me, he might fold right there on the spot."

Rising from the couch, I start to pace. Wearing a hole in the floorboards as I consider his suggestion. "No, I don't think that'll be enough. Not if Giselle is still an option."

If Dad has held on to this delusion about me and Giselle getting married and creating this medical and pharmaceutical empire with an exchanging of rings, he's not going to let it go just because I got a girlfriend.

"You're right," RJ says with an oddly gleeful smile in his voice. "She has to be off limits too."

"Is she dating anyone?" I already know the answer before I finish asking the question, but RJ confirms it.

"Nah, from what I can tell Oscar and Dad have shut down so many of her dates no one even bothers to ask anymore."

"Damn." A thread of sympathy runs through me for Giselle, the only person in this entire situation who has it worse than me. While

I've been here in New Haven, she's been stuck in Boston, being kept on the chopping block by our fathers.

"Yeah," RJ agrees, sighing sympathetically. He's always had a soft spot for Giselle, and I guess that hasn't changed. "I might be able to help with that though."

"You?" My brows fall together in confusion. "How?"

"Don't you worry your pretty little head about that. Just trust that I have it and focus on growing balls big enough to stand up to your daddy once and for all."

The line goes dead, and I stand there shocked at the mess I just set into motion. It's one thing to lie to Mallory's meathead ex about being her boyfriend, but to lie and tell my brother, who will undoubtedly tell my father, that we're together and in love is something completely different. It's a larger, way more in-depth, commitment I don't even know she'll be willing to make.

"Shit." Scrolling through my contacts, I pull up her number to send her a text. Drafting it proves to be hard because I don't know how much to say. Do I lay it all out there? Tell her that the hole I dug for us last night just got a million times deeper?

Chris: I'll pick you up for dinner at 7:15.

Mallory: Okay.

Mallory: Thank you.

Mallory: Really.

Despite the stress turning my stomach into knots, I can't help but smile at her triple text. Most girls would be self-conscious about texting back too quickly and would die before they sent three responses back to back, but not Mallory. She's just so completely herself.

It's one of my favorite things about her.

Chris: Don't thank me just yet. I have a favor to ask. It's not as payment for this, because you're right, I did make this mess and I'll happily help clean it up, but it is related.

Again, she texts back immediately and back to back.

Mallory: Related? In what way?

Mallory: What do you need me to pretend to be your girlfriend to save you from a creepy ex too? 😉

A gruff laugh escapes me as I type out my response, impressed by her ability to hit the nail right on the head.

Chris: Let's discuss it after dinner.

15

MALLORY

The restaurant Tasha chose is in Fairview. It's thirty minutes away from campus on a good day, and forty-five minutes to an hour on a Saturday evening when everyone is out doing cute things like going on dates. Given my aversion to dating, Saturday night traffic hasn't been a concern of mine in quite some time, but tonight, as I sit in my dorm and watch the clock creep towards 7:15—the time Chris said he would be here—it's the only thing on my mind.

Not the anxiety that twists my gut every time I think about our text conversation. Not the excessive amount of time I spent doing my hair —using flexirods and setting lotion to turn the straight braids into wavy tresses that I piled on top of my head in a sexy, messy bun with some of the curled ends left out of the elastic to create a faux bang that frames my eyes. Not the butterflies dancing on top of my anxious intestines, making my hands shake as I swipe on some of the expensive ass lip gloss Sloane gave me for my birthday in October.

Just as I finish closing the tube, there's a knock on my door. I allow myself one last look in the mirror, appreciating the way my blush, one-shoulder top hugs my breasts and the curves of my torso before disappearing inside the waist of my light-washed jeans. It's a simple look, but it'll work for whatever the vibe is in the restaurant Tasha chose. The only thing I'm not sure about is the one shoulder because even though it's been warming up, with February giving way to March, it still gets pretty cold at night.

"Maybe I should—" I glance around the room, searching for a cardigan or jacket to put on that won't ruin the look but another knock sounds, interrupting the thought. With a resigned sigh, I grab my things and head for the door, sending up a silent prayer that it won't be too cool tonight.

I open the door, and my senses are immediately bombarded with all things Chris. He's got the whole layered look going on with clothes that look casual but are clearly expensive. Dark-washed jeans with a strategically placed rip in the knee, a crisp white shirt that makes the gold of his skin pop, and a camel-colored, suede bomber jacket that looks softer than anything I've ever owned.

Absently, as I finally draw my eyes away from his clothing and meet his gaze, I note that the color of the jacket matches the rich depths of his irises. And if that isn't bad enough, he smells amazing. Like leather and freshly fallen rain soaking into sun-kissed soil.

It's mouth-watering.

"Hey."

His greeting pulls me out of my reverie, and I manage to give him a smile that doesn't betray my thoughts.

"Hey."

"These are for you." Taking his hand from behind his back, he presents me with a small vase with water in the bottom and a bouquet of white and yellow flowers sprouting from the top. The sweet, floral notes hit me, and I instantly recognize them. Eyes stretched in surprise, I meet his soft, serious gaze and he nods, answering my silent question. "Jasmine."

"My favorite. How did you know?"

"You always smell like it." He licks his lips, like talking about my scent makes his mouth water, and I blush because the thought makes the ball of desire low in the pit of my belly start to unfurl. "Like jasmine and citrus."

"I—" Don't know what to say. Because once again I'm shocked at all the things he notices about me. "Thank you, Chris."

I step back into the room, turning to place the vase on my desk, which is closest to the door, and coming back to him, still blushing like a fool. He steps back, making space in the entry for me to pass through and pull the door closed behind me. My fingers shake as I fiddle with the handle, making sure it's locked, and when I'm finally done, Chris is standing just a few inches away, waiting patiently for me.

"Ready?"

I nod, trying to appear confident even though internally I feel like I'm a second away from crumbling. The date hasn't even started, and I'm already losing it. I shudder to think what my reaction will be when he starts touching me, or doing all the other things boyfriends do like calling me baby and kissing me.

"Yeah." The word gets caught in my throat and is barely discernible when it hits the air, so I drive the point home with another nod and try again. "Yes, I'm ready."

"Well, let's go." With a dramatic flourish that makes me smile, he gestures for me to go ahead of him, and I'm hyper-aware of him walking behind me as we make our way down the hallway to the bank of elevators that will take us to the first floor. That awareness kicks up another notch when he leans over me to press the button for the elevator, his hard chest brushing my shoulder.

Thankfully, the elevator comes quickly, and I'm able to put some space between us as we step into the car. Chris presses the button for the first floor, and we ride down in silence. It's weird, the quiet between us, and I'm anxious to fill it with something.

"Was everything okay?" He turns to me, brows pulled together like he doesn't know what I'm talking about. "Earlier," I clarify, "when you got that phone call. Was everything okay?"

A dark cloud descends over his features belying his easy response. "Oh, yeah. Everything was good."

I purse my lips, fighting the need to call him a liar, especially after all the time he's spent demanding that I tell him all of my truths.

Unfortunately, I'm not any good at hiding my thoughts and feelings, and he sees it on my face immediately.

A frown tugs on his lips. "What?"

"Nothing."

"No, it's something. Tell me what it is."

Shifting on my feet to angle my body towards him, I give in to the order. "Fine. You're lying. Everything clearly wasn't fine."

Chris tucks his hands in the pockets of his jeans. "If you already knew that why'd you bother asking?"

"So you could *experience the relief of telling someone the truth*," I say the last part in my best impression of his voice, which is terrible at best and offensive at worst, and hate the way my heart flutters when it makes him smile.

"Well played, Ms. Kent, well played."

"Does that mean you're going to answer my question honestly then?"

The elevator dings, signaling our arrival on the first floor, and when the doors open, Chris places his hand on the small of my back and ushers me out. I'm momentarily stunned by the firm, possessive pressure there, and as we move through the lobby of the building all I can concentrate on is the low current of electricity thrumming between us.

"Let's discuss it after dinner," Chris answers as we step into the cool night air and make our way to his car, which is parked on the curb in front of the building.

"But we're supposed to be discussing the favor you want to ask for after dinner."

We approach his car, and I stop. Chris' hand leaves my back as he walks around me and opens the passenger door. He stares at me expectantly, waiting for me to get in, but I'm still processing. If he wants to delay the conversation about his phone call until after dinner when we're supposed to be discussing his need for me to reprise my role as his fake girlfriend, then the two things must be connected.

"*After dinner*, Mallory." Leaving the door open, he closes the distance between us and grabs my hand. The contact sets off a thousand sparks that crackle and set the air between us on fire. Our eyes lock, and I swear I see the same storm of emotions coursing through me in his eyes. But he drops my gaze, and when he looks back at me, it's gone. "Let's go. We don't want to be late."

"Fine but just be prepared for me to be all in your business like you've been all in mine lately. I want all the truths, mister, no if, ands or buts about it."

Heat from his body bleeds into my skin as I brush past him and slip inside. To my surprise, he leans forward and bends down slightly to take my purse and my keys from my hand so I can buckle my seat belt. While I get settled, he tucks my keys into the side of my purse. His knuckles graze my thigh as he sets the whole thing on the floor between my legs, and his breath is warm on my face when he says, "I don't have an issue with giving you my truths, Mallory. I'll start right now with the most obvious one. Do you want to hear it?"

I'm trapped in his gaze, drowning in soft and serious ochre eyes and trying to appear unaffected. "Sure."

"You look beautiful tonight."

My throat is dry, so the chuckle I force out is raspy. "Just tonight?"

"No." His eyes glow. "Not just tonight."

My chance to respond is lost in the sound of the passenger door slamming. While he rounds the car, I pull out my phone and see a text from Sloane. She's asking if I want to come over and watch a movie with her because Eric and Nic are at Mama's painting the kitchen. I type out a quick response, asking her for a rain check, and then tuck my phone under my thigh.

Chris settles into the driver's seat and cranks the engine, turning the heat on low and pressing a button on my side that has warmth spreading through the leather underneath me and making me feel less anxious about going to dinner with Tasha.

Well, at least a little.

As Chris weaves through the quiet streets of the city, following the GPS instructions to the address I gave him, a ball of dread sits at the bottom of my stomach. Sending waves of nervous energy flooding through me as my brain tortures me with unlikely scenarios that all involve Trent showing up to dinner, demanding we catch up in private so he can say all the things he didn't get a chance to when we ran into each other at the game. I can already hear the questions.

Why'd you disappear like that?

You just cut me out of your life like we were nothing.

Tasha said you did the same thing to her.

What's up with that, M?

A shudder runs through me, and it draws Chris' attention away from the road. He glances over at me. "You okay?"

"Yeah, I'm good." I swallow past the lump the lie leaves in my throat. "Just a little nervous."

If Chris is surprised I'm giving him answers he didn't have to pry out of me, he doesn't let it show. He just nods like he understands. "About the dinner?"

"I'm scared he'll be there."

The dark cloud appears again, taking over his face with thunderous emotion. "If he is you just let me worry about him, okay?"

"Okay." I fold my hands in my lap. "I'm probably just being silly. Tasha wouldn't invite him."

"Does she know—" The opening he leaves at the end of the sentence makes me feel transparent. Like wafer-thin glass floating on top of crystalline blue water. And my heart thuds against my rib cage as I wait for him to finish, to say my truth, which I'm now certain he knows, out loud. "—about the way you two left things?"

"No." I focus my attention on the wood grain embedded in the dash. "I stopped talking to her around the same time I stopped talking to him."

Tingles of awareness skitter along the line of my jaw, alerting me to his eyes on my profile. "You just cut them both off?"

"Yes." *And I used the shards Trent left me in to do it.*

We're both quiet for a second, and I use the moment to remind myself that no matter how nice it feels to let my guard down, to show him just a glimpse of my shattered soul, I can't do it fully. This arrangement, even if it's only going to last for tonight but especially if it's going to go beyond that, doesn't change anything. It can't.

Because he's still him—a light-hearted, playful guy with little to no cares in the world—and I'm still me: the girl who can't afford to be lured in by a bright smile and charming demeanor again.

Right now I just need to focus on getting through this dinner without being overly affected by how well Chris plays the dutiful boyfriend.

"Tell me something about you."

"Something like what?" I ask, exchanging my view of the interstate for the strong line of his jaw and the goofy smile taking over his face that tells me he's trying to lighten the mood. Even though I'm still anxious, I decide to let him.

"You know, something that your old best friend would know and your boyfriend should too."

"What like my favorite color?"

"No." He shakes his head, looking exasperated. "I already know that."

"You do?"

"Yeah, it's pink. But not like bubblegum pink or salmon pink, it's a very specific shade. Softer." He gives me one of those infectious smiles, the ones that make it impossible not to smile back. "Lighter," he continues, "like a blush."

I swallow past my shock and the delicious heat coursing through my veins and moistening my panties at the mere thought of being known by him. *He's just playing a role.* I remind myself, but it's so hard to believe when there's no one else around to witness it.

Doesn't matter. It's not real. None of this is real.

"Okay, so you know my favorite color. You know my brother and my mom and where I go to school and what I'm majoring in. What else is there?"

Chris looks at me like I've just asked the dumbest question known to man. Like there are so many other things to know about me, like I contain multitudes, caverns of interests and ideas and thoughts that have yet to be explored.

"Everything, Mallory."

"Like what, Christopher?" Frustration claws at my chest, and I'm unfairly aiming it all at him. It's not his fault I don't know who I am anymore, that when you strip away the obvious things like the people I love and the things I value there's not really a person underneath it all. "Tasha knew me years ago, it's not like she's going to interrogate you about my interests and ideas. She'll be more interested in whether or not you kiss me and hold my hand under the dinner table."

As soon as the words leave my mouth, I want to suck them back in, but I know it's both impossible and impractical. We do need to discuss how far we're comfortable going tonight as far as physical touch is concerned.

My leg starts bouncing, one of my more obvious anxious tells. "Are you comfortable doing that? Um, the kissing and hand-holding stuff, I mean."

It feels stupid to even have to ask considering what we're about to do, but I have to ask. The last thing I want is to lean in for a kiss and have him cringe and go the other way.

"Yes, Mallory," Chris says tightly, like the words are being forced from his mouth. "I'm happy to do whatever we need to convince your friend that we're a couple."

The butterflies that have been living in my stomach since he text me and said he would do this choose that exact moment to take flight. Their wings flutter around my stomach, inciting and soothing my frayed nerves at the same time. An unbidden wish is whispered from the depths of my soul, lifted up by the constant flapping and expelled with the sigh of relief that leaves me.

A wish for his kiss, for his hands on my skin, for his eyes, soft and serious and all mine.

It's a dangerous wish, made by a desperate girl, but I shouldn't be surprised because only desperate girls get themselves into situations like this. For all its negative implications, the wish does have one positive thing going for it. It forces me to remember a girl who used wishes like prayers, like spells and incantations that didn't need a special occasion to be uttered.

Drawing in another deep breath, I call on the energy of that girl, that version of me, and use the strength of her carefree spirit to share a piece of me with Chris I've never given to anyone else.

"Between the ages of six and eight, I used up all of my wishes on a dream that never came true."

Those three little wrinkles between his brows are back. "*All* of your wishes? How many wishes does a person get in a two-year span?"

I can't help it, I smile. At the wonder and intrigue in his response. At the easy smile pulling on his lips that I know is inspired by mine. "Between birthdays, shooting stars, and repeating numbers on the clock? A lot."

"Repeating numbers?"

"You know, like 11:11."

He nods. "Gotcha. So what did you wish for?"

"Promise not to laugh at me?"

"No," he snorts. "I can't promise you that, but you have to tell me anyway. For the sake of the mission."

I roll my eyes. "Okay, but just keep in mind I was deep in my Disney era, and they were hitting us with goodies left and right. Plus, when the version of Cinderella with Brandy and Whitney Houston came out, every girl in my class was obsess—"

"*Mallory.*"

"Fine." I sigh heavily. "Every time I made a wish, I wished to be a princess. And I'm talking waking up the next day in a castle with a fine ass prince at my beck and call and tiaras and ball gowns for days."

"A princess? *How original.*"

"Shut up!" I laugh, and my hand shoots out. Before I know it my splayed fingers are colliding with his chest. I snatch it back quickly. "Sorry."

He shrugs, still laughing. "No worries, Your Highness. All of your servants should be so lucky to find themselves swatted by your royal hand."

"Oh my God," I groan. "You're going to make me regret telling you that, aren't you?"

"Oh, most definitely."

I try to look annoyed. I do. But I just can't pull it off especially when Chris decides to talk in a surprisingly good British accent for the rest of the ride. Making me laugh and smile and all around forget the worries I had about this dinner. It's not until we're seated at the table, and I catch a glimpse of Tasha and her date walking through the front of the restaurant, that I start to feel nervous again.

It's unfounded. Especially because I can clearly see that they've walked in alone, but it's still there, and Chris seems to be aware of it instantly. He settles one of his long arms over the back of my chair and leans in close.

"We've got this," he whispers, lips brushing my earlobe in a gesture that feels just as intimate as it must look. "I'm right here with you."

And then for good measure, and probably to stop my heart from beating altogether, he presses a quick kiss to my temple. It's the same spot he kissed me last night in front of Trent, and I force myself not to think too much of it. He's playing a role, and so am I.

Tasha and Vaughn—a short, bald-headed guy with a jet black beard that blends into his deep ebony complexion—weave through the tables and make their way to us. Chris stands and pulls my chair out from the table so I can too. Tasha comes over to my side first, her arms open wide, and we hug while Chris and Vaughn do that manly dap up thing guys like to do. Then we switch, Tasha making funny eyes at me over Chris' shoulder while she hugs him, and Vaughn giving me an awkward one-armed hug that, thankfully, ends quickly.

We settle in our seats and wait for the waitress to take our drink and appetizer orders before we move from small talk to the reason we're all here tonight.

Trent.

"My brother didn't lie," Tasha says, batting her eyelashes at Chris. "You *are* pretty."

A grimace tries to curl Chris' lips, and I watch him turn it into a big, genuine smile. It's kind of impressive how quickly and easily he does it, and it makes me wonder how often darker emotions preface the bright smiles he's known for.

"Well, I'm glad you're not disappointed."

"I'm not at all. Honestly, I don't even think Trent did you justice when he described you. But then again he was a little drunk and maybe a little jealous that the love of his life has moved on."

I balk. "The *what* of his life?"

Tasha turns to me. "Come on, Mal. You know how he felt about you. My brother has always loved you, and that never changed, not even when you cut us out of your life."

"Damn, Tash," Vaughn mutters, shifting uncomfortably in his seat. "Go easy."

"I am, baby." She assures him, but there's a cattiness to her tone that makes me think otherwise. "I just don't know why Mal is acting like she doesn't know how Trent felt about her. They used to be all over each other, Chris."

"That was years ago, Tasha. And *I* was too young to be the love of anyone's life."

"Not too young to break his heart though," she tosses back. There's a bitterness shimmering in her eyes that I don't understand. She called me and invited me out to dinner. And at Mama's party, she was so pleasant and excited about reconnecting. It's hard to reconcile the angry, mean girl sitting in front of me now with the person from those encounters.

"Is that why you wanted to have dinner, Tasha? To bring up a bunch of old shit that doesn't matter to anyone anymore?"

"It matters to me!" She hisses, her tiny hand slapping the table with a soft thump. "And it mattered to Trent. You destroyed him, Mal. After you cut him out of your life, he just stopped being him. He stopped going to class, started drinking all the time, lost his football scholarship and any chance of going to the NFL. We were going to be sisters and you just messed it all up and for what? So you could go to college and date pretty boys with trust funds?"

All words are lost to me. They flit through my mind in a whirlwind, and I try to grab for them, but no matter how quick I am or how tight my grasp is, every time I open my hands they're empty. Tasha's still ranting, spilling years' worth of venom onto the table between us, and Vaughn just sits there, looking disgusted at playing a part in this ambush. I can't bring myself to look at Chris, especially when she starts to talk about the intimate parts of my relationship with Trent.

"….did you forget what it was like between you two, M? Cause I don't think I'll ever forget the time I woke up in the middle of the night and came downstairs to find you on your…."

"That's enough."

I've never seen Chris angry, and I certainly never imagined that the first time I did witness it, it would be because someone was disrespecting me, but that's exactly what's happening right now. And he's not just angry, he's *pissed*. Waves of fury roll off of him in lethal waves that are all aimed at Tasha, and she rears back as if he's hit her.

"Stay out of this, Chris."

Chris rises from his seat, leaning across the table with his lips curled in disgust. "No, I don't think I will. If you wanted a chance to get at my girlfriend without any interference, you shouldn't have extended an invitation to me. And since I'm here, I'm going to clear some shit up for you."

"*Chris.*"

I don't know why I'm saying his name, what I'm asking him for or begging him not to do, but when he looks at me, I can see that he understands. Chestnut eyes make me a promise that doesn't pass his lips. He won't go too far. He won't say whatever it is he thinks he knows about me and Trent.

And, despite all the lessons I've learned that suggest I shouldn't, for the briefest of seconds, I trust him.

"Your brother is a grown-ass man who preyed on a girl *that was your age*. Excluding that disturbing fact, whatever happened or didn't happen between them is none of your business and, as Mallory pointed out a few minutes ago, not at all relevant to anyone's life here today, least of all yours. If your brother wants someone to blame for his life going down the shitter after their breakup, then tell him to look in a goddamn mirror because as far as I can tell, he's the one who tried to destroy her, not the other way around."

Somehow, some way I'll have to get used to the surge of intense gratitude that seizes me every time this man steps up to the plate for me. Solving problems I can't wrap my head around. Formulating responses when I can't speak. Defending me without having a full understanding of why I needed it. After years of hiding my hurt and inadvertently robbing myself of the chance to get this kind of vehement protection, it feels good to watch Chris give me just that. So good, in fact, I almost forget it's just an act.

A role. A part he's playing that doesn't at all relieve me of the burden of having to stand for myself. I move to stand, attempting to push away from the table on my own, but Chris' hand is on the back of the chair before I get the chance, pulling me back and leaving enough space for me to rise. Tasha and Vaughn, who looks like he wishes he was coming with us instead of staying with his date, stare up at us. I make sure to meet her eyes as I round the table.

"This is why we stopped being friends when things ended. You love your brother, and I get that. I love my brother more than anything in this world, but the difference between you and me is that I know Eric isn't perfect and I have never felt the need to fight his battles for him because he's man enough to fight them on his own. Your entire family has always operated like the world revolves around Trent, and it's no wonder he grew up to be an entitled asshole who doesn't know how to take responsibility for anything, including the end of us."

I glance over my shoulder to see if Chris is ready and find him dropping a wad of cash on the table. It's definitely more than enough to cover our half of the food and drinks we ordered but didn't get a chance to enjoy, but I don't say anything about it because I don't think he's in the mood to argue about money, and although I'm a little turned on by the dark intensity swirling around him, I don't want to be on the receiving end of it.

Slipping his wallet back into his back pocket, he meets my eyes, lifting an inquisitive brow. "Ready, princess?"

A slight shiver rolls down my spine at the nickname, and I have to avert my gaze to hide my reaction to it. "Yes."

Without another word, or a second glance at the other half of our disastrous double date, he strides over to me, placing his hand on my back and guiding me out of the restaurant. There's a slight chill in the air as we walk out of the glass doors, and I decide to blame it for the goosebumps pebbling my skin because otherwise, I'd have to acknowledge that Chris' fingertips digging into the tender flesh around my tailbone and the vein throbbing in his temple as we walk to the car is the true culprit.

Keeping his hand on my back, he pulls his keys out of his pocket and presses a button to unlock the doors. I'm acutely aware of his heat and scent filling the air around us as our matching strides carry us closer to the car. Just as we're about to arrive at the door, Chris stops, slips one of his fingers through my belt loop, and spins me around to face him. Startled, I let out a soft yelp and throw my hands out, reaching for the closest thing to me, which happens to be his arms, to stop myself from falling over.

Warm, syrupy sweet eyes scan my face, ghosting over every one of my features. "You good? Or do we need to go back in there for round two?"

A laugh bursts free from my chest, and I feel like a weight I didn't know I was carrying has been lifted off of my shoulders. "Yeah, I'm good. No second rounds necessary. Although, I do wish she had waited until after we ate to turn into a raging bitch."

"Same," Chris sighs, his hands still on my waist. "You down for a ride?"

My heart twists and abandons my chest cavity altogether, performing a perfect nosedive because of the playful light washing over Chris' features. I should say no. I should thank him for his help for the millionth time this week and let us both go back to whatever we were before we were fake boyfriend and girlfriend.

But instead, I return his mischievous smile, feeling carefree and adventurous and completely down for a ride with him. Especially if we're going to a place that I'll always—even in the years that he's gone from my life, absent like the parents we both grew up without—think of as our spot.

"Curly's?" I ask, hopeful, excited, foolish.

16

CHRIS

"So let me get this straight," Mallory says, smacking her full, perfectly glossed lips together to clear any remnants of the cookies and cream milkshake from her mouth. "Your dad wants you to get married? At twenty-two years old?"

I should be more into this conversation, but the moment her lips wrapped around the bright red straw, I was done for. An uncomfortable and inconvenient erection tented my jeans and forced me to shift in my seat to make space for it. It had made focusing on my explanation of my fucked up family situation hard as hell, but somehow I'd managed to do it, and she listened.

Intently.

Those perfect amber eyes stayed glued to my face, even when Jalisa dropped a plate of delicious-smelling curly fries in front of her. They went round and wide when I told her about my recent conversation with RJ, especially when I mentioned I had already told him we were together, and then turned into narrow slits that threatened to slice through me when I mentioned the problematic Johnson family tradition.

It was surreal, sharing all of the shit I usually keep buried deep inside myself with her, but it also felt right. Safe. Like I was hoarding secrets, carting them around in my head and letting them take up space in my soul, for the sole purpose of sharing them with her.

"Well, not right this minute. He'd probably be open to a long engagement, postpone it until I graduate medical school, so the wedding invitations can say *Dr.* Christopher R. Johnson."

"R? What's your middle name?"

Curiosity shines in her eyes, and I smile, loving how hungry she is for information about me. I've always known she had a love of learning, of taking in new information and mastering it, making it a part of the impressive store of facts and figures she keeps locked inside her brain. Most days in class I get distracted watching her soaking in Richardson's lectures. Biting on the end of her pen in a way that's completely sexy even though she doesn't intend it to be.

"Reese," I answer finally.

She squints, recalling a piece of information from earlier in our talk. "Wait, so your middle name is Reese, like your dad's? And your brother is RJ, as in Reese Junior?"

I nod, a paralyzing amount of desire flooding my brain as I watch hers work. "Yep."

"And your little sister, what's her name?"

"Te*res*a." I emphasize the middle syllable, letting her hear the similarity between Ter's name and our dad's. "Real creative, right?"

"Creative?" Mal scoffs and plucks a fry from the plate between us. "More like narcissistic."

"That too, but as far as megalomaniac tendencies go, that one's quite mild."

She nods her agreement, still chewing. I watch her, fascinated by the sight of her jaw working and the muscles in her throat constricting as she swallows. Suddenly, I'm hit with an image of her kneeling in front of me, her nails digging into my thighs as her lips slide off of my well-spent dick and stretch into a proud smile as she swallows my....*Fuck. Don't think about that shit right now.*

Channeling every ounce of self-control I have, I will myself to keep my attention on this conversation, on the deal Mallory and I are in the midst of making. That's the only reason why we're here. I roll my head from side to side, releasing the pent-up sexual tension and regaining focus.

This is just a business deal. Two parties coming together to discuss an arrangement that will be mutually beneficial. There's no space for fantasies or distractions that will blur the lines and jeopardize our goals.

"Okay, so your family is officially worse than Sloane's," she says, leaning back in the booth. "Tell me how you see this going."

Steepling my fingers in front of my face, I take a moment to gather my thoughts. I want her to understand that this isn't just about getting out of marrying Giselle, it's also about getting out from under my dad's thumb altogether. About finding a way to stay out of Boston until I have an MD I earned—*with a specialty I chose*— through hard work instead of nepotism.

"Like it did tonight, minus the ambush and drama."

She arches a brow. "Are you really comparing Tasha's little hissy fit to the reaction your dad will have when he realizes you're trying to upend a decades-long family tradition?"

"No," I pause, reconsidering. "Yes, but I didn't mean to. The thing is, RJ and I think my dad will be more open to letting go of this engagement thing if he believes that I'm in love."

"Why?"

"Because he upended the decade's long family tradition first."

Once again her big, beautiful brain fills in the blanks I left open for her. "Your mom wasn't from one of Boston's elite families?"

"No, she was a foster kid with no family and a full-ride scholarship to my dad's fancy private school."

"Let me guess, they met, fell in love, and the rest was history?"

"Pretty much. He forced my grandpa into giving him his blessing to marry her after he proposed."

"You're not planning on doing that are you?" Concern is etched into her features. "Because I can be your pretend girlfriend, but I draw the line at being your fake wife."

"No," I assure her. "I have no plans on proposing to anyone."

"Cool, so the plan is to play on your dad's non-existent emotions to get you out of getting married."

"Yes."

"Okay. Do you think it'll work?"

"Honestly, I don't know but with graduation only a few months away, I have to try."

Her head bobs up and down, signaling her understanding, but I can see she has more questions, and I wait patiently for her to ask them. I won't rope her into this without giving her all of the things she needs to make an informed decision.

You already did, asshole.

Right. I guess that is true, so technically I'm just giving her all the details she needs and hoping she'll go along with a plan I've already made her an accomplice to.

"And how do you see this working when you graduate? Am I supposed to keep rocking my Mal and Chris 4Eva chain until you have an MD behind your name?"

"A chain?"

"Yeah." She shrugs and pulls a face. "Was that not a thing when you were in high school? Boys buying their girlfriends gold necklaces or bracelets with the engraved charm that says…." The sentence breaks off, and she waves her hand, dismissing her own thought. "Never mind, I can tell by the look on your face it wasn't. Maybe it was just at my school. All of my friends had one at some point or another, but I never got one because no one could know about my relationship."

All the muscles in my body go stiff at the thought of her, so young and in love with the wrong guy, longing for tokens of affection she could never have. It makes me angry for her, for the girl who trusted a guy who never deserved her. For the young woman the destructive relationship turned her into. Her high school years should have been filled with young love bordering on obsession. With guys beating down her door, braving the wrath of Eric and Nic, just to take her out on a date. Instead, she got Trent fucking Davis and years' worth of shame that she should have never felt let alone carried.

Mallory must take my silence for lack of understanding or judgment because she cringes and shakes her head. "Forget I said that."

But my brain doesn't want to forget it. Unbidden, it plays images that want to be memories. Teasing me with possibilities and what ifs I can't entertain. Forcing me to envision going back in time and meeting her before he ever got the chance to know her. Kissing her against lockers and searching for her face in crowded hallways. Praying to have the same lunch period as her and sneaking out of study hall to see her when it didn't work out that way.

In a matter of seconds, I hallucinate giving her everything she never had, when I know that my ambitions will only allow me to give her this.

A business agreement masquerading as a relationship.

I recognize that it's not much, but it's more than I've ever given anyone or anything else. Everything else is reserved for my goals, for building a legacy and career of my own, and honoring my mother while I do it. And even though I don't have any reason to ask, I know this is probably all she'll ever want from me. The most she'll ever be able to give when she's still trying to heal from being hurt so badly by someone she trusted.

We're quite a pair, Mallory and I, both unavailable and seeking asylum from former connections in the safety of each other.

I pull a face, feigning confusion. "Said what?"

She smiles, but it doesn't reach her eyes or activate either of her dimples. Reaching over, I steal a fry off of her plate and decide to get back down to business. The sooner we get this conversation over with, the sooner we can begin.

"We'll break up after I start school in the fall," I say, my tone thoughtful even though I've already planned this all out.

"That long? I thought you were just trying to make it past graduation."

"I am, but I'll still need the cover until I'm in classes at MUSC." Her brows furrow, and I continue. "My dad has this thing about finishing what you started. He never let me quit anything as a kid. Ever. And it'll be the same way with school, especially medical school.

Once I start at MUSC, he won't want me to transfer to Harvard because the optics will be bad."

"*Harvard?*" Her mouth drops open. "You're giving up Harvard for MUSC? Please tell me how that makes sense."

"Because it's my choice and not his." My tone is rough and defensive, and I force myself to fix it because she doesn't deserve my irritation. "And MUSC has Dr. Francine Suffrant."

"You say her name like she's important, but I've never heard of her."

"That doesn't surprise me. She's an OBGYN who specializes in high-risk pregnancies. A lot of her recent research has been on lowering maternal mortality rates through the use of inter-professional teams trained to address issues that commonly lead to maternal death during, and in the days after, birth."

Vague interest. That's what I expect to see on Mallory's face when I finish my explanation, but instead I see a serious, almost severe, curiosity. It sparkles in her eyes and takes over her features, tugging her lips down into a straight line.

"Is that what happened? With your mom, I mean."

Once again I'm shocked at how quickly and thoroughly she puts the pieces of my puzzles together. Even more shocking, is that she's the only one who ever has. My father, who was there in the room, watching his wife bleed to death or suffer from heart failure brought on by cardiomyopathy, has never even asked if that's why I'm so hellbent on my chosen specialty. Tears burn at the back of my eyes, but they don't fall. They never do. All the crying I do for my mother is reserved for my dreams.

"Yes."

"Chris." She reaches across the table, her elegant fingers grasping my hand. I turn my palm over, resting my knuckles against the cold linoleum table while the feel of Mallory's skin against mine makes irreparable changes to the structure of my DNA. It's like she's writing herself into my very being. "I'm so sorry."

Weeks ago we sat here, in this exact booth and she spoke those same words. Her sorrow and hurt for me evident in the wrinkles in her forehead, and I had marveled at her then, struck by the depth of feeling she—a girl who, up until the moment we kissed, had always felt so far removed from the emotion riddled and logicless plane the rest of us mere mortals operated on—had for me. Now I'm not surprised by it at all.

Because Mallory might be able to hide her worries, her stresses, and her heart from the rest of the world, but she's never been able to hide them from me.

"Thank you."

Brows lifted in surprise, she pulls her hand back from mine and tucks it into her lap. I wonder if she's rubbing at it with her other hand. If her pulse is racing as her thumb traces over the place where we were just touching.

Probably not.

As I study her face, I realize my subconscious might be right. She looks completely unaffected. I guess that's the one good thing about getting into a fake relationship with the most level-headed person on the planet: I don't have to worry about her confusing the act we'll have to sell for the real thing.

"Alright," Mallory says, her voice all business. "We'll pretend to be together until you start at MUSC in the fall, then we have a huge falling out, your fault, of course."

"Naturally."

She smiles. "And you'll be a free agent."

"Right."

"What about your ex-girlfriend/future wife? Won't your dad just go back to hounding you about marrying her?"

"That's possible, but we're hoping by then she'll be busy with another suitor."

"Who's we? And please don't ever say suitor again. This is not the 1800s."

My shoulders shake with laughter. She's so damn snarky. "My brother, RJ, and I."

She takes another long pull of her melting milkshake and holds her finger up for me, indicating she'd like me to wait. When she's done, she licks her lips, and my dick twitches.

"Is RJ married?"

"No."

"Why not? Doesn't your backwards ass family tradition have some kind of rule about marrying off the firstborn *first?*"

"You would think so, but things with Dad and RJ are complicated. He's not exactly his biggest fan."

"So no well-bred, high-class wife for him?"

"Not yet, no."

"And you trust him to have things covered on his end? Keeping your ex distracted and all that?"

"Do you see a reason why I shouldn't?"

It's a genuine question for one of the smartest people I know. Mallory's brain is always working, always turning at a million miles a minute and right now I'm psyched to be standing in the middle of the whirlwind.

She shrugs. "I don't know. What's your relationship with him like?"

Adversarial. "We're not as close as you and Eric."

"Eric and I are twins. There aren't many siblings who are as close as we are. What's it like with you and RJ though?"

"Let's just say, we're not always the best of friends, but right now we're good. Working towards a common goal."

Her lips twist to the side. A show of skepticism if I've ever seen one. "What's he getting out of it?"

That's the question I've been asking myself since RJ first called warning me about the ring and volunteering to put himself on the front lines of the Boston side of this operation. No matter how I cut it, I can never come up with anything that doesn't make him sound like some nefarious villain. And although our history is fraught with sibling rivalry and unfounded jealousy on his part, I'm not quite ready to cast him in that role yet.

Especially when I don't know what he gets out of helping me keep my freedom besides more time with Dad, and judging by the way he's been drinking lately, I don't think he wants that.

"I don't know yet," I admit, and Mallory nods, so understanding in the face of a situation that might have sent other girls running for the hills. "But we don't really need to worry about that right now."

She holds her hands up in mock surrender. "If you say so."

"I do."

"And what about my brother?"

"I doubt Sloane would let him date my ex to save me from being a child groom."

The surprised yelp/snort she lets out is both hilariously obnoxious and unfairly adorable. "Oh my, God. Shut up!" She snorts again, and Al and Jalisa glance over at us to make sure she's not dying. "You're definitely too old to be a child groom."

"I'm not that old."

"You're twenty-two. That's nowhere near childhood."

"You're right."

"I was trying to say that we'd have to tell Eric, Nic, and Sloane we're together. They'll have to think it's real or else we'll have to explain why we're doing this and I don't want to get into the whole Trent thing with them."

Her concern is palpable, slithering across the table and wrapping around my lungs. Reminding me that I'm not the only one with a lot riding on this fake relationship.

With a sigh, I sit back in my seat and scrub a hand over my face. "I agree. Plus, the fewer people that know about this, the better." We're both quiet for a moment, absorbing this new reality of having a shared secret. "Do you think they'll buy us as a couple?"

"Yeah, I think they will," she says confidently, a slight blush adding a red tint to her mahogany skin.

"You seem pretty certain."

"I am."

"Care to elaborate?"

"No, I don't think I will." When I lower my brows and frown at her, she rolls her eyes. "Just trust me, okay? I'll tell Sloane first and then, because she can't keep a secret to save her life, she'll tell Eric. And he'll tell Nic and Mama and the rest of the world. How are you planning on telling your dad?" This time it's her brows sinking down, knitting together to form an urgent, worried line. "Please don't tell me you're leaving that to your brother too."

I burst out laughing, amused at her immediate distrust of RJ. "Well, I expect he's already laid the groundwork after our call earlier today, and now that it's out there, we'll keep the narrative going using social media."

"Does your dad spend a lot of time on Instagram?"

"No, but all of my friends and family back home do. The news will reach him in no time. As an added bonus, making things so public will remind Trent that you're unavailable and encourage him and his sister to move on."

I wait for her reaction, holding my breath to see if she's satisfied with this plan. If it will work for her as well as I know it will work for me. Finally, after a few long moments, she gives it her reluctant approval with a nod, shrug, and an outstretched hand.

"It's been a pleasure discussing business with you, *boyfriend*."

Taking her hand in mine, I apply the slightest bit of pressure and marvel at the way her eyes flare with something that looks a lot like heated desire when I say, "The pleasure is all mine, *princess*."

17

MALLORY

We shook on it.

We shook on it, and now I have a boyfriend. *A fake boyfriend*, I remind myself for the millionth time since I woke up this morning. For some reason I expected to feel different, to feel less like an island and more like a landlocked city, tethered to something and someone on every side.

Instead, I just feel like me. The same old mask-wearing, secret-toting Mallory, except now the secrets don't weigh so heavy on me. I don't feel like my chest is going to cave in from the pressure of carrying them, and I guess that's the relief I anticipated feeling when Chris offered to listen to my problems on the way to Mama's party that day.

No, it's not just relief, it's the first breath after being submerged in water. When your lungs are so greedy for air they expand and expand and expand until they're well past their full size and still trying to grow. When they swell with the possibilities of finally, mercifully, operating without constrictions.

Okay, so maybe I do feel different.

So different in fact, it hasn't bothered me in the slightest that Tasha has sent me messages on Facebook and Instagram. I've left them sitting in my request folder, unread, because I'm not interested in anything she has to say on behalf of her brother, who thankfully hasn't reached out to me yet. Knowing Trent, though, it's only a matter of time before he does. He won't be able to resist the chance to act like the good guy, the hero here to save the day after his sister went off the rails.

Normally, I'd be worried about it. Somewhere curled up in a ball, letting anxiety get the best of me until he finally decides to strike, but I've decided I'm not going to do that. I've given too much time and energy to that problematic sibling duo, and they don't get any more.

Apparently, my brain agrees because last night is the first night since Mama's party that I have been nightmare free.

A development, which has already worked wonders for my skin. I lean in close to the mirror, noting the absence of bags under my eyes and smiling to myself as I rub in moisturizer. With my roommate, Alexis, gone for the weekend, I'm able to play music as loud as I want and dance around as I pick out an outfit for the day. Sloane and I are supposed to be going to the nail salon and then over to Chris' to hang out.

According to our well-thought-out plan, I'll have to find a natural way to bring up our relationship to Sloane, so she can disperse the information to Eric who will, undoubtedly, bring it up to Chris.

Once that's done, we'll be free to step fully into our roles and do the hard work of convincing his dad we're in love from over nine hundred miles away.

I've just settled on a pair of hip-hugging jeans and a soft, white tank under a blush cardigan when there's a knock on my door. I toss all the clothes on my bed and run over, opening it without looking because I know that it's Sloane.

"Hey!" I chirp, sounding overly excited.

"Hey," she says slowly, giving me a weird look as she walks in and presses an iced coffee and chocolate croissant in my hand. I close the door and turn just in time to see her checking out my outfit. Her brows shoot towards her hairline when she sees the jeans I chose.

They're my favorite jeans. Ones she always tells me make my butt look amazing. Suspicion lights her hazel eyes, and I know we're on the right track. "Why are you wearing your 'look at my ass, it's amazing' jeans? We're just going to the nail salon."

Sloane is impatient as hell, so I make her wait for her answer on purpose. Taking my time unraveling the paper from my straw and pushing it into the plastic lid of my cup. Drinking a big gulp of my iced coffee and sighing in delight when I take a bite out of the croissant. It's still warm, so the chocolate is gooey and perfect. It oozes down my fingers, and Sloane glares at me as I lick it off.

"What?"

"You know what! Answer my question, hussy!"

"Hussy?" I scrunch my nose, fighting back a laugh. "How old are you again?"

"Old enough to know that you don't wear jeans like this for a regular ole trip to the nail salon." She plops down on the foot of my bed and crosses her arms. "Who are you trying to impress, Mallory Pearl."

"No one, Sloane Elise."

"Liar."

"Your mama."

She laughs and sticks her tongue out at me. "No shit. Now tell me something I don't know."

"Hand dryers in public bathrooms are hella unsanitary."

"Everyone knows that, Mal."

"Really?"

We stare at each other. Her, glaring even harder than before, and me, feeling like I'm going to burst at the seams if she doesn't ask me the questions I need her to ask, so Chris and I can move to the next stage in our plan.

A stage that involves a lot of PDA, which we'll have to document religiously. I told Chris our best bet would be Instagram because most everyone our age is on the app, posting pictures of their food and day-to-day life. Talking about our relationship publicly on any other social media platform would look like we were trying too hard to get in front of his dad, and this can't work if he suspects that we're pandering to him specifically.

Like with my side of things, we'll count on chatty siblings, namely Chris' little sister, Teresa, and friends to disseminate the information we put out there to the necessary sources. And once we've got their attention, we'll really put on a show.

My stomach flips every time I think about Stage Two because it means letting Chris get close. Letting him touch me and kiss me and freezing those moments in time, putting them on display for everyone to see.

But that's the point. Being seen. By Trent, by Chris' dad, by all the people who stole our control and are forcing us to wrestle it back with our bare hands.

I walk over and sit on the top of the bed, closest to my desk with my legs dangling over the edge. She's still looking at me suspiciously, so I decide to tip my hand. Reaching out, I brush my hands over the petals of the flowers Chris gave me.

"What movie did you end up watching last night?"

The faint scent of jasmine fills the air, and I smile. A real smile. Because these flowers truly are lovely, and I'm touched that they made Chris think of me. Sloane tracks the motion of my fingers.

"Some Lifetime movie about a lady whose nanny stole her husband," she mutters. "What about you? What were you doing that was so important you couldn't come watch movies with me?"

"Oh, I was just studying." The lie is an easily believable one, and it's also essential to letting Sloane feel like she's figuring this all out on her own.

"I didn't realize they had a garden at the library."

I pull my attention away from the flowers and turn it back on her. "What?"

She tilts her chin, inclining her head to indicate the bouquet on the desk. "Where did the flowers come from?"

"Oh—" I pretend to be stumped, caught up in trying to formulate another lie, and I know I've got her when she snaps her fingers and jumps up off the edge of the bed.

"You were with a guy, weren't you?!" She's pacing now, brain moving a million miles a minute. "But who? You don't hang out with anyone but me, Eric, Dominic"—a slight eye roll when she says Nic's name—"and….Chris."

Triumph shines bright in her eyes, and I make a halfhearted attempt to extinguish it by calling her name. "Sloane."

"Oh my God, Mal!" She's squealing now and clapping her hands together happily. "I knew it. Damn, I should have seen it before. The way he was acting at the game the other night, like he wanted to duel with me for the honor of running after you when you went to the lobby."

"What?"

My question gets lost in the sound of her rambling. "God, it makes so much sense. You've both been acting weird ever since the kiss, and when y'all are in the same room it's like he can't take his eyes off of you."

Leave it to Sloane to turn a situation where I'm supposed to be feeding her information into one where she's telling me things I didn't know. The way she's describing things makes it sound like Chris and I are actually together. Like in a real way. Her hands wave around animatedly as she gives me all the clues she looked past because she thought I wouldn't give him the time of day.

Clues that when named, make my heart beat a mile a minute.

Clues that I have to ignore, to write off as Sloane's love-struck ass misconstruing the tiniest things and making them bigger than what they are.

Yeah, I assure myself, *that's exactly what it is.* Everyone knows people in love want everyone else to be in love too. And Sloane is in love, embarrassingly so, which means she's prone to seeing hearts in everyone's eyes.

"And last night," she continues, on a roll, "you weren't available and neither was he."

"How do you know Chris wasn't available?"

"Because Eric texted and asked him if he could help them paint the kitchen, and he said he had plans."

"He could have had plans with someone else, Sloane."

"Yeah." She grins, plopping down on the bed right beside me and bumping me with her shoulder. "But he didn't have plans with someone else, Mal, he had plans with you." An anticipation filled pause stretches between us, and Sloane groans loudly. "Please, just put me out of my misery already!"

"Fine." I lean into her, giggling despite myself. "Chris and I are dating."

* * *

SLOANE DID EXACTLY what I knew she would do: took the first chance she got to text Eric and tell him the news. I knew she'd done it when Chris sent me a message while I was getting my pedicure. It was a short text, just a thumbs up and a smiley face, but my heart still tried to beat out of my chest when his name popped up on my screen.

I told myself right then and there that I needed to pull it together. I mean, I can't be having heart palpitations every time he texts me because that begs the question of what will happen when he does something drastic like kiss me in front of our closest friends.

Again.

As Sloane and I approach the entrance to Chris' apartment building, I'm running through all the possible scenarios, weighing the likelihood of him kissing me as soon as he opens the door to let us in or delaying the kiss until some other, more strategic time. Usually, I find calculating probability soothing, but today it makes me feel even more flustered. Which is funny because Sloane is practically floating. She's so happy to see me happy that it almost makes me feel bad about lying to her.

It's better than her having a truth I can't live with her knowing, though, and that makes it all worth it.

Warm air greets us as we cross the threshold to Chris' building and enter the quiet lobby. There are a few residents milling about, checking their mail, or chatting with the concierges who don't bat an eye when we walk through. They know us just as well as they know Chris, but it doesn't stop me from being surprised when one of them calls my name.

"Ms. Kent."

Sloane and I both pause and turn towards the desk, approaching the stout older Black man with neatly trimmed salt and pepper hair and a matching goatee. His name tag says Carl, and he smiles pleasantly as I approach with Sloane at my back.

"Yes?"

With white-gloved hands, Carl reaches into the pocket of his uniform shirt and pulls out a small, yellow envelope. It's not big at all, probably only has enough space to fit a small note but I'm still shocked when he places it on the marble counter of the desk and slides it towards me.

"Mr. Johnson asked that I give this to you when you arrived."

"What is it?" I blurt the question out, causing Carl's wrinkled features to collapse into a disapproving stare.

"I wouldn't know, Ms. Kent, I'm not in the habit of opening pack-ages meant for tenants. Unless, of course, they request that I do so."

"But I'm not a ten—"

"Thank you, Carl." Sloane says as she reaches over me to take the tiny envelope off of the desk. Carl gives her a relieved smile and turns his attention back to the computer in front of him, probably checking giving me this mystery package off of his to-do list.

"Yeah," I mutter, backing away from the desk. "Thank you."

Carl gives a curt nod of his head and switches from his computer to picking up the phone as Sloane pulls me by the arm to the bank of elevators. Before she presses the button to go up, she puts the little envelope in my hand and smiles.

"I think I know what it is, but you have to be the one to open it."

The doors in front of us slide apart, and we step on. Sloane presses the button for Chris' floor while I slip my freshly manicured nail under the envelope's sealed seam. It gives easily and in no time at all, I'm pouring its contents out in my hand.

Well, content, because there's only one thing in this envelope.

A key.

It's shiny and silver with ridges and grooves I can only assume match the internal mechanisms of the lock in Chris' front door. My breath catches, shock coursing through me in thick waves that replace my blood. We never discussed him giving me a key, and I can't see one good reason why I would need it.

Sloane's gasp is audible, and when I look up at her, her mouth is comically wide. "He gave you a *key*? How serious are y'all?"

I bite my lip, forcing back the instinct to deny, deny, deny. "Pretty serious."

Her lips part again, and I know she's about to ask if I love him. Chris and I agreed that we would keep mentioning the depth of our supposed feelings to a minimum with the people in our day-to-day lives while playing it up for everyone else, but him giving me a key in front of Sloane definitely makes that hard to do. Before she can ask, the elevator dings, letting us know that we've arrived at our destination.

We step out together, but I beat Sloane down the hallway. My strides long and eager. My mind spinning with thoughts that whisper and yell about doubts and surprises and dependability. None of it makes sense. They're all jumbled together, wrapped up in panic that marks Chris as an outlier, a rogue wave that will abandon even the best-laid plans and wipe out everything in its path.

That's when I realize it's not about the key. Not really. It's about him improvising even though we have a script. It's about him deviating from the plan and forcing me to doubt his intention to follow it in the first place. It's about him robbing me of control even though he's supposed to be helping me get it back.

I stop in front of his door, fist poised and ready to knock, when it pops open like it did yesterday. Only this time, Chris isn't on his way out. He looks, for all intents and purposes, like he was expecting me, and I yelp in surprise when he slips his arms around my waist and pulls me into a tight hug. A rumble that turns into a soft growl escapes his chest as he buries his nose in my neck. I'm aware of Sloane somewhere behind me, and so despite my annoyance, I let myself melt into him. Wrapping my arms around his neck and returning his embrace.

"Princess." He mumble-growls into my ear, lips brushing over my lobe. "I've missed you."

"You just saw me last night." My voice is shaky, and I'm annoyed by that. By the easy way he undoes me. Chris pulls back, his smile bright as it shines on me, blasting away the rest of my short-lived annoyance with a simple curve of his lips.

"Wow." Sloane sighs as she walks up behind us and slips through the doorway using the small space we've left open. "I can't believe I missed that."

Her footsteps echo down the long hallway, and I wait until I'm sure she's gone to let Chris go. Dropping my hands from around his neck, I try to take a step back, but he's still holding on to me.

"Where are you going?" He sounds put off by me trying to put some space between us, but his eyes are doing that thing they do when he thinks I'm running from him. Chestnut gives way to a warm, rich shade of browned butter that says he'd enjoy chasing me.

"We're alone," I remind him, using my shaky fingers to remove his hands from my waist and ignoring the twinge of disappointment that moves through me when they fall back to his sides.

"Right." He glances behind him then turns back to me with a sheepish grin. "Sorry about the ambush, I just didn't want walking in here to be awkward for you."

Oh. I'm oddly touched by his foresight. I didn't expect anyone to be aware of the worries swirling around in my mind today, but Chris was, and that knowledge makes me want to hug him again. For real this time. Instead of acting on that impulse, I hold up the key in my hand and arch a brow at him.

"I could have just used my key."

Something about my tone must clue him in to how I feel about the key because his smile falls away, leaving only concern etched into his features. "You're mad?"

Mad sounds like the wrong word, but I don't have a better one for how I feel right now. "Yes, Chris. We never discussed you giving me a key to your place. Let alone doing so in front of Sloane."

He takes a step forward, coming out into the hallway with me and closing the door softly behind him. "Princess."

That damn nickname does something to me. Fries my brain cells and makes a full breath of air hard to come by, which is terribly inconvenient given how much I've grown to like my recently nonconstricted airways.

"Don't *princess* me," I hiss, which makes him start smiling all over again. Infuriating man. "We had a full-blown conversation about how this was going to go just last night. An entire plan put in place, and now you're just going rogue. Why?"

"You're right, we did have a plan, but last night after I dropped you off I started thinking about things we didn't cover in our discussion."

"Like what?"

A vein in his temple starts to throb. "Like your ex being on campus regularly. We don't know if he knows where you stay. There might come a time when you need somewhere to feel safe and you won't be able to go to your brother or Nic or Sloane without having to tell them things you don't want them to know. This can be that place."

Anxiety winds its way through my chest, wrapping around my breastbone. I hadn't thought about what I would do if Trent did come on campus for the sole purpose of finding me. It wouldn't be hard, especially not with his cousin Jamar, who lives two buildings away from me, to help him figure it out. Once again, I find myself thankful for Chris' attention to detail, a trait I never considered he might possess. Still though, I'm feeling petulant and apprehensive about thinking of a space he's probably used to fuck multiple women just this week as a safe haven from Trent.

"Let's say I did use this key and come here to feel safe or whatever," Chris nods, listening attentively. "What happens when you come home with one of your little fuck buddies and I'm here?"

In an instant, his features cloud over. A swirl of dark, thunderous emotion moving over his face as he steps closer to me. "What?"

"I said what happens when—"

"No," he cuts me off, a laugh escaping his lips that's just as dark as the look on his face. "I heard exactly what you said, I'm just confused as to why you think I'd be bringing girls here, or anywhere, when we're together."

"But we're not," I stumble over my words, caught off guard by the ferocity of his response. I pause, lower my voice to a whisper. "But we're not really together."

"Mallory, as long as we're doing this," he gestures between the two of us, "I can promise you that you won't see or hear about me being with anyone else. All of my time, attention, and affection is yours."

I swallow past the lump in my throat. "Chris."

"I'm serious," he whispers, and I believe him. I've never seen him look more sincere. "You don't have to worry about that, ever."

"Okay," I concede, mostly because I can't take another second of him looking at me like this.

"So you'll use the key if you need it?"

"Yes. I'll use the key if I need it." But even as I make him the promise, I'm praying I'll never need to. Having such unbridled access to his personal space feels like a step too far.

"Okay. Any other grievances you need to air out?"

"No, not unless you've gone and made some other drastic decision that impacts our plan without consulting me."

He licks his lips and gives me a wry grin. "Nope. That's all, princess."

"Good," I croak, that stupid nickname making my heart squeeze uncomfortably in my chest. "Now let's go in before they start to get suspicious."

With a slight, and very dramatic incline of his head, Chris opens the door to the apartment and gestures for me to go in. "After you."

As I get closer to the living room, I hear the deep rumbles of Eric and Nic's voices mingling with Sloane's lighter one. They're listening to her recount the movie she watched last night, and even though I've been a part of a scene like this a million times, today I feel nervous about heading into it. I stop short in the middle of the hallway, doubt swirling in my gut about being able to actually pull this off.

Sloane's words from earlier echo in my mind. Her certainty about our chemistry and the overly in-depth analysis of the way Chris looks at me. They should bolster me, make me feel more confident, more comfortable with letting the electricity that runs between us—that probably stems more from me than it does from him—carry us, but all they do is fill me with dread. If she was watching that closely before, she'll be watching a hundred times closer now, and I just don't know if I can sell it now that I'm supposed to be.

Despite the crush I've had on Chris, I'm embarrassingly out of touch with the dating world. I haven't been in a relationship in years. I don't even know how I'm supposed to act around him or what the official girlfriend protocol is these days. I mean I see Sloane with Eric all the time but he's my brother and she's basically my sister, so I spend most of my time trying to dodge their public displays of affection, not study them for future reference.

"Shit." I spin around and find myself face to face with Chris. "I don't think I can do this."

"What?" He doesn't look angry, not like Trent did that night when I was naked on his bed with him hovering above me, and I said I didn't want to go any further. No, Chris looks worried, and not for himself, just for me. He puts his hands on my shoulders and pulls me a little further down the hall, closer to the door we just walked through.

"I don't think I can do this," I repeat, eyes wide. "I don't know how to act like a girlfriend. I haven't been anyone's girlfriend in years."

"And I haven't had a girlfriend in years." He shrugs, "Who cares? There aren't any rules for how you have to act. Just do what's comfortable, and I'll follow your lead."

"That sounds good in theory, but what if I do something wrong that makes it obvious this isn't…you know? I think I might need specific instructions."

"Mal, there isn't a playbook for fake dating."

"Well, there should be!"

Humor shines in his eyes, and I appreciate the effort he puts into not letting it take over his whole face. His hands, which have been applying the most delicious pressure to my shoulders, start to slide up my neck. I suck in a deep breath as he brushes a few of my still wavy braids away from my face and cups my jaw.

"Rule number one," he says, gazing heavenward for a thoughtful second then looking back at me. "Hold my hand."

"Now or just…?"

"Whenever you want," he clarifies, folding the laugh I know he wants to let out between his full lips.

"What if you're not in the mood for holding hands though?" That happened sometimes with Trent, but I guess it was just one of the perks of being in a secret relationship.

"I'll always be in the mood to hold your hand."

My heart does that crazy squeeze thing again. "And what about kisses?"

This is my second time asking him about kisses in twenty-four hours, and I can tell that that's not lost on him. His eyes drop down to my lips. "Kisses are always on the table. Especially when the plan necessitates it."

"Is that rule number two?"

"What?" His gaze returns to mine, and I swear I see a hunger in it that wasn't there before. "Oh, yes, that's rule number two."

"Can you kiss me right now?"

The words pop out of my mouth all on their own, but as soon as they hit the air, I know it's exactly what I need to calm my nerves. To get the first kiss over with and remind myself I still know how to do it right. Specifically when there's not a dare involved.

"Princess." He looks uncertain, and I hate it. The idea of him hesitating to kiss me now when just a few weeks ago he had no problem with it. With his hands still on my face, I rise up on my tiptoes and grab the collar of his t-shirt, pulling him down so we're just inches apart.

"Kiss me. You just said they're always on the table."

"When the plan necessitates."

"Well, the plan does necessitate it. Right now, I'm doubting whether or not we can pull this off in front of the people that know us best, and if we don't get this first kiss out of the way then the one you inevitably try to lay on me in front of them will be awkward and suspicious, so kiss me and do it like you mean it."

His fingers tensing against my face, gripping my jaw a little tighter to hold me in place, is the only warning I get before his lips are on mine. My eyes go wide with surprise and then fall shut with a soft moan that Chris swallows whole. It feels like he's trying to swallow *me* whole, but in the best way.

Our lips move together, and there's not even a second of awkwardness or hesitancy, just magic. Sparks flying. Electricity pulsing. Tongues colliding and retreating in a carnal dance that speaks of hunger and desire and soul-deep yearning that has no place in what we're supposed to be.

"Ohhh, gross. Get a fucking room!" The voice—which I know belongs to Nic—causes Chris and I both to jump. He releases my face and I let go of his shirt, and in the space of a heartbeat, we're on opposite sides of the hall acting like we've just been caught doing something much worse than kissing.

Chris recovers first, pushing off of the wall I just had him pinned to and reaching out for my hand. I give it to him and allow him to pull me down the hallway. A wave of heat washes over me, turning my face, neck, and ears warm. I have to force myself to look at Nic, who's coming from the guest bathroom at the end of the hall closest to the living room.

"It's my house, man," Chris says, smiling. "Every room is my room."

Nic rolls his eyes. "It's a damn hallway, ass hat. Next time you kiss my sister and I'm in the general vicinity, do it behind a door."

"Please!" Eric yells as we enter the living room.

I laugh and shake my head at them. "Both of you need to shut up. How many times have I had to see y'all put your tongue down some poor girl's throat?"

Sloane cuts her eye at Eric. "Yeah, Eric, how many?"

"I'm gonna plead the fifth on that one, baby."

"A lot, Sloane," I say as Chris leads me over to the large sectional in the middle of his living room. It's feather-soft in a light cream color with chaise lounges on both ends. Eric and Sloane are cuddled up on one end, and Chris pulls me down onto the other.

She fake gags, and Eric throws down the remote in his hand and tugs her into him. He rains kisses on her face while she squirms and giggles and pleads with him to stop. When he finally does, she's red in the face and gazing up at him like he hung the moon and the stars. Out of the corner of my eye, I see Nic watching them, his dark eyes swimming with something close to tortured jealousy.

Chris rests his arm along the back of the sectional right near my shoulders, and his proximity makes me wonder how this feels for Nic. He went from being an occasional third wheel with Eric and Sloane—a problem easily remedied by the appearance of Chris or me—to now being a fifth to two couples.

It must be awkward.

As if he feels me staring at him, Nic turns his head, giving me a questioning look. There are layers to it, multiple questions that I know I can answer for him without saying a word. That's the good thing about growing up with a person, being as close as two people can be, you develop your own language. Right now Nic is asking me if I'm happy with Chris and why I'm staring at him. With a tiny nod and a smile, I tell him that I am happy and that I'll stare at him as long as I damn well please. He rolls his eyes, turning his attention back to the show playing on TV, and that's that.

The rest of the afternoon goes by quickly. With Eric and Sloane making everyone sick with their lovey-dovey nonsense and Chris keeping me tucked into his side. Gifting me with casual touches and loving looks that make me stumble over my words and smile like a fool while Eric questions us about how things started between us. Chris lets me take the lead, and I give the simple answer we rehearsed last night at Curly's: it all started with the kiss—that was followed by a triumphant shout from Sloane the Instigator—and things just naturally progressed from there.

No one seemed to question it, probably because everyone but Chris was aware of the crush I've had on him since last year, and when they're all walking out the door a few hours later, leaving me and Chris alone, all three of them take turns telling us how happy they are about us being together.

It feels weird, accepting their congratulations and encouraging their excitement, but it's all part of the job. A requirement of the roles we signed up to play. And I'd rather let them believe that I'm happy and in love than have them know the ugly truth.

18

CHRIS

The door closes behind Eric, who left me with a whispered warning to never hurt his sister, and I flip the lock, pulling in a deep, steadying breath. Mallory is in the living room waiting for me to come back, but I need a second to recover from the past few hours of having her glued to my side. Her curves pressed into my body. Her elegant fingers threaded through mine. Her laughter ringing in my ears while we watched TV and ate food I ordered just because she said she was hungry.

I'm fucked.

This plan felt like such a good idea when my mind was soaked in doubt and worry for Mallory and for myself. I wanted to protect her, to solve both of our problems in one fell swoop, but I think the only thing I've done is create another problem.

One that starts with Mallory's full curves and ends with her sweet, perfectly kissable lips.

Lips I've dreamed about tasting again for months and yet, still wasn't ready for.

I scrub a hand down my face and try to prepare myself for walking down my hallway—which now smells like jasmine—and going back into the living room where we'll discuss the long-distance public displays of affection that will sell our relationship to the person that will be hardest to convince.

My dad.

Just the thought of him, and the lengths he's willing to go to in order to take control of my life, is enough to get me moving. I let it carry me down the hall and set my head back on straight, forcing out the distracting thoughts of kissing Mallory again and concentrating instead on getting back to business.

Mallory is on her feet when I come back into the living room. At some point today, she kicked off the ballet flats she had on and now she's wearing a hole in my hardwoods with her bare feet. I like the sight way more than I should.

"You good?" I ask, taking a seat on the edge of the couch opposite her. She's tapping her index finger on her lips and mumbling about something I can't quite make out, but I still try to listen. My ears perk up when I hear something that sounds like Trent's name. I push to my feet, crossing the room to stand in front of her. "Hey, tell me what's going on."

She pauses, looks up at me. "Trent messaged me. He wants to meet up. Alone."

I don't even have to think, the answer just comes. "No."

"I wasn't asking you for permission, Chris."

Her words cut me deep, and I have to stop myself from reacting like it hurts. Mallory is panicking and not thinking clearly. I know she doesn't actually want to see Trent, so I just have to remind her of that.

"Right. You're right. I'm sorry. I just didn't think you'd actually want to see him."

"No," she sighs. "I don't. I just can't believe he has the nerve to reach out to me after that stunt his sister pulled."

Her words go a long way towards alleviating the tension knotting the muscles in my neck. The idea of her and Trent alone anywhere makes my stomach turn. If I had my way, he wouldn't even remember that he ever knew her, let alone be in her inbox demanding a meet-up.

"Can I see the message?"

Mallory hesitates, her eyes bouncing between my face and her phone which is still lying on the couch. I could get to it easily enough, but I don't move a muscle while she weighs her options. The last thing I want is for her to think I'm taking her ability to decide away from her.

Finally, she nods and moves around me to grab it. I watch her type in her passcode and then fiddle around on the screen for a few seconds before turning it towards me. It's open to a message thread on Instagram, and I clench my jaw to hide the rage I feel at seeing the proof of him invading her personal space. Even on a digital level, it feels like a massive violation.

Trent: M, let's get together for lunch this week. I miss you and would love to catch up without any interruptions this time.

I grip the edges of her phone so hard I swear I hear the metal and glass creak under the pressure. Mallory places her hand over the screen, sliding the phone out of my grasp and putting it in her back pocket.

"What an asshole," I growl. "He knows you're in a relationship and he's still trying to take you on a trip down memory lane?"

"That's Trent for you. He's used to getting everything he wants." She gets this look on her face, like her mind is carrying her somewhere away from here, away from me.

"And what happens when he doesn't?" I ask softly.

She snaps out of her reverie with a small jolt. Silence stretches between us as she considers her answer, and it's not long before she crosses her arms over her chest and gives me a sad, resigned smile.

"Nothing good."

It hurts to see her like this, all wrapped up in years-old turmoil I can't pull her out of because she won't let me. I could stand here all day holding out my hand, offering to help her, and she still wouldn't take it. That's how tight this guy's grip is on her. How deeply he's buried his claws in her flesh.

For a second, I imagine prying his fingers off of her, pulling his talons from her skin, and setting her free, but then the image changes. Suddenly it's not good enough to just remove his fingers from her, I need to break those fingers. Hear his bones cracking and the wet squelching of his flesh as blood pours from his wounds. I don't just want to set Mallory free, I want to destroy Trent, to wipe his very existence from this earth.

"Chris?" Mallory's head is tilted to the side, her eyebrows knitted together. "I asked if you wanted to get started with Stage Two?"

I give myself a little shake. "Yes. Let's do it."

"Do you want to use your phone or mine?"

"Mine," I answer immediately, knowing if I find myself in possession of her phone again I'll do something stupid like text Trent and tell him that contacting her again will end with me rearranging his face. "I'll tag you in everything and send you ones you can post."

Stage Two is all about establishing our social media presence as a couple. Mal suggested we spend whatever time we got after the rest of the crew left taking pictures at my place to start laying our digital foundation.

"Okay," she agrees quietly, watching me dig my phone out of my pocket. "We could start on the couch if you want."

"Yeah, that sounds good. Go ahead and take a seat." She gives me a puzzled look, but she still sits down and waits for me to explain. "I want to get some pictures of you first, then we'll do some together."

"Makes sense."

She slides back on the couch, curling her legs under her. With her bare feet and worn jeans that are form-fitting yet relaxed, she looks right at home on my couch. Like she belongs there. I open my camera app and take a test shot while she's staring right at me. Serene features, soft and a little self-conscious. I examine the photo, and amber eyes trace my movements in person while they haunt me from the screen of my phone.

My chest burns, a fire sparked inside of me because of her beauty.

"Perfect," I breathe, and she beams at me. I snap another photo, this time of her smiling and tucking a braid behind her ear. She turns her head, suddenly shy, and I take a photo of that too. Happy to capture whatever part of her she's willing to give. "Okay, I think we got it. Do you want to see?"

"No. I'll look at them when you post them."

That surprises me, she's usually so adamant about being in control of things, so it strikes me as odd that she's not trying to oversee every aspect of this. "You sure?"

"Yeah," she nods, beckoning me to the couch. "I trust you."

The easy way she says it, without prompting or pretext or any other kind of caveat, adds kindling to the fire already roaring inside of me for her. I try to breathe, but my lungs are ash, and I feel hollow as I sit down beside her. Like she's used those three words to scoop out everything inside of me and fill it up with nothing but her and the gift of her trust.

She leans in close to me, her breath skating across my jaw, as she smiles big and happy for the camera. "This angle is weird," she says through clenched teeth, holding the smile. "We might have to change positions."

"Come here."

Leaning back into the cushion of the couch, I pull her into me with an arm around her waist. Her leg bumps mine, and a flash of uncertainty crosses her face before she expels it and drapes that same leg over mine, popping her hip out and turning an innocent pose into something else. The small shift in our positions makes it so her head is level with my chest and this time she doesn't look unsure at all as she rests her head there with the top of her crown brushing the underside of my chin.

With my arm outstretched, I take in the sight of us through the lens of the front-facing camera. Mallory glances up, her eyes half hooded, and signals her approval with an incline of her head. We both make subtle changes as I capture the pictures, but mostly we stay in the same position. At one point I use the hand not holding the phone to tickle her ribs and she explodes with laughter.

It makes for beautiful candid photos, especially because in every photo that she's giggling, I'm smiling down at her like a lovestruck fool.

"I like this one best," she says, tapping her finger on the screen of my phone to indicate a particularly cozy photo of us. "You should post it."

We've already got the Instagram app open, so I select that picture and watch it expand until the square is filled with us. "Whatever you say, princess." With her watchful eyes on me, I type in a short caption —***All my best days are spent with you***—tag her using her handle and hit post. I close out the app and glance over at Mallory who looks like she's glad that we're done with today's photo shoot.

"How often do we have to do these again?" she asks.

"Two or three times a week, in and out of the apartment."

"Right." She bites her lip. "The dates."

"Yep," I murmur. "The dates."

She twists on the couch, angling her body towards me. "Well, I hope it's okay that I'm going to leave the date planning to you, boyfriend."

The sass in her tone coupled with the indentations her teeth are leaving in her flesh have tingles spreading down my spine. I want to kiss her again, to pull her body back against mine, and do all the things we just did for the camera again, but this time just for us.

I shake my head, setting the thought free because it has no place here. Not inside my mind or out of it. The reminder doesn't sit well in my soul, but I force my brain to accept it and will my body to do the same.

Otherwise, this relationship will end up causing more problems than it solves.

19

MALLORY

Monday morning starts with my roommate, Alexis, giving me the stink eye and tossing her pillow over her head as I walk out the door. I can't really fault her for being upset with me. I've been up since around five this morning, gathering all of my study materials so I can get to the library and get one of the good study rooms. The ones on the third floor with windows that let a ton of sunlight in so I don't feel like I'm in a prison while I prepare for midterms.

When the door closes, I sling my book bag over my shoulder and make sure that it's locked. In my hand, my phone vibrates and my heart does a little two-step inside my chest. One glance at the screen shows a good morning text from Mama, and while I'm glad to hear from her, I'm disappointed it isn't from someone else.

Not just someone else, Chris.

Normally I wouldn't be expecting texts from him at any time, especially not this early in the morning, but today, when I slapped the screen to turn off my alarm, I saw a message from him. It was a short message, just a simple good morning, but it had turned into a full-blown conversation when I texted back.

Chris: Good morning, princess.

Mallory: Good morning.

Mallory: You know you're not the first person to start calling me princess after they heard about my Disney obsession, right?

Chris: I figured. But something tells me I am the first person you've ever liked to hear it from.

The stupid smile that took over my face when I read that one was embarrassing, even more so because I was in the middle of brushing my teeth and a little bit of the foam spilled down my chin. I had to wipe it up with one hand while I texted him back with the other.

Mallory: Are you always this cocky so early in the morning?

Chris: What do you think?

Mallory: I'm going to go with yes.

Chris: Good answer. :) Why are you up so early?

I was washing my face when that one came in, and I guess he took my silence as hesitancy because there was a follow-up message waiting for me.

Chris: Another nightmare?

Mallory: No.

And then, because that reply felt too short, and I didn't want him to think I was lying.

Mallory: I haven't had a nightmare in a while. I always wake up early and go study in the library during midterms.

Chris: Getting there early to get one of the coveted third-floor rooms with windows?

Mallory: Yep.

Chris: Smart.

Thinking the conversation was at a natural end, I sat my phone down on the counter and prepared to hop in the shower. Just before I hopped in, I doubled back and picked it up again. I didn't even know what I wanted to say. All I knew was, I didn't want the conversation to be over just yet.

Mallory: Thanks. There's nothing smart about getting up this early without at least one cup of coffee within reach, though.

Steam fills up the small space that is the bathroom Alexis and I share with two other girls who live in a dorm on the other side of this suite while I stare at the screen waiting for Chris' reply. I know he got the text—the small subtext underneath the blue bubble where my message resides said *read*. I waited a full two minutes before getting in the shower, checked my phone after getting out, and eyed it suspiciously after getting dressed, but he never responded.

Now, as I'm heading out the front of my building and texting Mama back, I'm trying to push away the inevitable embarrassment that comes from being left on read. It's hard to do, though. Especially when that unease and awkwardness clings to your veins and infects your bloodstream, poisoning everything with self-consciousness that's impossible to shake.

After I finish my text to Mama, I slip my phone into the back pocket of my jeans and push through the double doors. Warm air, with only the slightest chill to it, greets me as I step out into the sunshine, and while it's a beautiful day, I can't bring myself to notice anything but the familiar figure leaning against the light post right across from the entrance.

My breath catches as I take him in. The mussed curls that say he's just rolled out of the bed. The gray sweatpants that leave so little to the imagination I have to force myself to move past them and focus on something else. And even that turns out to be a mistake because the something else I choose is his torso—the defined abdomen and pectoral muscles that taunt and tease me through the fabric of his white shirt.

Once again, I shift my attention, moving to his face. His sharp jaw, darkened by the stubble of a beard he always shaves. His golden skin that somehow looks even better in the early morning sunlight. Honey bourbon eyes that crease at the corners when a smile takes over his full lips.

A smile that's just for me.

A smile that's so distracting, so disarming, I don't even notice the things in his hand until he's a hairsbreadth away, long arms reaching out to give them to me.

"Got you some early morning brain food plus the coffee you requested."

Wrapping my fingers around the cold plastic and the warm paper wrapped around what smells like a bacon, egg and cheese sandwich, I give him a puzzled look. "I didn't ask you to bring me coffee."

It's the wrong response, but Chris looks completely unbothered by it as he puts his fingers through the loop at the top of my book bag and lifts it from my back. I slip my arm through the one strap I was using to keep it up to help him out and watch as he swings the entire thing—which has my laptop, several textbooks, and a million and one notes in it—onto his shoulder like it weighs nothing.

"You're welcome, Mallory." I give him a funny look because I haven't even said thank you yet, and he laughs. "I'm just pretending like you have manners."

"I do have manners. I tell you thank you all the time."

"And yet," he sighs, slinging his arm around my shoulder and starting us down the path that will take us to the library, "somehow you still haven't said it."

The man is a furnace. That's all I can think about as we stroll down the sidewalk, my body pressed into his side. His arm around my shoulder. The heat rolling off of him. The waves of his scent flooding my senses with every step we take. I take a sip of my coffee, hoping like hell it will help orient me. It doesn't.

"Is this a—" I hold the cup out, turning it to inspect the drink name and additions included on the label, and find that he's brought me my favorite drink.

"Iced shaken espresso with dark caramel sauce and a splash of milk?" He finishes for me, pride stamped across his features as he beams down at me. "Yep."

"How'd you know?"

"Sloane's always getting them for you. You seem to enjoy them, so I figured it must be the coffee you were craving."

There isn't a word good enough to describe how I feel in this moment. Shock. Awe. Happiness. They all swirl together, expanding in my chest to create a new sensation that isn't at all like anything I've ever felt before, and I have to look away from Chris to keep it from showing in my eyes.

"Thank you," I say finally, forcefully, like it's a struggle to let those two words out and keep all the other ones—that are laced with adoration and appreciation that have no place here—stalled in my throat. I don't know if Chris notices, but it's evident to me that my gratitude isn't just about him getting my coffee order right.

It's also about him caring about whether or not I had a nightmare and getting out of bed early just to do something nice for me. Something that isn't a part of our agreement and, as far as I can tell, doesn't benefit it in any way. I mean it's not like he snapped a photo of me walking out of the building with the plan to make a post about how he's a good and supportive boyfriend making sure I'm well prepared for a study session.

And he could have.

In fact, he would have been well within his rights to, but he didn't, and that means something to me even though I wish it didn't.

"You're welcome, princess."

A shiver moves down my spine, leaving goosebumps in its wake as the perfection that is Chris saying his nickname for me in his rough, early morning voice that's somewhere between a growl and a purr settles in my bones. A rush of heated liquid pools in my core, and I clench my legs together, which makes the last few steps I have to take to make it to the library's threshold very awkward.

And by some miracle—probably bestowed on me by one of my ancestors who was also dumb enough to agree to be in a fake relationship with a man she's always found ridiculously attractive—I make it. Once we're right outside the entrance, I slip out from under Chris' arm and turn to face him.

"Thanks again, for the coffee and the sandwich. I do appreciate it."

"I know you do. You just have a hard time saying it."

I roll my eyes at him, backing towards the door. "Bye, Chris."

"See you later, Mallory."

Something in the finality of his tone makes me spin around. "Later? Do we have plans I don't know about?"

"No. Nothing but Richardson's class this afternoon."

My jaw drops, and it feels like the happy little bubble I was just existing in pops. Sending me plummeting towards the ground. "Shit. I forgot all about Richardson. We didn't account for him in our plans."

"Because there's no need to. We're not breaking any rules by dating. I checked the student handbook and his syllabus three times just to make sure."

While his thoroughness is appreciated, I'm still not convinced it won't be an issue. Especially after the tangent he went off on, on the first day of class.

"But you also sat in the same class I did where he made a point of telling everyone not to date you. He was talking to me specifically, Chris, and I don't need to give him another reason to dislike me."

My voice is high. Shrill and panic-laced. It's starting to get embarrassing to even think about the number of times I've let Chris see me like this. He doesn't look phased though or the slightest bit annoyed as I dissolve into a pile of worry right in front of him.

Trent hated when I would worry, especially about people finding out about us. He would minimize everything, discount all of my emotions, and then dismiss them as small and insignificant. I search

Chris' face to see if there's any sign that he's about to do that, but he looks just as miffed as I am that we didn't discuss Richardson when we were planning things out.

"I can talk to him," he offers, and I shake my head immediately.

"No. He can't know. He'll fire you and make the rest of the semester hell for me. Maybe we can hide it from him."

He purses his lips, considering my solution for a moment before shaking his head. "Mal, the whole point of this is for us to be public. We're posting pictures online together and going on dates, we can't hide this from anyone."

I know he's right. Most everyone on campus already knows we're together thanks to the ridiculous amount of followers Chris has online —which includes current students, alumna, and some professors—but it still sucks to think about giving Richardson more ammunition against me.

Taking a step towards me, Chris lifts his hand and cups my jaw. It's such a soft, intimate gesture that I almost forget we're talking about making our relationship known to a racist and sexist asshole who probably thinks all women of color sleep around to get the things they want.

"Let me talk to him. It'll all work out and none of it will blow back on you." He's serious, eyes soft and sincere as they search mine, seeing worries I haven't even voiced. "I promise." The last two words, coupled with his tender touch, are more than enough to do me in, and I find myself doing something I haven't done in a while: trusting someone enough to hand over the reins.

"Okay," I breathe, leaning into his palm despite my brain screaming for me not to.

"I'll handle it this afternoon before class," he says, leaning in close and planting a soft kiss on the corner of my mouth so quickly I almost think I imagined it. "I'll see you then. Good luck with studying."

He's gone before I manage to formulate a response. Stunned, I run my index finger over the place where his lips just were and head into the building. Thankfully, I have no trouble getting the study room I wanted, but as I settle into my seat, with all of my notes and books spread out on the table before me, the reassurance Chris' touch and promise gave me start to slip away, leaving only doubts and worry.

My mind starts to spin with all sorts of scenarios. Situations where things end up the exact opposite of how Chris said they would: with all the blowback and shame on me. I know it's just my experience with Trent talking. The trauma left in the wake of a relationship that should have never been. And despite all the time I've spent comparing the two of them because of their charming nature and carefree attitude around most things, I have to admit to myself that Chris isn't like Trent at all.

He's too thoughtful to cover his own ass and leave mine hanging in the wind, and all I have to do is look at his actions this morning to support that fact. He left his bed to do something nice for me. To solve a problem I had inadvertently brought to his attention even though it had nothing to do with him or our arrangement.

It was just a nice thing he wanted to do for me.

Blowing out a slow, steadying breath, I eye the coffee and sandwich on the table in front of me and feel another swell of appreciation run through me, but this time it's tinged with a little guilt because right next to them is my phone. This is the exact kind of thing I should document and post online to show everyone that we're so in love, but I selfishly want to keep it to myself.

Something that's just between the two of us.

Maybe that's how Chris wanted it too. I think, picking up the sandwich and unwrapping it. It's still warm as I sink my teeth into it, and I reach for my phone, intending to text Chris and thank him again for being so thoughtful and handling the Richardson situation, but as soon as I pick it up I see a notification waiting for me.

Instagram: Chris Johnson tagged you in a photo.

My heart sinks, and my fingers shake as I tap the banner and wait for the app the open. Deep down, I know what the photo is before it even loads, but I still want to see it. The proof that directly contradicts the foolish and hopeful thoughts I just had about a moment that felt special to me but clearly wasn't anything more than an opportunity to him.

Sure enough, the photo finishes loading, and there's Chris, standing in front of a coffee shop right around the corner from campus, smiling wide for the camera while he holds the sandwich I'm currently eating and the coffee I'm too embarrassed to drink up next to his face. Slowly, I scan the picture and then the caption: ***Early morning coffee run for my princess.***

It shouldn't hurt.

It doesn't hurt.

This is what you signed up for. I remind myself, repeating the three phrases over and over. Once while I close out of the app. A second time as I push up from the table and grab the sandwich and coffee. Another time as I toss them both in the trash can. And then again, as I sit back down and open my textbook, focusing on notes for the exams I'll have all week.

I say the words until I believe them. Until they've dug a hole in my chest and created a crater that they can live in forever. Because this *is* what I signed up for. A public relationship, where nothing is, or ever will be, private, sacred, and just for us.

20

CHRIS

"**Y**ou got a girlfriend and didn't even tell me?" Teresa squeals, her clear excitement overriding the sternness she's trying to inject into her voice. At seventeen, almost eighteen, years old, she's a spitfire. A short little thing with tawny brown skin, dark eyes, and the facial structure most of the women we grew up around pay their doctors a hefty sum to have. Not that she cares about superficial things like physical beauty. Like me, Teresa is more concerned with leaving the world better than she found it, but instead of using science and medicine, she's determined to use art to do it.

Lucky for her, as a Johnson daughter, there are no grand designs on her life. No hand-picked husbands waiting in the wings to sweep her away and lay waste to all of her dreams because as a woman she's not burdened with the glorious purpose of contributing to the Johnson legacy.

I remember the first time I realized our family's sexist tradition didn't apply to the women. We were at my Aunt Clarice's wedding. All of my uncles were there with their wives, and despite them being younger than their older sister, they'd all been married for years. RJ asked Dad why Grandpa Joe didn't push her to get married sooner, why he didn't choose a partner for her like he'd done for his sons, and

Dad's answer was simple: *Because daughters don't continue legacies, sons do. Any child your aunt has with her new husband will carry his last name, not ours. By getting married, she's agreed to be absorbed into the legacy of her new family and do what she has to in order to continue it.*

Aunt Clarice never had kids with her husband, Vince, but she does look happy. Happier than any of her brothers who cheat on their wives and neglect their children. I want that same happiness for Teresa, and I'm relieved to know she won't have to go to the lengths I'm going to, in order to have it.

"Sorry, Ter." I stretch on the chaise lounge Mal and I cuddled on Sunday, which is now my favorite spot because even after nearly forty-eight hours I can still smell the faint scent of her here. "Mal and I have kind of been keeping things under wraps since we got together."

"And when exactly was that?"

"The beginning of the semester, but we've known each other since last year."

"So you've always liked her." There's no inflection in her voice, so I know it's not a question and that makes me smile. My little sister is as straightforward as they come, and she doesn't ask questions when she already knows the answer to them. As it is, her non-question forces me to think back to the first time I met Mallory and how I felt about her then.

'Like' isn't the right word.

I was mesmerized by her. Drawn in by her beauty and held hostage by the serious frown tugging her lips down into a pretty pout while she waited for Eric to get his key from me. Nic had already moved in the day before, and as we walked to a party that night, he told me his roommate, Eric, wasn't moving in until later that week. That's why I was surprised when I saw him come up to the table I was manning right outside the dorms. He was smiling brightly while Mallory stood behind him looking annoyed and impatient. Her amber eyes scanned the busy sidewalk, taking in the families carrying boxes and bedspreads into the building with marked efficiency, while I watched her.

It wasn't a conscious thing, watching her, but it felt necessary. Imperative. Like if I took my eyes off of her for even half a second she would disappear forever and that was the last thing I wanted.

"Yeah, I guess you could say that."

Ter snorts. "I've seen the way you look at her in those pictures you posted, and RJ told me how grumpy you got when he said how pretty she was, I most definitely would say that."

"She's my girlfriend, of course I'm going to be protective of her."

I don't mention the pictures because I know what she's talking about. My entire heart shows when I look at Mallory, that's the whole reason why I snapped a picture outside of the coffee shop yesterday morning instead of taking it with her. I knew it needed to be done, knew she would hand me my ass if I missed a chance to make our relationship look even more real to my dad and her ex, but I couldn't take it with her because I was afraid she would see that the only person I did it for was her.

Four days. It's been four days of this, and I'm already losing my grip. How am I going to make it to August without fucking this up and pushing her for things she's not interested in giving me?

"Sure. But the whole alpha male protective act plus the lovesick puppy dog look you've got going equals feelings that have been brewing for longer than two months. A year and some change sounds about right, especially if you've loved her for most of that time."

Her succinct tone makes me laugh. "When did you become such an expert in love equations?"

"I'm seventeen, Chris, all the conversations I have with my friends involve analyzing the behavior of teenagers with more hormones than sense. No one knows how to just come out and say they like you and ask you to the movies, so we have to sit around breaking down text message conversations and five-second interactions in the hallway to glean any type of understanding about how to move forward."

"Mhmm. Well, if art school doesn't work out, maybe you have a future in matchmaking."

"Definitely not. I don't have the patience for that. I give Leah them ten minutes of my full attention and then I break out my sketchbook and tune them out."

"I saw the sketch you posted last night, the one of the pregnant woman." The words try to get stuck in my throat, but I force them out. Ter started asking me about Mom a few months ago, it was her questions that led me to the conversation with my grandpa, and ever since then she's been sharing sketches of pregnant women. I know she's thinking about Mom, about the knot of complicated feelings linking her birth and Mom's death. "It was beautiful."

The line is quiet for a moment before she says, "Thank you."

"We can talk about her, if you want. I don't remember much, but I can tell you more about what Grandpa knew or we can ask Dad together."

"No, it's fine. I kind of like not knowing. Is that weird?"

"Nothing you feel about her could ever be weird."

"You have to say that because you're my brother." There's a forlorn smile in her voice, and I imagine it turning her sharp features sad, grief-stricken. "It's just that when I think of her, she can be whatever I want her to be. A mom who baked cookies and brushed my hair, who tucked me into bed every night and rubbed my back until I fell asleep. A mom who hung my drawings on the fridge with those ugly alphabet magnets and put them in boxes in the attic when the fridge ran out of space."

Again, the line is quiet, filled with the wistful and heartbreaking wishes of a motherless daughter.

"Nothing Dad or Grandpa can tell me will help me know that stuff, you know?" She sighs. A long, heavy, sad sound that cracks my chest open. "They would just talk about her brilliance or all the ways she contributed to *the Johnson family legacy*. They wouldn't have paid any attention to the kind of mother she was. They wouldn't have placed any value on the way she loved you and RJ. On the way she would have loved me."

"The way she *did* love you," I correct her gently. "You didn't get the chance to know her, but she knew you. She carried you for nine months, felt every kick and turn and hiccup before you even took your first breath outside the womb. She laughed at you and sung to you and plotted a big, beautiful life for her baby girl. You're everything she could have ever dreamed of, of course she loved you."

"Yeah?" She asks, voice small like she was when Dad brought her home from the hospital that day.

"Yeah."

Neither of us speak, a comfortable silence spilling across the line until Ter finally sighs and expels the sadness from her body.

"Well, I'm not going to hold you hostage on the phone any longer."

"You're not holding me hostage," I say, even though I'm supposed to be heading to campus soon. "We can talk for as long as you want."

"No, I've gotta go too. Dad wants me to come with him to lunch at the DuPonts today."

I refrain from letting out the enraged growl building in the back of my throat. Dad and his obsession with the DuPonts is ruling everyone's life, and it's not fair.

"Sounds like fun."

"If you call eating cucumber sandwiches and listening to everyone faun over Giselle, fun, then yeah, it's fun."

"Try to make the best of it?"

"I will. Let's hope RJ comes, then Dad and the DuPont's will be too busy listening to him talk about himself to pay me any mind."

I sit up, hoping that RJ does show up to offer Teresa a reprieve and do whatever he's planning to do to make it so my dad no longer thinks Giselle is an option. "Here's hoping. Love you, sis."

"I love you too, Chris, and I can't wait to meet Mallory. She's really lucky to have you. I hope she knows that."

The last part is rushed, like she's embarrassed to say it, and she hangs up before I can respond, but my heart lurches at the statement all the same. At the idea of Mallory having me and me having her. It's only been four days of this fake dating situation, and I'm already doubting my ability to get through these conversations that require me to layer real emotion over lies that feel less false with each passing day and every new person I tell.

It had started with Trent, fueled by panic and the frantic need to protect Mallory. Then my brother and Trent's sister and Mallory's family who are some of my closest friends. Then it was the awkwardness of talking through it with Dr. Richardson, whose thin lips turned into a grim frown as soon as I finished explaining the situation.

He wasn't happy about me being involved with Mallory, I could tell from the way his nostrils flared when I said her name, but in the end, he admitted there wasn't much he could do besides prohibit me from grading any of her assignments.

I left his office relieved because everything had turned out fine, but I was also confused because it had all felt too real.

The words and tone I used to convey the depth of my feelings.

The fierce, angry growl in my throat that dared him to say something disparaging about her. *He was familiar with that one, having come into contact with it on the first day of class when I overheard him trying to make her drop the class.*

The warmth in my chest when I thought about how happy she would be to know we were in the clear.

Except she didn't look all that happy when I told her. I waited down the hall, posted up by the door she always comes through just so I could see her face when I said it. When she finally entered the building, we locked eyes instantly, and I could tell something was off. Thinking she was worried about going into class, I rushed through my explanation and watched for any sign that my words were helping whatever was going on inside of her.

They didn't.

And when I tried to push for answers, hoping like hell it didn't have anything to do with Trent, she just said she was stressed and walked into class. Keeping my eyes off of her proved to be a challenge I wasn't prepared for, and I'm lucky Richardson was too busy running a review session in preparation for this week's midterm to notice me staring.

Not that it would have mattered. I don't even think one of his speeches could have gotten me to take my eyes off her. Especially when she kept raising her hand, wiggling around those elegant fingers to signal that she had the answer to the question, which happened a lot.

I marveled at her. Impressed with the way she seemed to shed all of her stress and worry the moment she was presented with a problem to solve. I had already known that about her, had already developed a healthy appreciation for it, but that was back when I only knew her in the most superficial sense of the word and thought all there was to her was the single-minded focus she displays in the classroom. Now, I know there's more to her than that—a girl who dreams and jokes and makes wishes to become a princess when she was born to be queen— and knowing that all of that is there inside of her, makes her ability to shift and compartmentalize that much more impressive.

I think I recognized that in her that first day. Her determination and strength. It signaled to me, called to the part of me that won't stop, won't rest, won't yield to any outside forces threatening to derail it from achieving its goals.

It's just another way that we're evenly matched. Compatible. The kind of congruence Mallory and I share isn't like anything I've ever experienced before. Not even with people who grew up in the same world I did, with powerful parents and private schools and trust funds with more money than we could ever spend in a lifetime. And I'm hungry for more of it, for something beyond this arrangement we have that could have been real, *could still be real*, if she trusted me.

Although she didn't say it, I think that was the issue yesterday. I obsessed over it all last night after I came home. We were supposed to hang out after she finished class, but she put me off, saying she had to study and asking to meet up for lunch today. All I could think about was how things were fine until I said I would talk to Richardson.

She was fine when she walked into the library, but the hours in between left plenty of time for doubt to brew. For her to convince herself that she couldn't trust me to take care of a situation we created together.

Maybe that was her experience with Trent. After meeting the guy and his sister, I wouldn't be surprised by that. They don't seem like the kind of people that value accountability, but that's not me.

I would hope that by now she knows that, but if she doesn't, I'll prove it to her.

* * *

BOTH OF MALLORY'S dimples are showing, little potholes in her face
that I want to kiss because I know that they only come out when she's
happiest. Right now, she's sitting at one of the round tables in the
middle of the dining hall laughing with Sloane who's doubled over in
her seat, jet black curls nearly falling into the food on her plate as she
gasps for air. Sunlight from the glass panels in the ceiling streams in,
bright strips of gold hitting the two of them, but all I can see is the way
it hits Mallory. Turning the bundle of wavy, plaited tresses sitting at the
top of her head into a glowing crown.

My phone, which I had taken out just a second ago to call and ask
which side of the cafeteria she was on, burns in my hand, begging for
the opportunity to capture her like this. Happy. Open. Joyful. And God
help me, but I can't stop myself from honoring the request. Because
the need to have a photo of her that isn't posed, that isn't a public thing
pretending to be private, is suddenly the most important thing to me.

I try to do it quickly and casually, snapping a few while she tosses
her head back and her shoulders shake from the force of her amusement. I have no idea what Sloane is saying to her, but whatever it is
I'm thankful for it, because it gives me the best pictures of her.

Ones that aren't for anyone but me.

I'm just about to congratulate myself for being the stealthiest moth-
erfucker on the planet when Mallory looks up and our eyes lock. She
instantly drops my gaze, trading it for a quick examination of my
phone in my hand, raised and pointed directly at her in a way that
makes what I just did obvious as hell. I see the moment it dawns on
her, and for a second there's a flicker of something that looks like
annoyance dancing across her features, wiping away the happiness that
was just there, but it disappears as quickly as it came. A thin smile
graces her lips, and she waves me over.

"Hey, Chris." Sloane smiles, as I sit down beside Mallory.

"Sloane." I offer her a greeting but my eyes are all for Mallory,
skating over the rigid line of her jaw that tells me her teeth are
clenched. Taking full advantage of the parts we agreed to play, I lean in

close, brushing my lips over her skin and planting a kiss where her jaw is firmest. "Princess."

"Hey." Mal doesn't look at me, which makes Sloane's eyebrows raise. She shoots me a 'you fucked up' look and grabs her plate.

"I'll see you guys later."

As soon as she's out of earshot, I put my hands on Mallory's chair and turn her towards me. The sound of the metal scraping against the tile floors is swallowed by the voices of the dozens of students in the room, but I still hear the gasp that escapes her lips when we're face to face.

"Let's try that again," I say, placing my hand on her chin and forcing her to look at me. "Hi, princess."

"I already said hello to you, Chris."

"Yes, but it was as dry as that chicken on your plate. What's wrong?"

With a flick of her chin, she's free from my grasp. "Nothing. I'm just stressed because of exams."

"Are they that bad?"

Imagining her struggling is hard, but I know even the strongest people hit road bumps sometimes, especially when they're under stress. I can't see maintaining a fake relationship and fending off a crazy ex during midterms lending itself to any kind of relaxation.

All the uncertainties swirling around us must be frustrating for her, especially given her love of control. On instinct, my hand reaches out for hers, and I lace our fingers together. She stares down at the place where our hands are joined for a second before pulling away, looking around as if to remind me that there's no one here but us.

Her withdrawal is a stark and necessary reminder of our circumstances and the hard rules around the roles we play. I can't keep letting the lines get blurred, not with both my and Mallory's future on the line.

"No." She shakes her head. "They're actually going pretty well, I think I'm just tired from worrying about Richardson's exam. I can't shake the feeling that he's going to try to find a way to use our relationship against me."

"Mal." Maintaining an even tone is hard, especially in the face of the grim certainty coating her words. They hit me like a kick to the gut, and all my hope around gaining her trust, which was just so high a few days ago, lands on the floor with a dull thud. "You don't have to worry about that, he's not a problem."

"For you."

I scrub a hand over the lower half of my face. "For us. He's not a problem for us."

"Chris, please. Now is not the time for you to do the whole 'we're in this together' thing. We both know he won't come after you because you're young and rich and male, but me on the other hand? I'll be the one dealing with his wrath."

"And if that happens, he'll be dealing with mine," I growl, and her head snaps around, eyes wide as she takes in the anger rolling off of me in waves. It's not for her, it's for Richardson and Trent and all the other assholes who wronged her and made her think she can't trust anyone, but especially me. I study her face, and where I expect to find soft understanding, I only find hardened resolve.

"You think I need you to fight my battles." It's a statement that should be a question just like when Teresa told me I've always liked her. I was hesitant to admit it then, but looking at Mallory now, all stern features and steely determination, I can admit it to myself: I've always liked her, and now I like her even more.

"No." *But I want you to let me, you've been fighting long enough.*

The words don't leave my lips, but I try to convey them with my eyes, with my tone, with my clenched fists made of fingers that itch to touch her again.

"Good." She lifts her chin. "Because I don't."

"I know." The words taste like acid on my tongue, but she needs to hear them. And they're not untrue. I know she doesn't need me. I just wish that she did.

The desire is old, yet new. It's fresh and sweet, and, somehow, also made bitter by age and time. Months. Weeks. Days. Hours. Minutes and seconds of knowing her and not. Of wanting her and fighting it. Not just because of our arrangement or her valid trust issues, but also because of the things within me that have held me back. Kept me in a space where casual hookups are king and true connections are unheard of. Where the lie I'd told myself about relationships being a distraction from my goal to honor my mother's life with my own could stand up tall because it didn't have to face any scrutiny.

That lie is crumbling now, under the weight of amber eyes and my desire, not just for her body, but for her brain and her secrets and her trust, and the only thing left when it falls away is regret.

That I didn't realize what we could have had, what we could have been, sooner.

Now every part of our would-be beginning is wrapped up in complications I don't think we'd be able to get past because even if I told her how I feel, she wouldn't trust that any of it was real. She'd always look at me like she's looking at me right now, with doubt dulling the light in her eyes.

After a moment passes without either of us saying anything, she shifts in her seat, angling her body towards me. The pent-up tension she's been holding in her shoulders since I sat down starts to dissipate.

"Any update?"

"Update?"

"On how things are going on the social media front? With your dad and the rest of your family."

"Oh." I nod, understanding dawning on me even as the abrupt change in our conversation grates on my nerves. "I haven't talked to my dad yet, but RJ and Ter have called about our pictures so I'm sure he knows by now. I'll know for sure after our call on Friday."

She scrunches her nose, taking one last bite of the chicken and tossing the fork on the plate in front of her. "I still think it's weird that you guys schedule calls."

"It is." I shrug. "But I'm used to it now. What about Trent?"

Every muscle in her body tenses for a second at the mention of his name, and I watch with piqued interest as she gets them all back online one by one. "Haven't heard from him."

"Good. I'm glad to know you're getting what you need from this." Several emotions flit across her face, but they move too quickly for me to identify any of them.

"Yep," she says, pushing up from her seat and grabbing the plate off the table. "I have to get to class."

"Oh," I move to stand too, but she's already moving, leaving me behind. "I'll see you later?"

We don't have any plans on the books. Since we're both studying for exams, neither of us proposed a meet-up. She stops, turns around to face me.

"Yeah. Later." Then she's moving again and calling out over her shoulder. "Make sure to tag me when you post the picture you took earlier."

My brows dip, pulling together in confusion before I remember the photos I took when I first walked in here. I fish my phone out of my pocket and pull them up, surprised to find they're more stunning than I remember. In every single one, she looks like joy personified. The physical embodiment of radiant delight, and I know in an instant that I won't be tagging her in any of these photos because I won't be posting them at all.

Without a bit of reluctance—and only a little bit of shame because I'm breaking our 'post everything, all the time' rule—I move the photos from my camera roll and into an album that's currently untitled but holds all of the solo pictures I took of Mallory on Sunday.

The ones that are just for me.

21

MALLORY

A bead of sweat rolls down my spine, and the sliver of brain space I dedicate to wondering why I noticed it when the rest of my back has been soaked for the last thirty minutes of this class gives my sparring partner— a tall, shapely girl named Rae with medium brown skin and the body of a dancer—the space she needs to make her first successful advance of the night.

Her open palm collides with my chin and my head snaps up and back from the force of the blow. I let out a growl of frustration and glare at her. Her eyes glitter with delight as she steps back and resumes her fighting stance, palms up, hands raised as she bounces around on her feet. I adjust my stance as well, holding my hands up and mirroring her footwork in practiced movements that probably aren't half as graceful as hers are.

All around us, other women grunt and yell and strike at each other. The sound of their victories and failures echoing around the gym, bouncing off of the cement walls with posters and banners sporting the Legacy Training Center logo and reverberating off of the padded floors that bear the same insignia although it's slightly faded now.

When I first found this place last semester, I'd forced Sloane to come with me because I was scared to check it out alone. The pictures on the website were less than awe-inspiring, but the moment I walked in here and met Hunter Drake—a big, burly brute of a man with mocha skin, a bald head, and haunted eyes that made the tattoos covering every inch of him the least interesting thing about him—I knew I was in the right place.

Hunter wasn't nice and the gym wasn't exceptionally clean, but from the start of the very first class, I could tell he was just as serious about teaching women to keep themselves safe as we were about learning. Well, at least some of us were serious. Sloane made it through one demonstration about how to get out of a front choke hold before she leaned over and asked me if I was good because she wanted to go to the fair with Eric.

I was too focused on what Hunter was saying—a speech about open palms being more useful than fists sometimes—to listen, so I just nodded and shooed her away. She was gone before Hunter finished his sentence, giving me a short sideways hug and telling me she would leave the keys to her car in my gym bag.

When it came time to execute some moves, I was slightly annoyed about her abandoning me for funnel cakes and fried Oreos, but that feeling quickly faded away when I found myself standing in front of Hunter, heart beating out of my chest as he peered down at me with hard eyes that kicked my pulse up several notches. Sending me back into the body of the girl who couldn't find a single ounce of fight inside of herself when she needed it most.

Hunter had ordered me to focus, to breathe, and trust my body to do the work. I had to admit that I didn't trust my body or myself at all. He didn't need an explanation—you don't spend years teaching women and girls how to defend themselves without learning the shorthand of trauma—and instead of sending me to the back of the line until I pulled myself together, he wrapped his hands around my wrists and lifted my arms for me. His touch, fast and impersonal as he spread my fingers and reminded me of what I needed to do. We ran the drill a million times over the course of the hour, and when we were done, I walked outside and threw up in the parking lot.

It would have been hard to explain such a visceral reaction to

Sloane, especially when I didn't quite understand it, so I was glad she had ended up leaving and I never asked her to come to a class again.

"Focus, Mallory!" Hunter's gruff order rings out, pulling me out of my head and back onto the mat where Rae is still circling me. I'm glad he called my name because she's closing in on me, preparing to land her second blow.

We've got one point each, so if she gets it, she'll walk away the winner of our two-point sparring round and I'll go home even more agitated than I was when I came in here.

Rae is in front of me now, held off by my outstretched arms. When I was coming to class regularly, we'd spar all the time, so our breathing is in sync, both of us hyper-aware of the other's movements, waiting to see who will strike first. I decide to.

Using our height difference to my advantage, I drop my left hand and swing it up, breaking through the shield she tries to create with her forearms to strike her chin with the heel of my hand. She stumbles back, clearly surprised at the force I managed to put into the blow despite using my non-dominant hand.

We both drop our palms at the same time, and she grins at me, shaking her head as she comes across the mat to bump me with her shoulder.

"Damn, girl, I really thought I was going to get you this time."

Adrenaline courses through my veins, and I soak up the feeling, the exhilaration that can only come from besting someone who's just as good as you are. "The hand switch got you, didn't it?"

"Hell yeah, it did." We both turn to look at Hunter whose rugged face is screwed up in an expression as close to happy as he gets. "Switching hands was smart, Mal. It almost makes up for you dropping your palms and letting her land that first blow in the first place."

I bend down and pick up my water bottle, pouring the rest of the lukewarm liquid down my throat and rolling my eyes. Hunter never actually tells you that you've done a good job. Maybe it's his rumored military background or just his personality, but every would-be compliment that comes from him is followed so closely by critique it negates the positive words altogether.

"Thanks?"

"Next time," he continues, ignoring my reluctant gratitude, "make sure you keep your head in the round. A guy on the street won't wait for you to get your bearings before attacking. He'll happily…."

"Exploit your distraction and use it for his advantage," I say, mimicking his rumbling baritone. "Yes, I know."

He narrows his eyes. "Next time let your actions match your knowledge."

Rae and I share a look as he marches off, heading towards another group of women huddled close together laughing and talking.

"Next time let your actions match your knowledge," She says mockingly, wagging a finger at me as I grab my gym bag and dig out my phone. "He's so damn grumpy."

"Yeah," I sigh, opening up my messages and texting Eric to see if he's on the way. "But he's good at what he does so he knows we're not going anywhere else."

"True." She lowers herself gracefully to the floor and starts to stretch. The artful lines of her arms and legs reflecting the love of dancing I suspect lies deep in her history. It's just a suspicion, one that will never be confirmed because most of the women who frequent Hunter's gym are here to avoid reliving their pasts, not discuss them at length. "You really should stretch after class, you know. I can lead you through a few that help with the soreness."

I arch a brow at her, dragging my eyes away from my phone where Eric has yet to reply. "No, thanks. You'd probably end up pinning me to the mat just to get your lick back."

She snorts, and even that sound, which is horrific on anyone else, sounds graceful on her. "Probably. I am a sore loser."

"Yeah, I know." My phone dings, and I assume it's Eric telling me he's outside. He hates when I make him wait, so I toss my bag on my shoulder and wave at Rae. "Catch you later."

"Byeeeee!" She sings, holding the note long enough to draw the attention of everyone in the gym but capturing Hunter's most effectively. He glowers at her, and then rolls his eyes when she sticks her tongue out at him. I laugh at their exchange and head out the door, stopping short on the sidewalk when I don't see the Toyota Corolla Eric and I share idling in front of the building.

"What the hell?" I mutter under my breath, opening the message he just sent.

> Eric: Did you run over something the last time you drove? The car's got a flat. Nic and I are on the side of the road changing it.

Now I feel like Hunter, giving my phone the same stink eye he was giving Rae as I stare at the message and the one that follows.

> Eric: Called Chris to come pick you up since he's closest. Why didn't you just call him in the first place? That's literally what boyfriends are for.

I stare a hole through my phone, cursing Eric, the stupid tire that's probably flat because of him, and whatever part of his brain told him that calling Chris was a good idea.

Oh, yes, that would be the part of his brain that's buying the act we've been selling for two weeks now. We've been peddling it all over town, campus, and the internet, putting it on at Mama's house on Sunday when we all went home for dinner, using study sessions and group outings as opportunities to take all the pictures we could ever need to sell our relationship to his family and my stalker of an ex who won't stop writing me asking to meet up.

Trent's incessant messages had been a key component in me coming back to the gym, but that was only a part of the reason I've been a fixture on the mat lately. The other parts were wrapped up in Chris and the safety net he'd built around me without me even noticing.

When we were sitting in the cafeteria during midterms and he got all growly and protective, it became quite clear to me what had happened. Somewhere along the way—between our first kiss, that night at Curly's and him witnessing the aftermath of my nightmares— he got it in his head that I was weak.

Those words never passed his lips, of course, but I could see it written all over his face. His determination to keep me safe, his unwavering belief that I needed him to be my sword and shield for the duration of our act. I couldn't even bring myself to be angry about it because that's the role I've been playing: the damsel in distress. Passive and afraid, depending on the presence of one man to keep me safe from the malice of others. Sitting around waiting for the other shoe to drop, for Richardson to say something—so far he hasn't—for Trent's increasingly belligerent behavior to manifest outside of my private messages.

I guess it's not all my fault. It's kind of hard to feel like the only person who cares about your safety when you've got someone like Chris in your life.

Everywhere I go, he's there. Bringing me coffee in the mornings, watching over every interaction between me and Richardson, holding my hand while we walk to class when neither of us is able to hold a phone let alone take a picture, and staying on campus late just to make sure I get back to my dorm safely after lab on Fridays.

It's almost like out of all the other things he's worried about—gaining his father's acceptance, solidifying his spot at MUSC, and taking full control over his future—making me feel safe is the most important of them all.

And that's *exactly* how I have been feeling. Secure. Guarded.

It pissed me off and prompted me to take my safety and well-being into my own hands. To come back to this place where I first found my power and reclaim it as my own. Everything was going great. Weeks have passed with me fitting in classes during the days and evenings when Chris and I don't have plans. I haven't told him about the gym, or the new, nastier messages Trent has been sending, because I didn't want to have another conversation about how he doesn't think I can take care of myself. But I guess that's all gone out the window now that he's on the way to pick me up.

As if I've conjured him up, my phone lights up with Chris' name flashing across the screen. He's probably calling to ask me how to find the gym. It's in a sketchier part of town, housed in a big, brick warehouse that used to be a factory or some shit. Hunter converted it into what it is now, using the majority of the space for the gym and renting the rest to a guy who teaches karate to kids in the neighborhood for free.

Pushing out a hard breath, I accept the call.

"Hello."

"Princess," he rasps. "Where exactly is this place?"

I close my eyes, absorbing the gravel in his voice that's wreaking havoc on my body. My heart squeezes and fire heats my blood. "You don't have to come."

"Did Eric get the tire fixed?"

"No."

"Then how are you getting home?"

My teeth sink into my bottom lip. "I can ask someone—"

"Why would you do that if I'm already on the way?"

It's a good question. A great question, even, asked with the right inflection and the perfect amount of concern, but it still grates on every one of my nerves because it forces me to come to terms with the other reason I had for hiding this from him.

These classes still leave me hollow, operating in the vulnerable space I have to maintain access to in order to absorb the information Hunter gives us and execute the moves. Some of the women here come just for fun, to feel cool and powerful and get in a good workout, but then there's the rest of us—like me and Rae—that have already had the thing our lucky counterparts only think of in the hypothetical sense happen to us.

And we use it as fuel.

We picture our assailant's faces as we throw blows and land punches on the hard slabs of muscle that are Hunter and the other male instructors who help out at the gym. We smell their scents—sour and always alcohol laced—when the men who have dedicated their lives to showing us how to protect ourselves come up behind us, padded forearms at our throats to protect their skin from the claws they encourage us to unsheathe.

It takes a while to climb out of that space, to rid your brain of the chemicals that rush through your body while you're in the midst of simulated danger, and I don't think I'll be able to keep where I am mentally from Chris.

He just sees too much.

Even when I'm trying to hide from him, which I've made a habit of doing ever since I realized this relationship is feeding my crush on him. Actually, gorging is the more accurate word. What was once a small, infinitesimal infatuation, has expanded into something more. Affection with an insurmountable wingspan. Feelings with roots that only dig deeper the more I try to yank them up. I don't want it, or maybe I do, but either way, it doesn't matter because I can't have it.

I can't have him, not in any real sense of the word, because he wants my truths and I know that if I ever give them to him, he won't want me. Guys like him, who do hookups and fun situationships, don't know what to do with girls like me who have baggage for days and trust issues for miles.

"Because I don't want you to get lost down here. The gym is kind of hard to find."

The line goes quiet, and I try to envision what his face looks like right now. Chestnut eyes narrowed, jaw clenched, wrinkles of confusion and impatience formed between his brows. "Give me the address, princess. I won't have any trouble finding you."

There's nothing special about the way he says it, and that only makes the sudden rush of arousal slicking my underwear that much more embarrassing. I should have this under control by now. After weeks of touching him and kissing him in public, I should be perfectly capable of having a conversation with him without turning into a puddle, but the time we've spent pretending has only made it harder.

I mean it took me two days to pull myself together after he posted that picture of the coffee and sandwich he got me on our first Monday, and I was only able to do that because Sloane's overly observant ass kept asking why I was so mad at him. In order to protect our agreement, I had to tuck my feelings into a tiny little box at the back of my mind that I try to only open when I need to.

Most of the time I fail.

"Mallory." His voice is a low growl that demands my acquiescence, and I cave, rambling off the address to the gym and listening as he plugs it into his GPS. It says he should be here in five minutes, which confuses me.

"How are you so close?"

"Eric called a while ago and told me I needed to pick you up from the gym. He assumed I knew the name of the place, since you're my girlfriend and all, and he hung up before I could decide whether I should tell him I didn't know where you were or that you were taking self-defense classes at all."

I'm going to have permanent indentations in my lip from my teeth by the time this conversation is done. Guilt tugs on my heartstrings, but I push it away. I don't have anything to feel guilty about. Chris and I are not actually together, which means I don't owe him any explanations about what I do outside of the time we agree to spend together.

"You didn't need to know."

"Obviously, I did."

"I couldn't have known Eric was going to get a flat and end up calling you to come get me."

"You're right. You still could have told me though." He pauses then adds, "If only to keep me from looking like a clueless, self-centered boyfriend in front of your brother."

Something inside of me, that was being fed by his concern and nourished by the possessive thread weaving its way through his voice, deflates when he says that last part. And it's like I'm back in that library study room, hoping for private regard while he's occupied with public perception.

"Right," I stumble over the word. "I guess I wasn't thinking."

On his end, I hear the telltale ticking of a signal light that causes me to scan the road for any sign of him turning onto the short drive that connects the building to the main road. It doesn't take me long to locate the car, and I watch it sail down the road smoothly and then come to a full stop in front of me.

Pushing off the wall, I end the call and start to walk to the car, intending to hop in and get this ride done as quickly as possible, but

Chris surprises me by putting the car in park and getting out. He strides around the car, looking good as hell in a pair of black track pants with a matching moisture-wicking shirt that hugs his pectorals and torso, showcasing abs I've dreamed about licking more than once.

Heat creeps up into my cheeks as he approaches me. His presence makes the complex work of freeing myself from that vulnerable space simpler than it ever has been, and I'm thankful to find that he looks significantly less irritated than he sounded on the phone. He even graces me with one of those panty-evaporating smiles as he takes my gym bag from my shoulder and places his hand on my back, ushering me over to the passenger door and opening it for me.

It's only as I'm settling into my seat, feeling the damp coolness of my sweat-soaked shirt pressing into my skin, that I consider I might smell. Trying to be covert, I sneak a sniff of my armpits while Chris stores my bag in his backseat, but I can't get a good read on the odor situation before he gets back into the car. Just in case I do stink, I tuck my arms into my sides and cross my legs at the ankles.

Chris gives me a weird look, assessing eyes moving over every inch of me. "Did you have a good workout?"

My eyes bulge. "Why? Do I smell?"

"Let's see." To my absolute surprise and misplaced delight, he leans over the console and pauses with his face inches from my neck. "May I?"

I swallow audibly as his question makes my core contract. "Uh, sure."

He comes in closer, crowding my space, and with his nose millimeters from my neck he breathes me in. Seemingly pulling every molecule of my scent out of the air and into his nostrils with an inhale so deep my lungs hurt just listening to it. Then, as if he hadn't already turned my underwear into a sopping mess, he lets out a low, satisfied growl and pulls back a bit. I turn to face him, my eyes wide with shock and shining with unspoken desire I don't care if he sees.

"Well?" I ask, voice barely above a whisper. Something close to hunger glints in his eyes as he stares back at me, lips parting.

"Perfect," he says simply.

Tension crackles in the air and it doesn't fade, doesn't even consider becoming something less, when he moves all the way back, settling in his seat. I watch him shift the car into gear and then press the gas, long fingers gripping the steering wheel.

"Liar," I mutter under my breath, which makes him smile.

And just like that, we're back in that weird space we always seem to occupy. Together but not. Flirting but only when our arrangement necessitates, and, on the not-so-rare occasion that the flirting happens without any thoughts of the plan at the forefront of our mind, acting like it never happened.

Chris is good at that, probably a leftover skill from the many years he's spent sleeping around, but I am not, and every time something like this happens, the barrier between my very real feelings and our fictional relationship gets a little thinner. I know I can't afford to lose it completely. If I do, I'll be broken all over again by the end. A victim of unchecked charm and charisma.

As he drives back towards campus, I busy myself with a mental review of the class, playing back the moments Rae got the better of me and repeating Hunter's tips for increasing reaction speed.

"How come I never knew you took self-defense classes?" Chris asks, turning down a road that will take us to the back side of campus and bring us closer to my dorm.

"I don't know. Maybe you don't pay enough attention to me."

It was supposed to be a joke, but the way he looks at me, with a soft gaze that's unfairly serious, suggests he took it as anything but. "No one gets as much of my attention as you do."

My mouth goes dry. "I was joking, Chris."

"It was a bad joke, princess. Now stop deflecting and tell me why I've been walking around for weeks not knowing that my girlfriend could lay me out if she wanted to."

My girlfriend.

A thousand butterflies take flight in my stomach, feather-light wings flapping against my ribcage. "I don't know, probably because I just decided to go back a few weeks ago."

"What made you want to do that?"

"I guess I just wanted to brush up on my skills."

He glances over at me, and it only takes him a second to pick apart my answer and get to the truth of the matter. "Trent's still writing you."

"No," I lie, the word like sandpaper on my tongue. Images of the thread of messages from Trent that I've left unanswered flash through my mind. The last one was mean, desperate: *Stop ignoring me, bitch, you know you're dying for another chance to suck me off.* I shudder. "No, I haven't heard from him in a while."

It's stupid to lie to him about it, but if I tell Chris how dark the messages from Trent are getting then he'll want to step in and be the hero. That will probably involve doing something dumb like going to the police or confronting Trent himself, and I don't want him doing either of those things.

When I decided to go back to the gym, it wasn't just because I was scared about getting too comfortable behind the shield Chris offered me. It was also because I wanted to be prepared when I inevitably have it taken away from me. This relationship, and the comfort it has offered me is temporary, but the impact it has on my life doesn't have to be.

If we're successful, Chris will walk away from us with the kind of freedom he'd only ever dreamed about, and I want that for myself too. I want to come out of this feeling stronger and more powerful than I have in a long time, and the only way to do that is to use Trent's obsession with us to draw him out.

Clearly, our relationship isn't the deterrent we thought it would be, but I'm more than happy to adjust, to allow it to be a catalyst, moving us towards the kind of closure the broken girl who froze when she should have fought, who stayed silent when she should have screamed, could have never imagined.

22

MALLORY

The next afternoon I get an email from Dr. Richardson that gives me the distinct feeling that the shit that's been up in the air since Chris told him about our relationship is finally about to hit the fan.

If someone had asked me to describe the feeling, I wouldn't have been able to put it into words, but it starts when I open the curt email—*Ms. Kent, my office. Now.*—and clings to me as I walk across campus and text Sloane to tell her I'm going to be late to our study session. And when I finally step inside his office, taking in the folds of saggy skin and thin lips with creases around them that I'm sure come from frowning instead of smiling, it's still with me.

He doesn't even look up from the papers he's shuffling through on his desk when the door closes behind me. "Take a seat."

Despite the streak of rebellion rushing through my veins in response to his order, I lower myself into the chair in front of his desk. It's diagonal to the table that Chris usually occupies when he's in here doing office hours after class. Since it's Thursday, he's not there, and I can't help but wonder if Richardson chose this impromptu meeting time because he knew Chris wouldn't be available.

It doesn't matter, Mal, you know how to handle yourself.

The internal reminder is all I need. Sitting straight up, I decide to take control of the conversation instead of sitting here playing this intimidation game with him.

"What did you want to talk about, Dr. Richardson? I was just on my way to the library to study for the exam I have in Data Analytics tomorrow."

I make sure to keep my voice even, but when he lifts his head to look at me, glasses falling down the bridge of his hooked nose, he still looks like he doesn't appreciate my tone. With a long sigh and a resigned shake of his head, he sets the papers down and sits back in his chair, lacing his wrinkled fingers together and resting them over his stomach.

"I was recently made aware of your relationship with Mr. Johnson," he starts, sending my heart spiraling through my chest and down into the pit of my churning stomach.

"Chris told me he informed you during midterms."

He nods, the ruddy skin of his jowl jiggling with the motion. "He did, but we're not discussing him right now, we're discussing you."

My brows fall together. "I'm not sure I understand what you mean."

It's the most reasonable thing I can think of to say, but it still doesn't feel like it conveys the depth of my confusion. Any conversation about me in regards to my relationship with Chris, is a conversation about him as well.

Condescension laces the chuckle that fills the air between us. "That doesn't surprise me, Ms. Kent. I imagine you'll also be confused when I say I called you here to ask you to withdraw from my class."

"Withdraw? From a course I'm already halfway done with? Why would I do that?"

"Because your relationship with Christopher has become a distraction for the other students."

This is news to me. No one seems to pay any attention to us. Sure we get some looks when we're together on campus, but it never happens in the classroom. I'd venture to say most of them don't even know we're together.

"A distraction," I say slowly, laser-focused on the anger swelling beneath my breastbone.

"Yes. It appears the hearts in your eyes from the first day of class have only grown bigger and more ridiculous. It's to the point where students are complaining to me. There have been rumblings about favoritism and unfair academic advantages."

"And your solution is to remove me from the class."

"To *ask* you to remove yourself from the class, yes."

A loud, disbelieving snort erupts from my nose or my mouth or maybe both. I can't be sure because it's all so ridiculous. The man. The conversation. The reality of what he's asking me to do.

"No." Richardson lifts a brow, and his cheeks turn red. He doesn't like to be told no, especially by women, so I say it again. "*No.* I will not remove myself from the class. If you want me out, then you're going to have to do it yourself."

"I—"

"Don't have the ability to do that, do you?" I don't really need to ask, I know he doesn't. Professors can't withdraw students from classes after the final drop period is over unless they have cause. Cause being, excessive absences, and missing assignments, not imaginary complaints from students who don't give a damn about who my boyfriend is. *Fake boyfriend,* my subconscious reminds me.

Right, yes, students that don't give a damn who my fake boyfriend is.

"You know quite well that I don't."

"Well, then, I don't know what else we have to talk about here." I start to stand, but his next words force me to plop back down in my seat.

"We have plenty more to discuss, Mallory. Let's start with the paper you submitted at the end of last month. The one that was turned in over forty minutes after the deadline."

Now, my heart, which has been chewed up by the blades of anxiety oscillating in my stomach, is in my throat. It's been so long since the thing with the paper that I kind of forgot about it, and I hope that right here, right now, isn't the moment when it comes back to bite me in the ass. I school my features into a mask of indifference, running through all the steps Chris told me he took to cover our asses.

"What about it?"

I wait for the flare of panic to come. The one that used to show up every time I was forced to revisit a lie I told to keep my relationship with Trent safe. I always had to wonder if he'd done what he needed to do, said what he needed to say to make sure we were good, and while it always turned out fine, in the moment, I never trusted that he had us covered.

As I sit here, waiting for Richardson to answer my question, all I feel is certainty that Chris does. Realizing that I've added another person to the small list of people that I never doubt would normally be an unsettling sensation, but right now it just feels good. And I can only guess that it's because Chris has been working on gaining my trust for a while. Slowly. With patience and precision.

In the last few weeks, I've grown to depend on him and the easy way we exist together. When he tells me he's going to do something, I don't doubt that he will. And before, like literally just yesterday, I would have been berating myself. Screaming silently that walking around without even a flicker of uncertainty where a man—any man, really, but especially one who can charm the panties off a nun with a single smile that, these days, he only gives to you—is concerned is a stupid thing to do.

But I don't feel stupid, I just feel excited and open. Capable of taking care of myself but also comfortable in the knowledge that I don't have to do it alone.

For right now.

Dr. Richardson sits up in his chair, straightening to his full seated height which tells me he thinks he's about to make a big, important point. "I find it awfully convenient that you were the first student to turn the paper in after the deadline was adjusted. Given what we now know about your relationship with Christopher, I have to wonder if you were the real reason for the change."

There's no arguing with the facts or his logic, largely because I know for a fact I was the reason for the change, but I can't admit to letting Chris alter the submission settings for me.

"Was I the only student who turned in the assignment after the original deadline?"

He visibly deflates, and I want to laugh in his face because he clearly thought I'd be too flustered to use my common sense and ask the most obvious question. "No," he admits, eyes darkening. "You were not the only student to benefit from the change, but it still doesn't explain how—"

"You know what I don't get, Professor?" I cut in, slicing his sentence in half. "I don't understand how you thought calling me into your office to have this conversation was smart or necessary. You're clearly on a warpath, looking for any and every reason to get me out of your class and, more than likely, the department."

"No!" He bellows, face turning beet red. "Don't try to turn this into some ridiculous vendetta. I know Christopher changed the deadline for you. I know you are receiving unfair advantages—"

"And *I* know that your dislike for me started well before I began dating your TA." The color in his face and cheeks starts to take over his neck and ears when I cut him off again. He looks ready to stroke out, but I don't care enough to stop. "I *know* that the way you feel about me and the way you've treated me ever since I started this program is rooted in misogyny and racism. And I also know that I wouldn't be hard pressed to find another Black woman in this department that you've subjected to this same harassment."

"*Harassment,*" he sputters. A nervous hand coming up off of the desk to tug at the neckline of his ill-fitting shirt.

"Yes, Professor. Harassment. Well-documented harassment, thanks to your very public speeches about hormones and propositions and such on the first day of class. Harassment that's now turned into behavior bordering on sex-based discrimination because you are trying to force me out of a class I'm passing because you don't like that I'm dating your TA. A TA, who is suspiciously absent from this meeting despite the topic being our relationship and the alleged complaints you've received regarding it." The words are flowing freely. Each point piling on top of the other until it builds a mountain of hard-earned malice on his desk. "Which only further proves that you are not concerned about a moved deadline or distracted students, *you* are out to punish me, a *BLACK WOMAN*, for something you probably haven't even had the balls to bring up to my male counterpart."

"I'm not....You have this all wrong, young lady."

Tossing my head back, I let out another peal of laughter. "Let's say that I do have it all wrong. Tell me, Dr. Richardson, what are Chris' repercussions for engaging in a relationship with me? What's his punishment for distracting my classmates and allegedly adjusting a deadline that more than half of the class, not just me, benefited from?"

I watch his jaw work, and this time I wait for him to come up with something to say. Because surely such a learned, accomplished man would be able to hold his own in a verbal exchange with a young woman such as myself.

"That's between Christopher and me."

I roll my eyes. "Sure, let me take a guess though? You'll give him a good ole pat on the back and the 'boys will be boys' speech and that'll be it right? Done. Handled. You'll both go on with your lives while I, if I *was* going to submit to your asinine request, have my entire under-graduate career derailed, not to mention what your petty gossip will do to my reputation."

"It would all be confidential," he mumbles, unable to meet my eyes.

With another derisive snort, I push to my feet and fix him with a hard stare, feeling more powerful than I have in a long time. "It doesn't matter because it's not happening, and if you call another one of these little meetings or so much as look at me the wrong way, I'll lodge a complaint with the department chair and the Title IX Coordinator. I'm sure Dr. Wilson would be happy to usher out a cranky, old dinosaur such as yourself. Have a good day, Professor."

I don't bother glancing at him again as I dip to pick up my bag off the floor and march out of his office with my head held high. It feels good, slaying a dragon on my own. Walking away from battle having benefited from the solid foundation I trusted my partner to lay. I feel like I'm floating, walking on a cloud made up of all the parts of myself I thought would be lost to me forever.

The brave, daring parts that whisper quiet questions under the chorus of victory. Questions about Chris and me and this arrangement that I think could be more if we let it. I'd be willing to try for him, and maybe, just maybe, I can convince him to try for me.

23

CHRIS

I don't need convincing.

When Mallory shows up at my door in a crop top that bares a sliver of her midriff and skin-tight jeans that hug her waist and make the lush roundness of her belly even more prominent asking if I want to come on a ride with her, I say yes immediately. And it doesn't matter that we don't have anything planned or that, thanks to spending all of December trying to teach Teresa how to drive, I have a slight passenger seat phobia.

The only thing that matters is that she wanted an adventure today, and she came to me. I tell myself not to read too much into it. Remind myself there are several good reasons why she chose me instead of Sloane, Eric, or Nic.

1. They're all busy.
2. I'm her fake boyfriend, so it might look weird for her to be doing whatever we're going to do without me. She probably felt obligated to invite me because of the big deal I made about not knowing about her self-defense classes.

3. This might have something to do with her ex, which means
   I, the only person in her life who knows what he is to her,
   was her only option.

But as I look at her, none of those options feel right. She just looks happy, more relaxed than she ever has around me. The last few weeks have given me plenty of opportunities to see her in various states of repose. With all the time we spend at my place, either alone, trying to figure out why my dad hasn't asked about us yet, or with the rest of the crew, I've seen nearly every mood Mal has, and this is just different.

The windows are rolled down, warm air laced with jasmine and citrus floating around the small space of the Corolla. Her hair, which has been freed from the confines of her protective style and is now flowing loosely in wild, sexy coils that are thick and puffy, whips around her face, hiding those amber eyes from me for seconds at a time. Music blasts from the stereo as she takes a sharp curve with only one of her hands on the wheel because the other is hanging out the window, riding invisible waves of air that swallow her happiness and push it back into the car where it invades my lungs.

"You're in a good mood today."

She arches a sassy brow at me. "Are you suggesting I'm not usually in a good mood?"

"I didn't say that, but you are a little grumpy sometimes."

"Grumpy?" She gapes at me. "I'm not grumpy. A little too serious maybe, but never grumpy."

"Maybe," I agree, folding a smile between my lips because she's cute when she's in denial. "So what gives? I thought you were studying with Sloane today." Knowing she had a date with the library and passed it up for a chance to spend time with me makes me happier than I care to admit.

"I just felt like having some fun. The library has seen enough of me, and I've seen enough of it. I'm so glad spring break is coming up."

"Me too." *Because it means I get more of this.*

I leave the last part out and study her profile. I've got every line of her face memorized. I know every expression. The unique way each emotion plays across her features. Right now there's a serenity to her I haven't seen before, and I want to know where it came from, so I can do everything in my power to give her more of it.

Reaching out with one hand, she turns the volume down on the radio. "Just so you know, Richardson called me to his office today."

My jaw immediately tenses. "What did he want?"

"To ask me to withdraw from the class."

She says it so casually. Like a professor requesting a student remove themselves from a class is a normal thing when we both know it's not. Rage swirls around in my gut, asking to be set free, but I tamp it down.

Weeks ago I promised that Richardson would feel my wrath if he came at her, and she got angry at me for wanting to fight her battles. I promised myself then and there that I wouldn't make that mistake again, and now I find myself presented with the opportunity to make good on that promise.

Mallory is silent as I think of an appropriate response, and I wonder if she's waiting for me to make the same mistake. Although it pains me, I force myself to stay calm and continue the conversation. "What did you say to that?"

The mischievous sparkle in her eye and the dangerous curl of her lips tells me everything I need to know, but I listen intently as she recounts the entire story. Starting with the lies about student complaints and ending with her handing him his ass and walking out before he got the chance to respond. And when she's done, she looks so fucking proud of herself I want to lean across the console and kiss her.

"I'm proud of you."

The words pop out of my mouth of their own volition, but it's the most honest, most true thing I've said to her today. Mallory must hear the meaning in the words because she bites her lip, several emotions swimming in her irises before she pushes them all away and says, "Thank you. I'm proud of me too."

I stare at her, allowing myself to imagine a world where this feeling

—this sudden and intense onset of euphoric emotion—can last forever. Where it doesn't have to be swept away by an ill-timed reminder that we're nothing more than scene partners.

I let the moment go on too long, my silence stretching between us until it borders on awkward. Part of me wants the awkwardness, to see where it will take us, but I'm still not sure that Mallory is ready for where I want the conversation to go.

So I do the nice, honorable thing, and lead the conversation back into safe territory.

"You're welcome. Now, are you going to tell me where we're going?"

She glances over at me, flashing a full smile that activates both of her dimples. "Nope."

And just like that, I'm sucked back into the whirlwind that is her. Not even caring she won't give me an answer because being around her is one of my favorite pastimes. Doesn't matter where we're going or what we're doing, if Mallory is involved, I'm there.

"Fine, but at least slow down a little? I'm pretty sure you're not supposed to go above forty miles per hour with a donut on your car."

The small, temporary tire was the only thing that had made me doubt getting in the car her and Eric share. Mal sticks her tongue out at me and slams her foot down on the gas, propelling us further down the empty back road that seems to be taking us towards the side of town where her and Eric grew up.

"Jesus, Mal." I throw my hand out to stop myself from flying into the dashboard I'm precariously close to. How Eric, or Nic who's taller than all of us, fit comfortably in this car I'll never know. "If I knew you were going to drive this recklessly I would have made sure you got behind the wheel of a car where all four tires were the same size."

"Sloane would kill me if I drove her car like this."

"I wasn't talking about her car." My foot presses into the floor-board, trying to hit a brake I don't have as we round another curve.

She throws me a puzzled look, which is troubling because I'm pretty sure we're riding in both lanes right now. "I know this might come as a surprise to you, growing up with a fleet of cars at your disposal and all, but most people can count on one hand the number of cars they have access to and still have three to four fingers left. That's how I can say with absolute certainty there are only two cars on campus I can drive."

The road straightens out, and I relax a little. "First of all, we didn't have a fleet of cars." Mal opens her mouth, but I lift a finger and continue. "Second of all, you are always more than welcome to drive my car, which means at any given time there are three cars on campus available to you."

"Yeah, right. You're way too uptight about your car to let anyone behind the wheel."

"You're not just anyone, though."

There's a world of meaning in those five words, and I want to kick myself for letting them slip out. Keeping my feelings from showing in the things I say and do have been a huge struggle lately. I've tried to keep it in check, but this version of Mallory—this vibrant burst of sunlight that's been waiting to shine—makes it hard.

It just adds another layer to her personality, gives me another piece of her to appreciate, to covet, to obsess over.

"Chris, please," she scoffs, "there's no way on Earth I'd ever get behind the wheel of your luxury car."

Now, it's my turn to look puzzled. "Sloane drives a Lexus, that's technically a luxury car." She takes the one hand she had on the wheel and waves it dismissively at me.

"Boy, please. Everybody knows that a Lexus ain't nothing but a Toyota with a different logo."

"Mallory, put your damn hands on the wheel!" I try to reach over and grab it, but she swats me away, using her knee to maneuver the car. Exasperated, I lean my head back on the headrest. "You're a terrible driver."

"And yet, you want to let me drive your car that costs as much as two years of tuition." Licking her lips, she gives me a teasing smile. "You'd probably have a heart attack if you saw me sitting in your driver's seat."

My brain chooses that exact moment to conjure an image of her doing exactly that. A skimpy skirt pulled up around her torso, baring the decadent place where her tummy falls over her mound, thick thighs parted to make room for my fingers that are desperately seeking her slick heat. A dizzying amount of blood leaves my extremities and floods my groin, causing my dick to swell.

Mallory's laughter pulls me out of my sordid thoughts. "See, you can't even picture it."

Being as subtle as I can in this cramped space, I shift in my seat to make room for the erection I hope will be gone by the time we get to where ever we're going. "I can picture it just fine."

"I'm sure. I can tell by the look on your face that whatever you were picturing wasn't good. Did it start with me totaling your baby and end with you never speaking to me again?"

"It would take a lot more than you crashing my car to get me to stop speaking to you."

"Chris, please, it's an eighty-thousand-dollar car."

I cringe. The number is a reminder of my father's wealth and the power that comes along with it. The power that he wields with an iron fist and uses to crush anyone who won't fall in line. A fist that's looming over my head, coming in closer and closer the longer we continue with this struggle for control over my life.

I'd thought that by now he'd have brought up my relationship with Mallory on one of our calls, but so far he hasn't said a word, which means I'm no closer to the autonomy I crave than I was when we started this.

And the only thing that stops me from thinking this was all a waste of time is her.

Her peace of mind.

Her safety.

Her constant presence in my life.

"What's that supposed to mean to me, Mallory?"

"Oh, shit." Her mouth drops, and her eyes go comically wide. "I'm sorry, I forgot I was talking to the heir of the Johnson legacy. Eighty thousand dollars doesn't mean a damn thing to you, huh?"

"It's eighty thousand dollars, of course, it means *something* to me. Not more than you though. A car can easily be replaced, but a person" —I let the words hang in the air, fighting back the urge to say 'especially if that person is you'— "a person isn't."

24

MALLORY

Breathe.

I force air out of my lungs, but it doesn't do anything to calm the rapid beating of my heart as Chris' words layer themselves in between my skin and bones. Coiling around my veins, seeping into my bloodstream.

I'm reading too much into it. I know I am. Because he finished his statement—the one where he said his car, which everyone knows he loves more than anything, didn't matter more than me—with a broader, more generalized version of a sentiment, that when boiled down, only means we shouldn't value things over people.

Not a surprising take coming from someone who lost his mom at a really young age and has, for all intents and purposes, removed himself from the superficial world of Boston's elite.

So stop obsessing over it, Mallory, I scream to myself, pretending to be too focused on turning into Skate World's parking lot to respond to Chris. Which is fine because he's not paying attention anyway. His thick brows are knitted close together, chestnut eyes sweeping over the empty gravel lot of what appears to be an abandoned building. The old neon sign, which I imagine saw its best days when Mama was still a teenager, has busted bulbs and one red letter that's precariously close to slipping right off the white brick exterior.

Chris is quiet as I park the car, and I allow myself one minute to push away the nerves threatening to overtake my body. The whole purpose of this outing was for me to try and figure out if he's on the same page as me when it comes to us.

Us.

The word sounds funny, almost foreign, in my mind, but I kind of like it. I'd left Richardson's office with enough confidence in my feelings for Chris and his feelings for me to fill the entire roller skate rink in front of us, but somewhere between texting Sloane and saying I was blowing off studying to hang out with Chris and getting here, I've started to doubt the wisdom of that decision. I feel like I'm existing in a tiny, airless bubble that's being volleyed between optimism and hopelessness, and all of it depends on the things that come out of Chris' mouth.

An unfortunate thing, really, since everything he says seems to be some mixture of things that mean everything and nothing for us all at the same time. It's exhausting trying to decipher it all while not overplaying my hand. The last thing I would ever want is to pour my heart out to him and find out his affection for me doesn't go any further than our farce.

"Is this place even open?" Chris asks, hopping out and rounding the car to open my door before I get a chance to do so on my own.

"Yes, it just looks abandoned because no one comes here during the day."

He arches a brow, holding out his hand to help me out. I take it, loving the secure feeling of his rough fingertips wrapped around my wrist. I love it even more when he doesn't let go, and I'm forced to lock the door and secure my purse with one hand. When I'm done, Chris gestures for me to lead the way.

"You sound quite certain, princess."

I shrug. "I do my research."

"Sounded more like you're speaking from experience." He smiles down at me, inching up on another one of my secrets. He's gotten too good at that, filtering through my words to find the truth. It makes me grateful my break up with Trent hasn't been the topic of conversation for quite some time.

"Maybe I am."

Using his left hand because the fingers of his right one are still laced through mine, he opens the door and lets me pass through first. When I glance back at him, I swear I catch his eyes studying the sway of my hips, but he shifts his gaze too quickly for me to be sure.

"Do you come here a lot?"

"Eric, Nic, and I used to come here all the time in high school. It's *the* date spot for Lakewood students. You weren't official until you…" I trail off, thankful for the darkness of the rink because it hides the blush creeping up my cheeks. Here I am rambling about this being the premier spot for high school couples while trying not to expose my feelings for him. Chris looks thoughtful as we approach the skate rental desk, but outside of that, I can't really tell what he's feeling.

The desk attendant—an older Black lady with a jherri curl and a name tag that says Lorraine—gives us a big smile and immediately starts pulling down skates when we stop in front of her. Surprisingly, she got our sizes perfect and shooed us away when Chris pulled out his wallet to pay for the rentals.

"Go on and have fun, babies. No one here is worried about a few dollars."

"They probably *should* be worried about a few dollars," Chris whispers under his breath as we sit down on the benches and trade our shoes for skates. My laughter bounces off of the half wall in front of us, and there's so much warmth in his eyes when he gazes over at me it's hard to think I'm in this alone.

"I—"

"So—"

We both start and stop at the same time, an awkward silence falling between us as we wait to see who's going to start up again. When neither of us does, I shake my head and smile.

"What were you going to say?"

"Are you sure you didn't want to go first?"

"No, it's fine. I don't even remember what I was going to say."

"Oh," he sighs, tightening the string at the very top of his skate. I didn't even ask him if he knew how to skate before we came here. I just assumed that this, like everything else, was something he knew how to do, and I was right. "I was just going to ask if you were any good on skates. Because if you're not, and you're one of those people who drags the person closest to you down with you when you fall, then I might need to get a helmet. And maybe some knee pads."

I've become quite fond of Chris' sense of humor lately, and right now I'm really enjoying the way his lips curve while he takes a shit on my skating abilities. Instead of answering his question, I push to my feet, giving my body time to adjust to the feeling of the wheels beneath me. When I'm steady, I make a show of skating backward, letting my ass pass by his face before spinning to face the opening to the rink and stepping on. Getting my bearings on the slick wood only takes half a second, and it's not long before I'm zooming around with the lights from the disco ball in the middle of the ceiling scattering colors all across my body.

Music blasts through the speakers, and I do two laps around the rink before I feel Chris' presence on the floor. He's somewhere behind me, moving slower than he needs to, and I glance over my shoulder to try to catch sight of him. The moment our eyes lock, he flashes me a smile that can only be described as deliciously primal. It only adds to the sensation building in my chest. The ringing of alarm bells that alert me to the fact I'm being chased. I look back at Chris again, just to be certain, and he smiles again, this time running his tongue over his teeth like a hungry predator preparing to take a bite out of its prey.

Hunted. I'm being hunted.

Despite the safety of my surroundings and the trust I have in the person shadowing my movements, the feeling builds and builds. All of the training I've been doing at Hunter's gym pushes to the surface, heightening my senses and allowing me to filter out everything that isn't the smooth glide of his skate and the hairs standing at attention at the back of my neck.

There's a tightness in my chest that takes over all of my muscles, including the ones in my pelvic floor which are clenching and releasing furiously, completely at odds with my brain which is telling me to prepare to fight not fuck. Usually, I'd be inclined to let those instincts override my sexual desire completely, but today I'm just not strong enough. And instead of one negating the other, the two things mix together, creating the burning, urgent need to do both.

To be caught.

To fight.

To win and be rewarded with the sight of his eyes on fire for me as we lap at the wounds we inflicted on each other. Bites and scratches. Flesh parted by claws tipped with desire, laced with trust and something we can't name.

While I'm deep in thought, Chris closes the distance between us. He's completely in tune with my movements, fluidly following my weaving lines across the floor as my heart beats out of my chest. I can't help but wonder if he feels it too, if he knows what this chase is doing to me.

God, I hope he does.

The song changes, making a transition from a dance song to some smooth R&B that makes zipping around the floor at breakneck speeds seem a little ridiculous. I'm making a mental pros and cons list for slowing down first when two hands close around my waist pulling me back into a set of arms I've spent a lot of time studying. Chris hugs me to him, and I lean my head back against his chest, achingly aware of the way being caught by him only magnifies my desire as our movements sync.

"So you do know how to skate," he murmurs against my ear.

"Told you."

"Actually,"—he spins me around so I'm facing him and then pulls me in again. I'm skating backward now, determining the direction of our glides while he follows—"you didn't answer me before you took off."

"I guess I was in more of a 'show don't tell' mood."

"It was quite a show."

I'm barely biting back the urge to ask him if he's complimenting my ass, and the amusement stamped across his features makes me think he knows it. I don't know how else to respond, so I just say the first thing that comes to mind. "How'd you get so good at skating?"

He shrugs, and the motion causes his hands to lift a little. I suck in a sharp hiss of air when his fingers find the inch of skin between the hem of my shirt and the band of my jeans.

"Skating rinks were a regular hangout spot for us too, princess."

"Oh, right. That makes sense." A smirk curls his lips, and I know he's laughing at me, but it doesn't feel mean or wrong. It just feels nice to bathe in the warmth of his gaze. "I always had to be the third wheel with Tasha and her boyfriend. Or the fifth if I came with Eric and Nic and they had dates."

God, it all sounds so fucking sad. All the things I missed out on because I was dating someone no one could ever know about. My heart aches for that young girl who didn't know any better, who couldn't be bothered to consider what she was missing because she was in love.

Chris studies my face, accurately reading the emotions swelling in my chest. "Do you regret it?" I don't even pretend like I don't know what he means. I'm done hiding from him, acting like he doesn't see me when these days he's the only one who really does.

"Sometimes."

His brows lift in surprise, and I know he wasn't expecting an honest answer. I like that I can still shock him, and I decide to do it again by asking him a question related to a topic I try not to think too much about.

"Do you regret your last relationship?"

I'm deliberately vague because as far as I can tell Giselle—the girl he broke up with before leaving Boston for New Haven—was his last real relationship. I've been curious about what happened between them for a while now, but I've refrained from asking for obvious reasons.

"With Giselle?" A fierce pang of jealousy goes through at the sound of her name on his lips. It sounds too right. Like she belongs there, in his mouth, on his tongue. Biting my lip, I nod and watch as his eyes take on a faraway look. Wisps of honey and bourbon being clouded over by something dark. "The only thing I regret is leaving room for misinterpretation. When I broke up with Giselle, I should have made it clear I wasn't ever coming back for her or the life our parents want so badly for us to have."

"Why didn't you?"

"Because I was stupid enough to think the distance and time would be enough. I thought everyone would just move on, but it seems like leaving just made them even more concerned with getting me back there to honor the family tradition."

Sarcasm coats the last five words in the sentence, and he rolls his eyes when he's done. Chris always seems angry when he talks about the way his family does things, but it just makes me sad for him. Growing up without any true examples of love, or relationships that weren't formed based on what one party could do for the other, must have made dating hard.

It strikes me then that even our relationship is like that. Transactional. An exchange of time, energy, and effort benefitting us both in different ways. It's hard to reconcile that cold, hard fact with the way he's holding me right now though.

"Can I ask you something else?"

"Of course, princess."

"Why haven't you dated anyone since Giselle? Like actually dated, not just…" I pause, unable to say the word out loud.

Chris smirks again, but it falls away a lot quicker this time. His face turns serious. "Honestly, finding someone to date for real seemed like it would take too much energy, and I didn't want the distraction. Preparing for all the things I want to do— the specialty I've chosen, the lives I want to save—has demanded all my attention. A relationship would have gotten in the way of that." Golden eyes bore into mine, imploring me to understand his logic. I nod, letting him know I get him, even as the words deflate the tiny bubble I was occupying. It was hovering over-optimism, but now, as it's sinking to the ground, it's sliding towards hopelessness.

Hearing the man you want refer to relationships as a distraction he can't afford while he's standing on the cusp of a life that will only demand more from him, is a different kind of heartbreak. It's the loss of a thing that never was. The last breath of an idea that doubles as its first. Inside my chest, my heart cracks open, and my next question comes out dull, lifeless.

"So sleeping around was easier?"

"Until it wasn't."

I want to ask when it became difficult, but I can't spend another second talking about the women who have gotten parts of him I want for myself.

"Right. And then you ended up here with me." In the only kind of relationship he, by his own admission, can do right now. Fake. Transactional. Confusing as fuck.

"Yeah," he says softly, hands flexing around my waist. "Then I ended up here with you."

25

CHRIS

Right where I've always wanted to be.

That's what I should have said to Mallory while I had her body pulled close to mine, holding her gently, possessively, but the words never came. Now the time for them has passed. It's a whole day later, and I haven't seen her at all today. She did text me this morning saying she didn't have lab today, so I could go home when I finished with class.

I was actually grateful for the chance to leave campus early because sleep had evaded me last night, forced away by the nightmares about my mother that have recently shifted to become even more gruesome.

I didn't think it was possible since they're already so fucking brutal, but my brain proved me wrong. Taunting me with images of her being pulled out of the door by disembodied hands that didn't stop dragging her away even as she cried out for me.

It was the sound of her screaming my name that woke me. That stuck with me all day, making it close to impossible for me to focus on the words of the email Dr. Richardson wrote to the class announcing that he was leaving the department for personal reasons. Mallory had sent me a screenshot of the email with a smiling emoji, and I pretended to be surprised even though I know it's been in the works for months.

She'll never know, but after witnessing the interaction between her and Richardson on that first day in class, I decided Richardson wasn't going to be a problem for her, or any other Black female student, anymore. It took some thought, but eventually, I came up with a solution that would keep my hands clean, and after multiple calls—one to my personal banker to make a withdrawal from my trust and another to Lyla to get her to send the email—the ball was rolling.

And by ball, I mean a seven-figure donation made to the business department in Lyla's name with a single stipulation: a team of equity consultants be brought in to run a series of mandatory workshops to educate professors about the ways their race and sex-based biases harm their students. In addition to the workshops, I had Lyla specify that the department would need to keep the consultants on and have the older, white males—specifically Richardson—submit to mandatory audits that would look at their past and present interactions with students to determine what changes they needed to make.

I knew Richardson would never go for it. He's too old and set in his ways to ever respect the very real and valid points made by people who have dedicated their lives to leveling the playing field. Years ago, when I was a freshman hanging out with upperclassmen Business majors, I heard them talking about him threatening to quit when the university took away the option to submit hard copies of grades directly to the Registrar. If that simple change could get him up in arms, I figured having his unfair treatment of students like Mallory put under a magnifying glass would put the nail in the coffin.

And I was right.

He's been battling it out with Dr. Wilson since the second week of the semester when the check was cashed and consultants were hired. The workshops are set to start after spring break, so I guess quitting in the middle of the semester is his final 'fuck you' to the department and 'their new obsession with political correctness.'

His words, not mine.

Now Mallory can rest easy knowing she doesn't have to deal with him for the rest of her undergraduate career, and I can feel okay knowing she'll have that peace when I leave for medical school.

Rubbing at my tired eyes with both hands, I push that thought away. I don't want to think about leaving her or this place that's become home simply because it's where she exists, so I focus on my computer screen instead. My dad should be logging on any minute now, and I'm eager to talk to him about me and Mallory. He's had weeks to bring our relationship up, and even though I know he knows, he hasn't so much as hinted at me seeing someone. I'm tired of waiting, so after all the pleasantries and updates about Giselle I never ask for are out of the way, I'm bringing it up.

The Skype app dings, signaling that he's logged on, and I straighten to my full height. Dad's face comes into focus, and he's sitting at his desk in the home office like he always is. Papers and stacks of folders scattered around the edges of the frame while he rubs at his temples with one hand and holds the glasses he always wears to do paperwork in the other. He looks worn out, and it almost makes me feel bad I'm about to bring up a conversation that will almost certainly lead to an argument between us.

Almost.

"Hey, Dad."

"Son." He sounds as tired as he looks, and I feel a familiar pang of concern go through me. Whatever else my father may be—controlling, stubborn, relentless—he's still the only parent I have left in the world, and turning off the part of me that cares for him isn't something I think I'll ever be able to do. "It's rare that you log on before I do. I assume it's not because you were eager to talk to me, which must mean you're finally ready to discuss the recent developments in your personal life."

My brows shoot up, surprise surging through me as I wipe my suddenly sweaty palms down the legs of my jeans. "How long have you known about me and Mallory?"

"Teresa's been keeping me up to date on your social media presence for years now. She was extremely excited to find out that you've been dating and has made it her job to notify me every time you post something new about this young lady."

"*Mallory*," I say, wanting him to say her name, needing him to see she's a real person I care for, not just some nameless, faceless girl he can dismiss. "Her name is Mallory." He inclines his head, eyes shining with genuine interest because of my hard tone. Maybe RJ was right about the severity of my tone being the thing to seal the deal.

"Mallory," he repeats.

"If you knew about her why haven't you brought it up? All you've been talking about for weeks is me and Giselle, but you know that I'm in a relationship."

"The better question, son, is why have you been sitting on those calls listening to me talk about your future with Giselle and then climbing into bed with Mallory?"

A humorless scoff escapes my lips because the only time I've ever shared a bed with Mallory has been in my dreams. It'll probably stay that way too since I'm still not sure how she'll receive a declaration of my feelings. She looked like she understood my logic a little too well, like her experience with Trent had bought her a VIP ticket to the 'No Love, Just Goals' section I'd been comfortable running up until the moment I tasted her lips. That look of understanding in her eye stopped me from explaining I had a change of heart because of her. My dad clears his throat impatiently, snapping me out of my thoughts.

I take another second to formulate my response. "I assumed if you wanted to discuss it, you would have made room for it on the agenda you always seem to have for these calls."

Now, I see that was a mistake. I could have been capitalizing off of the work Mallory and I have been putting into this relationship for weeks now, but instead, I've been waiting around like a little kid hoping his dad will notice he cleaned his room.

"And I assumed the same thing. If this…" I narrow my eyes, daring him to say 'this girl' again, and he clears his throat. "If *Mallory* is so important to you, you should have brought it up to me sooner. Never wait for someone to open the floor up to you, son. If you have something to say, storm onto the stage and take the mic. Demand your right to speak your truth."

"Speaking my truth only matters if my audience is open to hearing it." Something in his expression softens marginally, and a tiny, almost infinitesimal, bubble of hope springs in my chest.

"I'm sorry if you feel like I haven't been open to hearing you, Christopher."

Ignoring the inclusion of the word 'if' in his apology is a battle, but I manage to do it because I don't want to derail our conversation by being nit-picky about his choice of words. "It's all good, Dad."

He leans back in his chair, leaving his glasses on the desk so he can lace the fingers of both hands in front of his stomach. "So it's serious then?"

"Yes. It's serious."

"You in love? Because I never brought any woman to my father's attention if I wasn't in love with her."

As far as I know, the only woman he brought to Grandpa's attention was Mom, and he did that with a ring on her finger and the promise of forever stretched between them. Just the thought of Mom's ring, altered for the woman my father's determined to see me marry, makes my throat tight. The gravity of this moment weighs on me because even though he hasn't said so, I know my answer to this question can change my entire life.

"Yes." The conviction in my tone isn't lost on either of us, and I have to school my features into a neutral expression to hide the shock radiating through me. Once again I find myself caught off guard by the pure emotion coating my words when I talk about how I feel about Mallory. Even more worrying is that those feelings run deeper now than they did when I told Richardson about us just a few weeks ago.

Dad is quiet as he considers me. I don't flinch under his examination because there's nothing to hide. My feelings for Mallory are real, and once I'm certain my dad believes me, I'm going to see to it that she does too.

Trent Davis, and the trust issues he left her with, be damned.

"I don't think I've ever seen you so serious about something that isn't medicine," Dad says finally. "Which is why I still can't understand why you would keep it from me for so long, Chris."

I resist the urge to point out the obvious and give him another honest answer. One that's not just about Mallory, even though having her in my life brought me to the realization. "Because I didn't want you to take it away."

Honesty has never been a huge part of my relationship with my father—mainly because dictators don't want truth from their subjects, they want blind loyalty—but saying these words to him don't feel as scary as I thought they would.

When I was a kid, I never imagined being so candid with him about all the ways he stripped joy from my life in service of legacy. Not when he refused to sign me up for piano lessons and enrolled me in a science camp instead. Or even when he made me stop being friends with a kid named Jonah because he wanted to be a teacher and suggested I become one too.

It feels good to let it out now, to watch his face as he absorbs my words and the meaning behind them. I don't get to see the full range of emotion though, because his processing is interrupted by the sound of his phone going off. The ringtone is specific and familiar, taking me back to the days when dinner would be interrupted by an emergency that could only be solved by his capable hands.

"It's the hospital," he says, leaning forward to snatch the phone off the desk. Before I can respond he's on his feet, grabbing his glasses, wallet, and keys. For a second, I think he's going to rush out of the office without even ending the call or addressing what I just said, but to my surprise, he doesn't. Pausing so his body is held just inside the frame, he sighs. "All I've ever wanted is what's best for you, son."

And then he's gone, the slamming of the office door against the wall the only sound coming through the speakers as I stare at the bookshelves behind his desk. It's not exactly the resolution I was hoping for, but I feel good about the conversation. Certain that he understands how much Mallory means to me and will now back off of the whole Giselle thing.

This is good.

Great.

Better than I could have expected it to go, and the only person I want to see, the only person I want to share it with, is Mallory. I close my computer and glance at my watch, it's only five-thirty, so I know she's not asleep. Without a thought about the exhaustion I was feeling just a few minutes ago, or the weird energy that lingered between us when we parted ways last night, I grab my keys, slide on my shoes and head out the door.

The drive to campus takes over forty-five minutes. An unexpected inconvenience since most of the student body skipped classes today, so they could start their spring break early. When I get to Mallory's dorm, the security guard waves me through without me even having to take out my student ID, and I give him an appreciative nod. Pretty soon, I'm standing in front of her door, heart beating a rapid tattoo of anticipation as I knock.

I hear shuffling behind the door and my pulse quickens then falls when it swings open and Mallory's roommate, Alexis, is the one standing in front of me. She's wearing her signature disinterested look, and her lips are turned down in a line as she stares at me. Over her shoulder, I can see a suitcase sprawled out on her bed, which means I interrupted her packing.

"Mallory isn't here."

I'm momentarily taken aback by the lack of greeting, but I brush it off. "Oh. Sorry. She told me she was going to be—"

"Yeah, well, just like I told the other guy who was waiting outside the building for her, I don't know where she is."

"Guy?" My brows fall together as a sick feeling of dread winds its way through my gut. There's only one guy who could have come looking for her that Alexis wouldn't have known. But, no, it can't be him. Mallory said she hasn't heard from him in weeks. "What guy?"

Alexis heaves a long-suffering sigh. "I don't know, Chris. I didn't exactly ask him for his name and birth date."

"Can you describe him?"

"Tall, light skin, muscular," she pauses, squinting like she's trying to remember something else. "He had on a letterman jacket. I remember thinking it was weird because it had Lakewood or something on it?"

Time stops, and I stop right along with it, existing in the stillness of a frozen hourglass. Staring at a broken clock with warped hands that spin endlessly, making aimless revolutions and never landing on the numbers I need to orient myself.

Trent was here.

Trent was here, and he was looking for Mallory and now I don't know where either of them are. I didn't see him when I was on my way in, so he either gave up on ambushing Mallory outside of the building or he found her.

The thought, coupled with the image of Mallory's fear-stricken features the first and only time I've seen her with Trent, sets me in motion. I spin on my heel, turning my back on Alexis and heading down the hall.

"*You're welcome!*" She yells behind me.

"Yeah, thanks." I toss over my shoulder loud enough for her, and then, under my breath. "For nothing."

When I get back outside the building, I crane my neck, swinging my head from the left to the right for any sign of Mallory or Trent. As I expected, both sides are empty, so I yank my phone out of my pocket and call her. The phone rings for forever before going to voicemail, and I let out a string of curses as I run for my car. I don't even know where I'm going, but I know I have to be moving. Have to be doing something to find her and make sure she's safe, and I have to do all of it without alarming anyone.

The car's engine roars to life, the gentle purr doing little to soothe my nerves as I dial Sloane's number. She's more likely to know where Mal is than anyone else, and as the call connects, I find myself doing something I rarely do these days: praying.

That they're together doing something silly like watching Lifetime movies and eating their weight in popcorn. That she's happy and smiling and has no idea there was a literal monster waiting on her doorstep.

"Hello?"

Relief floods me at the sound of Sloane's voice, and I close my eyes, thankful that she picked up even though she sounds like she has no idea who's calling. "Hey, Sloane. It's Chris. Is Mallory with you?"

"Hey, Chris! No, she's not with me."

My hand clenches, turning into a tight fist. "Have you seen her at all today?"

"Yeah, we've been together most of the day. We went to the mall, got some food, and came back to my room, but she left a while ago."

"Did she say where she was going?"

"Is everything okay, Chris?" Sloane asks, her voice taking on a suspicious tone that suggests I should pull back a bit if I don't want to alarm her.

"Yeah." I open my eyes, draw in a deep breath. "Everything is good."

The line is quiet, and I allow the silence because it gives me time to think of my next move. I almost forget Sloane is there and then she starts talking again. "I'm sure whatever is going on with you guys will turn out fine. Mal is stubborn, and too serious for her own good some- times, but she's happy with you. Happier than I've ever seen her, and I don't think a little argument, or whatever is going on right now, will change that. You'll find a way to fix it."

The last part is more of an order than a reassurance, and if it had come at any other time, I would have laughed, but I'm not feeling humorous right now. "Thanks, Sloane. I gotta go."

"Let me know when you get a hold of her, okay?"

"Okay."

I end the call before she can issue any more edicts and try Mallory again. Her phone rings and then goes to voicemail, so I call Eric and then Nic. A paralyzing feeling of helplessness envelops me as each call ends with no one offering new information, and while it's a common sensation within my nightmares, it's unlike anything I've ever felt in my waking hours. I don't know what to do with it. Where to put these unsettling emotions that have replaced my blood, making it so nothing but fear and rage and panic course through my veins.

With all my options exhausted, I throw my phone carelessly into the passenger seat and run my hands, which are still curled into fists, over my head before slamming them down into the steering wheel repeatedly.

"*Fuck!*"

26

MALLORY

5:40 p.m.

The melody of birds chirping happily is the only sound on the quiet path besides my footsteps as I walk from Sloane's dorm to mine. Beams of late evening sunlight filter through the treetops above me, bathing the sidewalk in the last bit of warmth it'll get today before the moon comes out to illuminate the shadows, and the idyllic scene makes me glad I decided to take the long way home. I went out of my way to take this path, zigzagging across campus just so I could be reminded of the night Chris literally ran into me and took me to Curly's.

My whole life changed that night, and I didn't even know it. The girl who said yes to him, who wanted to feel that same zip of spontaneous energy down her spine could never have imagined that the spark between us would have turned into this.

This, being a confusing array of emotions that refuse to be tamed no matter how much space I put between me and Chris. After yesterday at the skating rink, I decided I needed a step back, and the universe seemed to agree because it presented me with two canceled classes and no reason to see Chris at all today.

It didn't stop me from texting him about the Richardson resignation, though, but texting is different than being in the same room with him. Touching him. Hugging him. Kissing him. The space I took today was good for my brain, but it wasn't good for my heart.

All day long, when I was with Sloane, I missed Chris. I couldn't stop myself from thinking about him, wondering how his day was going, if he was missing me. It was an unproductive train of thought, and yet, I couldn't stop myself from indulging in it.

Gazing heavenward, I will myself to give the pointless thoughts a rest. For all I know, Chris spends all the time he isn't with me planning out his life as a world-renowned OBGYN. Normally, I wouldn't hold being goal-oriented against a guy, especially not someone like Chris who, just months ago, was nothing more than a careless playboy to me. Now I know there's so much more to him, and I want it all. The playful jokester who makes me smile. The soft, serious man with eyes that see through the smoke and mirrors down to the parts of me I hide from everyone, including myself.

I just don't know if I can have it.

Up ahead on the path, I see a form lingering close to the opening leading to the set of buildings I live in. From this far back, I can't make out who it is, but I can tell that they're staggering a bit. Immediately, the hair on the back of my neck rises. I can't exactly put a finger on it, but something about this person—this guy—feels familiar to me. And the closer we get to each other, the more the feeling intensifies. Suddenly, I'm hyper-aware of the fact we're the only two people on the path, and despite me not knowing who this guy is, he seems to know me.

I'm staring at him, so I can see the exact moment that he notices me. Something about his posture changes, his head snaps up and he stands up taller, starts to move faster. My pulse begins to race, but my feet don't stop moving. They're carrying me forward, towards this person whose face is becoming clearer with every step I take.

Trent.

My heart recognizes him before my mind does, and there's a part of me, a very loud part, screaming for me to turn around and go the other way. The other part, the part that's been training and waiting for him to do exactly what he's doing right now, is giving me strength. Fortifying me.

And I'm not afraid.

The realization rings through me just as the distance draws shorter. I stop walking first, so I can control the amount of space between us. Trent's face spreads into a wide smile as he stops in front of me.

"Mallory," he drawls, the slight slur of his words reminding me of the night I worked so hard to forget. "Don't you look beautiful today?"

Leering eyes skate down my body, and I fight to hide the shiver it sends down my spine. I can't believe there used to be a time when I loved his eyes on me. Now, they just make my stomach turn.

"What are you doing here, Trent?"

He takes a step toward me, and I take a step back. My hands coming up to put space between us. His brows rise as he takes in my new stance, and the laugh that escapes his curled lips mocks me. "I came to talk to you. You haven't responded to any of my messages."

"Because I didn't want to talk to you."

His smile shifts, turning cruel. "Funny. You used to love to talk to me. I remember when you used to cry when I couldn't call you, throw fits when I used to take too long to text back."

Shame washes over me. His words triggering memories of a girl who didn't understand that the joy he got from watching me pine for him was nothing more than a sign of toxicity.

"That was years ago, Trent. I've moved on."

"Right, right. With your new boyfriend who likes to post pics of you to remind the world that you're *his* slut now." He takes another step forward, angling his body to the side to try and create an opening that's not blocked by my palms. I turn too, remembering Hunter's instructions from a lifetime ago to shadow your would-be attacker's movements. "You forgot who taught you all the tricks you use on him, huh?"

One of his hands comes up, thick fingers outstretched and reaching for my face. I slap it down forcefully, and his brows pull together as his eyes harden. I'm so concentrated on the fact that I actually hit him, that I don't see his other hand come up. His fingers wrap around my wrist, squeezing tight and yanking it down to my side. With a hard tug, he pulls me into his body, and I gasp, pushing against him. It's only then that I smell the alcohol on his breath, the rancid scent spilling out of his pores and flooding my nostrils. My stomach heaves as my brain flits between reality and memory.

The bright path and the dark dorm room from all those years ago.

The solid ground I'm standing on and the soft mattress that offered no comfort when he was hovering over me, taking things I didn't want to give him.

Tears blur my vision, and I hate the way the sight of them makes his eyes shine with glee. He leans in close, inhaling my scent while I struggle to break his hold. "When I met you, you didn't even know what to do with a dick. I taught you how to suck one, showed you how to take one like a good little girl, and now you think you're hot shit because you're dating some rich boy from up north? Can't take the time to write me back, but you can pose for his camera?" Another cruel laugh. "If I knew you wanted to put on a show, I would have brought mine to the bed for you."

"Let me go." My voice shakes, but there's strength there.

"See that's the problem, baby." His sweat spreads across my skin as he presses his forehead to mine. I can practically hear Hunter shouting in my head about letting him get this close, but I couldn't stop it so now I have to find a way to use his proximity to my advantage. "I can't let you go. Ever since you snuck out of my bed that night, I can't get you out of my head. You were my life, Mallory, and you just left. Why the fuck would you do that?"

"Because you…" The words are there, in my head, on my lips, but they won't come out. "You know why, Trent. You know what you did to me."

But the wild confusion etched into his features suggests that he has no clue. *That* makes me want to laugh and scream and claw his eyes out. How is it possible for someone to be so blind? I guess I shouldn't be surprised, he didn't know, or care, that I didn't want it when he was right there in my face, as close to me then as he is now.

Unknowing, uncaring about my pain.

His hold on me grows tighter, and I feel the bones in his hand grinding against the ones in my wrist. "I gave you what you wanted."

"I said no." A tear slips down my cheek. "I changed my mind and you…you kept going."

Each word feels like it's being ripped from my body. The truth burning my throat like acid and fire. "You knew I didn't want you to—"

"Don't try to rewrite history, Mal. We both knew that you were there to get fucked."

The only upside to his nasty reply is that he pulls back, creating the space I need to breathe, to think. His throat is exposed, and although he's still holding my right hand, the left one is free. It's pinned between our bodies though, which means I can't do much of anything yet.

"I was there because I trusted you. I was there because a naive sixteen-year-old was the only girl you could trick into thinking you were a good guy."

"I am a good guy."

"*You're a rapist,*" I hiss. Anger bubbling in the pit of my stomach finally forcing the words up my throat and past my lips. Trent flinches, like being defined by the horrific thing he did to me is an affront to his character. I use his momentary discomfort to my advantage, yanking my arm down to break his hold on me and taking several steps back. Hunter says this is the point where you need to incapacitate your attacker and run like hell, but I'm not ready to do that just yet. "You raped me, and no matter how you try to frame it, that's the truth. I told you I didn't want to go any further, and you ignored me. I—"

"Laid there and took it," he bites out, moving towards me again on staggering feet. His hands are extended, and I know with a sick certainty that if I let him get his hands on me again, I won't be able to break free. All the muscles in my body tense as I prepare for him to strike. I can see from the way he's eyeing the puffs of black coils floating around me that he intends to grab my hair, so I decide to strike first.

My hand flies out and strikes at his neck, hitting him right in his Adam's Apple and sending him stumbling back. The vibration from the sheer power I put into the blow echoes through my hand, but I don't stop hitting him. I *can't* stop actually, and it's not long before the open palm strikes Hunter taught me are out the window and pure instinct kicks in. Soon, I'm just wailing on him with closed fists that strike at whatever they can reach.

Beneath the sound of the blows landing, Trent grunts and groans but stays on his feet. For a man who smells like he's got enough alcohol in his system to stock a hotel bar, he's got great balance and manages to slither out of my reach.

"You stupid bitch." He glares at me, putting his hand to his lip to try and staunch the blood flowing freely from the cut there. "You cut my fucking lip."

"And you deserve a million times worse, you pig," I spit at him, chest heaving from exertion. "You should be in jail for what you did to me!"

"I swear to God if you go to the cops, I'll—"

"You'll what?" I taunt him, eyes stretching wide to emphasize a point I have no desire to actually make. Going to the cops now would only make my life and the lives of the people I care about the most a living hell. I won't ever give him that. "Send Tasha to tell them I'm a liar? Show up here and get your ass handed to you *again*?"

I watch his eyes narrow into slits and finally his transformation into the monster I know him to be is complete. "Shut the fuck up."

"Go suck on a dick and die, Trent."

I don't know what it is about that specific phrase that sends him over the edge, but suddenly he's lunging at me. His torso parallel to his bent knees as he runs at me with his arms open, ready to wrap around my waist and take me down with a tackle he was known for in his high school days.

Panic clogs my throat, and I curse at myself for not getting away when I had the chance. Trent aims for my left side, so I jump to the right, twisting away from him and leaving the momentum he's built up with nowhere to go but down. He hits the ground with a thud but recovers quickly, muttering something about teaching me a lesson as he clambers to his feet.

Adrenaline pumps through me, and my fight-or-flight instincts beg me to choose flight, so I do. I can tell Trent knows I'm going to run. Judging by the way his unfocused eyes are bouncing between me and the path leading to the dorms, I see that's where he expects me to go, so I feign interest. Making subtle shifts to my body language to make it seem like he's right. A gross smile takes over his lips as he watches me prepare to run, and the next time he lunges at me, I strike him right in the face. The heel of my hand colliding with his nose and causing it to spray blood that has him reaching blindly for me in the wrong direction. His pained groans are the last thing I hear as I head down the opposite side of the path, going back the way I came.

I run blindly, listening for any sign that he's behind me as I dig my keys out of my purse and find the car in the spot I left it in when Sloane and I got back to campus earlier. My brain screams at me, repeating Hunter's directions to 'move fast and get safe' over and over again.

My hands shake as I unlock the car doors and throw myself into the driver's seat, not even bothering to hook my seat belt completely before reversing out of the spot and gunning the engine, heading for the only place, the only person, who can make me feel safe right now.

27

MALLORY

C hris isn't home.

I can feel his absence in the quiet, stillness of his apartment when the door closes behind me. My head hurts from the enraged screams and sobs that poured from my throat on the drive over here. Coming face to face with Trent, speaking the words that barely captured the damage he did to me, unleashing my rage on him, it was all too much. All of my senses were overloaded, every nerve ending alive and firing on all cylinders.

And they're just calming down.

Soothed by the hum of the air conditioner and Chris' scent tickling my nostrils as I walk through the hallway into the living room. Today is the first time I've used the key he gave me, and despite knowing he gave it to me for situations exactly like this, I still feel weird being here without him. I don't know what to do with myself, so I stride over to the kitchen island and collapse into one of the bar stools. My purse slips from my arm and lands with a thud on the floor, and even though I spent my whole life listening to Mama say leaving your purse on the floor will keep you broke, I don't bend over to pick it up.

Uncurling my aching fingers, which have been grasping the cool metal of the key to Chris' apartment like a lifeline, I drop them on the counter and take a look at my hands. There are small cuts and scratches along my knuckles from repeated collision with parts of Trent's body, and there's some stiffness to the tendons linked to my middle and ring fingers that's starting to hurt like a bitch. I eye them both, stretching them out to see if there's any swelling and whimpering when the movement sends pain radiating throughout my hand. I have no idea if they're swollen now, but something tells me that if I don't do something now, they will be soon.

I drag myself off of the stool and over to the freezer only to find it empty except for an ice tray that has no cubes in it. Then I switch over to the fridge and let out a frustrated growl when there's nothing useful in there either. I slam the door closed and wince when it sends another jolt of pain through my trembling hand. I stare at it for a minute, imagining I can hear the rattling of my bones as the entirety of my body shudders and shakes as the last of the adrenaline leaves me. Suddenly everything in front of me is moving, swirling around me in blurry waves that make my head spin and my knees feel weak.

Lowering myself to the ground slowly happens on instinct. One minute I'm standing, watching the stainless steel appliances doing a line dance, and the next I'm sitting on the hardwood floor with the refrigerator at my back. I draw my knees up to my chest, resting my elbows against my thighs so my hurt hand is slightly elevated, and close my eyes. I don't know how long I sit there like that, but the next time my eyes open, Chris is there.

"Princess." He's crouching in front of me, concern etched into his features as he examines me. Chestnut eyes with heated anger singing the corners sweep over me and catch fire when he sees my hand. "*What happened?*"

With gentle fingers he captures my wrist, pulling my hand closer so he can examine it, and I'm so overwhelmed at the sight of him, at the presence of his fury and concern, that I can't say anything. I just stare at him, stupid tears turning my vision fuzzy as my brain and heart scream that I'm finally safe.

Chris doesn't seem to mind the quiet, and I watch him inspect my hand with the kind of precision I would expect from a doctor's son. His deft fingers run over my wrist, testing its mobility by gently bending it forward and then backward. Then he moves on to the top of my hand, rubbing at each tendon and knuckle and pausing at my sharp intake of breath when he gets to the ones that are swelling.

"It's not broken, but it may be sprained."

"I tried to ice it, but you don't have anything in your freezer." He flicks his eyes at me, still silent as he isolates the two fingers that hurt the most and tests their range. It hurts when he moves them, but I don't think it's bad enough to indicate a break. He seems to agree. "I was looking for peas or steak or something, but it was just empty. You don't even have ice." I scrunch my nose up. "Who doesn't even have ice in their freezer?"

"Can you stand?" He asks, ignoring my question as he pushes to his feet.

"Uh, yeah."

He takes a step back and holds out his hand. I place the one that's not hurt in his, and he helps me up. As soon as I'm standing, his palm comes to rest on my lower back and he walks me over to the couch, settling me on the chaise lounge I always occupy when I'm here.

"I'll be right back," he says, walking away before I can even respond.

He's only gone for a few minutes, but it's more than enough time for me to think about how weird this must be for him. Coming home and finding me nearly passed out on his kitchen floor with a busted hand can't be the start to his spring break that he envisioned. When he walks back into the living room, carrying what looks like a first aid kit, I stand up.

"I should go."

"No."

"*No?*"

"No." He repeats, sitting down on the ottoman in front of me and gazing up at me. "The only thing you should be doing right now is sitting down and letting me take care of your hand. And then, either while I'm wrapping it up or after it's done, you should tell me what the hell happened between you and Trent."

I don't know whether it's the shock from him somehow knowing that I ran into Trent today or the sheer power in his voice as he tells me what to do, but I sit back down. My ass sinks into the plush cushion while he pulls alcohol wipes, a roll of gauze, and some other stuff out of his first aid kit.

"Give me your hand, princess."

I do as I'm told, extending my arm so he can start working. The alcohol burns as he swipes it across the open wounds, but I barely feel it because as soon as he pulls the wipe away he starts to blow on it. Steady streams of warm air floating across my skin, soothing the burning sensation in one part of my body and sparking flames in others.

That familiar burst of electricity crackles in the air between us, and I wonder, like I always do, if he feels it too. If he would do something about it if he did. If I would be able to let him if he tried.

"I don't like ice," Chris says, eyebrows knitted close together as he applies some ointment on my knuckles. "The cubes make my teeth hurt."

"Oh, so that's why there's no ice in the freezer."

"Yep." Holding my hand in one of his, he reaches over and picks up the gauze. I watch with a little too much interest as he uses his teeth to start unraveling the roll. It's not the most sanitary thing, but it's sexy as hell, and I have to look away to hide my reaction.

"What about when you have people over?"

"I've never gotten a single request for ice from you, Sloane, Eric, or Nic."

I guess that's true. Most of the time we order out and get drinks or just take whatever he has chilling in the fridge. "Right, but we're not the only people you have over. What about your other company?"

The wrap he's creating with the gauze starts at my wrist and loops around my palm and fingers. It's secure but not tight enough to cut off my circulation, and I appreciate the pressure it's placing on the injured fingers. He lowers my hand into my lap, drawing my attention back to him as he starts putting things away.

"What other company?"

I blink slowly, wondering why I even took the conversation in this direction. "I don't know their names, Chris."

He's placed all the items back in the first aid kit, but he's still moving things around like he's looking for something else. "Me either. Probably because I don't have anyone else over here."

"I'm sure you don't now, but you obviously did before…"

"No." He shakes his head finally pulling out the thing he was looking for. An instant ice pack. Chris squeezes the white and blue package with his hand then lays it vertically on top of the bandage, so it's touching my fingers and knuckles. "Not even then. You're the only woman I've been involved with that's spent time here."

His response reminds me of the day in Richardson's office when he told me that the girls he sleeps with never make it to his bed. I walked away thinking he meant that he fucked them in other places inside his apartment, but now I know I was wrong.

He doesn't bring girls here, but some days I spend more time here than I do in my own dorm.

He doesn't bring girls here, but I have a key.

I shut down the part of my brain trying to draw additional meaning from those words and focus on giving him a response that won't betray my thoughts or prolong this conversation.

"My hand feels a lot better. Thank you."

"You don't need to thank me, princess, but you do need to tell me what the hell happened." All the calm energy that's been emanating around him since he got me up off the floor dissolves, leaving only the thinly veiled rage I'm happy to know isn't actually aimed at me. I bite my lip, considering downplaying the situation because I don't know what he'll do with the whole truth. "Don't think about lying to me. I already know Trent was on campus. Alexis told me he was outside your dorm waiting for you."

My heart does a somersault in my chest. I hadn't considered that Trent knew where I lived. When we met on the path, all I could think about was that I was alone with him. I hadn't considered the implications of the direction he was coming from.

"He knows where I live," I murmur quietly, dread coating the words.

"You didn't see him outside your building?"

"No. We…I ran into him on the path that leads to the parking lot. I was just walking, and then all of a sudden he was just there." A shudder rolls through me as the gravity of the situation I was just in finally dawns on me. "He was drunk and angry because I wasn't returning his messages—"

"Messages? I thought you hadn't heard from him in weeks."

I can't look at him because now I know that at least some part of the heat in his voice is for me. "I might have downplayed it a bit."

"You think?" He laughs roughly, leaning forward and cupping my chin with his hand. He turns to my head until I'm facing him. "He could have hurt you, Mallory."

I hold my hand up, letting the ice pack fall off. I feel its absence almost immediately, the cool relief fading away the second it slides off, but it's worth it to see the pride that shines in Chris' eyes as he regards my injury. "But he didn't."

He leans between us to pick up the pack and grabs my hand, cradling it with reverent fingers as he sets the pack back right. I expect him to let go, but he doesn't. Instead, he uses his other hand to hold the ice pack in place, so it can't fall again, which means, for all intents and purposes, he's holding my hand. It's not the first time we've held hands or even the first time we've done it without anyone around to see the show, but this time feels different. There's a tenderness to his eyes, mingling with the pride and some other emotion I can't name to make a complex, layered expression I want more of.

"Yeah," he says with a rough edge to his voice, "this time he didn't. Is that why you started going back to your self-defense classes?"

"That was part of it, yeah."

"What was the other part?"

"You." I blow out a breath, and Chris' eyes stretch.

"Me? Did I…have I ever made you feel unsafe?"

He starts to release me, and I use what little range of motion I have in my hand to grasp his fingers because I don't want him to let go.

"No! I didn't mean it like that at all." He doesn't exactly look convinced but he stops trying to pull back, which helps me find the right words to explain. "You never make me feel unsafe. Honestly, I think I feel too safe with you sometimes."

"Too safe," he repeats the words, the lack of understanding evident in his voice.

"I was getting too comfortable. Feeling like I didn't have to worry about this thing with Trent because we're together."

"You say it like it's a bad thing instead of the entire reason why we're doing this." Of course, he would be confused by me being upset about getting the returns I was promised when I agreed to invest my time and energy in this relationship.

"Right. That is why we're doing this, but it doesn't mean it's smart for me to put all of my eggs in this basket. There were no guarantees this relationship would keep Trent away, and I wanted to be prepared for the moment he stopped being deterred by your presence in my life if it ever came."

"*When* it came, you mean."

"No." I shake my head. "I didn't know this was going to happen, Chris."

"But you knew there was a good chance it would, and you wanted to be able to face it on your own." It feels like he plucked the words right out of my mouth, and all I can do is nod. Another cloud of conflicted emotion darkens his features before he settles on reluctant acceptance. "Was it as satisfying as you hoped it would be?"

"Ask me tomorrow. Right now all I feel is this,"—I tilt my head, gesturing at my hand— "and the uncomfortable sensation of my stomach touching my back."

I hold my breath as I wait for his reaction, sending up a silent prayer he will take the out I've just given us. Talking about Trent with him hasn't been nearly as traumatic as I thought it would be thus far, but if we keep talking I know it'll only be a matter of time before he's asking harder questions. The ones he really wants the answers to. After a few long seconds of intense eye contact, Chris nods, seeming to understand my silent plea.

"What do you want to eat, princess?"

WE DECIDE on Chinese food and eat on the couch in front of the TV because Chris refuses to let me move a muscle. When he fixes my plate, he brings me a glass of water and some painkillers for my hand and watches while I swallow both pills. The food is good and goes a long way towards helping me feel less shaky, but after multiple episodes of Living Single and a second serving of shrimp fried rice, I'm exhausted and in desperate need of sleep. It's dark outside, and anxiety has already begun to wind its way through my chest at the thought of leaving here to go back to campus where Trent could still be waiting for me.

I reach over and pull my phone out of my purse, which Chris picked up off the floor after he nearly tripped over it when he was bringing in the food, to check the time but end up seeing a few notifications instead. Most of them are missed calls from Chris while the other ones are texts from Sloane, Eric, and Nic asking if I'm good. My leg starts to bounce as I text each of them back, letting them know I'm fine, and then I turn to Chris who's already muted the TV because he noticed that something's up.

"You good?"

"Yeah, I was just texting everyone back. They all wanted to know if I was okay." There's an edge to my voice that he picks up on immediately, he shifts in his seat, which is right next to mine, so now our knees are bumping.

"I didn't tell them what was going on with Trent. I never even mentioned his name."

As soon as I hear the words, I breathe a sigh of relief. I don't think I actually thought he had told them about Trent but it feels nice to hear him say it. "Okay, but what did you tell them?"

"Nothing, but when I couldn't find you or get a hold of you, I was kind of freaked out." My heart squeezes at the thought of him being worried about me. "As soon as Alexis described the guy who was waiting for you, I knew it was him. I looked for you, but I couldn't find you. I called you but you didn't answer."

His throat bobs and he swallows against what I can only imagine must be a lump there. I'm suddenly overwhelmed with the urge to kiss him there, to use my lips to soothe away whatever feelings are brewing inside of him. I wish he would name them, so I could use them to gauge the depth of his feelings for me.

I reach for him, placing my uninjured hand on top of his. He turns his palm over, linking our fingers together. "I know. I'm sorry."

We'd already gone over the timeline, figuring out how we'd missed each other despite being in the same places within minutes of each other. My phone had been in my purse the whole time, and between fighting with Trent, getting away from him, and basically passing out on Chris' kitchen floor, I hadn't thought to check it until just now.

"Don't apologize." His voice is soft as he scoots in closer. "I'm just glad you're safe. You have no idea how relieved I was to walk in here and see you."

"Even though I was on your kitchen floor?"

"Yes." The smile he gives me melts me from the inside out. "Even though you were on the kitchen floor."

The air between us crackles with tension and unspoken desire I'm sure isn't just one-sided. I want so much for him to close the space between us, to press his lips to mine and make me forget what brought me here to the safe haven of his home, but the moment is broken when my phone vibrates. The loud sound shatters the silence in the room and makes both of us jump back.

Chris looks like he's thankful for the interruption and while I read the message from Sloane—who's, unfortunately, joking about me and Chris having make-up sex—he stands and grabs our empty plates from the coffee table.

I hear the clinking of dishes being placed in the dishwasher and sigh. Being here with him this evening was so nice, I felt safe and protected and wanted, but I know I need to go. The little moments that keep happening between us are nice but hoping that they will become more is pointless.

With a heavy sigh, and a ball of dread in my gut, I grab my purse and push up from the couch to search for my shoes. Chris insisted I take them off and get comfortable, but I didn't see where he put them. They're not in the living room at all, so I start to head for the hallway to see if I can find them.

"Where are you going?"

I turn just in time to see the unfairly attractive sight of Chris drying his hands on a dish towel. It's such a regular, everyday thing to do but seeing him do it and knowing that no other woman he's been with has, makes my core clench in a dangerous way.

"Home," I answer, my voice thick.

He looks at me like I just told him I'm taking a trip to the moon instead of back to my dorm. "Mallory, you're not going back to campus tonight."

My brows fall together, a streak of rebellion running through me. Even though I don't want to go back to campus, I don't love the idea of him telling me where I can or can't go. "What?"

"You heard me." He strides over to me, taking my hand in his. "I don't think it's safe for you to go back there. It's dark and for all you know Trent could still be out there waiting."

I had the same concern but hearing him say it makes my pulse race. "Well, I don't have anywhere else to stay, Chris, and I'm not going to let the possibility of running into Trent keep me from going on campus forever."

"It doesn't have to be forever, princess, but for tonight just…" he pauses, warm brown eyes pleading with me, "stay with me. I know you don't need me to fight your battles, but I need you to do this for me. I need you to stay here, so I can know that you're safe."

The idea of him needing anything from me has warmth spreading from the place where our hands are joined, up my arms, and then through my chest where it makes a home right underneath my breastbone.

I want it too much though, him needing me, so I do what he would normally do in a moment like this: make a joke.

"Why does it sound like you're planning on sleeping by the door with a baseball bat in your hand?" Humor shines in his eyes, and it only intensifies the emotions rolling through me.

"If that's what it'll take to make you feel safe, I'll do it."

"No." I laugh, shocked at the truth ringing in his words. "You don't need to do that."

"Stay, Mal."

"Where would I sleep? You don't have a guest room."

His second bedroom is empty. There's not even a single pillow in there, which means he isn't prepared for a sleepover, least of all a platonic one.

"You can have my bed, I'll take the couch."

"I don't want to put you out."

"You're not putting me out, I'm offering."

"Christopher." I pin him with my most serious stare, which has no effect on him anymore.

"Mallory, if you really want to go, I'll take you home. I'll sit outside your building all night just to make sure you're good, but I would feel better knowing you're here."

I would feel better being here too. There's no sense in denying it especially since I ran here, to him, when I was at my most vulnerable.

"Okay. I'll stay."

The smile spreading across his face makes my heart swell. He pulls me back through the living room towards the short hallway that leads to his room. I've never been down here, never had a reason to since there's a guest bath in the other hallway near the entrance, so it feels like I'm about to walk into his inner sanctum. He stops just outside his bedroom door, still holding my hand.

"I'm just going to show you where everything is, so you can shower and get settled."

Again, I'm hit with the urge to kiss him, to show him just how much I appreciate his careful approach to a situation that would be uncomfortable for me if I was with anyone but him. I nod, knowing he needs the reassurance more than I do.

"Okay."

Chris turns the knob and guides me into the room, flipping on lights as he goes. There's nothing shocking to me about the cream-colored walls or the large windows that bracket the headboard of his king-sized bed, letting light from the buildings around us spill into the room. It feels more like a luxury hotel room than the dwellings of a twenty-two-year-old man, but I'm not complaining. Every surface is clean. There's no trash on either of the nightstands or the matching dresser across from the bed with a TV mounted over it, and his scent is everywhere. The smell of leather and earth wrapping around me like a warm hug.

"So the bathroom is over there." He points to a door to his right. "If you want to go ahead and shower, I can get you some stuff to change into."

I make a point of glancing between him and me. Chris isn't a small guy. He's taller than I am with well-defined muscles along every inch of his frame, but we both know that while I'm shorter by at least six inches, I'm bigger than he is. The curves of my stomach and breasts would shred any little t-shirt he could pull out of his drawer, and if it made it through being stretched to its limits by them, it would certainly give way when it encountered my arms. My size has never been a problem for me. I've always been a bigger girl navigating a world made for smaller people. I've learned to adjust, to love myself despite all the messages from society telling me I shouldn't, which is why I don't have a problem with pointing out the flaw in his reasoning.

"Nothing in your closet is going to fit me," I laugh.

He raises a brow, chestnut eyes roving over my curves as he turns and heads for a door that must be his closet. "I wouldn't be so sure, princess."

Intrigued, I walk over to his bed and sit down on the edge of it, listening as he rummages through his things, closing and opening several drawers before emerging with a pile of neatly folded clothes that still have tags on them. They don't look like things he'd wear at all, and as he hands the stack to me, I realize they aren't his.

Everything—including the buttery soft t-shirts, matching leggings, and lacy boy shorts—is in my size. I hold a pair that's fire engine red up at him and arch a brow.

Both of his hands come up, his face serious as he says, "I didn't pick those out, Sloane did."

"Sloane?" I give him a disbelieving look. "When did you and Sloane go shopping?"

"We didn't. I gave her my card and asked her to pick some stuff out for you to have at my place."

"She wasn't the least bit curious why you needed her to do that?"

He shakes his head. "Nope. She was just happy to help me do something nice for you."

"And why did you want to…." I gesture at the clothes, heat rushing to my cheeks.

"Do something nice for you?"

"No." *Yes.* "Why did you want me to have clothes here?"

"For the same reason, I wanted you to have a key."

I appreciate the thoughtfulness behind the gesture, but something about knowing Trent was the reason for it makes it hard to. "Oh, yeah, I guess that makes sense."

A semi-awkward silence falls between us for a few seconds before Chris breaks it. "Okay, well, I'm going to grab a few things, and then I'll be out of your hair."

"Cool."

While he moves around the room, going from the bathroom to brush his teeth to the closet to change his clothes and coming back to the bed to grab one of the six pillows piled on top of each other by the headboard, I stay seated, scrolling through my phone just to have something to do besides stare at him.

It's weird being in his space while he does such domestic things, but he doesn't seem bothered by my presence. When he's got everything he needs, he strides over to me on bare feet that speak of the intimacy of this moment. He stops in front of me, staring down at me while I gaze up at him.

"Towels and washcloths are in the bathroom. There's body wash, lotion and toothbrushes on the counter for you."

"Toothbrushes? You think I need more than one, huh?"

He smirks. "It's a new pack, I didn't want to assume which color you would prefer."

"How thoughtful of you."

"I told you a while ago I do take some things seriously, princess."

"And overnight guests just so happens to be one of them," I quip, trying to hide the fact that his deep timbre is turning my blood to fire.

"No." He frowns. "You, princess. Your happiness. Your safety. Your well-being. I take it all very seriously."

My voice comes out low, just above a whisper. "Oh."

Several emotions pass over his face, and he looks like he wants to say more, but he pushes those words away, trading them for a question. "Do you need anything else?"

"Nope. I think I'm good."

"Okay. Well, goodnight." He's backing away, and every part of me is seized with the desire to ask him to stay but I manage to keep my mouth shut while he walks out the door. Just before it closes, he calls out. "Don't get your hand wet."

"Yes, Dr. Johnson," I say sweetly, a smile playing on my lips when I hear his light chuckle echoing around the hall.

28

CHRIS

I'm exhausted, but I can't sleep.

Mallory has been out for hours, and I've been on the couch continuing to watch Living Single without her. The late nineties sitcom is a welcome distraction from thoughts of her jasmine-scented skin wrapped up in my sheets and the events that made her spending the night a necessity rather than one of my deepest desires. Wanting that from her was unfair, especially when I have no idea how to keep my nightmares at bay, but knowing that hasn't done a damn thing to rid me of the craving.

I turn onto my back and stare up at the ceiling, allowing my mind to replay the events of the day. Getting my dad's reluctant approval, deciding to finally tell Mallory as much of the truth as she could possibly handle, and then immediately being thrust into a walking nightmare that, for once, wasn't my own.

I still don't know everything that happened between her and Trent, not on the path today or all those years ago when he tried to break her. There's a part of me that recognizes I might not ever find out, and I've come to accept it. She doesn't need to detail her trauma for me to believe her, and I don't want, or need, the full story to know I want her.

The fear in my heart when I thought she was in danger and the relief I felt when I came home to regroup and found her on the kitchen floor only solidified the fact, but I'll have to wait to broach the topic with her. All she needs right now is somewhere to feel safe and secure, and even if I can't ever be all the things I *want* to be to her, I'm at least going to be that.

The volume on the TV is turned down low, so the first time Mallory cries out I hear it loud and clear. I jump off the couch and run towards the room, willing myself to remember she's not actually in any danger despite the realistic quality of her heart-wrenching screams. Everything is quiet as I approach the door, so I stop and knock, hoping maybe she's woken herself up like she did the last time, but then I hear it again.

Her sobbing.

Begging.

Pleading with him to stop.

Something inside of me cracks open, and I rush through the door over to the bed, turning the lamp on one of the nightstands on, so she doesn't wake to complete darkness. It'll already be disconcerting enough to wake up in a strange room with me at her side, I don't want to scare her more.

The faint light from the lamp bathes the room, outlining her frame and allowing me my first glimpse of her in my bed. She's curled in on herself, knees drawn up towards her chest while she lays on the side of the mattress I tend to favor. I don't let myself think about what I want that to mean though because now she's whimpering, her hands clenched into tight fists as she murmurs incoherently.

"Mallory." With a tentative hand, I reach out and shake her shoulder. She shrugs me off, shuddering away from my touch. "Princess, wake up."

Since she doesn't want me touching her, I nudge the bed, hoping the movement will help jar her awake. She groans, her face screwed up in pain.

"Please....*don't.*"

The words shatter me, and it takes every ounce of control I have left to stay on the side of the bed when what I really want to do is grab her and shake her. I try touching her again, tentative fingers nudging her shoulder at regular intervals while I whisper that she's okay, that I'm here and she's safe.

But it feels like hours go by with her thrashing around before the nightmare finally breaks. I can tell it's reaching its natural conclusion because she goes stiff like she's tensing for a fight and then her mouth opens and she screams the word no so loud she jolts herself awake.

Her body flies into motion immediately, wild eyes searching and unseeing as she scrambles out of bed with one hand clamped over her mouth like she's going to be sick. She turns to me, panic creasing the corners of her eyes that are leaking fresh tears, and I point towards the bathroom door.

"Right there."

She spins on her heel, sprinting the short distance and managing to slam the door before the sound of her retching fills the room. My own stomach heaves, not because of the vomiting itself, but because of the agony she's feeling that I can't take from her. Can't save her from because despite the satisfied gleam in her eyes when she showed me the knuckles she busted pummeling his face, Trent is still with her, haunting her in her dreams, and, I don't know how to set her free.

I pull myself up from the floor and head into the kitchen to grab her a glass of water. By the time I get back, she's out of the bathroom, sitting on the edge of the bed with shame slumping her shoulders. I cross the room, moving slowly so as not to alarm her, and set the glass on the nightstand. Her eyes are on the ground, but I want her to look at me, so that's where I go, dropping down on my haunches to steal her gaze.

"Princess." I don't touch her even though I want to. My fingertips are hungry for the slightest brush of her skin. My palms ache for her curves and the comfort I could press into her body. "Tell me what you remember."

"I don't...." She shakes her head, fingers digging into the side of the mattress. "They're always the same. It's always him and me and he's—" Fat tears slip down her cheeks, and she finally looks at me. "I don't want him in my head, Chris. I just want to sleep without having to see him, without having to feel him."

Her voice breaks on the last word, and I feel myself break right along with it. I would give anything to be able to hold her right now. To take away the horror of being haunted by images that refuse to leave your brain.

"I know, baby," I whisper, the words leaving my lips on a rough exhale. "What can I do? Tell me what you need."

"Hold me."

I'm shocked by her request—specifically that it aligns so perfectly with what I want to do right now—but I don't let it show. She's feeling scared and vulnerable and the last thing she needs right now is to be worried about whether or not I want to comfort her. Especially when it's all I want to do. Pushing to my feet, I hold her stare, letting my intent shine in my eyes.

"Scoot over, princess."

The sight of her scrambling over my sheets to the other side of the bed is one I won't ever forget, but I store it away for now. The spot where she was sleeping is warm and it smells like her. Mal watches as I push the pillows on my side up against the headboard, so I can sit up instead of laying down completely. I know that she asked me to hold her, but I don't want to freak her out by making it feel like we're going to bed together.

She waits until I settle into my spot before sliding over to me slowly. Uncertainty clouds her features, and I lift an arm to welcome her in. It's all the invitation she needs. In the space of a heartbeat, she's nestled up against me. Her head on my chest, tucked under my chin while my arm wraps around her waist, holding her to me. It's only as she tangles her legs with mine that I realize she doesn't have anything on but a t-shirt and a pair of underwear.

Heat from her thick thighs seeps into my skin through the fabric of my basketball shorts, and even though I don't know if she's cold, I lean forward and pull the covers up over the both of us. Mal lets out a soft sigh, like laying here on my chest is bringing her the kind of peace people like us can only hope to find in our dreams, and my heart pounds, smacking against my ribcage while I try to even out my breathing.

"How much did you hear?"

"Enough." She tries to sit up, but I shake my head, the hand I have at her waist applying the gentlest pressure to let her know she doesn't have to move. Doesn't have to explain. Doesn't have to do anything but be here with me. "I'm sorry you have to live that moment over and over again. I'm sorry you had to live it at all."

I feel the moment the tear drops. The hot liquid plopping onto the cotton of my shirt and soaking through until it hits my chest, marking my heart with her sadness.

"I guess I have to tell you now. Since I brought all of this to your doorstep, I probably owe you the truth."

"You don't owe me anything."

"What if I want to tell you?" she asks softly. "I've never talked about it, but you've seen and heard the nightmares, you already know."

This is the first time she's been so candid about how the nightmares relate to everything else. And she's right about me knowing already. I'd put it all together the second I saw her with Trent.

"If you need to talk, I'm here to listen, princess." I run my hand up her side and then back down just to test her reaction. She doesn't shrink away from me or ask me to stop. In fact, she leans in closer. Her arm stretching across my torso, so she's holding me just as tight as I'm holding her.

"You already know how things started with us."

My jaw clenches. "Yeah, when you were just a kid."

"I didn't feel like a kid with him. Having his attention, being the girl who meant the world to him, it made me feel mature, sophisticated." She's barely started telling me the story, and my chest is already tight. "I didn't think the age difference was that bad. I mean it was only a few years, but when you're a sixteen-year-old with no romantic experience and the guy you're dating is nineteen with an intimate knowledge of the crush you've had on him since middle school, a few years goes from being an age gap to being a fucking cavern."

She pauses, and I can't see her face but I can tell she's chewing her lip, thinking about what to say next. If it were anyone else, I would make them stop. I would tell them I don't want their trauma because I already have enough fucked up shit in my head, but for Mallory, I'd absorb a lifetime's worth of pain and heartbreak. Pull the images from the wrinkles of her brain and fold them into myself.

"I didn't realize it when we started dating, but he'd been grooming me for a while. Spending all this time pretending to be interested in my life, giving me sips of his dad's beer that he snuck from the refrigerator, coming up with little jokes that were just for us. It was stupid, but I felt special."

"You are special, and there's nothing stupid about believing that."

"It is if it makes you trust the wrong people."

"Someone breaking your trust is a reflection of them, Mallory. Not you."

"At some point, we have to take responsibility for trusting the wrong people, though. Trent was the lesson I learned the hard way, and I won't make that mistake again." Her tone brooks no argument, so I don't give her one. When she's sure I'm not going to reply, she continues. "He started pressuring me for sex before he left for college, but it got worse once he was there. According to him, all of his teammates were having sex all the time. Fucking random girls at parties. Spending the night in their girlfriend's dorms. Everyone was having sex but him, and he was angry about me wanting to wait to lose my virginity."

I swallow the string of curses that claw their way up my throat. She was a virgin. Her nightmares are about having her first time stolen from her. "Jesus, Mal."

She pulls back, concern wrinkling her brow. "Do you want me to stop?"

The irony of her being worried about me when she's in the process of baring her soul makes me want to smash my fist into something hard and kiss her at the same time.

"No, as long as you're talking, I'm here to listen."

"Tasha talked me into going up there to visit him. She said we could tell Mama I was staying the weekend at her house, and I could just drive up to see him so that's what I did. He was so happy I was there, and I remember being high on that feeling, being the person to put such a big smile on his face. On Friday night, he took me around campus and introduced me to all his friends. We went to a party on Saturday, and we were both drinking, dancing, and kissing. He kept whispering in my ear, telling me he was happy I was finally ready but I never said I was. By the time we left the party, he'd gotten me to say it though."

My hand turns into a fist at her side, and she tenses so I force myself to relax it. The tension fades from her body, her softness melting into me. "Everything between leaving the party and getting back to his dorm is kind of blur. I was so far in my head, trying to convince myself that I was ready and it was okay because I loved him, so in my mind one minute we're at the party, and the next he's taking my clothes off and telling me to lay back on the bed. We'd done other stuff before, so I wasn't scared. He was a bit rougher than usual, more impatient, but I chalked it up to him being drunk and tried to relax. I even managed to come, but then he got up and got the condom, and I just lost my nerve."

"That's normal, princess. You were about to take a big step and you needed more time."

More tears fall, and her body shakes. "I told him I wanted to wait, but he was already on top of me. He said it was too late and then….he was inside me."

I squeeze her so tight I think she might break from the pressure. I know I should pull back, should think about the way her brain might misconstrue the strength of my grip, but when I try to she shakes her head. A wild cloud of black coils brushing my nose and chin from the motion.

"Please don't let me go."

"I don't want to hurt you."

"You won't." She's gripping as much of the fabric of my shirt as she can with her bandaged hand, speaking with the kind of certainty I don't even have right now. I don't know if it's trust or just her need for comfort speaking, but I listen. "He kept saying I wanted it, that I knew what I came there for, and I didn't say anything, Chris. I didn't say no.

After I told him I wasn't ready and he ignored me, I just laid there and let him…"

"You were in shock. Someone you thought loved and respected you was violating you in the most horrific way. It's not uncommon for people's brains to shut down in moments like that."

"I let him hold me after he finished. He fell asleep beside me, and I laid there until the sun came up. Why would I do that?"

I press a kiss to the crown of her head. "Trauma induced shock doesn't stop once the trauma stops. Your brain needed time to recover, to get to a point where it was functioning and able to get you to safety."

"You say all the right things."

"I'm just telling the truth, princess. The question is: do you believe me?" Reaching between us, I bring my hand under her chin and tilt her head back, so she's looking at me. "Tell me that you know none of this was your fault. He took advantage of you. He coerced you into giving him something he could never deserve and when you changed your mind he stole it from you. Those were his actions, Mallory, you don't have to carry around the shame of what happened that night. It was never yours to begin with, it was always his."

The fire glowing in her amber eyes makes my heart swell with the fiercest pride. She nods her head. "I know that now, but sometimes I forget. Before I ran into him at that basketball game, I always thought our first encounter would go like the one today did. I thought I would knee him in the balls and call him out for what he did to me. And not just the rape, but the experiences he stole, the version of me he destroyed in a single night. But when I ran into him, I froze. It was like I was back in that dorm room, laying in his bed pretending like everything was fine when it wasn't. I hated feeling like that girl again, you know?"

I don't know, but I can imagine. After what Trent did, she worked hard to put herself back together all on her own. She buried the trauma deep inside and, through the sheer force of her will, crafted a new life from the wreckage of the old one. At sixteen, she reinvented herself, morphing into the beautiful, complicated and serious woman I've known for almost two years now. Having Trent reappear must have felt like going back to a time when she didn't have the power and control over her life she does today.

"I can only imagine," I say finally, smoothing a hand down her back. "Can I ask you something?"

"Why didn't I go to the police?" The sass underscoring her tear-clogged voice makes the corners of my mouth twitch, an inappropriate smile trying to curve my lips. I stop it from taking shape, but Mallory still sees it, and to my surprise, and delight, she gives me a small, watery smile of her own before her features turn serious again. "Because Eric and Nic would have killed Trent, and I couldn't let Mama lose her sons when I wasn't sure she was going to be able to keep her daughter."

I don't mean to react, but my brows raise on their own volition. Surprise stamped across my face at her inadvertent omission. I can't imagine a world where she isn't in it. Shame flits through her eyes, and she pulls her chin out of my grip. At first, I think she's going to pull away completely, but she surprises me by burying her face in my neck.

When she starts to speak again, it's with her lips brushing against my pulse. "I was never going to hurt myself, but by the time I realized that it was too late to go to the cops. All the evidence was gone. No one even knew we were together except for Tasha and his friends, but I knew they would all lie for him. It just felt like this insurmountable thing, something I wouldn't ever be able to get on top of, so I made myself forget about it. Most of the time I'm able to do exactly that, but then I'll have a nightmare and—"

"You're back in it."

"Yeah, something like th—" A big and loud yawn escapes her lips, cutting off the last syllable of her response. I glance at the clock on my nightstand and see that it's almost four in the morning. Usually, I don't sleep after my nightmares, but that doesn't seem to be true for Mallory. Her breath is already coming in slow, steady puffs that send warm air skating across my pulse.

I don't want to leave her, but after what she just told me, I don't want her to feel pressured to share a bed. I try to sit up and pull my arm from around her waist, but she moans in protest.

"Stay," she says, sleepily. "Please."

I can't find it in me to say no, so I don't. "Okay."

I hold her until she falls asleep, and then I hold her some more. For two hours, I sit in bed, holding her and contemplating solutions to this Trent problem. Mallory thinks their showdown on the path means he'll stop coming for her, but I don't think that's the case.

I need to nip him in the bud quickly and quietly, so she can move on with her life. I knew that their history was a sordid one, but I wasn't prepared for what it would do to me to hear Mallory confirm every horrible suspicion I had. A wide range of reckless emotions rushes through me as I listen to her breathe, swirling in my veins and conjuring images of the unspeakable things I would do to Trent if I ever got my hands on him.

All of the scenarios I imagine end in death though, and that's too peaceful an ending for a piece of shit like him. He deserves to suffer. To have his life ripped to shreds, to have his name ruined, to have his family and friends, who hold him in such high regard, shunned from society for even knowing him. To sit in a cell and spend every day wondering if someone is going to violate him the way he violated Mallory and, undoubtedly, other women.

That would be justice.

The word resonates deep inside me, and suddenly I know exactly what I need to do and who I need to call. Mallory whines in her sleep as I settle her on the pillows and slip out of the bed, turning off the lamp as I go. The sun is coming up now, which means she won't wake up in the dark. I don't know if she's the type to sleep in, so I move quickly, closing the door behind me and rushing to the living room to find my phone.

I take a seat on the edge of the couch and pull up the contact information for the only person I know who has the kind of connections I need to make sure Trent is held accountable for what he's done. I'll have to stress to him the importance of leaving Mallory out of it. She doesn't want her family knowing, and I'll never dishonor that request, but if my suspicions are right about Trent, and they have been so far, she's not the only woman he's done this to.

The people he'll call will find those women, and some of them will be willing to talk. Some of them will want justice, and when they get it, it will provide peace for every woman that's survived him, including the one I love.

That knowledge is more than enough to make me push down my doubts about asking him for a favor and dial the number. It's early, but I know he'll be up. The line rings twice before the call connects and his voice pours through the speakers. He's surprised to hear from me, but I don't let that deter me.

"Hey, Dad...."

29

MALLORY

Everything smells like bacon and my head hurts.

That's the first thing I think as I crack my eyes open and take in my surroundings. Luckily, I remember that I stayed the night at Chris', so I'm not too freaked about not being in my bed. What does kind of freak me out is the bits and pieces of the conversation we had after my nightmare flashing through my mind. I laid all of my truths out there for him to see, and it felt good to let them go. To share and trust him to understand.

To trust him period.

He didn't disappoint at all, meeting all of my needs without question even when he would have been well within his rights to do so. Like when I asked him to hold me, or begged him to stay in bed. He just did it. The kind of comfort I took from being in his arms should be illegal, especially because I don't know if I will ever have it again.

People tend to act different once they know your deepest darkest secrets, and I wouldn't put it past Chris to start handling me with kid gloves. The thought comes to me as I pull myself out of bed, careful not to put too much pressure on my hand which is less achy today, and go through my normal morning routine.

Chris didn't mention it, but when I took my shower last night I noticed that he also had Sloane pick up all of the toiletries I use. There was even a brand new bonnet waiting for me on the counter beside my toothbrush, extra large to fit all my curls. When I climbed in his bed last night, I felt safe and comfortable, and I was touched that he'd gone through so much trouble to make sure I would be if worst came to worst.

Now, as I prepare to step out of his room and investigate the delicious scents teasing my stomach with the promise of breakfast, I send up a silent prayer that nothing has changed between us. Even if I have resigned myself to never truly having Chris, I know I can't survive him looking at me with pity in his eyes when there used to be awe, respect, and sometimes, desire.

The hardwood floors are cool against the soles of my feet as I walk out into the living area. I adjust the band of my leggings, blushing again when I think about how I was wrapped around Chris wearing nothing but a t-shirt and some panties. He's standing over the stove with his back to me and turns around when he hears me coming, a tender smile taking over his face.

"Good morning, princess."

Hearing his nickname for me spoken in that half teasing, half serious voice makes my heart stutter to a stop and then start beating again, my relief and excitement bubbling up in my chest to make a dizzying cocktail of hope.

"Morning." I sit down at the island, and he slides me a plate with bacon, eggs, and toast on it. I lift an impressed brow. "I didn't know you could cook."

A bashful smile graces his lips as he shrugs. "I can do a little something, something."

I pick up a slice of perfectly crisp bacon and take a bite, noticing how his eyes trace the motion, and then drop to the countertop when a happy little moan escapes me. "Mhmm. I think you can do more than a little something."

When he brings his eyes back to my face, I blush from the intensity of his gaze. "How did you sleep?"

"Pretty good after….you know."

"Good." He nods, turning back to grab the plate he fixed for himself off the counter by the stove and setting it down across from me. A comfortable silence descends between us as he digs in and I keep eating. The food is really good, not as good as Mama's obviously, but impressive as hell for a senior in college who had no food in his fridge just a day ago.

I swallow the last of my eggs and wash it down with a sip of orange juice from the glass that was waiting on the counter for me. Now that I'm done eating, I don't know what to do with myself. Should I leave? Should I offer to clean up the kitchen since he cooked? Should I just sit here and stare at him, obsessing over the way he licks his lips after every few bites, treating me to flashes of his tongue that make me want to kiss him just so I can have the chance to suck on it?

"Mallory?"

I jolt at the sound of Chris calling my name, and the humor in his voice makes me realize that he's been calling it while I've been zoned out, staring at his mouth. "Yeah? What did you say?"

"I asked what you had planned for this weekend."

"Oh." I shift in my seat, wondering if this is the start of the conversation that will end with me leaving the security of his home. "Nothing, really. I was going to go to the gym but since my hand is still a little sore, I think I'll take the week off."

After he made sure I was good, Hunter would hand me my ass for letting my training fly out the window the second I was in danger. I don't feel like hearing his fussing or Rae's teasing, so I'll use this week to do something I never do: rest.

Chris frowns, setting his fork down on his plate and rounding the island to stand in front of me. He turns my stool around, the same way he did the first time we kissed, and takes my hand in his, examining the bandage that's still secure despite the night's events.

"Are you in pain now?"

I blink up at him, a lump swelling in my throat. "No, I'm okay."

"You sure?"

"Yes, Chris." I roll my eyes, trying to take my hand back. He lets me go instantly, and there's a part of me that knows his hypervigilance is because of what I told him last night. I don't know how to feel about that. I don't hate it, but I don't love it either. While I appreciate his thoughtfulness when he touches me, there's a part of me that wants what he knows about me not to matter. He's back to looking all concerned and worried, so I give him a reassuring smile and change the subject. "What are you doing this weekend?"

"Taking a trip to Florida."

"Florida?" I ask, heart sinking at the thought of him being states away. "What's in Florida?"

"Back in your princess-obsessed days, did you ever want to go to Disney?"

"Yeah," I say slowly, wondering why he's answering my question with an unrelated one of his own. "Of course."

We never got to go though, because Mama could never afford to take us. Making the trip to the happiest place on Earth was on my bucket list for a long time, but I let go of that dream a long time ago.

"Would you want to go?" Chris is asking now, eyes searching my face. "With me?"

"What?" My voice is shrill, full of confusion that makes him laugh.

"Do you want to go to Disney with me, princess?"

"We can't just go to Disney, Chris."

"Why not?"

"Because...." But I don't have a single reason why we can't, and the excitement blooming like wildflowers deep in my heart keeps me from looking too hard for one. "I don't know."

The teasing smile curling his lips amplifies my excitement even more. "Damn. If I had known you wouldn't be able to come up with a single reason, I wouldn't have spent the morning crafting the perfect responses to your objections."

I narrow my eyes at him. "Don't tease me. I'll come up with a million questions just to spite you."

"Do it. I don't want you to have any doubts when you say yes."

When you say yes, not if. I like how sure he is, how certain he is of the amount of thought he's put into this, so I take a moment to pull my own thoughts together. Pushing aside the initial excitement to think critically for a second.

"Why do you want to take me to Disney?"

His voice is silk and butter as he answers me. "I've heard it's the happiest place on Earth, and I thought you could use a little happy right now."

My heart does a flip in my chest, and I have to fight to keep myself from jumping out of my seat and kissing him. "That's really sweet, Chris, but you don't have to take me to Disney to make me happy." I bite my lip, hating the way it sounds like there's a link between his actions and my happiness.

"I know I don't have to, Mallory, but I want to. Is that okay?"

All I hear is he wants to make me happy, and that thought coupled with what he said yesterday about taking my happiness seriously has things happening in my core that shouldn't be possible after everything that happened last night. I never would have thought that vulnerability would have deepened my attraction to Chris, but it has.

"Yeah, I guess that's okay."

"What other questions do you have, princess?"

"Florida. Is that Disney World or Disney Land?"

"World. I figured a trip to Florida was more manageable than a trip to California."

"Where would we stay?"

"One of the resorts close to the parks. We'll have separate rooms, of course."

Separate accommodations didn't even occur to me, which is how I know I'm too far gone for this man. "Of course. How long would we be gone?"

"I booked the rooms for a week, but your ticket is open-ended so you can come back whenever you want."

A week. A week of being in another state with Chris on what will essentially be a couple's vacation. I press my lips together, absorbing the information and paying no mind to the fact that I can't even come up with a single scenario that would result in me leaving early.

"I would need to call Mama. She wouldn't appreciate it if I left the state without letting her know."

"Eric will tell her. I talked to him first thing this morning to let him know I was surprising you with a trip."

My brows fall together. "Did you sleep at all?"

"I got about an hour before I woke up to cook." He shrugs like he's used to running off of little to no rest. "Any more questions?"

I shake my head. "No, I think I'm good."

The questions I have left aren't about the trip so much as what it could mean for us, but I'm too scared to ask those because I don't think the answers he has will be the ones I want.

"Ready to give me an answer then?"

There's an earnestness in his expression that touches me deep down in my soul, healing the part of me that was wounded by my relationship with Trent long before he violated me in the worst way. Before this moment, I never knew what it felt like to have someone do something just to see me smile.

"Yes."

Satisfaction swirls in his irises, turning chestnut to a warm, liquid honey. "Yes, you'll go or yes, you're ready to give me an answer?"

"Yes, I'll go."

* * *

"HONESTLY, I'm so jealous right now. The only thing Eric and I have planned for spring break is…." Sloane trails off, trading the rest of her sentence for a suggestive wiggle of her brows that makes me gag.

"Ugh, Sloane, please I don't want to hear about you and Eric spending the week in bed."

She rolls her eyes and throws another lace thong in my suitcase, which I promptly pull out and stuff back into my drawer. "Why do you have all of these sexy underwear if you're not going to wear them for your boyfriend?"

Heat rises to my cheeks, and I turn my back to her, focusing on folding the dress in my hands neatly. I can feel her staring at me, and I know the question is coming even though I can't see it written all over her face.

"Are you and Chris having sex?"

All of my muscles go tense. "That's not your business, Sloane."

"I bought underwear for him to keep at his place for you, I think it is."

"It's not, and he shouldn't have asked you to do that."

She walks over, reaching around me to put the thong back in my suitcase. I don't bother to remove it. "Don't tell me you got mad at him about that. I thought it was really sweet of him."

"It was, and I appreciate you helping him out."

"You're more than welcome, babe. Now answer my question."

With a resigned sigh, I close the suitcase and start to zip it. Sloane waits patiently for my answer, completely undeterred by the steps I'm taking to try and avoid giving it. When I can't do it any longer, I turn to her and shake my head. "No, we're not having sex."

Her mouth drops. "How is that even possible? You guys are always all over each other, and you're always so happy."

"Because he makes me happy, Sloane." I laugh, grabbing the suitcase off the bed and rolling it towards the door. Our flight leaves at four thirty, and Chris will be here soon so we can get to the airport early. He was reluctant about letting me come back to campus to pack my bag on my own, but I needed the time to get my head on straight. Promising to stay on the phone with him as I walked from the parking lot to my dorm was the only way I got him to agree to it. I should have saved my breath though, because the few hours we've been apart haven't done a damn thing to calm my nerves or get my brain working right.

"So why are you waiting?" I narrow my eyes at her, and she holds up her hands. "I'm not judging, Mal. I'm just genuinely curious. Cause, I know attraction isn't the issue on either side."

I hate when she says stuff like that because they encourage the thoughts swimming around in my head. The ones that don't acknowledge the existence of our arrangement and completely ignore the possibility that no matter what Chris said about wanting to make me happy, this trip could very well be another ploy to sell our relationship to his dad.

"No." I sigh. "Attraction isn't the issue. I just haven't been ready."

Sloane gives me a sympathetic look. "Has Chris been okay with waiting?"

"Yeah," I say softly, my mind on how patient he's been with me over the course of our relationship. If it was real, if sex was on the table and I wanted to wait, I know he would be okay with doing so.

"That's good. You deserve someone who's willing to wait for you."

Unexpected tears spring to my eyes at her words. It's the second time in twenty-four hours that someone I care about has told me I'm worth waiting for. Chris probably had some idea how much it meant to me when he said it, but Sloane doesn't. It doesn't change its impact on me though, and I cross the room and pull her into a hug. She lets out a surprised laugh and hugs me back, her arms wrapped around my middle while she squeezes me like I'm going to war instead of on vacation.

"Have fun, okay? You've worked so hard this semester, and you deserve a break."

"I will."

"And if the timing feels right, go for it, but if it doesn't then don't."

I glance at the clock, wishing I had time to tease her about her motherly tone. "Okay, Sloane. I gotta go."

We release each other, and she helps me grab all of my things and follows me out of my room. When we get downstairs, Chris' car is parked on the curb. He hops out as soon as he sees us, taking the bags and loading them in the trunk. He waits by the passenger door while I say goodbye to Sloane. After I make her promise to keep Eric, Mama, and Nic from freaking out about me being gone all week, she gives me another tight hug before waving at Chris and leaving us alone.

I walk over to the car, stopping in front of him. "Ready?"

One of his hands come up, brushing a strand of hair that came out of my bun behind my ear. "Yep. Are you?"

"I am."

As soon as I get settled in my seat, the butterflies that seem to live in my stomach start to flap their wings, and they get more and more aggressive as we drive to the airport, check our bags and board the plane. By the time we're in our seats, they're fluttering so hard it feels like they have the strength to carry the plane to Florida all on their own.

My leg starts bouncing, already frayed nerves being shredded by the reality of being minutes away from being launched into the air in a metal tube. Chris grips my right hand, his hold loose to accommodate the tenderness that's still there even though the swelling was gone when he took the bandage off this morning.

Concerned eyes meet mine. "Are you okay?"

"Yeah, I just got nervous all of a sudden. This is the first time I've been on a plane."

I can tell he's shocked, but he tries to hide it. Probably because he doesn't want me to feel like a weirdo for having never been on a plane. I study his face, watching shock turn into a dismayed frown. "Princess, I didn't know. I wouldn't have booked a flight if I knew you were going to be nervous. I'm sorry."

"No, it's okay. You don't have to apologize. I think it's just hitting me that we're about to be thousands of feet in the air."

On our way to another state where we're spending an entire week alone.

His thumb runs over the inside of my palm, sending sparks down my spine. "Getting up there is the hardest part. After that, it's smooth sailing."

"That's easy for you to say, you've probably done this a million times."

"Something like that." He chuckles. "But that just makes me more qualified to tell you that everything is going to be fine." I twist my lips to the side, giving him a skeptical look that earns me another chuckle. This one dark and sensual. "Just trust me, princess. It's going to be a good flight."

I stare down at our joined hands, the image of our laced fingers reminding me of all the photos we've posted across our accounts doing this exact thing. And even though I don't want it to, my mind wanders to the arrangement, begging me to find out if our act has any place on this trip or if the only thing coming with us to Florida besides our luggage is this connection that feels more real with every passing second.

"I think I just need a distraction," I say, keeping my voice even. "Should we take a few pictures so you can post online before we take off?

The question catches him off guard, but he recovers quickly, going from surprise to some expression I can't read. He uses his free hand to rub at his forehead, and my heart slams against my ribcage as I wait for his response. I don't know what it says about me or my commitment to the goals I promised to help him reach, but I want him to say no.

Finally, he turns back to me. "No, I don't think we need to."

The relief that floods me is dizzying and almost enough to distract me from the unsettling feeling of the plane gliding down the runway. Chris doesn't flinch when I tighten my grip on his hand as we move into a surprisingly smooth takeoff, and he doesn't say a word when I keep holding it once we're in the air.

30

CHRIS

The flight was a little over two hours long, and Mallory held my hand through the whole thing. The weight of her hand in mine reverberated through me, rattling my bones, shaking my soul, and just like every other time I've touched her, I felt like the only thing right in my world was her.

Every scent, her jasmine-soaked skin.

Every color, the amber of her eyes, and the rich mahogany of her complexion.

Every sound, the sweet, melodic lilt of her voice.

Every beat of her heart, my reason for breathing.

It scares me, the depth of my feeling for her, because even though I feel closer to her than I ever have before, I'm afraid the things she revealed to me last night will make her pull back. So far that hasn't seemed to be a problem though. We were close on the plane and on the ride over to the resort. And the only reason I'm not with her now is because we decided it was best to get settled in the rooms and chill out, so we could be well rested for the parks tomorrow.

Our rooms are right next to each other, and we're sharing a wall, which means I'm standing in the middle of my room in the dead quiet, just to see if I can hear her when I should be calling Vanessa back to see how Margaret is doing. She called while we were in the air and then texted to say Margaret was asking for me. I know I need to call them back not only to talk to Margaret but to check on Vanessa who's acting as her caregiver, but the thought of hearing death in her voice stops me every time I try.

It's been that way for weeks now. Ever since Vanessa told me about the diagnosis I've found myself screening her calls and making excuses about why I can't call back. I recognize I'm cheating myself out of the time I do have left with her, but none of it seems to matter when I'm thinking about what it's going to be like to lose her.

All of my thoughts are plagued with grief, for the woman who birthed me and the one who raised me. For the lives ripped apart by their loss. The only time I get a break, the only reprieve I have, is when I'm with Mallory. Talking to her, laughing with her, touching the smooth skin of her cheek and fantasizing about caressing her in other places, watching her bite the supple flesh of her bottom lip while I memorize every curve of her frame.

The urge to be around her is so strong, I have to force myself to do something else. Calling Vanessa is out, so I put my phone on the charger and start to unpack my bag. Hanging up my clothes and storing my suitcase in the bottom of my closet after I get my toiletries out. I'm walking out of the bathroom, where I've just set my toothbrush and shower stuff on the counter, when there's a tentative knock on my door.

I'm there in an instant, pulling it open to reveal a smiling Mallory. "Princess. I thought you were getting settled in your room."

She shifts her weight from one leg to the other, suddenly looking shy. "I was, but I'm starving. Do you wanna go get something to eat?"

"You asking me out on a date?"

"I'm asking you to join me for a meal." She laughs. "But you can call it a date if you like. I'll even let you pay."

That makes me laugh because the whole time we've been doing this, I haven't so much as caught a glimpse of her debit card. I don't complain though, because that's exactly how I want it to be between us. Her trusting me to provide her with the things she needs, and me proving it's not a mistake.

"Sounds good, let me grab my phone." I step back and the door starts to close. "You can come in if you want."

"Oh, okay."

She looks uncertain, but then she's stepping inside. The door closing behind her as she moves into my space. Both of us stand there with a quiet awareness stretching between us, making the air thick. I scan Mallory's face, noting the way her eyes move from my face to the bed behind us, and comes back again. She bites her lip, and I drop my gaze to the base of her throat where her pulse is throbbing. I want to dip my tongue into that hollow place, to drink her sweat from it, and sink my teeth into her collar bone while pleasure pours from her lips.

I break the moment when I turn my back on her and walk over to the table where I sat my phone. The images that flashed through my mind sent blood rushing from my head to my dick, and the last thing I want is to be sporting an unsolicited erection while we're standing in the middle of a hotel room. I take my time getting my phone, subtly adjusting my dick in my pants before turning back around and facing Mallory. Her expression is a little less open now, but she still smiles at me before leading me out of my room.

"Where were you trying to go?" I ask, just to keep my eyes off the swaying of her hips.

"There's a few different restaurants around here. I was thinking we could just walk around until we find something that smells good?" She glances at me, and I can't help but smile at her. "Is that okay with you?"

"Whatever you want, princess."

I swear I see red tint her cheeks, but she turns away from me so quick I can't be sure. We walk for a while, taking one of the more scenic paths that wind through the resort, leading to the restaurants, on-site pool, and the play areas teeming with children and tired-looking parents. Eventually, we end up at a bar and grill with coastal vibes and an expansive patio area where Mallory asks to be seated. The sun is starting to set, but it's still hot and humid. I don't mind though because the faint strips of sunlight pouring through the slotted wood above us kiss every inch of Mallory's skin bared by the halter top and shorts she changed into when she was in her room.

She wasn't kidding about being hungry. When the server came to take our drink order, she already knew what she wanted to eat and ordered her meal right along with her water and frozen drink made with passion fruit, orange, and guava juice. Distracted by the thought of what her mouth would taste like with those exotic flavors on her lips, I ordered the same thing she got, and she teased me about being a copycat until the food came. Conversation flowed easily between us with her leading, moving us from topics like her favorite Disney movies to the stories behind the scars on her elbows and wrists— apparently, she's not a gifted bike rider—until eventually, we wind up talking about school.

"I just don't know what the rest of the semester is going to look like without Richardson. Like who's going to finish teaching the class?" Mallory asks as she pushes her empty plate away. She hummed and moaned her appreciation with every bite she took of her coconut shrimp and cilantro lime rice. I'm sure it was all delicious, but I was too focused on her to taste any of it.

"The head of the department will take it over or they'll ask Dr. Brennan to come back from sabbatical. Either way, they'll have it sorted by the time break ends, so you don't have to worry about his leaving impacting your early graduation date."

She tilts her head to the side. "You're weirdly cavalier about this. Almost like you know something I don't." Instead of answering her, I pick up my glass and take a sip of water. Her eyes shine with suspicion and intrigue as she leans forward. "You *do* know something. Spill."

I set my glass back down, holding up my hands. "I don't know anything for certain, but there were rumors about them bringing in a team of equity consultants to teach workshops and assess certain professors' interactions with students from marginalized groups. Apparently, the department is making the workshops and assessments mandatory, and Richardson has been against them from the jump."

"So he quit because he was going to have to hear someone other than me tell him he's a racist, misogynistic asshole." She nods her head, lips pursed with understanding. "That tracks."

"Yeah, it does."

"Let's hope the rest of his cronies follow suit. The entire department needs to be cleaned out, to be honest, with the exception of a few people."

"Besides Dr. Wilson and Dr. Brennan, who would you keep?"

"No one," she deadpans.

"Damn." I place my hand on my chest, feigning hurt. "Not even your favorite TA?"

That wins me a giggle that's coupled with an eye roll. "Please, you're about to trade your slacks and button-ups for scrubs and sneakers. You won't remember a single person in that department in a few years."

The reminder that in just a few months we'll be going our separate ways, our act complete, our lives changed, eats at me. Chipping away at the joy I've been feeling since we landed.

"You really think I could forget you?" Once again I'm putting too much meaning into my words, layering in complicated emotion where there should be simplicity. Mallory stares at me, her eyes turning dark to match the intensity of my gaze.

"No." She shakes her head, looking for all the world like a woman fluent in the language of things left unsaid. The expression takes over her face, clinging to her sunlit features for long seconds before fading away and leaving a teasing smile that feels forced. "I mean, you never forget your first fake girlfriend, right?"

Like every one that came before it, this moment loses its potential for realness to humor, and for the first time in my life, I understand the frustration Mallory must have felt during our first library encounter when I kept making jokes to hide that our kiss had turned my world upside down.

"Right." I smile back, keeping my tone light. "You'll be a tough act to follow."

She cocks a sassy brow at me. "You planning on having more than one fake girlfriend in your life?"

"No, but you never know what might happen."

"I guess that's true. Well, if you ever find yourself in need of one, I'd be happy to reprise my role."

Now I'm the one arching a brow at her, surprised, and a little annoyed, that she can offer me this so easily when what I really want is the real thing. "You'll be too busy dominating corporate America to have time for those kinds of shenanigans."

Her nose wrinkles. "You got the busy part right, but I will not be working in corporate America." A shudder rolls through her body, shaking her shoulders, and she pulls a face. "There isn't enough money in the world to make me want to spend the rest of my life living in microaggression hell."

The vehemence of her response makes me realize I don't know anything about what she plans to do with her business degree. I'd heard her talk about going back to school to earn her MBA after she graduates next semester but that was about it. I should have known she wouldn't be taking the same path as other business majors whose only aspiration for life after college is securing a position as an investment banker.

"Well, what do you want to do after you graduate?"

As soon as I finish asking the question, her entire demeanor shifts. Her eyes turn bright and warm. Pools of starfire and pure gold staring back at me as she sits up a little straighter in her seat and smiles wide, showing off both of her dimples.

"I'm going to help Sloane start an interior design studio. She'll handle the design side of things, and I'll manage all the behind-the-scenes stuff that no one cares about but will make sure we're growing and scaling at the rate of our competitors. Sloane is creative and ambitious as hell, but she doesn't have a head for business operations which is where I'll come in. I'll probably end up doing the same thing for Eric and Nic when they start their construction company, but it'll be a few years before I have to worry about them."

She looks so happy talking about how she'll use her degrees to help the people she loves achieve their dreams, but I can't help but think about how she never mentioned what she hoped to accomplish for herself.

"And when you're done?"

Both of her brows fall together. "When I'm done?"

"When you're done helping everybody else get what they want, what are *you* going to do?" Her mouth opens, but no words come out. I'm not surprised that my question has stumped her. Mallory has spent the last few years making decisions for her life based on what she thought the people around her *might* want or need.

As far as I can tell, no one forced her to do that. The people closest to her are some of the most loving and understanding folks on the planet. They uplift each other, encouraging one another to go after their dreams, and it never even occurs to them to try to impose their own will and desires on the people they love.

Mallory could do anything she wanted, and they would cheer her on without a second's hesitation, but she's so used to anticipating their needs and putting them first, she doesn't realize it. Or at least she didn't until just now. I can see the question taking root, sprouts of ideas and possibilities shooting from every part of her brain.

In that moment, I envy her and her newly realized ability to decide for herself what she's going to do with her life. Eventually, joy overrides that feeling, turning envy into excitement born solely from the knowledge that nothing will be able to stop her from achieving whatever goal I just watched her set.

"You can do it," I say, pulling her out of her head and away from the spinning wheels of her brain that are probably plotting how to take over an entire industry.

She gives me a quizzical look, but there's warmth in her eyes that lets me know my words are appreciated. "You don't even know what I'm planning to do. Hell, I don't even know fully."

"Doesn't matter." I shrug. "Whatever it is, you'll do it, and you'll do it just like you do everything else: *well*."

"You're something else, you know that?"

"I might have heard that once or twice in my life," I say through a yawn that catches me completely off guard. Mallory's eyes go wide, and the concerned frown that tugs her lips down makes them look even more kissable.

"Oh, no, I'm keeping you from resting again, aren't I?"

"Again?"

"Yeah, I stole your bed last night, woke you up in the middle of the night, and now I've got you out here having dinner at the late, late hour of,"—she taps the screen on her phone checking the time— *"nine-thirty p.m.*, I think it might be too much excitement for an old man such as yourself."

She chuckles, and I shake my head. "You really had me thinking you cared for a second there, but no, you were just setting up for a bad joke."

"A bad joke? I'm offended."

"No, princess, I'm most definitely the injured party here."

"That's unfortunate," she sighs. "Because you know resilience tends to fade with age."

This time I can't help but laugh. "You know I'm not that much older than you right?"

She turned twenty at the end of October, and I turned twenty-two in December, so there's just a few years between us. I wonder if that matters to her at all after dating Trent.

"I know, I just like making fun of you."

I lift a brow. "Ah, so you do have a sense of humor."

"Of course, I'm actually very funny when I'm comfortable around a person."

My heart flips as my brain tries to process the meaning behind her words. The hidden potential soaks into my bones, under my skin where I've worked to keep my hope for our future under wraps.

"Oh." I clear my throat, pushing a response out past the lump forming there. "And I'm one of those people now?"

There's barely a second between my question and her response.

"Yes," she says. "You are."

I open my mouth, preparing to let the words I've been wanting to say for so long tumble out, but before I get the chance her phone rings.

Even from across the table, I can see that the caller is her mom, and I know that the likelihood of her not answering is negative zero.

Proving me right, Mallory gives me an apologetic look and picks the phone up. She slides back from the table and starts to speak, her voice fading away as she moves through the patio to a quieter spot, turning heads as she goes.

She doesn't seem to notice all the eyes on her. All the people taking in her beauty, admiring her graceful stride and the compelling power of her bone structure. Her lack of awareness only makes her that much more alluring.

And the longer you stare at her, the more it mocks you, laughing in your face for ever thinking you could have her.

31

MALLORY

The look on Chris' face at the end of our first dinner has stuck with me for the entire week. Between spending all day at the parks, riding rides, eating the most expensive theme park food known to man, and getting pictures with all the characters, we haven't had a lot of quiet moments, but every time we do, I find myself wanting to ask him what that look was about. When I lay in bed at night, I replay the entire dinner in my head, imagining what would have gone differently if I hadn't answered Mama's call.

She's called every day this week just to chat, and while I've been a bit exasperated by the whole thing, Chris hasn't been bothered. He's even talked to her a few times while I've waited in line for the bathroom, and when I told him he didn't have to do that, he said he didn't mind. The solemn look on his face reminded me that outside the scheduled calls with his dad and the occasional texts from his brother and sister, no one really checks on him.

I never realized how alone he was. How many gaps existed in his life that the small family we indoctrinated him into filled. Even Mama is trying to adopt him, calling him son and telling him not to spoil me too much while we're out here. When she called today, we were spreading out a blanket on one of the patches of grass in the middle of

Magic Kingdom so we could watch the firework show, and after she finished talking my ear off about some drama at Aunt Mary's church, she asked to speak to Chris. They chatted and laughed until I made him hang up with her because the show was about to start.

Now, he's sitting next to me with his shoulder brushing mine, bleeding heat into my skin. The air is cool, so his warmth is welcome. Even more welcome is the leather and earth scent of his skin mingling with the smell of fried dough and powdered sugar from the funnel cake he got for me that I've been too nervous to eat. Tonight is our last night in Florida. In the morning we'll get on a plane and head back to New Haven, and I'm afraid that nothing between us will have changed even though everything has for me.

"Thank you for this week," I say, leaning in close so he can hear me over the excited chatter of the kids around us.

"You don't have to thank me, princess." His eyes meet mine just as the first firework lights up the sky, the blue and pink and purple sparks reflected in his eyes, and the crowd gasps around us, marveling at what I'm sure must be a beautiful sight, but I can't take my eyes off of him. Clouds of conflicted emotion play across his features. He looks like he wants to say something else, and I hold my breath, willing him to do it. "Your smile is gift enough."

"It is a nice smile," I quip, too afraid to let this moment go on without any levity. Chris doesn't so much as crack a smile. Waves of intensity rolling off of him as he searches my face.

"It's more than nice, Mallory. Your smile is the thing I want most in the world. I spend every waking moment trying to find new ways to get you to give it to me. I wish for it on every shooting star and repeating number on a clock." My chest is tight, lungs begging for air while he reminds me of our first date when I told him all the wishes I used up trying to become the thing he's told me I am since the very beginning. Chris shifts on the blanket, angling his body towards me while one of his hands grips mine. Long fingers thread through mine until his fingertips are brushing my knuckles. "I'll probably spend the rest of my life wishing for it to always be mine."

Another wave of color explodes above us, absorbing the sound of my audible gasp. My ribs hurt from how hard my heart is thudding against them, threatening to crack them open and let all the feelings I've been hiding come flooding out. Forcing air through my lungs, I look down at our joined hands, mesmerized by how right his skin feels on mine. I want to tell him that he can have my smile whenever he wants. That he's the only person I want to give it to, but I have to be sure I understand what he's saying.

When I look back up, his face is just inches from mine, and we're sharing air. Exchanging quiet desire and hopeful exhalations with every expansion and contraction of our lungs.

"The rest of your life, huh?" I laugh, voice trembling. "That's a long time to be in a fake relationship."

He shakes his head, earnest eyes boring into mine as he finally says the thing I've been wanting him to say for months. "Not fake, princess. *Real.* Everything I feel for you, everything I want with you is real."

"Real," I repeat the word, tasting the possibility, savoring the potential, the reality of us.

"Is that something you could want?" Doubt plays over his features, and seeing him so afraid that I don't want him, pulls my answer from my throat before I have the chance to think.

"Yes," I whisper fiercely, nodding to emphasize my answer. "It's all I want, Chris."

Pops of color and explosions that lace the air with the smell of smoke and gunpowder begin to build towards a crescendo that seems to be swelling just for us. Chris leans in closer, and I want to, but I can't move. His other hand comes up, gliding up my arm and shoulder, up the column of my neck, over my pulse where his thumb rests as he grips my nape and urges me forward.

The largest, loudest burst of sparks we've seen so far, illuminate the lawn, and the crowd gasps, children screaming their delight while Chris' lips crash against mine. I'm stunned by the force of the kiss, by the delicious pressure of his fingertips digging into my skin, holding me to him like he's afraid I'll float away if he lets go. When my mouth starts moving, they tell him that I'm not going anywhere because his lips are anchors and every carnal swirl of our tongues is the knotting of a rope, tethering my soul to his.

A feral growl that comes straight from Chris' chest echoes in my ears as he breaks the kiss, sending us both plummeting back down to Earth from the dizzying heights of cloud nine. It's only then that I realize the fireworks have ended, that there's nothing but white smoke in the air and the fading chatter of the families vacating the area to head back to their hotels. The park doesn't close for a while, but suddenly it's the last place I want to be. Chris is staring at me, waiting patiently for words he already knows are going to come.

"Let's go back to the room."

Once the words hit the air, we both jump into action, leaving the park in a mad dash punctuated with random kisses that are half laughs, half moans. The drive back to the resort is a blur of streetlights and anxiety that's tampered by the constant presence of Chris' hand in mine. His thumb running over the space between my thumb and index finger with strokes that soothe parts of me I haven't had to worry about in a long time. But once we get to my room, with my bed in front of me and Chris at my back, all of it comes flooding back.

My feet are planted firmly on the ground, and I'm blocking Chris from moving into the room any further, so he walks around me. Moving with the kind of slow precision that speaks of his awareness of my past and calms my racing pulse, reminding me I'm safe with him.

He reaches for me, both of his hands coming up and turning over so his palms are facing me. A silent offer. An extension of connection. A reminder that I'm the one in control. I take a step forward, placing my hands in his, my heart swelling when relief shines in his eyes. He flexes his fingers, giving mine a gentle squeeze, pulling me out of my head and back into the moment with him the way he did the first time we kissed.

"Nothing has to happen tonight," he says, and I know he means it. The air of calmness around him assures me of that, but the fire burning just inside the corners of his eyes belies the coolness in his voice. It tells me that somewhere under the tranquil facade I suspect he's putting forth just for me is a man starving for contact. For release. For me.

And that knowledge has my blood racing through my veins, abandoning all of my extremities and heading straight for my clit. Pulsing inside the greedy, swollen bundle of nerves that pounds out my desire in a steady rhythm that only Chris can hear.

"I know, but I want it to." My mouth is dry, voice raspy with fear and desire. "I think I'm ready."

Chris laughs, and I'm shocked by the dark, velvet sound and the way making the sound has forced his lips back, away from his teeth that look sharp and dangerous and sexy as hell because they're bared for me.

"Thinking isn't the same thing as knowing, princess."

I can't help myself, I pry one of my hands out of his. Raising it to his face and running one shaky thumb over his lips. My fingertip brushes over his top teeth, and a low growl rumbles from his chest, sending a rush of liquid arousal from my core to the boy shorts I'm wearing. What started out as a trickle of desire turns into a full-blown flood when he opens his mouth and pulls my finger into it, biting down gently at first and then harder when I moan at the sensation that's pain and pleasure wrapped into one.

His eyes glow, a wildfire roasting chestnuts. Turning shiny brown husks into the charred ashes of control that he seems hellbent on holding on to even though it's slipping through his fingertips. He drops my other hand and places his free one on my waist, gripping it tight. Then he brings the other one up to grip my wrist. Slowly, he pulls my thumb out of his mouth, letting his teeth graze over my skin before turning my hand over and placing a kiss into the center of my palm.

That kiss starts a trail up my arm that forces me to move closer to him the higher up he goes until finally my chest is brushing against his and he's leaning down to take my mouth again. I push up on my tiptoes, wrapping my arms around his neck to deepen the kiss, to show him I'm sure about wanting this.

"I want you," I whisper against his lips while I'm in the process of trying to scale his body. His hands snake around my waist, over the curve of my ass where he squeezes both cheeks hard before lifting me off the ground completely. I'm shocked by how easily he holds me up, not even a hint of strain in his muscles as he urges me to wrap my legs around him. I do it immediately, moaning into his mouth while he releases another decadent growl. "I've always wanted you, Chris. I've never been more sure about anything, about anyone, in my entire life."

Those words cause something to snap inside him because as soon as they hit the air, we're moving towards the bed in the center of the room. He lowers us down slowly, and even though I know that it's him, even though I know that I'm safe, the second I feel the mattress at my back and the weight of him at my front, a fierce wave of panic washes over me.

"*Wait.*"

He pulls back immediately, untangling himself from me and standing up in the space of a heartbeat. Even with my heart in my throat, and the confusing effects of being aroused and afraid at the same time, I manage to feel bad for him. There's an impressive erection tenting his jeans and hunger shining bright from his dilated pupils caused by the words I spoke just seconds ago in hopes of getting this exact reaction from him, and now I'm telling him to slow down.

I sit up, pulling my legs underneath me. "I'm sorry."

"*Don't apologize.*" Chris drops down on his haunches, studying my face. "What happened? Did I hurt you? Was I moving too fast?"

"No." I shake my head wildly, unable to live with the tortured look on his face. "You didn't hurt me. I just…" I blink away frustrated tears, hating how even in this moment it feels like Trent is here, stealing something else from me. "That position just isn't….I can't do it. I'm sorry. I thought I was ready, but I just can't do *that*."

"Stop apologizing, baby. I already told you nothing has to happen tonight."

"But I want it too." I'm whining, which takes the sexiness of this moment down another degree. Or ten. Chris stares, patiently waiting for me to make my point. I pull my hands into my lap and start picking at my cuticles while I wait for the words to come. "That time with Trent…it was my first time."

"I know."

Right. I told him that when I spent the night in his home, in his bed.

"It was my only time." Finally drawing my eyes away from my hands, I glance at him, trying to gauge his reaction. He doesn't seem surprised. "You already knew that, huh?"

"I figured as much. Everyone who knows you knows school is your top priority."

"It's also become an excuse to stop living. After everything that happened, I just wanted something I could control. Because that's what I felt like he took from me. My power over my life, my sexuality, my desire. It's like it's all still there in that dirty ass dorm room, and I want it back."

"Your life is yours, Mallory. You've already proven you can make it whatever you want it to be. No one could have come out of what you went through completely unscathed, but you picked up the pieces and built something beautiful out of the destruction."

"And what about the rest of it? I haven't been in a relationship in years. I can't stand to have you lay on top of me for half of a second. Nothing about that sounds like a woman ready to take control of her sex life."

Chris' eyebrows knit together. "Taking control of your sex life means knowing what you like during sex and what you don't like. The only thing this moment has taught us is that you don't feel secure being pinned down. Now, that can change or it can stay the same, but either way, the power is in knowing. In acknowledging that limit and seeking different ways to find pleasure while still respecting it."

"Different ways?"

My inexperience is showing, and I'm well aware of it but I can't find it in me to be ashamed. All of my experiences with Trent prior to that night either happened with me on my knees or on my back. There was never time to explore, to learn, to figure out if I liked anything different. Chris nods, understanding shining in his eyes as he scoots back from the edge of the bed a bit.

"Stand up, princess." I slide off the bed, pulling in a deep breath as the sight of him on his knees in front of me threatens to steal every bit of air from my lungs. He gazes up at me, ocher eyes serious and laced with desire. "You've said several times that you want this, is that still true?"

I nod, biting my lip. "Yes, but I don't know if I'm ready for…" Trailing off feels silly, childish, but saying the word feels hard. Chris inclines his head, acknowledging my unspoken request.

"We'll go as slow as you like. Whatever feels good to you is what we'll do."

"Okay." I'm surprised I can get the one word out past the lust clogging my throat.

"Good." Chris breathes, hungry eyes roving over my features. "Now tell me exactly what you want out of tonight, princess. You're in charge."

Heat floods my cheeks, and I feel suddenly shy in the face of his expectant gaze. "I don't…I don't know."

"Yes, you do, and you're going to say it."

The words come out in a soft growl, reminding me of the sound he made when he took a bite of his burger at Curly's that first night and sparking a request I'm too scared to speak. Chris waits quietly for my answer, and after a few seconds tick by, I decide to go with something simple, something safe.

"I want you to touch me."

"Where, baby?" He inches closer, shuffling on his knees until his face is just inches from my stomach. My dress rippling because of the warm puffs of air leaving his lips. "Take your hands and show me where you want mine to go."

Feeling self-conscious and more than a little turned on, I lift my hands from my sides and bring them up to my chest. Allowing my fingertips to caress the tops of my breasts and running them down my stomach. Chris tracks my movements with his eyes, and as my hands approach the apex of my thighs, fingers cupping my soaked sex through layers of fabric, he licks his lips.

Emboldened by his reaction, I let one hand stroke lazily at my throbbing pussy while the other comes back up to cup one of my breasts and pinches my nipple. A sharp gasp falls from my lips, and Chris' dark gaze moves to my face, holding my eyes.

"Am I free to do that now?"

I'm nodding before he's even finished asking the question. "Yes, please."

Even though he's on the ground, he has no trouble reaching my chest, and his palms are rough against my smooth skin as they follow the trail from my chest to my core, which is throbbing incessantly for him. When I was touching myself for him, it felt like it took me forever to get from one place to the other, but Chris does it in record time, leaving me hungry for more.

I let out a shaky exhale. *"Chris."*

"Would you like more, princess? Can I taste you?"

"Yes, please."

He reaches for me, but just before his hands land at the backs of my thighs he looks up at me and says, "Tell me if it's too much, and I'll stop, okay?"

"Okay."

Then he's gripping my legs, pulling me into him so he can bury his face between my thighs. While he breathes in a lungful of my scent, his hands move up my torso, taking the thin cotton of my dress with them. The fabric skates up my sides and suddenly the only thing I want is to be bared to him, so I reach down and pull it up over my head, tossing it to the side.

Chris must have known that I wasn't wearing a bra, he had to have felt it when he caressed my breast just moments ago, but he still looks absolutely feral at the sight of my bare breasts, heavy and swollen, swinging from the force of my throw.

His eyes roll into the back of his head for a second as another dark, guttural sound climbs from his chest and spills into the room. Turning the air thick with lust. When his irises are visible again, there are endless rings of gold and stardust. Swirling clouds of wonder and desire. Hope and fear. Disbelief and joy.

"You're beautiful," he whispers, fingers going to the waistband of the biker shorts I put on whenever I wear a dress or skirt because chafed thighs are not a good look. He pulls them down my legs, and I use his shoulders as support while I step out of them. Now, I'm in nothing but my soaked panties, heart pounding in my chest as his eyes sweep over me like he's trying to memorize every one of my curves. "So fucking beautiful."

"Thank you."

"I should be thanking you."

I run my hands over his head, and he makes a satisfied noise in the back of his throat when I grip his curls tight. "I can think of one thing I'd be happy to accept as a token of your gratitude."

Amusement shines in his eyes. "Just one? We can do better than that, don't you think?"

"Well—" I start, but he's already making short work of my underwear, pulling them down my legs slowly with a determined smirk on his face.

"I don't have a specific number in mind, but I know one won't be enough for you." He takes my left leg and hikes it up on his shoulder. His arm is looped around my thigh with his fingers splayed across my back for support while the other starts to trail up my right leg. "What do you think will be enough, princess? Five?"

He leans forward and places a kiss on the inside of my thigh, flicking his eyes up to me to see my reaction. I'm entranced, too turned on by the thought of him wringing pleasure from my body to contemplate whether I could actually come that many times in one night.

"Ten?" Another kiss, this one wet and hot and only a few millimeters away from my clit. My hips jerk forward, and I have to place my hands back in his hair to find my balance. When his fingers start to graze my pussy lips, I'm glad I did. "That might be a bit excessive," he sighs against my skin, sounding like he's disappointed.

"*Chris.*"

I can feel my arousal slipping out of me. In seconds it'll be coating my thighs, spilling out onto the places where his lips and fingers are teasing me. I rock my hips forward, hoping to make contact with some part of him that can give me the pleasure I so desperately need. My blood is on fire, and there's a heavy, low pressure in the pit of my stomach that's aching for him, for a release only he can bring me to.

"I know, baby. I can smell how turned on you are." To emphasize his point he runs his nose over my sex, flared nostrils taking in all of my scent as they move over my engorged folds. "You smell even better here, Mallory. There's no jasmine or citrus, just you."

His words distract me from his actions, from the feel of his thick fingers spreading my pussy open to ensure the first stroke of his tongue goes directly to my clit, and as my eyes roll back into my head, my back arching, forcing my hips forward and into his greedy mouth, I wonder if that was his intent. To keep me from getting too far into my head while he touched me in places that no one has since…

"That's right, princess." He murmurs against my sex, tongue still stroking relentlessly into me while I grind against him. "Fuck my face. Let go, baby. I've got you."

And he does. He's supporting the weight of my entire body while I writhe against him. Broad shoulders unyielding, rough fingertips firm despite the wildness of my movements as I follow the rhythm he's setting with his tongue. I'm so far gone, so lost to the sensation of heedless pleasure zipping up and down my spine, I don't register his fingers circling my entrance until he pulls back with the question in his eyes.

"Yes," I moan, certain the fullness his fingers will provide is the exact thing I need to go over the edge. "Yes, Chris." I yank his head back to my body roughly, and he groans his approval, rewarding me with a slow advance of his middle finger into my core.

In that moment everything stops. My body goes still, muscles tensing against the intrusion. Chris tries to pull back, and I know he wants to see my face to check on me, but I can't look at him. I don't want to see the concern or pity or whatever else in his eyes, I just want to feel this. To process the sensation of a fullness that I welcomed, that I wanted.

"I'm fine," I whimper into the air. "Please don't stop."

He hesitates but only for a second, and I appreciate him trusting me to know myself and what I want in this moment. He keeps moving forward, and my walls clench around him, sucking him into the heat of my body and gripping at him desperately when he starts to retreat.

All of the tension melts from my muscles as he repeats the motion, drilling in and out of me slowly, building unbearable pressure up to unimaginable heights while my pussy leaks juices all around him.

"It's not enough," I whine. "Give me another one. I need another one."

On his next advance, the pressure in my core is doubled as my body stretches to accommodate both his middle and ring finger. Chris twists his hand, screwing his fingers into me while I moan and rock against his face. When he's sure I'm fine with the addition, he adds his tongue back into the mix. Lapping at my cunt with renewed enthusiasm until my orgasm sweeps over me, bowing my back and pulling a scream from my throat while Chris licks up every single drop of my satisfaction with his tongue.

My chest is still rising and falling violently when he pulls back, face coated in my juices and stretched with a self-congratulatory smile. "You're incredible."

"All I did was come." I'm blushing and my leg shakes as he lowers my foot to the floor. I take a few steps back, grateful when the edge of the bed meets the back of my knees, and collapse. I stretch out on my side, so I can see him. Chris stands, bending over to pick up my dress and then striding over to me. His erection is even more prominent now, but he takes great care to keep it from touching me as he leans over the bed and plants a kiss on my lips.

"That's all you had to do. Seeing you like that? Tasting you, touching you? I didn't know it could be like that with anyone." That look of wonder is back in his eyes, and it has warmth spreading through my chest and the rest of my body as I sit up and slip the dress back over my head. When I'm done, I grab a fistful of his shirt and pull him down onto the bed. He lands on his side and props his head up on his hand, smiling at me.

"That's what I thought the first time you kissed me," I whisper against his lips, sliding closer to him.

"Really? You didn't seem moved by that kiss at all, meanwhile, my entire world was turned upside down."

My mouth drops, and I can't tell if I'm more shocked that his world was turned upside down by our kiss or that he couldn't tell mine was as well. "What? I couldn't even breathe when you were walking over to me. You had to tell me to! How could you not think I was affected?"

He shrugs. "I just thought you were nervous about completing the dare in general, not completing it with me."

"No, it was you. Sloane could have dared me to call Mama and tell her I was dropping out of school, and I would have been less nervous."

"Somehow I doubt that."

"Okay, you might be right, but I was nervous about kissing you. And then when our lips met, it just felt…." There are a million words I could use to describe the feeling I got that day, the feeling I still get when he kisses me, but it's all too big for this moment in our burgeoning relationship. I don't want to scare him. "Right. It just felt right."

He nods. "Yeah, that's how it felt for me too."

His confession sends a flood of emotions through me, and I lean forward and kiss him. Taking his lips in a sweet pressing of mouths that say things I can't yet. When I pull back, I think he understands, and my heart flutters.

"Are we really going to do this?"

Both of his brows fall together. "I thought we already established that we were?"

"We did. I just wanted to make sure that you were sure."

"Have I said or done anything tonight to give you the impression that I wasn't?"

I bite my lip, wondering if we're venturing off into territory that might ruin our night. "Not tonight, no, but you have said before that you didn't have time for relationships. That's why you haven't been in one since Giselle."

Chris sets his hand on my waist, pulling me closer to him. He doesn't look upset, just thoughtful, like he's trying to determine how much he wants to say. "After Giselle and I broke up, I did decide a relationship wasn't something I needed. Part of that was because I didn't want anything to get in the way of my goals, and the other part was being afraid of having something good and having it snatched away from me."

He told me this the other day when he finally revealed he'd told his dad about us and gotten a surprisingly good reaction from him. Apparently, his fear of having the good things in his life taken away because they didn't fit his dad's vision for his life had come up in conversation. I'd wondered how he managed to conjure up the emotions necessary to make his fears feel real to his dad, but now I think I know.

"Do those reasons still stand?"

"I'm still afraid of having good things taken away from me, yeah, but I'll do any and everything in my power to keep them. *To keep you.*" He lifts a brow, answering the question I didn't ask. "I don't know what a relationship with any other woman would have looked like, princess, but this thing between us is too good to ever be considered a distraction or a hindrance to my goals, especially when all of them include you now."

I open my mouth to speak, but no words come out, which is fine because I don't think there's a single word in the English language that will accurately convey the way hearing him say that his goals now include me makes me feel.

Chris laughs. "You okay?"

"Yes." I chirp, head bobbing up and down. "I'm fine."

32

CHRIS

Mallory looked anything but fine when I said those words. Her eyes stretched comically wide, her throat constricted, the muscles working to hold in words I hoped weren't something along the lines of *'are you crazy?'* or *'you are definitely moving too fast.'*

I couldn't decide which reaction was more likely before she excused herself to go to the bathroom and freshen up, and now I'm sitting at the head of her bed wondering if I am, in fact, crazy and moving too fast. I was only answering her questions, being honest with her about the way I felt while reassuring her that I had all the space in my life for her, for us, but I should have pulled back a little. She hasn't done this before, and honestly, neither have I.

What's happening between me and Mallory is different from anything I've ever had with anyone. The puppy love I had with Giselle. The casual hookups with girls like Alisha. None of it had ever come close to this, and I would bet my entire trust fund that this is how Dad felt about Mom. Despite what he said about Grandpa wanting their union more than him, it must have been.

He must have recognized that I was struck by the same reckless, desperate emotion that pushed him to put a ring on her finger and announce their union to everyone without his father's approval.

I'm glad I didn't have to go to such lengths to prove I was serious about Mallory. I mean, I wouldn't have been opposed to being tied to her in such a permanent way, but I know she's not ready for that, and I honestly would never want to go into something as life-changing as marriage to prove a point or appease someone else.

Luckily, I don't have to worry about any of that now.

Dad has accepted the relationship. Mallory knows how I feel about her, and by some miracle, she feels the same way. Everything is right with the world, and I can't remember a time when I felt as happy as I do right now.

The bathroom door opens and Mallory emerges, looking significantly calmer. She smiles at me and saunters over to the bed. The hem of her dress rides up her thighs with every step, inching up even more as she lifts one leg and climbs on the bed to sit between my legs. Her hair tickles my nose as she leans back on me, resting her head on my chest.

I press a kiss to her temple, and she sighs happily. "You good?"

"Yeah, you?"

"Perfect. I don't think I've ever been this happy to be someone's boyfriend."

She glances back at me. Scrunching up her nose and making that face she always does when she's trying to make a joke. "Boyfriend? You're my boyfriend now?"

"Unless I misunderstood what happened during the fireworks show, yes."

"No, I might be the one who's confused. I don't think I heard you ask me out."

"Mallory," I say, tone serious even though I want to smile. I love when she's happy like this, comfortable enough to crack jokes and laugh, even at herself.

"Christopher." She mocks me, dropping her voice several octaves and copying my inflection.

"You need a formal request to be my girlfriend even after I've had my face buried in your pussy?"

"Yes, I do actually because giving excellent head doesn't automatically get you the role. I might have let it slide if you had given me the five orgasms you promised, but…." She lets the sentence trail off and shrugs like her silence has made the point for her.

"Excellent point, Ms. Kent." I smile when she rolls her eyes. "Do I need to get down on one knee or will the question suffice?"

"The question should be more than enough, Dr. Johnson."

"Fine." I wrap an arm around her middle, pulling her closer to me. She gasps when I lean down and nuzzle into her neck, kissing and licking the spot where her scent is strongest before dragging my lips up to her ear. "Mallory Kent, will you please do me the honor of being my girlfriend? For real this time?"

A shiver rolls through her, no doubt inspired by the dark silk of my voice, but when she speaks her voice is even, unaffected. "Hmm, I don't know. I think I might have to explore some other op—" The words are cut off by shrill laughter as I tickle her sides and stomach. She squirms, her hands flailing wildly. "Okay! Okay! Chris, I give."

Her surrender causes me to pause instantly, but it takes her several minutes to stop wheezing. By the time she calms down, my cheeks hurt from smiling and laughing along with her. Her joy permeates the room, piercing everything around it including me, and I lean down to kiss her just because I can.

The kiss grows deeper than I intended it to, and it's not long before Mallory is scrambling up off of the bed and climbing into my lap. My hands bracket her waist, trying to keep her from coming into contact with my erection. I've been brutally hard all night long, swollen past the point of discomfort, and moving into some new place where the steady stream of precum leaking from my dick is a welcome relief even though it's soaking through my briefs.

She reaches down, moving my hands and gasping when she feels my reaction to her. We both freeze, but she's the one who breaks the kiss to look down between us. Her dress is covering most of the view, so she pulls it up around her waist, showing me a sight that's likely to drive me insane.

After I ate her out earlier, she didn't put her underwear back on, so there's nothing between her pussy and the dark denim of my jeans. Neatly trimmed tufts of soft, black hair cover her mound, but I can tell by the way she's sitting that her folds are spread over me. Her clit nestled against the flared tip of a dick that's weeping for her, desperate to be inside her even though I know it won't happen tonight.

She's not ready, and I respect that. *I will always respect that.*

But damn if the sight of her inspecting us doesn't make it hard.

"Princess." Her eyes are wild when they meet mine. They match the storm raging inside of me. "We can stop. I can go. I don't want you to feel like this means you have to do something you don't want to."

"No, I—" I watch her top teeth sink into the lushness of her bottom lip. "I'm not ready for that yet, but I don't want you to go. I want more, but not if it means you're going to be uncomfortable."

"Your desire will never make me uncomfortable."

"But doesn't it hurt when you get like this"—she rocks her hips against me, and I groan—"and you don't come?"

"Yeah." I blow out a harsh breath. "It does."

"Then me wanting us to do anything else will make you uncomfortable."

I don't know how she manages to be sexy and logical at the same time, but it only adds to her appeal. My dick twitches underneath her, and her eyes go wide as she lifts up and backs away, settling on the mattress across from me with her legs stretched out.

"I'm sorry. I didn't—"

"No." She shakes her head, eyes on the tent in my jeans. "No, I'm okay. I just…can you do that again? I want to see."

"Princess." The word comes out harsher than I intend it to, but I can't help it. I know that if I pull my dick out in front of her, we'll be cruising into dangerous, potentially triggering territory for her, and I don't want that. "I don't think that's a good idea."

"Please, Chris." She blinks up at me through those long lashes, but it's her legs that put a crack in my resolve. They're opening, slowly, treating me to a view of her pussy, the lips coated in her essence, while one of her hands slips down her thigh. "I just want to see."

I never thought I'd meet a person I couldn't say no to, but as I undo my pants and pull my dick out, I realize I finally have. Mallory Kent could ask me for the moon, and I'd find a way to get it for her. She could ask me for the stars, and I'd steal them from the sky. She could ask for my heart, and, well….she already has that. She just doesn't know it yet.

Quick as a flash, her tongue moves over her lips, and she gives me a look that promises one day soon, she's going to devour me. That promise, that thinly veiled, way too welcome, threat calls to the most primal part of me. The part that wants to be devoured and do the devouring. The part that has been denied the joy of being fully unleashed because I knew none of my other partners would want what I'm going to give Mallory. I already know how it will be with us. I can tell by the glint in her eyes and the dents she's leaving in her own lip at the sight of me.

I grip my dick roughly, dragging my hand from the root to the tip to spread the precum that's pooled at my base around. Mallory hisses, and I groan, the sound causing my dick to twitch again.

"Fuck," she moans, sitting up like she's going to come closer. "That's so fucking sexy."

"Stay. There." It's a struggle to get the words past my lips. I'm on the edge. Hanging on to the last shred of my control by a thread that will snap if she moves an inch. Her entire body goes still, worry stamped across her face, and I push out another breath, calming myself so I can reassure her. "You're safe with me, princess, but I'm…." I shake my head. Putting this feeling into words is impossible. "I just need you to stay there, okay? Touch yourself for me. Show me how you play with that pretty little pussy when no one's around."

Her fingers are at her clit now, swirling around the swollen bud. She's so wet I can hear it, see it with my own eyes. I lick my lips, tasting that same nectar on my skin, as my fist pumps harder, coaxing my release forward. Mallory doesn't take her eyes off of me, her busy hand moving in time with mine, her hips rocking as the muscles in her thighs tighten.

"That's it, princess. Does it feel good, baby?"

"So good," she murmurs, head lolling to one side. "I want to see you come, Chris. Go faster."

She's greedy and demanding. Beautiful and dangerous. And mine. All fucking mine, so I do as she asks. The increase in my speed causes my balls to draw up. A familiar tingling sensation originating in the base of my spine then climbing higher and higher, attracted to the throaty, pleasure-laced sounds spilling from Mallory as she works herself into a frenzy.

Her legs are spread wide now, both feet planted firmly on the mattress while she lays back with her eyes squeezed shut. She's close. I can tell by the way her legs jerk every time her fingers hit the right spot, so I move even faster. Twisting my wrist, running my thumb over the weeping slit in the center of my tip with every swipe until the sparks burning up my spine threaten to steal my breath.

Mallory arches up off of the mattress, her eyes flying open and finding mine just as her orgasm descends. It washes over her like a wave in reverse, starting at her toes and traveling up her thighs, caressing her stomach and breasts, laving at the base of her throat where a decadent whisper makes its escape.

"*Chris.*"

It's my name on her lips that does me in. It pulls an impossible, animal-like growl from my loins up through my chest as ropes of white, hot cum coat my fingers, turning them into a sticky mess that, despite the two orgasms she just had, she looks turned on by. Our pants fill the room for long minutes, until I finally find the strength to get up and drag myself to her bathroom to clean up.

When I emerge, fully clothed once again and more satisfied than I've been in months, Mallory is still stretched across the bed. Her dress yanked up over her hips, her hand still resting lazily against her sex.

She mumbles incoherently as I pick up her hand and wipe it off with the warm washcloth I brought from the bathroom, and then she moans when I take the same rag and wipe off the insides of her thighs and the warm softness at the center of her body.

Once I'm done, I pull her dress back down and take the washcloth back to the bathroom. She's sitting up when I come back out, half-lidded eyes dancing happily over my frame as she stretches and yawns. I check my watch. It's after midnight, and we have to be up early to fly back to New Haven.

"I should go." Leaving her is the last thing I want to do, but I don't want to push her too hard. She's already given so much of herself to me tonight, I don't want to ask for anymore.

Mallory pushes herself off the bed and crosses the room, wrapping her arms around me once she's in front of me. "You don't have to."

"I want to give you some space to rest and process everything that's happened. You can't figure out how you feel about things if I'm right here in your face."

"Chris, I'm going to sleep. I'm not about to be figuring out how I feel about anything besides leaving this mattress behind." She leans back and pushes her lips out, using the power of a pout I can't resist. "Stay, *please*. Hold me. Kiss me. Rub my back until I fall asleep. I promise I'm still going to want us in the morning, nothing is going to change my mind about that, especially not time away from you."

She seems so certain, so sure about us, that I can't even bring myself to argue. I'm nodding before I even realize it. She grabs my hand and leads me back to the bed, over to the side that we both seem to favor.

"Get comfortable. I'm going to go take a quick shower."

I arch a brow. "You're very bossy, you know that, princess?"

"I'm royalty, Christopher," she says in a fake posh accent as she backs towards the bathroom door. "Whatever did you expect?"

The door closes behind her, and I do exactly as she says and get comfortable. I slip out of my pants and shirt, and fold them up neatly. As I'm crossing the room to put them in the chair across from the bed, my phone falls out of my pocket. I lean down to pick it up and see a text from my father lighting up the screen. Dad never texts me, so I open it immediately, knowing inherently that it's about the favor I called in.

> Dad: Was able to dig up some information on this Trent Davis character. He had quite a few complaints on him at UNC, one as recent as last year before he came back to New Haven. Sent all the info to the DA, Charles Butler. He's a former patient of mine, so I trust that he'll make sure it's handled correctly. In the meantime, tell your student to seek out some counseling and call the cops if he ever contacts her again.

Telling my dad Trent had been involved with one of my students was a risky, but necessary, lie that had just paid off. After Mallory told me everything that he did to her, I couldn't live with knowing he was out there, able to hurt more women, but I couldn't break my promise to keep her secret. So I spun a web of lies and weaved them in with the truths I knew for sure: Trent Davis is a predator who hurts women, and he needs to be in jail.

Initially, Dad wondered why I was so concerned about something that didn't have anything to do with me. He wanted to know how I even knew about Trent, so I made up a lie about a student disclosing to me and he bought it. I could hear the pride in his voice when I asked him for his help. Of course, I didn't ask *him* to dig up any information on Trent because I didn't want any of his private investigator goons that close to someone who hurt Mallory. I wanted him to pass the name along to his contacts and have them do the case building, but I guess I'll have to take this win.

He didn't mention Mallory in his text, which means they must not have made the connection. I breathe a sigh of relief, thankful that I was able to keep Mallory safe without betraying the trust I've worked so hard to earn. With my heart lighter than it's been in a long time, I text Dad back and thank him then get in bed to wait for my princess to come lay down.

It's not long before she's climbing in bed beside me, a cloud of jasmine and lush softness surrounding me as she weaves her legs through mine and throws her arm over my stomach like she's done this exact thing every night for a lifetime.

Within moments of settling in beside me, her breathing starts to even out. I listen to the sound, allowing it to lull me to sleep. And when I wake in the morning to the sound of my alarm and Mallory's soft snoring, I realize that for the first time in forever, I slept through the night.

No nightmares.

No strangled cries from my mother's ghost.

Just the peaceful perfection of a heart that's finally found its home.

33

MALLORY

Hot oil sizzles loudly as I move the pan I used to fry chicken to the back eye of Chris' stove top and place the last batch of wings in the paper towel covered bowl sitting on the counter next to Eric's macaroni. Mama went out of town this weekend, on a trip to Atlantic City with Aunt Mary and some of her friends from church, so we decided to make Sunday dinner ourselves.

Everyone was supposed to have an assigned dish, but Eric and I ended up making almost everything while Chris and Sloane played the 'my mama never taught me how to cook' card. Even Nic, who spent just as much time in Mama's kitchen as me and Eric, flaked out on us, claiming he was more suited for cleanup than cooking before settling in on the couch and turning on the TV. I didn't mind being left in the kitchen with Eric, though, because it gave us some rare one-on-one time.

Since Chris and I came back from Disney a few weeks ago, we've been joined at the hip. I've spent more time at his apartment than I have in my own room, disappearing into the same bubble of happiness that absorbed Eric when him and Sloane got together. It's nice existing there, especially with Chris and his lips and hands that know how to make me forget everything including my own name, but I missed my brother.

Our twin bond doesn't need much maintenance. Even though we never have, I've always known we could go days or weeks without seeing each other, and nothing between us would change. That suspicion was proved to be correct when we took over Chris' kitchen, playing music loudly, laughing and joking, and reminiscing over our childhood days when Mama used to make us both sit at the table in the kitchen and clean greens with damp dishcloths. We always divided the stack and raced to see who could finish first.

Back then we were just childish, competitive kids and now we're two adults in serious relationships with people we could see ourselves spending forever with. Instead of turning green cleaning into a competition, we took our time. Standing side by side at the counter with our backs turned to the living room, teasing each other about who was more obsessed with their significant other. I insisted that it was him, and he was adamant that it was me.

Neither of us would admit that we're both sprung, but it was evident in the way we couldn't keep ourselves from starting at Chris and Sloane while we were supposed to be tending to the several different pots and pans we had going in the oven and the stove. Somehow we managed to pull it all off without anything getting burnt. A fact I'm more than grateful for as Chris sits the plate he fixed for me down on the table and takes his seat beside me.

I look over at him, an impossibly large smile stretching my lips. "Thanks."

"Anytime, princess."

Nic makes a gagging sound in the back of his throat and pulls a face when I glare at him. He's been like this all semester. Cranky, bordering on bitter when all of us are together. Most days I don't pay him any attention because I know Chris and I being together has changed the dynamic of the group, and it's possible he feels left out. Before we were together, Nic and I were the perpetually single ones. Now, he's all on his own which, speaking as someone who used to be a fifth wheel all the time, I know can't feel good. I just wish he'd get laid, or take any one of the girls he's always texting seriously, so he can be happy like the rest of us.

After a quick blessing of the food, we all dig in. I try not to focus on the sounds Chris makes as he eats because they're downright sinful, and the last thing I want to be right now is turned on. Still, I can't help but be tuned into him. The way the muscles in his jaw move as he chews, the hum of satisfaction that echoes in the back of his throat as he swallows. The flash of sharp, white teeth that, just a few hours ago, were grazing over my clit.

"Why aren't you eating, Mal?"

When I drag my gaze from my untouched plate to Sloane's face, she flashes me a knowing smile and takes another bite of her macaroni. Heat floods my cheeks as every man at the table, including my brother, looks up at me. I can only bring myself to look at one of them: the man responsible for my distraction. And he's got his eyes stretched wide, feigning innocence while he fights back a smile.

"Everything okay?"

"Yep," I say far too brightly, finally bringing a forkful of candied yams to my lips. Everyone stares awkwardly at me while I chew, so I force myself to swallow and say something else. Anything else, really, besides the fact that listening to Chris eat food I cooked reminds me of the sounds he makes when he feasts on me. "I was just thinking about exams."

Both Chris and Sloane look away, their faces telling me everything I need to know about what they think about my lie. Eric rolls his eyes. "Mal, exams don't start for another two weeks. You've gotta chill out."

"I think this is her version of chill, E," Nic says, cleaning off a chicken bone. "This time last semester she was living in the library. We didn't see her until she needed us to move all her shit out of her dorm."

He's not lying. Final exams usually send me into a tailspin. I'd spend weeks at a time in the library, my head tucked into books I'd already memorized because there was nothing else in my life I wanted to give my attention to. Now it's split between Chris and school. A combination that works surprisingly well since all the time we spend without his head between my legs is dedicated to studying.

"Well that won't be the case this semester," I say proudly. "Chris has promised to help me pack up all of my stuff, and I'm already ahead of schedule as far as studying goes."

"A study schedule." Nic shakes his head. "Sometimes I forget how much of a nerd you are."

"Some people just like to be prepared, Dominic," Sloane says.

Nic cuts his eye at her, an amused glare turning them into slits. "And some people know the difference between a joke and an insult, Sloane."

"Don't you two start." This from Eric who's pinching the bridge of his nose like he feels a headache coming on. There will be plenty of headaches in his future if he actually does plan to marry Sloane after graduation. Her and Nic just don't get along, and a ring on her finger won't change that.

Chris glances at me, a smile playing on his lips because he knows this whole conversation could have been avoided if I would have crafted my lie a bit differently. I hold his gaze for half a second and then drop it, so I can look at his hand, which is now resting on my thigh. I swallow hard, panicked desire clogging my throat and causing my eyes to flare.

He flexes his fingers, making the ones gripping the inside of my thigh dig into the tender skin. I squirm in my seat, so lost in calculating the distance between his pinky finger and my throbbing pussy I don't hear the question Eric directs at Chris, who not only hears it but begins to answer without a moment's hesitation.

I have to force myself to concentrate on the conversation, wading through the words that make up Chris' answer to determine what the question was. Judging by his repeated mention of MUSC, Harvard, and move-in dates, I can only assume Eric asked about his plans after graduation. My heart sinks as I watch joy line Chris' features. He's so excited about this next step in his life, and I'm happy for him, but I'm sad about what it means for us.

We've only just gotten started in this thing that's proven to be better than anything I could have ever dreamed of, and in August it'll all be changing. Sure, we'll be in the same state if he ends up going to

MUSC like he's planned, but no matter where he goes the distance and the demands of both of our busy schedules will make it nearly impossible for us to see each other. For all we know, this last part of the semester and summer break might be all the time we have left together.

My heart revolts against that thought. Fighting to reject the idea that Chris and I are coming to an end when we've just really gotten our start.

But no matter how hard I fight to free myself from the realization and the heart-rending bubble of sadness it has blooming in my chest, I can't get out from under it. It sticks with me through the rest of dinner and cleanup, through the solemn goodbyes I give to everyone as they leave. Through the redundant wiping down of already clean countertops while Chris wraps up a phone call with his sister on the couch.

Even with my back turned to him, I can feel his eyes on me. The weight of his gaze causing the hairs on the back of my neck to stand up as tingles of awareness dance down my spine.

"Alright, Ter, I'll talk to you later." There's a smile in his voice, reminding me of just how close he is with his little sister. The warmth in his voice when he talks to her is so different from the guarded coolness that's there when he chats with his brother and dad. "I love you too. Bye."

The call ends, and the energy in the room shifts as all of his attention is fixed solely on me. I feel him moving. Rising from the couch in one fluid motion that rolls into an effortless glide that carries him across the room to me. The heat of his body is at my back in the space of a heartbeat, and I look down to see the long, capable fingers of both of his hands gripping the edge of the countertop on either side of me. Despite having me caged in, he's left space between my body and his, ensuring that I could get away if I wanted to.

He drops a kiss on my shoulder. "Turn around, princess." Still clutching the dishcloth in my hands, I spin around to face him. He leans in close, capturing my lips in a kiss that's softer and more chaste than I want in this moment. "Tell me what's wrong."

"How's Teresa doing?" I ask. He narrows his eyes, and I can't help but smile. "I'm not deflecting. I just need a little more time to figure out exactly what I'm feeling."

Chris regards me for a moment, warm eyes roving over my features before he gives in. "She's good, ready for school to be out so she can spend more time in the studio painting. Apparently everything that doesn't involve a paintbrush and canvas is a distraction she doesn't have time for."

I laugh. "A girl after my own heart."

"Yeah." He smiles, pride shining in his eyes. "I think you two would get along really well actually."

"I'd love to meet her one day." The words slip out all on their own, and I immediately wish I could suck them back into my mouth. Chris doesn't look the least bit disturbed by the thought of me meeting his sister, though. In fact, his smile just grows wider.

"You'll get the chance to meet her at graduation. She's over the moon about meeting the girl who finally got me to settle down." He takes a step closer, turning the distance between his hips and mine into a sliver of space and heated potential.

"Is that what I did?" I ask. My voice small despite trying to convey how little I like that phrase and the way it makes it seem like our relationship was some sort of compromise. "Forced you to make a choice? Got you to abandon all your viable options?"

"There were no options before you, princess. No choices to be made. Just you, me and the connection that's existed between us since you chose dare instead of truth. You sealed our fate that day and neither of us knew it until our lips met." My breath catches, freezing in my lungs while Chris studies my face. I can see him detailing the way his words are affecting me. He moves closer, grazing my lips with his before planting a kiss on the corner of my mouth. "Now, do you want to tell me what's wrong?"

There was a time when I would have lied to him, would have hid the actual problem because I worried about what hearing my truth would do to someone else, but with Chris it's easy to let it all flow. He already knows the worst of them. Held them in his hands. Tasted them on my skin. Made all of my pain his own and proven time and again that any space that we exist in together is one where my heart and all the complicated truths that live inside of it are safe.

"You're leaving," I whisper, resting my forehead against his.

"Baby, I'm not going anywhere for months."

"I know, but the thought of you leaving when we've just gotten started makes me…" I can't finish the sentence because all the words that might come next would be far too serious for where we are in this relationship. Chris stays quiet, waiting for me to finish my thought, so I change courses, switching to a topic that safe but still gets me some answers. "And I don't even know if you're going to be at MUSC or Harvard."

"I'm going to MUSC, princess." His lips curl into a soft smile. "I already told you that."

"You told me you wanted to go to MUSC, but you never mentioned getting your Dad's approval to actually attend."

And that makes me worry. As far as I can tell, his dad has let go of the whole 'come home and get hitched' plan because he believes Chris is serious about me, but I don't know if our relationship—fake or real —will ever be enough to make Reese Johnson let go of the idea of having his favorite son graduate from his alma mater.

"My dad is never going to give me his explicit approval, which is fine because I don't need it." His right hand leaves the counter and goes to my waist while he tips his head back to look into my eyes. The dark intensity shining there speaks of his certainty, his full belief in his words, that I let comfort me. "All I need is for him to know that MUSC is the place for me."

"Because you'll get to study under Dr. Suffrant." His would-be mentor's name comes out shaky, quivering past my lips as a direct result of his fingertips ghosting over my ribs.

"Yes."

Knowing he'll be close has made my heavy heart significantly lighter, and made room for me to ask a question I probably shouldn't. "Is that the only reason why you chose MUSC? I mean you could have chosen other schools. Surely there were other options between there and Harvard."

The suggestion is clear, and even though I expect him to immediately dismiss it as the ridiculous question it is, Chris' brows furrow together, forming a thoughtful line. It takes him less than a second to figure out what I'm really asking, and when he's got it, his face transforms into an expression that's somehow serious and playful at the same time.

"Are there any other factors you think I might have been considering when I made my decision to stay in South Carolina?"

I twist my lips to the side, fighting the urge to squirm under the machinations of his busy fingertips. "I don't know, that's why I asked you."

"Well, I might have weighed out my options. Maybe even made a pros and cons list."

"Mhmmm." I hum. "A list. That doesn't sound like you at all."

He arches a brow, curling his fingers into my ribs and making me squeal. "Back to pretending like you're the only organized one in this relationship?"

"Pretending?" I gasp, wiggling out of his touch as he begins a relentless assault on my sides with both hands. My next words are spoken through ridiculous giggles. "I don't need to pretend when we both know it's an inarguable fact."

"Inarguable, huh?" He's doubling down. His hands moving in a frenzied blur that has me doubled over, stepping sideways to try and get away from him. By some miracle, I manage to break free and take off running without giving it a second's thought.

It's not long before the sound of his feet slapping against the hardwood floors hits my ears, and I look back at him. A hungry glint takes over his eyes as we enter the living room, and I manage to put the couch between us. I'm hugging my ribs and gasping for air. I feel like a frazzled mess, but Chris looks delicious. Every muscle in his body is relaxed, but I know him well enough to know they're taut, poised, and ready to spring into action the second I start to move again. I take a step to the side just to see how in tune he is with my movement, and he takes one to match it.

A vein in his jaw pulses as he studies me, trying to anticipate my next move, and I'm reminded of the day at the skating rink when we did a similar dance. Our physical connection is stronger now than it was then, and I can see that he's aware of how this little cat and mouse scenario is affecting me. My blood is rushing through my veins, most of it headed to my sex where liquid arousal is pooling in my core, and my nipples are tightening, forming painful peaks that poke through the fabric of my bra and t-shirt, begging for his attention. Hunger flares in Chris' eyes as he studies me, and I bite my lip, wanting his touch more than anything but also needing the thrill of the chase.

As if he can read my thoughts, Chris starts to move. His long legs taking slow, steady steps around the couch while I move backward in the opposite direction. My heart thuds in my chest, pounding against the same ribs he was just tickling, and he smiles. Actually, calling it a smile seems a bit tame. It's a wild, feral stretching of his lips over teeth he bares purposefully. Flashing them at me with the promise of burying them in my skin.

"Are you done running, princess?"

"No."

A low, tortured growl spills from his lips."Do you want me to keep chasing you?"

I bite my lip. "Yes, and I want you to catch me."

"I will." It's a promise as much as it is a threat, and it's so sexy I almost forget that we're laying out the terms for a game neither of us have played. "Tell me what you want to happen when I catch you."

I wasn't prepared for that directive. Hell, I wasn't prepared for any of this actually, but I appreciate Chris' ability to think on his feet. I'm even more appreciative that he's encouraging me to consider what I want from this moment and share it with him.

"I want to fight you."

"You want to fight me." He says each word slowly, tasting their meaning. Holding each syllable on his tongue.

I nod. "And I don't want you to *let* me win. I want to earn it."

To be sure that beating Trent wasn't a fluke. Obviously I know whatever Chris and I are about to do here isn't going to be the same as what happened on the path, but I don't want to spend any more time thinking the outcome was pure luck instead of a result of my strength and ability.

There isn't a hint of trepidation in his voice when he responds. "Got it. How do I know if you want me to stop? I'm happy to play this game with you, princess, but I won't let it go too far." Once again I'm struck by his thoughtfulness and impressed by his ability to make a conversation about safety parameters sexy. I purse my lips, thinking back to the way we signal overwhelm when we're running through scenarios at Hunter's gym.

"If I want you to stop, I'll tap out. Three times on your arm or whatever part of your body I can reach."

"Okay. Well, in that case, princess" —he licks his lips, smiles his most sinister smile—"*Run.*" I take off as soon as the word leaves his mouth, turning on my heels and jumping over the chaise lounge then cutting the corner that leads down the hall to his room. My heart finds a new home in my throat as his feet pound the floor behind me, echoing in the hall and crossing the threshold to his bedroom mere seconds after mine. I don't know where I'm going. I thought I would have time to get into his room and maybe take some time to hide, but now that we're in here together, I'm at a loss.

At the last second, I feint to the right, hoping to find safety in the bathroom, but just as I switch directions I feel his arms wrap around my waist. Suddenly, we're tumbling towards the ground. Chris twists us around, making sure that when we land on the floor by the bed his body absorbs the majority of the blow. We're both on our sides, and his arms are like vices, cinching around me while my breath leaves my lungs in a startled huff. I can tell he wants to ask if I'm okay, so I don't give him a chance.

I throw one of my legs around his hip, rocking back and then forward forcefully enough to roll him on his back and put me on top of him. His grip loosens, and I take the opportunity to gain control of my arms again. I grab hold of his wrists and pin them to the ground, stretching out over his body. My breasts swing in front of him, and his eyes leave my face, examining the lush curves just out of his reach.

"I thought you weren't going to let me win."

"I haven't yet." He bucks his hips. The force of the motion and the shock of his hardened length pressing against my core makes me gasp. He uses my surprise against me, slipping out of my grasp and putting his hands back on my hips. I'm on my back before I know it with Chris hovering over me. None of his weight is touching me, and I'm stunned by the amount of control and strength he must be using. Control I don't think he has considering the wild look in his eyes. "Is this okay?"

Over the past few weeks, we've found ourselves in all kinds of positions, but Chris has been careful to avoid this one. For some reason, it doesn't feel scary to have him on top of me now. I know he won't hurt me. Won't do anything that I don't want him to do. I wrap my legs around his waist, pulling him closer and nodding.

He leans in. His jaw tight like he's trying to concentrate on anything besides the heat between my legs which his dick is nudging against. "Are we done fighting?"

"I think so. Although, it was more like wrestling. You took it easy on me."

"I didn't want to scare you, but it's not like I let you win."

"You're right. I've never been so happy to lose."

I tilt my head up, offering him my lips. He dips down to take them in a kiss that floods my system with a drugging dose of fiery passion that burns through me. When he pulls back, I swallow hard. My pulse is erratic as I watch him try to reel it back in. The rough, primal part of him I only get glimpses of every now and then. The hungry, desperate animal that wants something it thinks only I can give. I don't know if I can, but I want to try. For him, for me, for the girl I used to be who lived for adventure and would try anything once.

"Don't do that," I whisper.

His fingertips dig into my flesh through the fabric of my shirt. "Do what?"

"Hold back." I surge forward and kiss him, catching him completely off guard when the kiss I initiated turns into a bite. My teeth sink into his bottom lip, and he growls into my mouth. One hand leaving my waist to find a home in the braids tied into a low ponytail at the nape of my neck. I got them in a little over a week ago, so my scalp is still a bit tender when he tightens his grip. But I'm too distracted by his tongue sweeping into my mouth to be bothered by the pain, and I stop feeling it altogether when he starts grinding into me. Slow revolutions of his hips that mimic the one thing we haven't done together yet and make me want it even more.

I run my hands up his sides, slipping them underneath his shirt, so I can feel his skin. Then I'm inching it up his body, baring his abs and the defined lines of his chest until he gets the hint and reaches backward, yanking it up over his shoulders and head and tossing it to the side. I can't stop touching him, can't stop rocking my hips up and into him, meeting every one of his would-be thrusts and imagining how they would feel inside me.

I break the kiss, desperate for a full breath, and Chris heads for my throat. Kissing and licking his way down my neck while I pant underneath him. "*More.*"

He doesn't acknowledge my request verbally, but I feel his movements get more frenzied. His hands are everywhere, wrenching up my shirt, grazing over my breasts through the thin lace of my bra, slipping over my stomach, and then down to the button of my jeans. My pulse kicks up another notch, arousal and the finest thread of fear running through me, taking over my churning hips until they're moving all on their own.

Another growl fills the air, vibrating against my throat where his lips are latched. The sound rattles my bones, and I clutch at him, trying to get closer even though there's hardly an inch of space between us. Chris' tongue lashes out, cutting a slick line over the tendon on the side of my neck at the exact moment his dick drives into my clit, sending a shock wave through me.

The pleasure is almost too much, but I don't want him to stop. I don't want anything but him and the passion his body has promised mine. He unbuttons my jeans, and then my zipper is coming down and my jeans are following suit. Shimmying down my hips and upper thighs until they're caught somewhere between Chris' legs and mine.

The small amount of space shouldn't be enough for him to do anything, but he manages to hook his fingers around the side of my panties, sliding them to the side and exposing the heated skin of my sex to the cool air. I open my legs further, welcoming his fingers into my soaked channel. He's rough as he pushes two fingers in me, rougher as he sinks his teeth into the side of my throat.

I whimper.

Not because I'm hurt or afraid, but because I'm so turned on. More turned on than I've ever been in my entire life, and yet, the moment Chris hears the sound, he scrambles off of me. Before I've even realized what's happening, he's kneeling at my side, brows wrinkled in a grim line of concern as he watches me sit up.

"I'm so sorry, princess." He pushes to his feet and begins pacing in front of me, running an agitated hand over his head. "Are you okay?"

"Yes, Chris. I'm fine." Sitting while he's standing feels awkward, so I fix my clothes and get up too. He reaches out to help. I take his hand, but he tries to let me go as soon as I've got my feet under me. I grip his hand tighter, pulling him closer to me. "Babe, I….I wanted more. I *want* more."

"Mal, I can't." He shakes his head and takes a step back, dropping my hand. A tempestuous cloud of emotion swirls around him, turning his dilated pupils into pools of melted gold with molten lava in the middle. "I don't want to hurt you."

The words hang between us. Their meaning exacerbated by the tortured emotion turning the handsome features I adore into a mask of pain that's fractured by the truth of my past. A truth I shared with him because I wanted him to know me fully. Because I believed that it wouldn't stop him from wanting me, from giving me everything I'm asking him for in this very moment.

All at once, my fears come back, winding their way through my chest like vines of poisonous ivy that crack my ribs and attack my organs. Piercing flesh, veins, and arteries until every beat of my heart, every breath in my lungs, every drop of blood in my veins is panic and then white-hot anger.

Chris watches me cross the room and sit down on the edge of the bed. There's a wariness in his eyes that tells me he knows exactly how this conversation is about to go, and I'm glad he knows I'm about to call him out for trying to handle me with kid gloves.

"You realize this exactly why I didn't want anyone to know about what happened with Trent, right? This—" I wave my hand, gesturing wildly between us. "—exact thing is what I have been trying to avoid. He's the last thing I want to be thinking about when you're on top of me, when I'm telling you that I want you inside of me. You and me. That's all I want to feel in those moments, and you keep reminding me that once upon a time I was a victim. Do you see me that way, Chris?" My voice breaks, but the words keep rolling. "When you touch me are you thinking about what he did to me, how he took the things I'm offering you? Because I'm not, and I don't think any other man in your position would be either."

I should regret bringing up other men, even in the most hypothetical sense, but I just don't. I'm frustrated and horny and in love with this stupid man who won't reap the benefits of the trust he worked so hard to earn. Chris stops pacing, folds his arms over his chest so his biceps are bulging, begging, even in this tense moment, for my teeth and my tongue. For harsh bites and soothing licks against sweat-slicked brown skin.

His eyes snap up to my face, and it takes him a moment to speak, but when he does his voice possesses all the might and intensity of a thunderclap. "You're right. Any other man in my position wouldn't be the least bit concerned about what you went through, princess. In fact, he'd be so lost in the way you smell, in the sounds you make he wouldn't notice, *or care*, about you tensing up under his touch. He'd be so wrapped up in trying to get his dick inside of you that he wouldn't bother to check if the position he has you in makes you feel powerless, if the things he's whispering in your ear make you feel worthless."

I'm not sure if he means for this little speech to be comforting, but it's not. Hearing about the laundry list of things he keeps at the forefront of his mind when I'm losing myself with him makes me feel like being with me is a chore instead of a pleasure.

"I don't need you to keep track of that. I don't *want* you to. Not if you're going to make it sound like some sort of job that's been forced on you." Tears start to blur my vision, and I want to swipe them away, but I've learned from previous experience that it only causes more to come.

"It is a job, princess." Chris' eyes glow. Frustration etched in his features as he thumps his chest. "Keeping you safe? Making sure you're okay at all times? It is a job, and it's *my* fucking job. One I signed on for long before you knew you were mine. One I'll keep doing even if one day, down the road, you decide I'm no longer fit for the role." His nostrils flare. "You're not just my girlfriend, Mallory. You're my mission. My purpose. The only thing in my life I can't afford to fail at, so forgive me if I don't give a fuck about what another man in my position would do because I can guarantee you there isn't a man in this world who…."

My throat aches. A pesky byproduct of holding back a sob that will come out sounding horrible and ugly despite being born of the purest kind of joy. No one has ever made commitment and obligation sound as romantic as Chris has in this moment. I'm sure of it. As sure as I am that the words he's just stopped himself from saying are going to leave me with no choice but to set this hideous, terribly sad sound free.

"Who what? There isn't a man in this world who what?"

"Loves you." He swallows. "There isn't a man in this world who loves you like I do."

"You love me," I say slowly. Incredulous.

He nods. A solemn, severe gaze burning through me. "I love you, Mallory."

"Really?" I ask, laughing. Crying.

Chris laughs too, and it's a rough, humorous rumbling sound from his chest that breaks all the tension in the room. "Yes. Fuck, was that not clear when I risked my job to make sure you could turn that paper in?"

Shock ripples through me. Him moving that deadline for me happened before everything else. Before we established our fake relationship, before it turned into something real. I brush the happy tears leaking out of the corner of my eyes away. "Even then?"

I can't believe how genuine his tone is when he says, "Always, princess."

More tears fall, followed by that sob I've been dreading hearing, and I cover my face. Speaking through my wet fingers when I finally give him the three words I've held inside of myself for so long. "I love you too."

I hear him moving around and the faint sound of a dresser drawer opening and closing before I feel him in front of me. He's kneeling on the ground, his fingers wrapping around my wrists to pull my hands away from my face. I let them fall because I want to see him.

"You do?" He's not even trying to be funny. I can tell he really wants the assurance.

"Yes." I reach up and place a hand on his cheek. He leans into my touch. "Was that not clear when I agreed to be your fake girlfriend?"

"Oh, no, it was. I was just hoping to hear you say it again."

I shove his shoulder, which makes him laugh harder. "You're such an ass."

"An ass that you love, right?"

"Yeah, an ass that I love." We stare at each other, and the happiness bubbling between us is tangible. A living, breathing thing.

"Then now seems like a perfect time to give you this." He reaches over, picks up the slim box sitting on the bed beside me, and sets it in my lap. I drop my hand from his face and run my fingers over the black velvet with gold lining. It's a jewelry box, and judging by the shape and size it's either a necklace or bracelet inside.

"No one besides Mama has ever brought me jewelry before."

"I know," Chris says, his expression soft, patient. "Open it."

I lift the top and gasp when I see the gold herringbone necklace nestled inside black tissue paper. It's thin, one of those classic chains that work with everything and will still be stylish years from now. "It's beautiful."

"Turn it over." His warm gaze follows the motion of my hands as I flip the chain to the other side, revealing a small inscription in slanted font I recognize as his handwriting. There, etched in the shining metal, are our names and words that make me laugh and cry for the second time today: ***MAL AND CHRIS 4EVA.***

I run a fingertip over each letter, and the tears won't stop. Chris brushes them away with his thumb then takes the box from my hand. I watch him pluck the necklace out of the box and move onto the bed behind me. The metal is cool when it hits my skin, and I fiddle with the chain while he fixes the clasp. He presses a kiss to the side of my neck, just above the spot where the necklace lies.

"Do you like it, princess?"

I lean back, allowing myself to relax against him. He wraps me in his arms, kissing my temple and down the line of my jaw. I turn and steal a kiss, all of the worry about the miles that will soon be between us and the doubt I felt when he pulled away from me earlier fading away.

"I love it, and I love you."

34

CHRIS

Mallory's ass jiggles beneath the light-washed denim of her jeans as she bounces on her toes, squealing and pumping her fists in the air because the bowling ball she just sent sailing down the aisle knocked over all the pins. Eric and Nic both shake their heads. Their eyes on the scoreboard, watching the points my princess just scored put her in the lead.

"Sloane, you're up," Mallory says, sliding onto the seat beside me. Her cheeks are flushed, her eyes alive with humor and mischief. She's been bragging all day about beating us at bowling, but I had no idea she would be such an obnoxious winner. It's as adorable as it is annoying.

"You don't have to announce it every time, Mal. The order has been the same since we started playing," Sloane mutters, rising from her seat beside Eric to pick up a ball. Apparently, she's just as competitive as Mallory is and isn't taking well to losing. A fact that has provided endless entertainment to Nic, who's been snickering into his soda every time she rolls.

This was the last full week of classes for the semester and exams start next Wednesday, so we all decided to use this weekend to have some fun before our professors take one last stab at crushing our spirits. Personally, I can't believe the semester is over. That my time as a student at NHU is coming to an end. I wouldn't have imagined wrapping up my senior year like this: in love, with a future I chose looming in the distance.

There are still some uncertainties. Some loose ends I need to tie up before graduation, so I can give Mallory the reassurance she needs about our relationship becoming long-distance. When she mentioned that my dad hadn't given me his blessing to attend MUSC, I told her I didn't need it, and I meant it. My spot in their upcoming cohort is solidified, all the fees paid and an apartment near campus rented with the money from my trust. But I would be lying if I said I haven't been hoping for my dad to acknowledge—and maybe accept—that I chose MUSC over Harvard. That what's best for me is a future with Mallory instead of the one he had planned for me and Giselle.

We haven't talked about her in weeks. During all of our catch-ups, he's been harping on the importance of me finishing the semester strong and avoiding any and all distractions. He even suggested Mallory and I stop hanging out until the semester was done. That had raised some red flags for me, but he let it go as soon as I told him it wasn't happening. Still, I can't help but feel like I'm just waiting for the other shoe to drop. Like he's used his silence to lure me into a false sense of security while he's plotted his next move.

I asked RJ about it, and he told me everything was fine. He even mentioned that with all the time he's been spending with Giselle, there might be a possibility of him being the son to make the Johnson-DuPont union everyone's been dreaming of for so long a reality. The idea of the two of them together was, and still is, strange to me. Not because I want Giselle, but because the excitement in RJ's voice when he told me made me realize his offer to help was never about me. It was about him and what he could get out of the deal.

I did a shit job of explaining that to Mallory, though, and she ended up asking me if I was jealous of my brother spending time with my ex. I assured her that I wasn't. I could tell she didn't believe me, but she dropped it and hasn't mentioned it since. I hate that I might have planted that seed of doubt, though. That my mixed up emotions might have made her think there's another woman in this world I want as much as I want her.

Because there isn't.

There's only her. And in this lifetime and every one after it, that's all there will ever be for me. Amber eyes that see into my soul. Lush curves I've made my home. Smooth mahogany skin that glitters like stardust. Long elegant fingers that one day, when she's ready and I'm braver than I am right now, will be adorned with my rings.

A symbol of our love, of the forever I won't give to anyone but her.

"Babe, your phone is ringing." Mallory taps my leg with one hand and holds the phone in the other. We both glance at the screen and when she sees Vanessa's name, her expression shifts. It becomes more urgent, more demanding because after I told her about Margaret's diagnosis and the calls I've been avoiding from Vanessa, she made me promise to pick up when they called again. "You need to talk to her, Chris. You don't want to miss your chance to say goodbye."

I know she's right, so I take the phone from her hand and push to my feet. By the time I make it into the lobby where it's quieter, the phone is no longer ringing. I consider going back in and telling Mal I missed them again, but something tells me she wouldn't be satisfied with that answer, so I do something I haven't done in months: call back. The phone rings twice before Vanessa picks up, and the instant she starts speaking, I know something is really wrong.

"Chris," she sniffles, her sadness almost palpable. "When are you getting here? The funeral is tomorrow, I thought you would have been here by now. We have to be at the…."

Vanessa keeps talking, and I try my best to absorb what she's saying so the grief-addled monologue doesn't fall on deaf ears, but it's nearly impossible. Everything after the word 'funeral' is drowned out by the sound of my heart pounding in my ears. Vanessa's voice is distorted. Her words a slow, gurgling mess that makes it sound like she's drowning in molasses and tears.

Nothing makes sense.

The entire world has shifted beneath my feet, and there's nothing I can do to right it. I stumble back, colliding with the brick wall behind me and sliding down until I'm as low as I can go. Only I wish I could go lower. That I could disappear from Earth altogether because the grief is so heavy, the weight of the guilt so impossible, I don't want to exist anymore.

"She's gone," I whisper the words, more to myself than Vanessa because it's clear from the way she's talking this is not news to her. They've already planned a funeral, which means Margaret has been gone for days. That my chance to say goodbye to the only mother I've ever known has been lost to me for longer than I could have imagined.

Vanessa stops talking. "You didn't know?"

Hot, fat tears roll down my face, and I can't even bring myself to wipe them away. Margaret deserves these tears. A public, outright display of my grief. Of my agony over losing her. My chest feels tight. I can't take a full breath, can't absorb the meaning of Vanessa's confusion.

"No." I shake my head even though she can't see me. "When?"

"Oh, Chris," she murmurs, and I hear the mother we shared in her voice. See her gentle face and soulful brown eyes in a flash of a memory that flits through my mind. "It'll be a week tomorrow. I thought—" She sniffles again, but I can hear her trying to pull herself together, trying to be strong for me even though I left her alone to deal with all of this."—your dad told me he would tell you, and I've been so caught up with funeral arrangements and packing up the house, I didn't realize he hadn't told you at all. Why wouldn't he tell you?"

"I don't know." And I don't. I have no idea why my dad would keep this from me, and I don't have time to think about it. Right now, all I need is to get to Boston in time to pay my respects to the woman who raised me. Who died without knowing how much she meant to me. I scrub a hand down my face, clearing my blurred vision. "Van, I'm so sorry. I wasn't there for you or her. I just....*fuck*." A painful sob shakes my body, rattling my bones. "She can't be gone, Van. I didn't get to say goodbye."

I take the phone away from my ear and bury my head in my hands.

Vanessa's voice is a distant, faraway sound that doesn't reach me, can't touch me through the storm of emotion raging around me. The only thing that does reach me is the sound of Mallory calling my name. The first time I hear it, I think I'm imagining it, but the second time I know that she must be close. My suspicion is confirmed when the swirl of her jasmine and citrus scent pierces my nose and her warmth is at my side. I drop my hands, shame clawing at my chest as I meet her eyes.

"I was too late."

"Oh, baby." She reaches for me, curling her body around mine. I twist around, wrapping my arms around her waist and hanging on for dear life. She hugs me back, squeezing me with all of her might and murmuring in my ear, telling me she's sorry. I know she means it. I can hear it in her voice, the anguish and pain she feels because I feel it, and she loves me. It makes me love her more.

I don't know how long we sit like that, on the floor of the bowling alley with my tears wetting Mallory's skin and her warm curves applying constant pressure to my wounded heart, staunching the flow of blood until I'm well enough to pull us both off the floor and pick up the phone to finish the call with Vanessa. I assure her I'll be at the funeral, and while we talk, Mallory stays close, rubbing small circles on my back while she texts Eric and tells him to wrap the game up. I'm not sure I want everyone to see me like this, but that choice is taken from me when the rest of the crew shows up in the lobby less than a minute after the message is sent with their sympathetic gazes trained on me.

They all take turns pulling me into their arms and giving me words of comfort. Nic's hug lasts the longest, and when he lets me go, he gives me a hard clap on the back that speaks of solidarity and under-standing. After telling Mallory about losing my mom, I opened up to the rest of the group about it. Having lost his mom not too long ago, Nic was especially sympathetic. He even understood how important Margaret was to me, and I can see in his eyes that he feels for me.

"I'm sorry, man," he says, stepping back to complete the circle of support they've formed around me. Eric shakes his head, his fingers linked with Sloane's. They both look like they're ready to cry. Just looking at each of them, seeing the depth of their empathy, mends a piece of my broken heart. I've always gone through life feeling alone. Solitary. Carrying the pain of loss and the burden of expectation all on my own. But right here, in this moment when the pain is only mine, I feel the relief of support. Of shared hurt and communal healing, and I've never been more thankful for my friends than I am right now.

Eric nods. "Yeah, C, let us know what we can do."

"And where we can send flowers," Sloane chimes in. Sometimes I forget that she's a born and bred socialite. The product of a well-to-do family that probably has its own fucked up traditions and expectations. That small reminder of our similar upbringing has my stomach twisting because it's just hitting me that I have to go back home.

"Thanks, you guys. Really." I glance at my watch. It's almost ten o'clock, and I still need to get home, pack and find a flight. "I need to go. Princess, can you ride home with them?"

I turn to look at Mallory and stop short when I see the frown tugging down her lips. "No, because I'm coming with you."

"Mal," Eric says gently, looking between the two of us. "He might want to deal with this on his own."

"I'm sure you do." She's directing her reply to me even though Eric is the one who turned my thoughts into words. "But there's no way I'm letting you fly to Boston all by yourself. You're still in shock, Chris, and I'm not going to let you navigate this alone."

"Princess—"

She holds up a hand, cutting me off. "No. I'm going and that's it. I already texted Mama and told her what happened, and she would kill me if she found out I let you do this all on your own. Now, let's go, so we can get packed and find a flight."

I look around and see that her no-nonsense attitude has shut everyone up, including Eric. He gives me a look that says he has nothing more to say, and although the last thing I want is Mallory in Boston around my dysfunctional family, I cave because I need her.

"Okay."

Relief smooths Mallory's features, and I realize how much it means to her to be able to be there for me. We hug everyone, say our good-byes, and then we're out the door. While I drive back to my place, Mallory uses my phone to book us on a red-eye flight to Boston and a hotel close to the church where Vanessa said the funeral will be held. As soon as we're inside the apartment, she pulls me in close for a long hug and kisses me.

"I love you," she whispers, her face buried in my throat. "And I'm so sorry."

I run a hand down her back, letting the solidity of her presence soothe me. "I love you too, princess. Thank you for being here with me."

"There's nowhere else I would be." She pulls back, tears glistening in pools of amber as she blinks up at me. "She knew how much you loved her, Chris, and I'm sure she understood that you were scared of facing the fact that she was going."

My eyes fall shut, closing out her words and the peace they're trying to bring me. I push out a steadying breath, willing the wave of despair trying to wash me away to subside. When I open them again, Mallory is still staring at me. "We need to pack."

She looks like she wants to say something, but she doesn't. And I'm thankful for her silence and understanding, but the second she pulls away from me, heading into my bedroom, I miss the comfort of her touch. I follow her into the room and head for the closet, and for the next fifteen minutes we're all frantic, but coordinated, movements.

Mallory selects a black suit for me, and I promise her we'll have time to find her a dress before the service. We pack toothbrushes and toiletries and double-check everything a million times before we finally head to the airport.

The process of paying for parking and rushing through the check-in is a blur. I spend the entire time in my head, letting Mallory handle everything while images of Margaret's frail body wreak havoc on my heart and mind. Images of her last days, days I wasn't there to witness because my fear and my father conspired to keep me away from her, haunt me.

Make it impossible for me to sleep or drink or talk for the duration of the flight. My silence worries Mallory, but she doesn't say it. She just threads her fingers through mine and squeezes tight, letting me know she's there.

That even when I feel like I have no one, I have her.

35

MALLORY

What kind of father keeps the death of a loved one from their own son?

That question keeps playing through my mind as I stare at Reese Johnson Sr, watching him move through the great room inside the sprawling mansion the Johnsons call a house. This is the home Chris grew up in. The place where Margaret raised motherless children while mourning her best friend. I hadn't realized Celeste and Margaret had been so close, but her niece, Vanessa, mentioned it several times in her eulogy about her aunt who also acted as her mother. Reese Sr. shifted uncomfortably in his seat when Vanessa mentioned their friendship. That struck me as odd, but that wasn't even the oddest thing about him.

Chris had warned me that his dad could be temperamental and abrupt, but when I met him outside the church just before the service started, that wasn't the vibe he gave off at all. He was nice, *charming* even, which had all of my alarm bells ringing. The ringing grew louder when he didn't apologize for not telling Chris about Margaret's death. Instead of addressing the lack of communication or the fact we weren't even supposed to be there, he hugged Chris and said it was good to see him and nice to meet me. Then he launched into a speech about paying for the entire funeral and the repast, which he was hosting at the house, and told me I was more than welcome to sit with the family.

Anyone else would have been grateful for his welcoming behavior, they might have even forgotten how fucked up it was that he participated in the planning of the funeral he hid from his son, but none of it sat right with me. And the longer I stand here, in the corner he stashed me in before proceeding to drag Chris around the room to talk to all the people who knew Margaret was dead before he did, the less comfortable I feel.

That discomfort, I tell myself, has nothing to do with their tour around the room coming to a grinding halt because the circle surrounding the DuPont family has expanded to make space for them. I looked up pictures of Giselle and her parents, but even if I hadn't I would have been able to identify them immediately. An air of sophisticated grandeur swirls around the trio, creating an impenetrable bubble that holds everyone around them at bay. It expanded when Chris and Reese approached, the long tendrils of old money and influence reaching out and wrapping around their bodies, escorting them into an inner circle that wreaks of exclusivity.

Oscar DuPont is a short man with light skin and neatly arranged features that would read as handsome if it wasn't for his beady eyes and creepy smile. His slick hair is black, too black to be his natural color, which suggests that he dyes it regularly. His wife, Ramona, is tall and thin. She has flawless ebony skin and the bone structure of a print model that she passed on to her daughter who is her spitting image save for her complexion, which she got from her father.

Giselle is stunning.

A natural beauty with a bright smile and perfect white teeth that are on full display while Chris greets her with a hug. I watch their embrace with red blurring my vision and vicious, white-hot jealousy searing my insides. She looks at home in his arms, and I can tell by the bliss taking over her features when she rests her head on his shoulder that she feels that way. I know I should look away, spare myself the horror of watching him with the woman his father wanted to be his wife, but I just can't.

I stare at them, studying their movements, the easy way their bodies curl around each other and stay close even when the hug ends. Chris keeps his hand on the small of her back, and she turns into him. Her pretty features sinking into a practiced pout while they carry on a conversation separate from the one their parents—who are watching their reunion with huge smiles on their faces—are having. I can't read her lips, but I can tell she's asking him how he's doing. A question I've been swallowing whole every time the words crowd together on my tongue because I somehow know he won't answer it.

After I tried to comfort him in his apartment before we packed, he'd shut me out. Saying next to nothing on the flight, or the cab ride to the hotel, then staying up when I went to bed. I tried not to read too much into it because I know he's processing this loss, but I'd be lying if I said it didn't hurt to be pushed away.

Especially when it seems like he's so eager to pull Giselle in. I watch his face as he answers her question, see his mouth moving and his brows wrinkling like he's accessing emotions he doesn't want me to know exist. She listens intently, sympathy pouring off of her that he's soaking into himself.

"They look good together don't they?" The smooth baritone makes my skin crawl, but the sound itself isn't as bad as the hot breath skating across my neck that accompanies it. I spin around, barely resisting the urge to cringe as I come face to face with RJ. We met outside the church, and I took an immediate dislike to him. Something about the way he leered at me when Chris introduced us set my teeth on edge. A large smile stretches across his face as he rubs at his goat tee with one hand, his eyes bouncing between my face and the couple we're now staring at together. "Makes it easy to see why my dad and her parents are so adamant about them being together."

My lips curl involuntarily, the disgust evident on my face as I look at him. There's a heinous smugness to his tone that's not reflected in his expression. In fact, he looks a lot like I imagine I do right now: worried, jealous, anxious to see Chris and Giselle go their separate ways. Seeing him look that way reminds me RJ is just as involved in this whole situation as I am.

He's the one who gave Chris the information that led to us putting on our act in the first place. And he's the one who's been spending time with Giselle, hoping his dad and the DuPonts would see him as a viable option for Chris' replacement. Since our first conversation about our fake relationship, Chris has maintained that his brother wanted to help him, to save him from having a future he didn't want forced upon him. I never trusted it though. I've always wondered what exactly he was getting out of helping his brother defy their father, and now I know.

"Sounds like you're excited about the future your father wants for Chris and Giselle as well." I lift a brow, taking a sip of the expensive champagne Reese has the caterers serving because today is all about celebrating Margaret's life. "Only, that doesn't make a lot of sense considering how *you* want to be the Johnson in the Johnson-DuPont union. Isn't that why you've been spending so much time with Giselle, so you can finally have your chance at one-upping your little brother?"

The smug smile falls off his face, and his eyes narrow. "Is that what Chris told you? He loves to make me sound like the jealous, overly competitive big brother. He'll say anything to hide the truth."

Despite my best effort, I can't keep his words from slipping underneath my skin. They touch on the deepest, most insecure part of me. The part that churns out a new worry every second we stay in Boston. In this place where Chris is quiet and distant and the differences in the worlds we grew up in are massive, glaring things that make it hard for me to see the future I just started taking steps towards securing.

"Which is?"

My voice wavers when I ask the question, and I hate it because RJ hears it for what it is. Weakness. Vulnerability. The soft underbelly of the hard facade I've tried to construct around myself. It's open, exposed to him, and his claws are out, ready to slice me in two. He smiles, and it's all sharp edges that press against my skin, threatening to make me bleed.

He turns his body towards me, making it so I'm caged between the wall and him, and my pulse shoots up. All of my fight-or-flight instincts triggered in an instant. I'm not afraid though, and it's not because we're standing in a room full of people, but because I know that if he so much as takes another step towards me I'll be well within my rights to knee him in the balls and haul ass out of here.

"That he's just as competitive as I am. Maybe even more so. When we were kids, he'd put down a toy and leave it for hours without so much as thinking about it, but the second I touched it, he lost his shit, crying and screaming to get it back. He says he doesn't want this life, doesn't want Giselle, but he does, Mallory. Because he doesn't know how to lose, especially not to me."

I bite down on the inside of my cheek to keep my jaw from dropping as RJ recites all of my worst fears like my internal monologue is a playbook he's memorized lines from. This is exactly what I've been worried about since Chris told me RJ and Giselle were growing closer. He was so agitated that day, struggling to articulate his thoughts when he's usually so good at communicating. RJ watches my face, a smug smile lining his lips as he continues.

"I bet you he started losing his shit the day I told him about me and Gi. He probably started thinking about the history between them. How they've known each other for their whole lives, and how perfect she is for him. And he's not wrong. She is perfect for him. She understands him. She knows what it's like to live in this world and put up with all of this." He swipes his hands through the air, gesturing to indicate the house we're standing in and the people in it. Members of the elite with their gold-soaked souls and silver spoons. RJ looks at home among them, and as much as it pains me to admit it, Chris does too. "This is his world, Mallory, and while I'm sure you two have had a lot of fun down there in New Haven, this is where he belongs. And she," —he shifts, giving me just enough space to see Giselle smiling up at Chris who's saying something to her father— "is the kind of woman he belongs with."

I toss back the rest of my champagne, needing every ounce of strength from the bubbles and alcohol to finish this conversation. "Was this you and your dad's plan all along? Separate us, orchestrate some scenario where I watch him with Giselle and start to doubt everything I know to be true about us? Let me guess, your whole 'they belong together' speech was supposed to be the final nail in the coffin, right? You were supposed to make me cry, storm out of here, embarrass Chris, and dishonor Margaret's memory while your dad kept his hands clean?"

RJ's jaw clenches, and I laugh. "Wow. You guys really don't give a shit about him, do you? First, you do everything you can to keep him from this funeral. Then, you use it as an opportunity to try and poison me against him. Why can't you just let him be happy?"

"Because his happiness doesn't matter."

"And apparently neither does yours! Otherwise, you wouldn't be standing here trying to free your brother up so he can marry the woman you love."

"You don't know what the fuck you're talking about."

The air between us snaps with tension that doesn't break, doesn't dissipate until Teresa waltzes over. Her long legs, clad in high-waisted designer slacks that have a creamy silk blouse tucked inside, carry her across the room and deposit her between RJ and I before either of us realizes what's happened.

She faces me, her dark eyes wide and kind while she wraps her arm around my shoulders. I'm several years older than her, but she's taller than I am and more self-assured than I probably ever will be. She's also the nicest member of the Boston-based Johnson clan, which is why I let her lead me away from RJ without a second thought. My heels clack against the expensive stone floors as we leave the great room and head down a hallway that, judging by the number of tray-carrying servers coming in and out of the double doors, must be the kitchen.

We sweep in, and no one even bats an eye as she deposits me at the large kitchen island and plops down beside me. Almost instantly, two glasses of ice-cold water and a platter stacked with various meats, cheeses, and fruits appear in front of us, dropped off by a server who moves so quick I don't even see them. My mouth drops, and it's one of the first times I've let my true reaction to the luxury surrounding me show. Teresa tosses her head back, her long, wavy tresses nearly touching her butt as she laughs.

"I know. It's so obnoxious, right?"

I pluck a strawberry off the plate and take a bite, covering my mouth as I chew. "It's something, but I don't know if obnoxious is the right word."

"Shit." She frowns. "Now I sound obnoxious. Like how rich do you have to be to complain about attentive kitchen staff?"

"Pretty damn rich." Another small snort escapes her as she fixes me a small plate and then herself. "You're not obnoxious though. You actually might be my favorite person here."

"Besides Chris, you mean."

I let out a weary sigh while my mind plays the images of Chris and Giselle together on a loop with RJ's words as the soundtrack. "Yeah, besides Chris."

Teresa cuts her eye at me. "Please don't be mad at him because of what RJ said. Him and Dad are weirdos, but Chris isn't like them at all. He doesn't subscribe to the patriarchal bullshit they do."

That surprises a snort out of me, and she laughs. "I know he doesn't."

"Then why do you look like you might actually believe that he prefers all of this to what he has with you in New Haven?"

Chris had told me Teresa was smart and perceptive. He called her a spitfire, and he wasn't wrong in the least. In a matter of seconds, she's seen right through the brave face I thought I was putting on. I press my lips together, attempting to come up with an answer that's honest but not too honest. I don't want to talk to her about these things before Chris and I have a chance to discuss them at length.

"It's not that I think he prefers all of this to what we have." Not completely at least. "I just worry that circumventing these long-standing family traditions is going to be a lot harder than he thinks. Chris has been under the impression that your dad has accepted our relationship and let go of the idea of him and Giselle being together, but after talking with RJ, I'm pretty sure that's not the case."

Teresa nods thoughtfully, and I'm impressed with how invested she is in this conversation when any other eighteen-year-old would be bored out of their minds. "To be honest, I've never understood the fathers choose for their sons thing. It's weird and sexist as hell, but my grandpa, dad, and uncles swear it's the only way to ensure the continuation of the *esteemed line of Johnson men*."

Her nose wrinkles, and sarcasm coats every word at the end of her sentence. "For a second there, I thought Dad was going to let it go. After I started telling him about you and Chris, I mean. He wasn't thrilled or anything, but it seemed like he had accepted that he wasn't ever going to get Chris back under his thumb the way he wanted."

My heart soars, hope bubbling in my chest despite the fact that her words suggest that Reese no longer feels that way. "Well, what happened?"

She shrugs. An apologetic look taking over her expression. "I don't know. And I wish I did because then RJ wouldn't be acting like an asshole, and you and Chris wouldn't be…."

The silence stretches between us, and I know exactly how she was going to fill it. I shake my head. "Chris and I are going to be fine. I mean it's not like your dad can force him to come back here and marry someone he doesn't love."

Teresa takes a sip of her water, refusing to meet my eyes. "Right. That would be ridiculous."

As ridiculous as hiding the death of a beloved surrogate mother while paying for the funeral and hosting the reception.

As ridiculous as concocting a fake relationship to fool a parent and fend off an ex.

"Right," I mutter under my breath, heart sinking because I know people do ridiculous things to get what they want all the time. "Ridiculous."

36

CHRIS

It takes me ages to disentangle myself from Giselle. She was too busy putting on a show for the small crowd of people that formed around us the second Dad and I joined her and her parents in front of the fireplace to notice my unease. Dad didn't look too happy when I excused myself, but I couldn't have cared less. I had lost sight of Mallory and missed out on several chances to talk to Vanessa who kept giving me meaningful looks from across the room every time our eyes caught.

Neither of them is anywhere to be found by the time I'm free to move through the crowd on my own, and I feel worry flare in my gut. I shouldn't have left Mallory alone. She doesn't know anyone here but me, and all of my instincts screamed for me to keep her close, but the second my dad snapped his fingers, I caved. I told myself it was just so I could spare her the awkwardness of standing there feeling out of place while my dad and the DuPonts did their nice-nasty routine, but I can't help but wonder if it's because I'm hardwired to obey him. To give into his commands despite knowing better or wanting different. Before I wouldn't have given it much thought, chalked it up to keeping the peace and going with the flow, but giving in to him this time just felt like it meant something different.

Like I was acknowledging his power over my life, deferring to him, letting him lead me to the very specific waters he wanted me to drink from. Waters that smelt like plastic and tasted like vanity and corruption. A scent that had leeched into my skin, going deeper and deeper the longer I stood next to Giselle.

The hallway is empty and quiet as I step into it, and I look both ways, trying to determine where Mallory could have gone. Normally the thought of hunting her down would have me slightly turned on, but right now all I want to do is find her and make sure she's okay. Deciding she wouldn't have sought solace in the kitchen, I turn left, heading towards the front door to see if she's outside.

"There you are!" I turn around to see Vanessa peeping her head out of the doorway of one of the first-floor guest rooms and immediately head towards her. She meets me halfway, pulling me into a tight hug. We hold on to each other, and the tears come, but they don't break us open like I thought they would. "I'm so glad to see you."

Behind her glasses, her bright almond eyes shine with fresh tears, and her lips tremble. She held it together at the funeral, got through her entire speech without so much as a wobble in her voice, but now she's all raw emotion she's trying to reel in.

"I'm glad to see you too, Van." I pull her into another hug, this one shorter than the first. "God, I'm so fucking sorry."

"Chris, you don't have to keep apologizing. Everybody deals with this shit differently."

"Yeah, but I didn't deal at all. I just checked out, left you to deal with everything on your own."

She shakes her head, tucking one of her wavy locs back behind her ear. "Everything was exactly how it was supposed to be. She wouldn't have wanted you to remember her like that anyway. She didn't want to be another ghost living in your head."

I don't feel like arguing, so I let Van win, let her think her words—which are most likely Margaret's—have absolved me of the guilt I'll carry for the rest of my life. It's the least I can do on a day like today.

"Yeah, I guess you're right."

"I am." She smiles. "Do you have a minute? I have a few things I need to give you."

I give her a look that conveys my confusion but nod anyway. "Yeah, I've got time."

"Good, come with me." I follow her back down the hallway and feel even more confused when I see the state of the bedroom we've just entered. It looks lived in. Framed pictures of Margaret and Vanessa on the nightstand and dressers. Clothes hanging in the walk-in closet, a neatly made bed with more clothes strewn across it.

"I've been staying here," Vanessa says as she walks over to the desk in the corner of the room and picks up a bag. "After it happened, I couldn't stay in the house, so your dad offered to let me stay here."

"That's....nice of him." Too nice. Weirdly nice. I've never known my father to open his home to anyone except employees who needed to be on-site to execute their duties.

She turns around, notes my confusion, and smiles as she sits down on the bed. "No, it's not. I think he only asked me to stay because he thought I would give him what I'm about to give you."

I watch her unzip the bag and pull out a handful of small, leather-bound notebooks. On top of the stack in her hand is a folded piece of paper with what looks like my name written on the front. "What are those?"

Vanessa pats the bed beside her, and I walk over and sit down. She places the stack on top of the bag, which still has notebooks inside of it, and looks at me. "Did you know that your mom kept journals?"

The question shocks me. My mom is the last person I expected to be talking about today, but I should have known she would come up again. After all, Vanessa made a point of placing emphasis on my mother and Margaret's friendship. I wish I could say with any kind of certainty that I knew my mother kept journals, but the truth is I don't know anything about her.

Even her voice, the voice I hear screaming my name in my night-mares, is a figment of my imagination. A sound my brain put together to fill in the blank spaces of my memory. The more I think about it now, the crazier it seems. The reality of growing up with no knowledge of her, with no pictures of her in the house and no videos of her singing to us even though RJ once told me she did. He's the only one of us who remembers her.

Besides my dad, of course.

But he never talks about her. In all the years I've been alive, I can only remember him speaking her name a handful of times. Almost like the moment her body gave out, everything she meant to him ceased to exist.

I shake my head. "No. I didn't know that. Where did you get these?"

"Margaret has had them for years, ever since your mom…."

I don't understand the silence. Vanessa and I have known each other all of our lives, she's never shied away from hard conversations, not even when it was about death.

"Died," I finish the sentence for her, giving her a weird look. "Margaret kept these for eighteen years?"

Vanessa nods. "She kept them in a storage unit a few towns over. A few weeks before she died, on one of her last good days, she told me where to find them, and she made me promise I would give them to you."

I run a finger over the crisp edge of the folded paper. "Why did she want me to have them?"

"She said you were the only one who still thought about her as much as she did."

My chest grows tight. "I think about her every day."

"She figured as much and thought you would appreciate these more than anyone else." I can't say she's wrong. Teresa never met Mom, and RJ acts like she never existed. I'm the one she haunts.

"Have you—" I clear my throat, trying to swallow past the lump of emotion that grows larger with every passing second. "Did you read any of them?"

"No, I didn't even read the note from Margaret. All of this is for you and only you. Margaret was very specific. She told me not to give them to anyone but you, especially not your dad."

"Damn." I laugh. "She really couldn't stand him could she?"

Van joins in, her shoulders bouncing as she shakes her head. "She really couldn't. I think he might have suspected she had something of Celeste's though. He's been hinting around about wanting to pay to get the house cleaned out and all of Margaret's affairs in order. He even had his assistant call and ask me if she owned any other properties they might need to send the cleaners to."

A wrinkle forms between my brows as I try to reconcile Vanessa's description of my father's actions of the past few weeks with what I know to be true about him and his attitude toward staff. He goes out of his way to remain impersonal with them, preaches constantly about maintaining professional boundaries and expectations. Nothing I've ever heard him say or seen him do suggests he would go to such lengths for someone who worked for him.

Hell, I don't even think he'd go that far for one of his own children.

"That's weird as hell."

"Right? I thought it was so strange, and she kept calling until I finally told her I wouldn't allow strangers to go through my aunt's personal effects. I felt kind of bad for yelling at the poor girl, but I just wanted her to back off."

"I'm sure Lyla is fine, Van," I say, eyeing the journals and the letter with renewed interest. We don't know if my dad wanted them, but just the thought they could mean something to him has my interest piqued. "She deals with much worse on a daily basis."

"You're right." Vanessa pushes to her feet, clearly aware that the brain capacity I was dedicating to this conversation has been directed somewhere else. "Well, I'm going to go make the rounds and maybe get some food. You can hang out in here and look through this stuff, I'll cover for you."

"Thanks, Van." I glance up at her. "If you see Mallory, will you tell her where to find me?"

A huge grin spreads across her face as she heads for the door. "Yeah, I guess I can do that for you. Congratulations, by the way. I've been stalking your Instagram for months, and you two look so happy."

I smile back at her, allowing myself to think back to the pictures littering my account. Most of them are from the time when we were faking it, but we've added in a good bit since then. Ones where the emotion in the photos matches the things we say and feel. I want more of those moments with her.

Actually, I want more of everything. The warm glow of happiness. The heated passion. The sad and quiet and everything in between. Whatever life looks like with Mallory, is what I want, and when we get back to our room tonight I'm going to make sure to tell her. To let my words close the gap I allowed my silence to put between us. She was so kind and understanding last night and today, but I know me shutting down like that has to bother her. I don't want her to think I'm pushing her away, especially when all I want to do is hold her close and never let go.

"We are," I say finally, and she smiles another soft smile before slipping out the door. Immediately, I turn my attention to the items sitting on the bed beside me. Even though I want to grab one of the journals first, I force myself to pick up Margaret's letter. Her apple and cinnamon scent bounces off of the page as I unfold it, revealing her flowing cursive.

Chris,

If you're reading this, then I'm already gone. I won't waste precious space telling you how angry I am that I had to leave before I got to see you become the man you dreamed of being. I guess I'll have to watch you flourish from the clouds above. (Lord, I hope I'm in heaven because me and the heat have never done well.)

Anyway, son, I want you to know I love you, and I have always known how much you love me. No amount of time or space could ever alter our bond, so you take it easy on yourself. Don't spend too much time regretting the decisions you made when it came to handling my diagnosis. We all do what we have to do, and I understand you felt like you couldn't survive seeing me like that.

To tell the truth, I didn't want anyone to see me like this.

I feel like this disease has taken away everything that made me, me. My hair. My breasts. My smile. The only thing it hasn't touched is my mind, and I'm afraid it's next. That's why I sent Vanessa to the storage unit to get these journals. They belonged to your mother. She wrote in them every chance she got. It's not much, but it's all that's left of her in this world besides you and your siblings.

Especially now that I'm going.

I know it hurts to think about her, Chris, but I need you to do it for me. I need you to read these and learn her. Discover how she saw the world. Find out her hopes, fears, and secrets. Carry them with you in your heart.

Because if you don't, she'll die with me.

Celeste was my best friend and the love of my life, but I don't want to take her memory with me. I don't want to be the last person on this Earth to utter her name, to be moved by her words and changed by her heart. Your father has tried to erase her since the day they met. Don't let today be the day he succeeds.

I love you, my sweet boy.

Margaret

A thousand thoughts move through my mind in the space of a second as I fold the letter back up. Nothing makes sense. Margaret held on to my mother's journals for almost two decades and then, while she was on her death bed, left them to me so I could what? Keep my mother's memory alive? I mean that sounds simple enough. I always wanted a way to get to know my mother that didn't involve going to biased sources like my grandfather or Dad, and I'm happy to now have that option, but everything else seems weird.

Especially the whole 'love of my life' thing. Was that something people said about their best friends or was Margaret suggesting her and Mom had a romantic relationship? And what about the thing she said about Dad trying to erase her? She couldn't have meant that literally, that sounded way too sinister, but figurative erasure is just as bad.

And definitely something he could do. It's basically what he did after she died. Erected a cone of silence around her existence no one around him ever questioned because they assumed it was a coping mechanism brought on by extreme grief.

Except Margaret has me thinking it could be more to it than that, and now I'm standing on the edge of a cliff asking myself if I should jump or step away. I stare at the journals, and my fingers start to itch, begging for leather and answers.

"Fuck it."

I swan dive off the cliff, reaching into the stack and plucking up the first notebook my fingers land on. I flip it open, turn to a random page, and start to scan through the unfamiliar handwriting. My heart lurches when I see my name.

Christopher will be an easy baby, of this I have no doubt. Even his birth was easy, quick, painless. The kind of birth you only hear about from those moms at the park who make you want to pluck their eyes out because everything sounds so fake and perfect. After Junior's birth, which was nothing short of horrific because Reese scared me out of getting the epidural, I was certain they were all lying to trick other women into procreating, but now I know they weren't. Now I know you don't have to labor for hours on end, wallowing in pain and your own filth while a baby with a head the size of a watermelon tries to split you in half.

This time was so different. Maybe because Reese was a few floors down operating, and I was <u>finally</u> able to get an epidural. I almost missed my window because I was dilating so fast, but the anesthesiologist got to me quickly. Perks of having the same last name as the man who owns the building. It gave me just enough time to rest and prepare for delivery, which was so easy it makes me wonder why I waited eight years to do it again.

Chris slid out into the world with a head full of jet-black curls and the cutest little scowl on his red face. And when they placed him on my chest, his weight grounded me. Anchored me to the world and helped me remember how much I love my children, how much I love my family. <u>How much I love Reese.</u> We aren't perfect, but I believe that we can be good together again.

We have to be, for our boys.

My fingers trace the page, and I try to imagine her writing this. It would have been sometime after she left the hospital, when she returned back home and was able to have a moment of private time. Time to write in journals she hid from her husband because she didn't feel comfortable saying the things she wrote in them to his face. That must have been awful for her. Being married to someone who didn't see you, who didn't listen to you, who couldn't truly love you because they refused to hold space for you.

And to have kids with them, to be tied to them by name and blood and soul. I can only imagine that it was unbearable at times, that she dealt with things she could have walked away from if it was just her. Or hell even if it was just her and RJ. But then I came along and the anchor grew heavier, tethering her to a man who was so different from the one she met, she had to convince herself how much she loved him. Feeling sick to my stomach, I drop the notebook and pick up another, flipping towards the end where the entries are shorter.

There's no warmth in his eyes when he looks at me. I wish he would let me go....

Her loneliness is evident in every word. And I don't need to finish reading the entry to know that this is why Dad was adamant about going through Margaret's stuff. He had to have known Mom kept journals, had to have wondered about where they went when she died. I'm sure it didn't take him long to suspect that Margaret took them. He would have been desperate to get them back, to rid the world of any evidence of his shortcomings. His failures as a husband that led to his pregnant wife feeling trapped.

Heavy footfalls echo in the hallway and voices I can't quite make out start moving towards Vanessa's room. In a panic, I start to shove everything inside the bag and zip it before turning an expectant gaze on the door. The voices pass by, and I breathe a sigh of relief. If that had been Dad or RJ, all of Margaret's work to keep the journals a secret would have been undone in an instant.

Picking the bag up and slinging it over my shoulder, I pull out my phone and call Mallory. She picks up on the first ring, her soft, sultry voice doing wonders to soothe the knots forming in my shoulders.

"Hello?"

"Princess, where are you?"

"In the kitchen with Teresa. Where are you?"

Despite myself, I smile, happy she's spending time with Ter. "I'm on my way to you, stay where you are."

"Okay." There's a hint of annoyance in her tone, but I don't get the chance to address it before she hangs up, leaving me to skulk down the hallway without drawing any attention to myself. When I enter the kitchen, she's standing next to the island, talking to Teresa and Vanessa. They're all laughing at something Teresa just said, but I can tell that none of them are as happy as they're trying to appear. Vanessa has frown lines notched between her brows. Ter's shoulders are high and tense, and Mallory's eyes have a sadness to them that wasn't there when I left her earlier.

I walk up to her, putting an arm around her shoulder and pressing a kiss to the top of her head. She leans into me, settling her weight against my body with a sigh that suggests she needed the contact just as much as me. "Ready to go?"

My fingers are gripping the strap on the bag so hard, it feels like all the blood is leaving them. I'm so desperate to get the journals out of this house I almost collapse with relief when Mallory nods.

"Yeah, I'm ready if you are."

37

MALLORY

After we say goodbye to Teresa and Vanessa, Chris and I drive back to the hotel in silence. It's not tense or awkward, it's just silence. The kind you get when there are only two people in a car and they're both too deep in their own thoughts to say anything to the other person. It isn't broken until we step into the bedroom portion of the suite, and he drops the bag on the bed. He starts pacing, which catches my attention immediately.

I glance at it and then at him. "Where did the bag come from?"

He pauses, scrubbing a hand down his face. "Vanessa gave it to me."

"Okayyyy," I say slowly. "Do you want to tell me what's in it?"

"Journals."

My brows wrinkle. "Vanessa gave you journals? Are they hers or....?"

"They're my mom's."

Nothing about that sentence makes sense. Even when I repeat it in my head over and over again, it still remains scrambled. Confused. Since I just came out of Mindfuck Mansion, I decide to give myself some grace and ask for clarification. "I'm sorry, what? How did Vanessa even get a hold of your mom's journals?"

A half-crazed laugh falls from Chris' lips as he starts pacing again. "Margaret had them. She kept them for eighteen years. Had Vanessa dig them up out of a secret storage unit a few weeks ago so she could give them to me."

Interest piqued, I gaze at the bag and try to school my features into an expression that doesn't make it look like I think Vanessa just handed him a ticking time bomb. *What good could possibly come from him having his dead mother's journals?*

"Have you read them?"

Chris walks over to the chair in the corner and plops down. He looks worn out and his suit is wrinkled, but he's still as handsome as he was this morning. I want to kiss him and tell him everything will be okay then slap him for leaving me to fend for myself all afternoon.

"I skimmed over a few passages," he admits softly, eyes on me. "She wrote about me. About the day I was born and how happy I made her."

My heart aches for him, for the way none of this seems to be bringing him joy. Only more pain. I get up off of the bed and stride over to him. As soon as I'm within reach, he yanks me down onto his lap, wrapping both of his arms around my body and pulling me in. I allow myself to relish in the feel of him, in the way his leather and earth scent mixes with mine to make a fragrance that is uniquely us. Chris buries his face in the crook of my neck, inhaling deeply.

I reach around and cradle the back of his head with my hand, rubbing my fingers into his scalp while he hums his approval. "What was it like to read that?"

"Heartbreaking. She wasn't happy with him. I'm the reason she stayed, why she decided to try harder instead of leaving."

"Where would she have gone?" Chris shared with me before that his mom was a foster kid. A poor girl with a big brain who fell in love with a rich boy who folded her into his world. His friends became her friends. His family, her family. Leaving wouldn't have been an easy choice, especially for a single woman with a kid.

"I don't know. Maybe she would have run away with Margaret."

"What?" There's no hiding the shock in my voice. When Chris

pulls back to look at me, his expression matches mine. "Were your mom and Margaret in love?"

"I think so. Margaret wrote me a letter and in it, she referred to my mom as the love of her life." One of his hands is moving down my back, taking the zipper of my dress with it. "Doesn't sound particularly platonic does it?"

"No," I whisper, breath getting caught in my lungs when I feel his fingers against my skin, blazing a trail from my spine to my ass. "What are you doing, Chris?"

"I just need to touch you, princess, to make sure you're real because nothing in my life feels real right now. Is that okay?"

"Yes." He leans forward and kisses my jaw, nuzzling into me while I keep rubbing his head. There's a quiet energy thrumming between us. We both feel it, know it could turn into something else, but neither of us do a thing to move it further. "I'm sorry you had to find all of this out today and on top of losing Margaret. That seems like information overload."

"It is, but I can deal."

"I know you can, but that doesn't mean you have to. And you certainly don't have to do it alone."

"I know, princess."

I want to lose myself in the circles he's rubbing along my back and the sporadic kisses he's planting along my face and neck, but I can't. Not when I have the chance to make sure he knows I'm here for him. "Do you? Because you haven't been acting like it."

Chris lets out a long sigh, and I expect him to argue with me but instead he nods his agreement. "You're right, and I'm sorry for shutting down like that. You were trying to comfort me, and I just couldn't accept it. You were right though, about her not being angry with me. She said as much in her letter, told me not to waste time beating myself up about not being there because I was doing the best I could."

He doesn't sound like he believes it yet, but I have faith he'll come around. One day he'll remember my words and reread Margaret's and forgive himself. "Margaret sounded like an incredible woman."

"She was."

We sit in silence for a moment, and I hold the woman who raised the man I love in my thoughts. Thanking her for all she did to make sure he was okay, that he survived what must have been a catastrophic loss for her as well.

"I'm scared of what else I might find in those journals. My mom makes it sound like my dad was some kind of monster."

"Maybe he is." I press my lips together, wishing I could take those words back. "I didn't mean that."

Chris snorts then leans back to look at my face. "Yes, you did, princess. You don't say anything you don't mean."

I love that he knows that. Love that he says it like it's one of his favorite things about me. "Okay, fine, I meant it, but I don't think it's a fair statement. I haven't spent enough time with your dad to call him a monster."

"Mallory, be for real. You haven't liked him since you found out he was planning on forcing me into marriage. There's not much he could do to redeem himself in your eyes."

I bite my lip. "I guess that's true. And this situation definitely hasn't helped, but the straw that broke the camel's back was him dragging you over to Giselle and her family, so RJ could ambush me."

The hand on my back goes still. "What do you mean?"

"While you were getting groped by your ex, I was in a corner being harassed by your brother." As he listens to me recounting the conversation with RJ, Chris' expression goes from anger to straight up rage, and when I add in the little bit of information I gleaned from Teresa about how his dad changed his mind about us, he looks ready to break something.

"Why can't he just let this shit go? If RJ and Giselle want to be together, then letting them ride off into the sunset together seems like the best solution."

An image of Giselle's face when she hugged Chris flashes through my mind. "I think you've only got half of that equation right, baby. I don't think Giselle wants to be with RJ, or at the very least she isn't ready to choose him when you're still an option."

His head snaps back. "But I'm not an option."

"*We* know that, but judging by the look on her face today when you hugged her, she doesn't think that's the case at all. And I'm sure your father's plotting isn't helping."

The unfair truth tastes bitter on my tongue. This shouldn't be happening. After all this time, we should be in a better place as far as his dad is concerned. Giselle and this forced marriage should be a distant memory. Something we laugh about when we think about how we fell in love and where the life we built together started. Right now it just feels so hopeless, like we're right back at square one with no options. No idea how to move forward. Only the desire to do so.

Chris' hand starts moving again, and I know it's his way of pulling me out of my head and back to him. But it's hard to unstick myself, to shake off the negative, despairing thoughts trying to take over.

"Hey." He blinks at me, chestnut eyes urging me to be here with him. "I love you, princess, and I'm not giving you up. I don't care what that costs me. My trust fund. My name. None of it matters more than you do."

I want to find comfort in his words, but I can't. Not yet. "Is that what happens when you break the family tradition? You get disowned and cut off?"

There's more hope in the question than necessary, but I can't help it. We never talked about what would happen if his dad believed that our relationship was real but just didn't care. If cutting Chris off is the worst Reese could do then maybe there is hope for us after all. I mean, Sloane's mom threatens to disown her every single day, and she's fine.

"No one has ever truly gone against it. I mean technically Dad did, but he still doubled back and got approval from his father. Everyone else has just fallen in line. I don't know what would happen if I refused, but I guess we're going to find out."

"You'd really do that for me? Give it all up?"

"Princess," he says, using a tone that admonishes me for even asking him that kind of question. "You're the only thing I have that's worth keeping."

Then he's surging forward with his mouth crashing into mine. I react instantly, moaning into his mouth helplessly while the sparks of electricity between us turn into a powerful, rushing current that's alive with desire and passion. Chris slips one of his arms under my legs and the other around my waist then pushes to his feet. He walks us over to the bed and lowers us down without breaking the kiss. I'm aware of the way he's hovering over me, holding his body to one side of mine while his busy hands grasp the cuffed sleeves of my dress and tug them down my arms.

The fabric pools at my waist, and I expect him to pull it all the way down, but he doesn't. Instead, he lifts up, eyes on fire as they skate over my body. Taking in the lace of my bra. I spread my legs, reaching down to yank the dress up and show him the matching panties. He saw them this morning when we got dressed, but it doesn't stop the sharp intake of breath or dull the glow in his eyes when his gaze reaches mine.

He prowls around the bed, stopping at the side that puts him closest to my head and lets him look down the length of my body. "I love when you spread your legs for me, princess."

"What about when I play with my pussy for you? Do you love when I do that?" I shift my panties to the side, run a shaky finger up and down my slit while he climbs onto the bed and urges me to sit up.

"I love everything you do." Once he's settled, I let my back rest against his chest. He runs his hands down my chest, pulling down the cups of my bra and pinching both of my nipples. I cry out, letting my eyes fall shut. "Open your eyes, baby. Look how fucking sexy you are."

I do as he says, realizing only then that he's positioned us across from the full-length mirror mounted on the wall. We're a ruffled, tangled, sexy, mess. Chris is still wearing his suit, his legs under mine, and I'm half naked. My breasts bared, nipples tightened into hardened peaks Chris keeps taking between his deft fingers. Pinching and teasing them while my hips writhe, rocking to the rhythm I'm creating with my own hand.

The sight of us makes me even more needy, and I spread my legs further. Chris sucks in another harsh breath as my berry brown folds part, revealing glistening lips and an engorged clit that's getting all of my attention.

Chris kisses my temple. A gentle press of his lips that doesn't match the rough way he's handling my breasts. I love the juxtaposition. The duality of being kissed like I'm the most precious thing in the world and touched with reckless abandon that speaks of unbridled passion and desire. My core clenches, reminding me of just how empty I am, how desperate I am to have him filling me up.

"I love you," he whispers in my ear, capturing the lobe between his teeth while he holds my gaze in the mirror. His words set another warm gush of liquid arousal free, coating my fingertips. I abandon my clit, running my fingers through my slippery folds until they're sticky and perfectly lubricated, ready to ease the pressure building low in my belly.

Chris knows exactly what I'm about to do, so he lifts his legs and bends his knees. The subtle change in his position pushes my legs up, bringing my knees closer to my chest and tilting my hips upwards so I can reach my opening more easily. He grunts in my ear, both of our eyes on the mirror as my middle finger disappears inside my pussy.

He growls, reaching down to stroke my breasts and then my stomach with reverent fingers. "I can hear how fucking wet you are, Mallory. It's driving me crazy."

I moan, desperate to tell him I'm being driven crazy too. Not by the sound of my finger moving in and out of my sex, but by him. By the things he's saying, and the sinful growls leaving his throat at regular intervals. They start deep in his chest, and I feel them moving through him, forcing their way out while he touches me like he can't ever imagine a world where he doesn't get to.

My head lolls on his shoulder, while I keep hazy, half-lidded eyes on our reflection. Chris is staring at me, his gaze moving between my churning hips and my face. Usually when we're together, I have my eyes screwed shut, lost to the things he makes me feel, so seeing us like this, getting to watch his reaction to me, has all of my senses heightened. Every touch, kiss, lick to my neck and nibble along my jaw is amplified. Every stroke of my fingers inside of my rippling walls is another drop in a bucket that's already threatening to overflow.

So when Chris moves his hand down further, capable and sure fingers working around my arm to find my swollen clit, I know I'm done for. He uses the pad of his middle finger to apply pressure, pressing down firmly and then rubbing in slow, perfect circles, setting a rhythm I follow with my hips while I add another finger to my ministrations. I raise my legs off of the bed, bending my knees further, so I can get deeper, and Chris uses his free hand to grip the back of one of my thighs for support.

Every one of my breaths is a moan. An audible representation of the pleasure rolling down my spine. The pressure building in my core, begging to be released. The clenching of my walls that increases as I start to massage my g-spot.

"*Oh my God.*" I arch up off of Chris, the sound of me panting my way to my release drowning out everything else.

"There it is." He smiles against the side of my neck, each word a brush of his lips that sends me sailing towards the finish line. "You're going to make a fucking mess of this bed aren't you, princess?" As he talks, he increases the movement of his hand and adds two more fingers so with every rotation of his wrist the most sensitive part of me is being caressed three times instead of one.

"Chris, please don't stop."

"I'm not going to stop, baby." I watch his expression in the mirror, the torrent of pleasure etched into his features emphasizing his words. "Not until you've ruined this bed like you've ruined me."

That's all it takes. The madness of his words, the dark timbre of his voice as he makes the most erotic promise, that's all it takes to send floods of heated pleasure through every inch of my body. My cries fill the room, echoing off of the walls while my orgasm spills out of me. Coating my fingers and the inside of my thighs on its way to soak into the expensive comforter and sheets beneath us. True to his word, Chris doesn't stop until the bed is past saving and I'm a boneless mess.

With a satisfied smirk on his lips and an erection tenting the pants of his suit, he untangles himself from me and heads to the bathroom. I expect him to come back immediately with a warm rag for me and a towel for the bed, but instead, I hear the sound of water running, filling the large soaker tub in the middle of the bathroom. I want to get up. The muscles in my legs and thighs ache to be submerged in hot water and bubbles, but I can't move yet.

When Chris returns, he's shed his suit and is wearing nothing but a white tank top and black briefs that hug his ass. He's still hard. The imprint of his dick evident through the cotton, and I have to avert my gaze to keep from dropping on my knees and begging him for more. Ever since our argument about having sex a few weeks ago, he's been so careful with me. Avoiding certain positions, making sure I come multiple times while refusing to let me do anything to please him. I get that he's afraid of losing control when we're together, but I wish he would hear me when I say I'm not scared of him or the things he wants.

He hauls me up off the bed and takes me by the hand, pulling me close and pressing kiss to the tip of my nose before he leads me into the bathroom. The lights are dimmed, and white bubbles float on top of the water. Chris stands behind me, making quick work of freeing me from my bundled-up dress and helping me into the tub. I sigh happily as I settle into the warm water. Chris kneels beside the tub with a wash-cloth in one hand and my bodywash in the other.

I arch a brow at him. "What exactly are you planning to do with those?"

"You know what I'm planning to do with these, princess. The only question is are you going to let me?" I have no qualms about him washing me. In fact, I welcome any act that involves his hands on my body, but the imploring look in his eye, the genuine desire to do this simple, caring task for me, makes me even more eager to say yes.

"I guess I'll allow it."

Chris shakes his head as he dips the washcloth into the water behind me and brings it back up, letting the stream of warm liquid trail down my back. He repeats the same process over each of my shoulders and arms. I relax into his touch, enjoying being cared for. "Thank you again, not just for being here but for being with me and putting up with all of the shit that comes along with it."

"We've both got our shit, babe. You've seen all of mine and loved me anyway. I'm just returning the favor." He opens his mouth like he wants to disagree with what I've said, but then he thinks better of it and closes it back. Our situations, the things that brought us together, are drastically different, but there's no denying that we've both dealt with monsters. That we were able to sort through all the bullshit and find each other is a miracle. A gift. A bright strip of sunlight in an otherwise cloudy sky.

We both deserve the happiness we've found. If we don't cherish it, don't spend every day feeling grateful for it, then people like Trent and his dad win.

And they don't deserve to win.

The thought has me feeling brave, a surge of hopefulness pushing words to the tip of my tongue that I wanted to keep to myself for just a little bit longer. "I need to tell you something."

Both of his brows pull together, as his gaze moves from the drops of water skating down my breasts to my face. "What is it?"

"It's nothing bad," I blurt out, laughing nervously. "I mean, I don't think it's bad, but I don't know how you're going to feel about it. I guess you could see it as a bad thing, but you'd have to have all the details before you decide that it is...."

"Princess." A small smile plays on his lips, and I can tell he's trying to hold it in because I hate how he laughs when I start rambling. "Just tell me what it is."

I take a deep breath, praying that he's going to see this as a good thing. "Well, you know that I only have one more semester left at NHU."

"Yeah, and I'll be in the front row screaming at the top of my lungs when you walk across that stage."

The image of him, Eric, Nic, Mama, and Sloane screaming down the walls when they hand me my degree makes me smile. "I know you will, but I haven't really been thinking about graduation so much as what comes after."

"You said you wanted to get your MBA, has that changed?"

"No." I shake my head, my heart starting to smack against my rib cage. "Not at all. I still want to get my MBA, but I don't think I want to do it at NHU anymore. I've been talking to Dr. Brennan about exploring different options since she came back to finish out Richardson's class, and she told me there's a great program at the College of Charleston."

I study his face, watching for any indication that my words have freaked him out, and see nothing but understanding tinged with happiness. He drops the washcloth, and it brushes my leg as it sinks to the bottom of the tub, but I don't care because now he's gripping my face and kissing me.

Water sloshes around, spilling over the edges as I move to my knees to hug him. His tank top is soaked in a matter of seconds, but he doesn't seem to care. He's just smiling down at me like I've made him the happiest man in the world just because I want to go to graduate school near him.

"How could you think I would take that badly? I've been dreading moving for months. I would love to have you in Charleston with me, princess."

His quick acceptance and clear excitement turn my heart into a warm pile of mush. Happy tears spring in my eyes as I try to tamper down my own excitement. "I haven't even applied yet. I might not get in."

"You will," he says, undeterred faith in me, bleeding into his response. I soak it in, let it become a part of me, allow it to wash away the seeds of doubt that his brother and father tried to plant before they can take root.

I know they're not done coming for us. They're not ready to let him go, not done trying to force him to accept a crown he doesn't want, but in this moment I feel sure we can weather any storm they throw our way because the future we've committed ourselves to protecting depends on it.

38

CHRIS

The text comes moments after Mallory falls asleep in my arms, and it physically pains me to leave her, nestled among the fresh set of bedding housekeeping put on the bed when we went out to dinner after her bath and my shower.

Our evening was so peaceful, filled with plans for a future I could see written in her eyes. Inscribed in amber like the letters of our name were etched into gold. We talked about being long-distance next semester, about her visiting me on the weekends, and the things she'd do to fill her days during the semester before her graduate classes started.

We talked for hours at dinner and then we came back to the room and talked some more, and I didn't think about my fucked up family or the grief trying to cave my chest in at all. I was all set to go to sleep and then my phone lit up the room, vibrating on the nightstand one time and displaying a text from my dad.

Dad: Downstairs. We need to talk.

I don't even ask how he knew where we were staying or why he thought I would want to see him at almost eleven o'clock at night. I just slip out of bed, pull on a pair of sweats and a hoodie, grab my key and leave the room. When I get to the hotel lobby, he's sitting at the bar sipping from a tumbler with dark liquid in it. He looks up just as I take the seat beside him, and I'm immediately reminded of the last entry I read in Mom's journal. The one about there being no warmth in his eyes when he looked at her.

There's none in them now, just a reptile-like coolness that sends a chill down my spine as he stares at me like he's waiting for me to open up the conversation.

I look at him blankly, refusing to start talking for fear of backing myself into a corner I can't get out of. He could be here to talk about any number of things—the funeral, Giselle, the journals I inherited mere hours ago he's probably desperate to get his hands on.

When it becomes clear I'm not going to say anything, he scoffs. "First, you slink out of my house without so much as a goodbye, then you refuse to greet me after I drive all the way over here to see you before your flight leaves in the morning."

It doesn't surprise me that he knows Mallory and I are flying out in the morning. After all, I told RJ, which means I might as well have said it to him. "I didn't ask you to come out here."

"And you didn't leave me with much of a choice when you left without saying goodbye to anyone." The bartender stops in front of me, and I shake my head before she has a chance to ask if I want a drink. I don't want anything that's going to prolong this conversation.

"I said goodbye to Teresa and Vanessa."

His jaw clenches, and his nostrils flare. "That's not the point, Christopher."

"Then what is the point, Dad?" I fight to keep my tone even. "And please get to it quickly, because I know you didn't come all the way down here to talk about the way I left a funeral you didn't even want me to attend."

"Is that what you're sulking about?" He takes a sip of his drink, a condescending laugh bouncing off the rim of the glass. "Not getting an invite to a funeral?"

The fingers on both of my hands ball into fists. "It wasn't just any funeral. It was Margaret's, and no matter how much you try to down-play it, you have to know how fucked up it is that she died and you didn't tell me. You were going to bury her without me being there even though you knew how much she meant to me."

"She wasn't your mother, Chris, and you clearly didn't think that much of her, or you would have made time to answer her phone calls." A triumphant gleam takes over his eyes, finally adding some semblance of warmth to them. "At any rate, I was planning on breaking the news to you after the semester ended. She was already gone, there was no use in distracting you when there was nothing you could have done. I wanted to tell you when you were back home. Here with your family and friends. Not hours away, with no one to help you through your grief but strangers."

Anger and frustration claw their way through my chest, begging for an out. Desperate for a chance to explode and destroy everything in this lobby including the man in front of me. There are so many things wrong with his statement I can't even address them all, so I just focus on the last part. My mind wandering to the circle of support my friends and Mallory formed around me when I learned about the loss he hid from me for his own selfish reasons.

"The people you're talking about are my friends, not strangers. They are my family. They've *been* my family for nearly two years."

"Two years?" He laughs, and the air from his mouth smells like the expensive Scotch he's drinking. "You say it like that's such a long time. You've been a Johnson for over twenty years. You've been my son, the heir to the throne, for ten times longer than you've known any of them, including *that girl* you brought into my house today."

Red starts to tint my vision. "Her name is Mallory, and if you're even considering saying something disrespectful about her, then I suggest you think again."

For a second, he looks impressed by the vehemence in my tone, and it reminds me of the way he looked when I first told him about Mallory. But then it fades away, leaving nothing but annoyance in its wake. "It's always been funny to me how self-assured a man becomes when he starts getting pussy on the regular." His vulgar choice of words sends shock coursing through me, making it impossible to respond. "So I'm supposed to believe you're a man now huh, son? You got a pretty little thing on your arm, sitting on your lap and looking at you with those big eyes that make you feel like you hung the fucking moon, and now I'm supposed to believe you don't need me behind you?"

"I don't." I grind out, the vein jumping in my temple the only physical sign of my outrage. I've always known my father could be ruthless, but I've never actually been on the receiving end of it. It's disconcerting, and it makes me think, once again, about how my mother said she felt around him towards the end of her life. "I've gotten by just fine without you for the last four years."

Another snort, this one loud and derisive, escapes him. "While you were driving a car I pay for. Living in an apartment I pay for. Wearing clothes, attending a school, eating food that I pay for. You haven't done anything for yourself over the last four years. I've paid for your entire life, Christopher, including your little excursion to New Haven."

"Because that's your fucking job." I slam my fists on the bar, hitting it so hard his empty glass shakes and the bartender turns to look at us. "And you know what? It's the least you can do. *Literally.* Do you expect me to thank you for doing the bare minimum? For throwing money at every problem and sacrificing the happiness and well-being of your children for the sake of a legacy they don't even want to be a part of? Well, thank you, Dad. Thank you for being the shittiest fucking parent to ever live."

"I'm the only fucking parent you have, Christopher." He turns in his seat and leans in close, so we're face to face. "No matter how many times you wake up from your nightmares, crying for your mommy, you can't change that I'm here and she's not. Call me a shit father if you want, but I've done more for you than that woman has over the course of her entire miserable existence."

"Mom died, Dad. *She died* giving you another slave to Johnson empire. Your fucked up parenting choices, and the way I feel about them, don't have anything to do with her."

Just a second ago he was seething, practically foaming at the mouth, but as soon as he processes my response the screw that must have come loose in his mind, clicks back into place. He pushes out a harsh breath and blinks rapidly, sitting back in his seat. He runs his hand over his face, and I can tell he's trying to regroup. To get some control over himself and the conversation that's gone so far off-topic.

"This isn't about your mother or whatever you think you know about our marriage. She's the past. You are the future of this family, and I won't let you throw it away for some girl."

I want to punch something. More specifically, I want to punch him for looping this frustrating discussion back around to Mallory. The future we were planning just hours ago flashes before my eyes as fear fills my gut. My dad has a history of taking the things I love, the things that make me happy, away, and despite what I believed to be true before, he seems determined to see history repeat itself.

And I just can't let that happen.

"She isn't just some girl, Dad. I *love* her, and I never said it was about her."

"You think I don't recognize a man destined for greatness being distracted from his true purpose by a nice ass? I've been there, son. I've made the mistake you're about to make, and I'm going to do for you what my father should have done for me, cut the problem out by the root."

The way he talks about my mother makes it easy to realize why he has gone so long without speaking of her at all. There's nothing loving or tender in his depictions of her and their marriage. In fact, it sounds like he spent more time hating her than he did loving her.

Now it makes sense why he wasn't moved by my attempt to recreate the circumstances that allowed him to circumvent tradition: he regrets the choice he made.

I just don't understand why.

And I don't have time to figure it out, right now I just need to focus on making him realize that Mallory and I are not him and Mom. "Mal isn't some problem for you to solve, Dad. She's my future."

"We'll see about that." I feel conflicted as I watch him rise from his seat. I don't really want to keep talking to him, but I hate that the conversation is ending when I'm trying to make sure he understands that I'm not letting Mallory go.

He throws a twenty on the bar and starts to move towards the exit. Just when I think he's about to walk out without acknowledging what I said, he stops behind my seat and claps me on the shoulder.

"Go back to New Haven, son. Ace those finals. Fuck that girl out of your system and enjoy it because once you walk across that stage you're coming back home to honor your commitments."

I shrug his hand off then hop out of my seat to look him dead in the eye. "Those are not my commitments, they're yours, and I won't walk away from the one good thing in my life to honor them for you. We've spent months going back and forth about this, which is dumb because I should have just told you I'm not doing it. *Any of it.* I'm not moving back to Boston. I'm not going to Harvard or studying cardiothoracics, sure not marrying Giselle DuPont, so you can take all of your talk about commitments and legacy and shove it up your ass."

Saying those words out loud is the greatest relief. I feel like a thousand-pound weight has been lifted from my chest, and I wonder why I waited so long to do this. To speak my intentions clearly and stand behind them fully. To show my father, once and for all, the days of him calling the shots for my future are long gone.

I get less than half of a second to bask in that feeling, in the shimmery glow of independence and self-actualized control. Because that's how long it takes my dad to curl his lips into a menacing smile and transform his gaze into a daunting dare that sticks with me long after he walks out of the lobby without saying another word.

I see it as I make my way back up to the room. Hallucinate that it's reflected back at me through the black screen of the TV in the living room as I settle on the couch and start thumbing through more of Mom's journals, looking for more instances of her being frightened by the monster I just went toe to toe with.

And when I finally fall asleep, with my mother's journals scattered on the couch around me and her words swirling in my head, that ominous smile appears in my dreams. Stretched across his face as his fingers wrap around a woman's arm, dragging her away from me while she kicks and screams and fights to break free.

At first, it's my mother, her face frozen in agony and her stomach sliced open. The gaping wound gushing blood that runs down her legs. It leaves a smeared trail of red, and I follow it, disturbed but also not surprised to see her in such a state.

But then the woman changes. Her frame fills out. Her curves are familiar, ones I know by heart. And instead of an open stomach wound, there's blood on her thighs and her tattered clothes.

My father stares down at her in disgust, barely touching her as he drags her out of my reach.

39

MALLORY

I wake up to the sound of whimpering. Desperate, guttural exhalations that pierce the darkness of the bedroom and pull me out of my sleep. I roll over, reaching for Chris and finding nothing but empty sheets that are cool to the touch. Confused, by the sounds filling my ears and his absence, I slide out of bed and head into the living room where I find a sight that breaks my heart.

Chris is curled up on the sofa. A stack of his mother's journals on the coffee table in front of him. One of them is open, lying face down like he just sat it there. Except I know that's not right because he's asleep, his handsome face twisted into a mask of agony while the sounds that woke me fall from his lips.

I stop dead in my tracks, and my heart splits open because I know those sounds. I mean I haven't actually ever heard them come from him, but I know what they mean. Everyone's nightmares are different, made of different haunting images, inspired by different monsters, but they all sound the same.

A soundtrack of despair that's recognizable to any person who's ever been unlucky enough to have their brains turn against them when they're at their most vulnerable.

Chris frowns and shifts around on the couch. His long legs are restless, like he's walking or running, but I don't know if he's moving towards something or away from it. Slowly, I pad across the room and lower myself to the floor in front of him. This close, I can see the way rapid rise and fall of his chest and the notches in between his brows. My hand shakes as I lift it up and run a tentative finger over his jaw.

"Chris," I whisper, my heart rate rising when he stirs. "Wake up, baby. You're having a bad dream." I repeat the words over and over again, keeping my voice gentle and even until he finally blinks his way back into consciousness.

As soon as he sees me, he reaches for me, pulling me into him while he sits up on the couch. I move with him, climbing onto his lap, my bare thighs bracketing his hips as he squeezes me tight.

"You're okay." His voice is thick, clogged with sleep and grief I don't understand.

I lean back to get a look at his face. "You were dreaming about me?"

"I thought he took you from me."

"Who?" My question is lost in the gasp leaving my lips when his hands come up to cradle my face, pulling me down to meet his mouth. The kiss is fraught with fevered urgency, and everything else falls away. The nightmare, the nameless, faceless man he thought took me from him. All of it stops mattering.

His lips and tongue overpower mine, leading the carnal rhythm that trickles through my body and inspires the swirling of my hips. I can feel Chris growing hard beneath me. All the sexual tension that's been stored in his body for weeks now rushing to his dick in an instant, creating a massive erection that feels like a rod of heated steel between my thighs.

I grind down on it, seeking friction that will lead to pleasure for us both. Chris' hands leave my face, trailing down my neck and over my breasts before coming to rest at my waist. His touch is just as urgent as his kiss. I can even feel the blunt edges of his nails through the thin cotton of my t-shirt.

They dig into my skin while Chris urges me to move faster, to press down harder because he's arching up to meet me. My mind is spinning, excitement swelling in my chest as my body responds to him and the silent message he's sending, telling me he wants this.

That he needs it as much as I do.

I reach down and grab his wrist, taking his hand off of my waist and guiding it to my core. He groans into my mouth when he feels that the moisture seeping out of me has coated the sliver of fabric making up the front of my thong. And then his fingers are curling around it, his knuckles brushing my clit as he gives one hard pull and shreds my underwear with minimal effort.

The thong gives easily, but the sound of it tearing shatters the spell we're under. Chris breaks the kiss, sending me plummeting head first out of the cloud of desire we just created. I groan when he looks down at the ruined thong and lets go of me to run an agitated hand over his head. I watch as the man that was just devouring me disappears, making way for the calm and considerate man I love but want no parts of right now.

He shakes his head, trying to regain his composure, to calm down enough to talk us out of something we both clearly want to do.

"Princess, I shouldn't have—"

"No." I cut him off, taking my hands off his shoulders to grab his face and force him to look at me. The glassiness that was in his eyes when he first woke is gone, but the shadows of his nightmares remain, lingering beneath the surface of conflicted pools of chestnut. "You can say anything to me right now. You can give me any reason why you don't want to go further tonight, and I promise I'll accept it. I can understand if you're not in the right head space. If you're not in the mood. But don't you dare make this about fear because I'm not afraid of you, Chris."

A vein in his temple jumps, activated by the tight clench of his jaw. "You should be."

"Why? Because you ripped my thong? Because you like to bite my neck and grip my waist so hard you might leave your fingerprints in my skin?" Even though he looks horrified by my words, his dick throbs. "Why should any of that scare me?"

"Because you deserve so much better than that, princess. You deserve gentle hands and loving kisses, and I can't give you that right now. I'm not going to take you while I'm like this. I'm not going to fuck you like some kind of…."

The fingers in the one hand still on my hip flex as he swallows the word that my mind fills in on its own.

Animal.

All at once, pieces of a conversation I overheard my former suite mate having with one of her upperclassmen friends come back to me. They were in our shared bathroom that connected our rooms, gossiping about guys they'd slept with while they got ready for a party. Despite being in a relationship with some guy named Ash, Jasmine was matching the girl she was talking to hook up for hook up. Somewhere along the way, Chris' name came up. I tried not to listen, but they were so loud. Laughing and cackling while Jasmine's friend dropped words like rough and wild as she described a late-night encounter with him.

Frustration winds its way through my body, unfurling in slow coils that make a home next to the ball of jealousy living in my stomach. I know Chris has slept with other women. He's never tried to keep his past a secret, but right now the thought of him with someone else makes me sick. Countless women have had this part of him, have been given the gift of his feral thrusts and untamed touch. All things I want from him but he refuses to give to me because he can't get over what Trent did.

"Do I even get a choice in the matter?" I grip his jaw harder, the pressure I'm applying making his pupils dilate.

"Of course, you get a choice, princess."

I lick my lips. "Then ask me what I want, Chris."

He shakes his head, already aware of the answer to the question he hasn't asked. "Mallory."

"Ask me what I want." He swallows, and I make a mental note to trace his Adam's apple with my tongue. "Ask me, baby. Don't be scared."

"What do *you* want, princess?"

I lean in and drop a kiss on his lips, every word of my answer a brush of skin that paints my desire on the canvas of his mouth. "I want you to fuck me like you know I won't break. I want it hard and rough and perfect. I want to be sore when I wake up in the morning, and then I want you to spread my legs and fuck me again. I want your teeth in my skin and your hands in my hair. I want us—our desires, our moods, our needs—to be the only thing determining how we do this. Not my past. Not your fears about hurting me or your thoughts about what I deserve. Because what I deserve is a partner who trusts me to decide what I want and how I want it."

"I do trust you."

"And you want me?" I have to ask, have to make sure I'm not reading this wrong, that I'm not stomping all over his boundaries. Chris nods, a humorless puff of air passing through his flared nostrils.

"I want you too much, Mallory."

"Good, because I want you too, Chris." I'm whining, and I don't even care. "I want you. However you are. Whatever you need to give me, where ever you want to take me. That's where I want to go."

Pulling back, I let go of his jaw and grip the hem of my shirt. Chris' hands turn to fists at my hip as I pull it up and over my head, tossing it onto the floor. My chest heaves, nipples tightening in anticipation as his hungry gaze sweeps over them. He sweeps his tongue over his teeth. A predator considering its prey and just barely resisting the urge to pounce.

I run my hands over my belly and palm my breasts, moaning when my thumbs brush against the hardened buds.

"I don't have a condom, Mallory."

His voice is tight, words coated with tension as he makes a last-ditch effort to talk me out of this. "You know that I take my birth control religiously."

A growl—low and feral with the promise of devastation—fills the air, and it's the only warning I get before he launches himself at me, flipping us over so I'm on the couch and he's kneeling in front of me. He gazes up the length of my body, serious eyes holding mine while he spreads my thighs.

"If it gets to be too much, princess, tap out."

I nod, lust clogging my throat. "I will. I promise."

I half expect him to say something else, to reiterate his point about signaling my overwhelm or ask me if I'm sure one more time, but he doesn't. As soon as I make my promise, he breaks the single thread holding up my ruined thong and tosses the scrap to the side. Then he's pushing my legs up, setting my heels on the edge of the couch so my pussy is on full display.

He dives for it, burying his head in my folds, his tongue lashing wildly while the most obscene sounds come from someplace deep in his chest. They move up his throat, echoing along my aching slit, adding to the pleasure he's working into my body with his mouth.

My hands go to his hair, fingertips gliding through curls that have grown longer in the time we've been together, nails digging into his scalp with enough force to elicit a snarl from him. He turns his head, warm lips grazing the inside of my thigh before he bares his teeth and sinks them into the soft flesh. I arch up off of the couch, a moan stuck in my throat as he returns his attention to my pussy, this time focusing on my clit while the rough pads of his fingertips find my entrance.

I open my mouth, prepared to beg him to put them inside me, but he beats me to the punch. Slipping in his index finger first, curling it so it touches all the right places, and then adding in another. When he gives me a third one, the pressure is almost too much. I feel my body resisting him, fighting against the intrusion even as the pleasure of being so full sends tremors of ecstasy down my spine.

"Breathe," Chris orders roughly as he scissors them in and out of me. Stretching me. Preparing me. Not just for his dick but for the reality of being fucked by something with more girth than my fingers, with more presence than my vibrator. I push out a breath, and a moan follows as the burning sensation subsides and the pleasure takes its place. "That's it. You're doing so well, princess."

I'm rocking into him, meeting each thrust of his fingers with a grind of my hips that pulls him deeper into me. With my hands still on his head, I guide his mouth back to my cunt, the slick skin slipping easily over his as I fuck his face. The combination of his fingers and tongue coaxes my release to the surface at a rate I didn't even realize was possible. Tears leak out of the corners of my eyes, accompanying the warm liquid that gushes from me in forceful, repeated streams that would be embarrassing if I had the capacity to care.

As it stands, the only thing I do care about right now is the way Chris' hums of approval vibrate against my clit as he laps up every drop, fingers still plunging in and out of my rippling walls. When he finally pulls back, his chin and neck are shiny, dripping with my essence, and his eyes are wild with lust.

"Next time I'm going to make you do that in a cup, so I can make sure I drink every drop."

I blush, feeling shy even though there's nothing but reverence in his tone. "I've never…that's never happened before."

He extracts his fingers and places both of his palms on the insides of my thighs. So close that his thumbs are resting on the outside of my pussy lips. I feel them flex, pressing into my skin as his eyes fall shut on a tortured groan.

"Don't tell me that, Mallory. I'm barely holding it together as it is." When he opens his eyes, he looks even more feral, and I smile, thoroughly turned on by the sight of him.

"I thought we agreed you weren't going to try to hold it together."

He lets go of me and pushes to his feet. I watch in awe as he starts to strip off his clothes, yanking off his shirt, pushing down his sweatpants and underwear at the same time to reveal his stunningly hard dick. He grips the base of his shaft in a tight fist and runs it from the veined root to the smooth tip that's dripping precum.

I gasp, and he blesses me with a devious grin I feel right in my trembling core. "We agreed that I'd give you what we both want. In order for me to do that and make it good for you, I need some self-control, baby. If only to keep me from blowing my load the second I get inside you."

"*Oh.*"

He lifts his brows, humor sparkling in his eyes. "Yeah. Now stand up, princess."

I do as he says, and he walks a slow circle around me. Biting his lip and pumping his dick with a rough fist while he examines me. A fresh wave of arousal washes over me, and the tingles of awareness skittering across my skin feel familiar. They're similar to the way I felt when he was following me at the skating rink and when he chased me at his house. Only this time, I'm not moving. I'm not running.

I'm caught. Trapped in his gaze. Held hostage by desire that I welcomed. That I chose. My heart swells with love for him, and I stand still, refusing to move even when he's out of my line of sight because I know he won't do anything to scare me.

"Turn around." The command comes from behind me, uttered in a low, decadent tone. I do as he says and find myself inches from his handsome face. The scent of my release wafting in the air between us. Chris takes a step back, eyes still on me as he sits down on the sofa, taking the seat that's wet because of me.

He spreads his arms out along the back of the couch, the golden inches of his skin made even more beautiful by the brown leather. I stare at his dick, the proud length protruding from between his hard thighs, and lick my lips, already imagining what he'll taste like on my tongue. Chris shakes his head.

"You can taste it later, princess. Right now I want you to sit on it."

Riding dick isn't exactly a part of my skill set, but I don't let my lack of knowledge stop me from walking over to him with a sultry sway. And it damn sure doesn't stop me from straddling him, my thighs framing his powerful hips as I hover above the flared crown of his tip.

Chris' hands go to my waist, but his eyes are on my face. I don't know what he sees there, but I hope it's not the panic flaring in my chest or the quiet fear trickling down my spine as my brain screams at me that I can't do this. That letting him fuck me with his fingers and his tongue are a far cry from *this*.

"Princess—" I can hear the acceptance in his voice, the understanding wrapped up in that one little word, and I don't want it. I don't want reassurance or pity. I don't want anything but him. So before he can finish his sentence, I lift my hips up and slam them back down. Thankful for the lingering juices from my orgasm that ease the way and allow me to seat him to the hilt with a single motion.

"Jesus!" Chris shouts, holding me so tightly I couldn't move if I wanted to. And I'm not sure I want to. My mind is spinning, disorientated, struggling to make sense of the pain and pleasure of being filled this way. Stretched past my limits with every inch of his thickness kissing the deepest, most sensitive parts of me. I squeeze my eyes shut, will myself to breathe, to remember that this is what I wanted.

That it's still what I want.

"Look at me." His words are strained, and they match the tension in his body perfectly. He's trying not to move, resisting the urge to thrust into me. "Mallory, *look at me*." My eyes pop open, and the faintest hint of relief winds its way through my chest when I see his calm features. "There you are. Do you want to stop?"

"No, please. I can do this."

"I know you can do this, but that's not what I asked."

"No." I'm relieved to realize it's not a lie. "*No*. I don't want to stop."

"Then keep your eyes open, baby." He leans forward and kisses me, moving from my mouth down my jaw and then to the side of my neck where he licks and bites me. "Stay right here with me."

I wrap my arms around his neck, holding him, keeping his earthy scent at the forefront of my mind as I start to move. Using his broad shoulders as support while I lift my hips and drop them back down. Once. Twice. Three times before I find a rhythm that works for me and allow myself to get lost in the scent of our lust filling the air, lighting up every nerve ending in my body until my soul is on fire with love and purpose.

Purpose that makes me think the only thing I was ever meant to do was sit on the throne that is his lap. His princess. His queen. Impaled on a scepter, stripped bare by the sheer power of his sword, ruling from the most primal, most possessive part of me.

Chris grunts as I clamp down on him, my body desperate to claim him as my birthright, to memorize every ridge and vein of the length that was made for me. I feel rather than hear the noise because it gets lost in the hollow space at the base of my neck, swallowed by the sound of his tongue lapping up the sweat gathering there.

His teeth knock against my collar bone, daring the skin to break so he can inject his need directly into my bloodstream, and then, when that's not enough, because it can never be enough, right into the marrow of my bones.

"Fuck, Chris," I moan into his ear, making sure he hears me over the sound of my ass slapping against his thighs. "It's so good."

"That's right, princess." His praise has bolts of lightning exploding inside my chest and trickling into all of my limbs. "Say my name. Don't ever forget that it's me inside of you. That it's my dick filling your pussy up."

My walls convulse around him, and I feel myself growing slicker as his words reverberate through me. The reminder that I'm safe, that I'm in control, isn't lost on me, and I loosen my hold on his neck, so I can dive for his mouth. My appreciation and love for him evident with each stroke of my tongue over his.

With his newfound freedom, Chris buries one hand at the nape of my neck, twisting his fingers through the braids flowing down my back and pulling hard while the other finds a home at my waist.

His grip is tight, commanding as he helps me keep the tempo I've set, and I relish in the feel of his flesh pressing into mine. Marvel at the pleasure being stoked into my body every time his dick slides in and out of me. I never imagined it could be this way, that I could feel this safe, this loved, in anyone's arms. Chris is an anomaly. A departure from all the meager expectations I had for my life. He made me want more. More goodness. More adventure. More passion and fearlessness.

More love.

"I love you." I slide my arms back around his neck, allow my fingers to sink into his sweat-dampened roots, and grip the curls there. I slow down, changing the rhythm to a slow grind that crushes my clit against his abs and creates the most lascivious squelching sound that makes us both moan loudly.

Chris' eyes lock on mine, and I know he sees it. What he means to me. What this moment means to me. He starts rocking up, deep, slow thrusts that are punctuated by his response. "I love you more, princess."

I don't get to tell him there's no way he loves me more because before I can respond he wraps his arms around my middle and tilts me back until I'm laying on the coffee table. He's half-kneeling, half-standing between my legs, still buried deep inside me. The rough way he grips my waist and yanks me down to the edge surprises a delighted yelp out of me, and he chuckles darkly.

"You like that, princess?"

"I love it."

His head dips down, lips, teeth, and tongue taking turns abusing and spoiling the lush curve of my belly and the undersides of my breasts. All the while his hips are pistoning in and out of me, dragging the head of his dick over my g-spot and tormenting my clit with the near-constant collision of his pelvic bone until his movements grow jerky and my body is clutching at him, pounding out the cadence of my release.

"Come, princess," he says hoarsely. "Come all over this dick because it's yours. It fucking belongs to you."

I place my hands on his forearms, scoring my nails into his skin while my body gives in to the orgasm curling my toes and forcing a long, strangled cry from my lips.

Chris pulls up to look at me, his face a mask of concentrated pleasure that shatters like glass when his release finds him. He roars my name as he floods me with hot ropes of white cum that scorch me. Branding me as his and promising that he will always be mine.

If only that were true.

40

MALLORY

After we return to New Haven, Chris barely lets me out of his sight. The only time we've been apart in the last week and a half is when one, or both, of us has to sit for an exam, or I go to bed and leave him up on the couch thumbing through one of his mom's journals.

I've enjoyed all the time we've gotten together—especially with graduation a few days away and his fall move-in date growing closer with every passing minute—but I'm also grateful for some rare one-on-one time with Sloane while Chris picks up his graduation tickets and takes his textbook rentals back to the on-campus bookstore.

We've been in her room all day, relaxing instead of packing, and she's listened intently to every detail I wanted to share about the trip to Boston, which was pretty much everything except what I learned about Chris' nightmares.

He told me about them after we made love and I pressed him for answers about the dream I woke him up from, specifically who he thought was taking me away from him. My heart broke when he said his mind had twisted his recurring nightmare about the last day of his mother's life into images of his father dragging me away while he ran to catch up to us.

It didn't take much to decipher the meaning of the nightmare, especially after he told me about their conversation at the hotel bar. He's afraid to lose me, and his dad is determined to take me away from him. Only I don't know how he plans to do it. Realistically, he can't force us apart. He can't lock Chris away in that big house in Boston or make him disappear off the face of the Earth, and that's exactly what he'd have to do.

He'd have to destroy every fiber of the connection between us, decimate every atom of our bond, and Reese Johnson might be a powerful man, but he can't do that. No one has the power to do that except for us. I know Chris won't do that, and I certainly won't.

"If you move to Charleston, how are we going to be roomies until Eric and I get married?" Sloane pouts, and I roll my eyes, forgetting that the last thing I said was about the possibility of me moving after I graduated.

Her words tug on my heartstrings, already making me miss the things I'll leave behind when I take this next step. Her, Eric, Mama, and Nic. The familiarity of New Haven—the place that's always been my home. I had all these plans for how my life was going to look once I finished undergrad, a million little dots connected together by string I was desperate to keep tacked to the board because holding it in place gave me some semblance of control.

I'm still a planner, still dependent on the dopamine hit that comes from knowing exactly how to solve a problem and what to do to avoid it next time, but the need for control has died down. Turned into a quiet hum instead of a raging storm of sound that was alive beneath my skin, drowning out everything else.

A lot of that change has to do with Chris, but more of it has to do with me. With who I allowed myself to become, the parts of my long-lost self that I gave permission to flourish and thrive under his careful touch. I'm not the girl I was before Trent, and part of me hates that I'll never be her again, but I like this new version of me. She's a nice mix of the girl who was hurt and the one who saved her, and I can't wait to see how she continues to grow and change.

"You and Eric could just move in together. That's what Chris and I are going to do." He already showed me the apartment he leased, told me all about his plan to turn the guest bedroom into an office where we can study.

Sloane rolls her eyes and bumps me with her shoulder. We're laying side by side on her bed, and she's scrolling through her phone while I flip through a magazine. "You'll be two hundred miles away, which means you can do whatever you want. If Eric and I move in together right under Mama's nose, we'll have to hear about how disappointed she is in us for shacking up every Sunday."

"Well, sounds like you two better have a shotgun wedding."

"Shotgun weddings are for pregnant girls with drunk daddies who have more guns than sense. I don't think that applies to us."

"You're right. I bet Mark doesn't even own a gun."

"He doesn't…..wait, Mal, have you seen this?" She slides her phone over to me, the screen open to an article on some online news site. The headline says something about a local New Haven man confessing to multiple rape allegations after several women came forward and compelling information was found in his home.

I'm about to ask Sloane why she thinks I'd be interested in this real-life version of a Law and Order SVU episode when I scroll down and see Trent's face staring back at me. His eyes are hollow, sunken into blotchy skin that makes it look like he's been crying.

"Where did you find this?"

"Eric sent it to me. He said this is your friend Tasha's brother?"

"Yeah." I try to force some kind of emotion into my answer, but it's hard when I don't feel anything. Well, that's not exactly true. I feel a lot of things. Happy Trent is finally getting what's coming to him. Relieved I didn't have to reveal what he did to me in order for that to happen. And a little sad I kept my secret and made it possible for him to hurt more women. It's a lot to process all at one time. "She's not my friend anymore though."

"Good. I would hate for you to be associated with the likes of him." She scrunches her nose up, taking the phone from me and closing the article. "God, what a gross fucking human."

Even though her outrage isn't for me, it still feels good to hear it.

To have someone else see the monster behind Trent's charming facade and name it. It makes me want to hug her, so I do, and she laughs as I squeeze her tight then let her go. She gives me a puzzled look as I roll off her bed and head to her door, giving in to the sudden urge to see the one person I can talk candidly with about this new development.

"I gotta go. I'll see you later, okay?"

The door shuts behind me, drowning out her response, but I don't care because the further I move away from her, the deeper the news sets in.

Trent confessed.

He admitted to being the scum of the fucking Earth, and he's going to pay for what he did to those girls. For what he did to me. Out of all the emotions moving through me as I drive to Chris' apartment, I choose to focus on the happy, on the peace settling deep in my bones yet somehow makes me feel lighter as I use my key to unlock his door and walk into his apartment.

I kick off my shoes by the door and head down the hallway. When I enter the living room, all thoughts of Trent's arrest fall by the wayside, washed away by the sight of Reese Johnson Sr. standing in the middle of the floor. His eyes, which are so similar to Chris' it's eerie, narrow as they land on me.

"Hello, Mallory."

A shiver rolls down my spine, inspired by the malicious smile lining his lips. I don't let it stop me from moving further into the living room, though. I'm not scared of him, and I want him to know it. "Dr. Johnson, what a pleasure to see you again. I didn't know you were in town."

He watches me cross over to the kitchen island with flared nostrils, obviously annoyed at how comfortable in his son's space. "Yes, well, I wasn't going to miss the chance to see my son walk across the stage and get his degree."

From the university you've disparaged for four years? I swallow the question, lifting my brows in faux understanding. "Chris is an extremely hard worker, and he'll make a hell of a doctor. You must be very proud he's chosen to honor your wife with his life's work."

A vein in his temple jumps, and I wonder if he's about to give me a speech about all the ways Chris is disrespecting the Johnson legacy with his choices. "I have never had any doubts about my son's capabilities as a physician, but thank you for giving me your opinion on the matter."

The way he says it, with sarcasm dripping from every word, makes it clear he places no value on my thoughts about his son. He flicks his gaze to the hallway that leads to Chris' bedroom, impatience clear in the purse of his lips.

"Would you like me to go see what's keeping him?"

I'm not trying to antagonize him, but I can tell by the way he scoffs that I have. "No, if I need to know what's keeping my son, I'll go see for myself."

I throw up both my hands. "Okay. Well, excuse me for trying to be helpful."

He gives a long-suffering sigh, eyes going to the hallway again, and this time I'm looking with him. I want to know where Chris is and what's taking him so long. For all I know, he could be in his room freaking out about his dad's sudden appearance.

They haven't talked since we left Boston. He didn't even think he was coming to graduation, and now he's here, standing in the middle of the living room being rude and impatient.

"Why are you here, Mallory?"

"I'm sorry?" Surely, I didn't hear him correctly. He didn't just make it seem like I'm unwelcome in a place I've practically been living in for months now. "I could ask you the same thing. It's not like you and Chris have talked since the funeral."

"There you go again, speaking on things you know absolutely nothing about." He folds his arms behind his back, and the motion pulls the expensive fabric of his jacket taut. "You think our lack of communication means something? He's still my son, the heir to a throne I've dedicated my life to preparing for him."

"A throne he doesn't want."

"Of course he wants it." He sounds so sure. Every word ringing with the same certainty that RJ's did when he cornered me at the repast. I try not to be shaken by it, but even I can't deny their knowledge of Chris runs deeper than mine.

They are the people that shaped him, molded him into a man with a love and dedication to medicine that rivals their own. A long time ago, Chris told me that his family chose medicine for him, and his desire to practice it, to save lives, grew to match their expectations. If they were right about that, they could be right about this too, about him eventually growing into the life they have planned for him.

"I know my son, Mallory. He's acting out now because four years of being in this town has made him lose sight of his purpose, but I'll bring him back into the fold and keep him from throwing away his future on the likes of you."

I open my mouth to respond and am interrupted by the sound of Chris coming down the hallway. Both Reese and I turn, but I'm the only one who sucks in a sharp breath when I see him appear in a khaki blazer with a black shirt, that hugs his abs, tucked inside matching black pants. He looks good—walking trust fund, good—and even though I've seen him in dress clothes before, there's something heart-breaking about the sight of him in them now.

And though I'm hesitant to admit it to myself, deep down I know. I know that this version of him, so close to the one I witnessed in Boston, is a living, breathing representation of the Chris that doesn't belong to me. My Chris smiles and jokes and laughs. He makes me see light in the world. He made me believe in the magic of wishes again.

This man is different. Serious in all the ways I used to think I wanted him to be. Power in every commanding stride of his long legs. Darkness cast over his handsome features. A reminder of the side of him I glimpsed during our very first kiss. I walked away from that moment thinking Chris would be my greatest mistake, another tragedy sealed with a kiss.

So far, I've been wrong, and I can only hope it'll stay that way.

He's fixing the button on the cuff of one of his sleeves, but as soon as he hears the hiss of air kissing my teeth, his head snaps up and he looks straight at me. A bright smile stretches across his face as he moves over and pulls me into a hug.

"Princess, I was just about to text you."

I feel Reese's eyes on us, watching as his son plants a kiss on my lips and shines his warm adoration on me. "You should have. I would have stayed at Sloane's until after you got back from dinner with your father."

"Why'd you come over early? Is everything okay?"

My mind immediately goes to Trent and the news I wanted to share with him, but I push it away. The last thing I want to do is discuss my deepest, darkest secret with his father in the room. "Yeah, everything is fine, we just got done early."

"Do you want to come to dinner with us?" He stretches his eyes, imploring me to say yes. Initially, I couldn't get a read on him to gauge how he was feeling about his dad being in New Haven, but now that he's staring at me, the silent plea stretching between us, I get it.

He's even less happy to see him than I am.

Reese steps forward, glancing at the watch on his wrist. "That won't be possible tonight, Chris. We have reservations, and we can't wait for Mallory to find an outfit that would be suitable for the restaurant."

Chris glares at him. "Seriously, Dad? Mallory has clothes here, she can be ready—"

"Chris." I cup his face, gently turning his attention back to me. "It's fine. I'm a little tired anyways, so I'll probably just lay down and see you when you get back."

"See, son. She'll be fine," Reese says, stepping forward to put his hand on Chris' shoulder and start leading him towards the door.

Chris gives me a disbelieving look, but after a few backward steps, he turns around and falls into step beside his father. I watch them go, their strides matched, and try to ignore the sinking feeling in my gut.

The one that tells me no good will come from Reese Johnson being in New Haven.

41

CHRIS

Mallory once accused my father of orchestrating ambushes, and as I look around the dimly lit restaurant inside the hotel where he's staying, making note of every familiar face at the dinner table, I can't help but think about how right she was.

Dad showed up at my door unannounced, acting like the fight we had after Margaret's funeral, and the cavern of silence that's been between us since, never happened. He asked me to come to dinner, so we could talk through things and come to a solution that would work for both of us.

Never once did he mention that Giselle and her parents would be joining us.

I should have turned around and walked out as soon as I saw Oscar and Ramona seated on one side of the table across from their daughter. But instead of doing that, I took a seat in the chair beside Giselle while my dad took a seat at the head of the table and prayed that whatever solution he was offering would be worth suffering through dinner with the DuPonts.

Small talk carried us through the first two courses of the meal with Dad and Oscar leading the charge. They talked about business and colleagues while Ramona chugged vodka martinis like a fish, and

Giselle and I pretended to be interested. Every so often, she would give a conspiratorial roll of her eyes, which made me laugh but do nothing to ease the tension in my neck caused by her and her parents' presence.

"I never got the chance to thank you for this," she says as the third course comes out, brushing her hand over the diamonds set inside the thin, white gold bracelet I bought her for the debutante ball. "When it arrived before the ball, I was so touched. I've worn it ever since."

"She has," Ramona adds in, smiling at me from across the table. "You picked out a wonderful piece, Christopher. It's classic, timeless."

Her words remind me of Mallory's description of the necklace I gave her the night I told her I loved her. Hours after I put it on her, I caught her in the mirror admiring herself and listened intently as she told me that her favorite thing about it was that it would never go out of style. The smile on my face isn't for them, but Giselle and her mother still light up when they see it, so I force myself to dial it back.

"Thank you, Ramona." I turn back to her daughter. "And I'm glad you like it, Giselle, but I can't take all the credit. Dad is the one who encouraged me to send something."

Her face falls, and I feel a twinge of regret go through me. I don't want to hurt her, but I do want to make it clear my father is the only reason I sent her that gift and every other one she's received from me over the last four years.

"Oh. I didn't know that." Her eyes are glassy as she averts her gaze to my father, who's just started paying attention to the conversation. "Thank you, Reese."

Dad waves his hand, a friendly smile on his lips that doesn't match the rage in his eyes at all. "It's no problem, sweetheart. You deserve all the best things. Christopher just needs a little reminder every now and again to give them to you."

I take a sip of water and place my glass back on the table with a little too much force. "I think you've got me confused with RJ."

"Now, son—" Oscar starts, but he's interrupted by the sound of Giselle's chair sliding across the floor as she pushes back from the table. We all turn to look, watching her move between the other tables on her way to the exit. Ramona starts to stand but begins to sway almost instantly. Oscar places a steadying hand on her waist to make sure she doesn't fall as she lowers herself back into her chair. Dad glares at me, his eyes commanding me to go after Giselle.

With a frustrated sigh, I push back from the table and head in the direction that I saw her go. As I search for her, I have to work hard to shut down the part of my brain that notices chasing Giselle holds none of the same power or allure as chasing Mallory.

I finally find her pacing outside the women's bathroom. Her long legs making her heels glide smoothly over the carpet, the hem of her dress swishing around her knees, her features scrunched together tightly in a mix of frustration and embarrassment I don't understand.

When she sees me approaching, her shoulders sink in defeat, and tears well in her eyes. "Reese told me you wouldn't find out about me and RJ. I swear nothing happened, Chris. I was just lonely and he was there."

My eyebrows knit together. I don't know why she thinks I would care if something happened with her and my brother. I mean, at first, I did care, but that was about me and RJ not about me and her.

"Gi, it's fine. You know I'm in a relationship, right? You saw Mallory at Margaret's funeral? What you do with RJ is none of my business."

She stops pacing. "But your dad said that you and Mallory were done."

"He said what?" Rage turns my vision red, and I have to force myself to calm down even though none of this makes sense. Less than an hour ago, Dad was standing in the middle of my living room talking to Mallory. He knows we're not done, so why would he tell Giselle we are? "When did he say that to you?"

"A while ago. That's why I was surprised when you brought her to the funeral."

I shake my head, an incredulous laugh leaving my lips. "Unbelievable."

Giselle walks over to me and grabs my hands. "Chris, he just wants what's best for you."

I pull away, taking a few steps back to put some distance between me and the wild, desperate look in her eyes. "Mallory is what's best for me."

"Is she though?" She tilts her head to the side.

Staying calm is becoming one of those impossible things. As hard to do as licking your own elbow or touching your nose with your tongue. Giselle didn't even speak to Mallory at the funeral, so her questioning whether or not she's good for me is laughable. Infuriating.

"Yes, she is. Why do I even have to explain this to you? You'll be just as trapped as I am if our parents actually get what they want. You should be working just as hard, if not harder, for your right to make your own choices."

She stares at me, an icy kind of determination hardening her eyes. "I made my choice a long time ago, Chris, and I thought you'd made yours too. We were supposed to go to college together, have the fairy tale romance you're supposedly having with Mallory. Everything you're giving her is what you were supposed to give me."

I feel like I've stepped into The Twilight Zone. Giselle and I haven't been together in four years, and I never promised her anything. I mean, we both thought we were in love. We even said the words, uttered them to each other when I took her virginity on prom night, but what we had isn't anything like what I have with Mallory. I don't see how she could think it is, how she could still be holding on to feelings from a lifetime ago.

"You can't be serious right now." I run a hand over my head, fighting the urge to walk away from her and this entire evening to go back to Mallory. "It's been four years, Giselle. I'm with someone else. *You're* with someone else."

"I'm not with him!" Up until now, she's spoken calmly, using that sweet, pleasant voice that reminds me why my dad wants me to be with her. I'm surprised that bringing up RJ could make her break form even for a second. She clears her throat, smoothing her palms over the fabric of her dress. "Look, Chris, I don't want this to keep coming up because whether you like it or not, our futures are intertwined. RJ and I spent time together, yes, but it was no more serious than whatever you have going on with Mallory. I'm willing to look past it, so we can build a life together. You loved me once, I know you can love me again."

I run a hand over my head, wondering where the hell all of this is coming from even though I already know the answer: my father. While I've been in New Haven trying to carve out a life for myself, he's been in Boston cultivating a reality everyone around him, including Giselle, has bought into.

"Giselle, I need you to listen to me, okay? I love Mallory. I'm *in love* with her, and I don't think there will ever be a day in my life that I don't love her, so you and me?" I gesture between us, hoping that the intensity of her gaze on me means she's following along. "We're not happening. Ever. I'm sorry I broke things off so suddenly, maybe you didn't get the closure you needed in order to move on, and that's my fault. But you have got to understand, no matter what my dad says, I'm not marrying you."

"*Christopher.*" I turn to see the puppet master himself walking up behind me. He's furious, his booming voice echoing through the hall. "You're out of line. Apologize to Giselle immediately."

I spin on him, years of anger and frustration layered into the movement. "I'm out of line? What about you, Dad? You said you wanted to come to some sort of resolution that worked for both of us, but here you are doing the same old thing. Lying and scheming to get your way. I already told you I'm done, but you just won't stop. What the fuck is wrong with you?"

He isn't the least bit phased, looking past me to Giselle. I guess the emotional compartmentalization skills he's honed over the course of his career as a surgeon has finally found a place in his personal life.

Or maybe it's always been there.

That's probably why it was so easy for him to treat Mom the way he did throughout their marriage. I've been reading her journals every night since the funeral and found multiple passages where she called him cold and distant. She also talked about how his emotional neglect led to the affair with Margaret, which started after I was born, and how he pushed her to get pregnant with me after she started talking about going back to school.

My mother wanted to be a doctor, and judging by the way Grandpa Joe talked about her academic performance, she would have been a great one. Maybe even better than Dad. She wanted to have a life outside of the gilded cage he'd built for her, and when she tried, he shut it all down. Forced her to have another baby when she only ever wanted one.

RJ was supposed to be an only child. That fact had thrown me at first, but when I sat down to think about the eight-year gap between us it made sense.

She wanted more. A big, beautiful life where she was more than a mother, than a vessel for the next generation of Johnsons to pass through. He punished her for that, and in the end—with a final pregnancy that wasn't planned or wanted after a series of miscarriages—it killed her.

He killed her.

I didn't want to believe it. I hadn't even talked to Mallory about it, but it was the truth. An ugly, tragic fate that I don't want to be tied to. And no matter how hard she fights for it, I won't rope Giselle into it either.

"Giselle, sweetheart." Dad places his hand on her shoulder, giving her a comforting pat. "Why don't you go find your parents? I've already taken care of the bill and ordered a car to take you all back to the hotel."

"Okay." She smiles weakly at him and glances at me as she walks by. "Goodnight, Chris."

"Goodbye, Giselle."

Dad waits until she's gone to turn to me. "Have you lost your damn mind, son?"

"No, it seems I'm the only person around here who's using their brain. I can't believe I wasted my entire evening on this bullshit dinner. I'm going home."

I start to move past him, but he stops me with a firm hand on my shoulder that I shrug off immediately. "You're not going anywhere until we talk."

"We've had all night to talk, Dad. You haven't said a single thing I'm interested in hearing."

"That's because the things I have to say to you can't be discussed in mixed company."

I roll my eyes at his ominous tone, but when he starts to make his way towards the bank of elevators at the end of the hall, I follow him. I want to know what exactly he has to say, so we can be done once and for all.

We ride in silence all the way up to the presidential suite, and when we get inside I take a seat while he heads over to the bar to pour a drink.

"You know, Chris, I've always thought you were the most like me. You're smart, driven, incredibly protective of the things that matter to you."

Ice cubes clink inside the crystal tumbler in his hand, swirling around in amber liquid the color of Mallory's eyes, but my eyes are on the laptop in his other hand with a small, blue box balanced on top of it. He sees me staring, a silent question in my gaze that he doesn't answer as he settles in the chair across from me.

"You're right, Dad. I am protective of the things that matter to me, and Mallory matters to me more than anything in this world. I thought you understood that. I thought you'd accepted it."

There's a thread of desperation weaving through my words, and it takes me back to the day when he told me I couldn't play with Jonah anymore. I sit up straighter and roll my shoulders back, so he knows I'm not a little kid begging for his approval. Maybe if he believes it, I will too.

"Giselle said you told her weeks ago that Mallory and I broke up. Why would you say that if you had just found out about us, if you had just told me you wanted what's best for me?"

If you knew my happiness is tied up in her.

He takes a sip of his drink, tongue kissing his teeth on a slick laugh. "I do want what's best for you son, and for a while there you had me thinking that she was it. I was prepared to let it ride, especially with Giselle and RJ getting close. He wasn't the son I envisioned bringing the two families together, but I was going to make do. Let you keep this life you're so desperate to have."

Every time he speaks in the past tense, my heart beats a little harder. Each thump cracks my ribs, knocking another shard loose until they're hanging precariously over the most important part of my anatomy. Hearing that Mallory and I's plan worked, that we had successfully convinced him to release the reigns, sends me floating up into the clouds. My ascent is marked with joy and love for the incredible woman who is more mine now than she was when Dad bought the act.

But I know, based on his expression and his tone, that the feeling will be short-lived. That whatever he says next will send me plummeting into the pits of hell, his words hot on my heels, ready to plunge the knife into my heart.

"What made you change your mind?"

His brows lift and an undeniably giddy expression takes over his face as he sets his drink down and finally reaches for the computer. My mind spins as I watch him work to pull up whatever it is he wants to show me. In the span of a second, I consider a million different things he could have on that computer, and yet, I'm not at all prepared when he spins it around and sets it on the table between us with the video already starting.

I lean forward, eyes squinting as I try to make sense of the fuzzy details in front of me. It looks like a college dorm, but not one I've seen before. There are clothes scattered all over the floor, food wrappers, and what looks like a box of condoms on a desk that's being used as a wardrobe. Confused, I look up at him. "What is this?"

He sits back, the same malicious smile that's been haunting my dreams since Boston stretching his lips. "Keep watching."

The video keeps going, and my confusion remains until the door to the dorm opens and a couple stumbles inside. They're kissing, just outside the frame, which makes it hard to make out any of their features. Then she steps back, walks over to the bed, and sits down, and I know her.

I recognize the features of the woman I love in the young girl sitting on the bed, looking uncertain and scared as she gazes up at the man standing before her.

Trent Davis.

A paralyzing, sickening chill creeps down my spine. It makes it impossible for me to move a single muscle, to even take my eyes off of the screen as he starts to remove her clothes.

"Turn it off."

I can't watch this. I can't violate Mallory this way, can't watch her be hurt by that fucking monster who recorded what he did to her. There's no way she knows about the video. She would have mentioned it to me if she did, and I would have destroyed it. I would have wiped it and Trent from the face of the fucking planet.

My father doesn't move. He just sits there with a sick smile on his face as he breathes in my agony. Then the room is filled with the sound of Mallory's moans because the video is now at the only part of the night she consented to.

He lifts his brows, feigning intrigue. "Sounds like she's having a good time."

I snap, picking the laptop up by the screen and flipping it over to snap it over my knee. The back doesn't disconnect from the front completely, but the video stops playing and that's all I care about. The only thing I register before I launch myself across the table and haul my own father up to his feet by his collar, shoving him into the wall behind him.

"WHAT THE FUCK IS WRONG WITH YOU?"

Shock, and a healthy amount of fear which he tries to hide, takes over his features for a second, but he recovers quickly. I watch him push up from the wall, let him get his bearings, and then swing on him. A full-blown punch that connects with his jaw and makes his head snap to the other side. He stumbles, and I follow him. Throwing one more blow and then another until he's on the ground, laughing like a madman with blood trickling down his lip.

He doesn't deserve mercy, from me or anyone, but I still stop because I have no interest in going to jail for beating him to death.

Though the thought does sound appealing. I take a step back, giving him a wide berth while he picks himself up off the floor.

"You're sick, you know that?" I lace my fingers together and plant them on top of my head just to keep myself from hitting him again. "Why would you show that to me? How did you even get it?"

Triumph blooms in his eyes as he wipes his lip with the handkerchief in his jacket pocket. "*You* told me where to look. You've always been good at that, telling me where all the bodies are."

I'm nauseous, keeping down what little food I ate at dinner feels like a challenge I'm not going to be able to complete. "What are you talking about?"

He walks back to his chair and plops down in it like I won't yank him out of it again. "You called and asked me to look into that young man on the tape. I had one of the private investigators I keep on staff look into him. He's good. One of the best investigators I know, and every time I have him investigate someone, I give him a blank check. Do you know why, Chris?"

"Get on with the story. I'm not playing Q and A with you today." But I will be playing it with the New Haven police department if I don't get out of here soon because the longer I look at him, holding the expensive crystal tumbler to his busted lip, the more murderous I feel.

"I give him a blank check because I don't want him wasting precious time calling me to get permission to utilize his various skill sets, most of which are not above board."

"Color me surprised," I deadpan. "A man who finds and distributes a tape of a woman being raped clearly isn't operating within the parameters of the law."

"If you wanted to be concerned with legality, you would have went to the police. Not me."

There go those shards.

Splintering away from my ribs and free falling from the sky right into my heart. Even though I hate him right now—and I do hate him, more than I've ever hated anyone in my life—I can't deny that he's right. I brought Trent to his attention knowing there was a chance he could discover his connection to Mallory. I didn't think it would turn out like this though, with my attempt to protect her exposing her truths to people who would exploit them to hurt me.

To ruin us.

I scrub my hand down my face, thankful none of my knuckles are bruised. "So what now, Reese?" He flinches when I call him by his given name, and I take an infinitesimal amount of joy in that. "Is this the part where you tell me what happened on that tape is proof she's not worthy of me? That she doesn't deserve to be a part of this fucked up family you're so hell-bent on continuing? You think that what happened on that recording says something about who she is, but you keeping it and sharing it with me as a way to finally break us up says more about you than it ever will about her."

There's nothing remotely human about him as he listens to me speak. No emotion. No indication that he knows or cares what I'm saying, which is fine because I'm about to be done talking. I'm about to be done with everything that has to do with him and this wretched family.

"I'm done, Reese. Do you hear me? Don't you ever contact me again. Don't you ever show your face in this city. Don't you ever come near the woman I love, because if you do I swear to God, there won't be enough doctors in all of the hospitals you own to save you."

Saying it in Boston had felt good, but it was a little bittersweet because there was a part of me that still loved him. That still cherished him as the man who raised me, but that part of me is dead now. Poisoned by the knowledge that that man never actually existed.

He was always a monster masquerading as a human, and that's all he'll ever be.

I feel the intense heat of his gaze boring into my back as I turn to head towards the door, to finally put him behind me. I don't need his approval or permission to live how I want to live, to love who I want to love.

"Is that what her family and friends will think?"

The words stop me dead in my tracks. My guts turn to ice that spreads out to my limbs. Still, I manage to turn around and look at him, to make sure I heard him right. That I read the intent behind his words correctly.

The deathly serious stare that greets me tells me that I have.

"When they see the video, I mean. Do you think Eric, Annette, Dominic, and Sloane will ever look at her the same? Or will they wonder the same things I did? Why didn't she say no? If it was rape, why didn't she go to the police? Why did she lay there in his arms for hours if she didn't want it?"

I shake my head. My heart, my very soul, shattering into fragmented pieces as his words reflect the same doubts Mallory voiced to me. The same reasons she never came forward, the same reasons she blamed herself for what Trent did.

"They wouldn't ask any of those questions." I know her family. *Our family.* They love her, and they'd sooner die than turn one of the most traumatic things she's ever gone through into an interrogation.

"You can't be sure though, can you? If this recording happens to find its way onto the internet with her name and address in the caption, you wouldn't be able to guarantee that it wouldn't have detrimental effects on her health and well-being."

I'm drowning without water, gasping for air my lungs continue to reject. I don't know what would happen if that video found its way online, but I know that I won't risk finding out. "You would really release a tape like that? You would leak footage of a minor being raped just to…"

I can't even say it, can't even fathom a world where this is my reality. Where my love for a person is being twisted, turned against me for the sole purpose of forcing me to make a choice between two impossible options.

Stay and let Mallory be destroyed by the video.

Leave her, and destroy myself in the process.

"I wouldn't what, Christopher? Go to extraordinary lengths to protect my son? Do everything in my power to keep him from making the biggest mistake of his life? I think we both know, I would. I think the only question to answer now is: are you going to make me?"

My answer is immediate and painful, like the onset of a migraine you could have avoided if only you'd heeded the warning signs.

"No."

"Good choice, son." He slides to the edge of his seat and smiles as he picks up the small, blue box he brought over with the laptop. I watch him crack it open and place it on the table again, turning it around, so I can see what's inside. "Now, sit down, so we can finally talk about the future of our family."

42

MALLORY

The necklace Chris gave me is nowhere to be found. I guess somewhere in between packing up my dorm, taking some of my larger things back home to Mama's, and putting together a quick bag to spend the night at his place, it must have gotten lost. Not knowing where it is makes me unreasonably emotional, exacerbating the strong sense of foreboding that's been with me since Reese showed up a few days ago.

I feel like I've barely seen Chris since his dad's been in New Haven, and when I do see him, he's not himself. He's always in his head, worrying about things he won't talk to me about. I can't help but think the distance between us is about Trent. I told him about his arrest and the charges as soon as he came back from dinner that night. That's when I noticed the shift in his mood, but no matter how hard I push, he won't open up.

I've tried to put it out of my head. To chalk up his odd behavior to the stress of having his father in town. I know I wouldn't be acting like myself if my shitty father invaded the city that's been my safe place for the last four years. And I'd be even more bent out of shape if he brought along my ex-girlfriend and her parents and left my siblings at home, preventing them from sharing in the day he says is meant to be spent with family.

That was the line he spun to Chris in order to get him to agree to spend the hours following his graduation with him and the DuPonts instead of with me. I wasn't hurt about being excluded by his father. The last thing I wanted was to spend time with that horrible man, but it did kind of sting that Chris went along with it so easily.

When I talked to Sloane about it, she said that he might have just been trying to spare me the headache of being around those people for an extended amount of time. Apparently, she does the same thing with Eric when it comes to her mother. I let her words comfort me even though deep down I feel like there's more to it.

Behind me, I hear the snap of a phone's camera. I turn around to see where the sound came from and find Chris leaning against the door jamb with his phone in his hand and shadows in his eyes.

"Hey," I say, breathless. Not because he caught me off guard, but because that's what the sight of him does to me. I hope looking at him always takes my breath away. "What are you doing?"

"Taking a picture of you."

"I figured as much." I walk over to him with a small smile on my face. He's been doing that a lot over the last few days, snapping random photos of me when he thinks I'm not looking. "Can I see?"

He hesitates for just a moment before placing the phone in my outstretched palm. I can feel his eyes on me as I look at the screen, his gaze a hot and heavy weight I can feel in my bones, sparking a longing inside of me. We haven't had sex since the morning before his dad showed up, and I'm desperate for him. For the physical connection we share to reinforce the emotional bond I feel slipping between my fingers.

The picture he just took is beautiful. Early evening sunlight streams through the windows behind me, bathing the side of my body in warm golden hues that highlight my curves. My face is calm—serene, even —not showing a hint of the turmoil happening inside of me. But all thoughts of it fade into the background when I see the title of the album he moved the picture to.

"Just for me?" I look up at him then back down at the phone, scrolling through what has to be a hundred or so photos. Random, candid photos of me studying, reading, sleeping, some that go as far back as March when nothing about us was real except for our feelings. "What is this?"

He plucks the phone from my hand and stashes it in his pocket. "It's you."

I laugh, but even as the sound of my amusement fills the air, tension begins to line Chris' shoulders. I close the space between us with one step and wrap my arms around his neck.

"I mean, I know that. Some of these are from before Disney though, back when our agreement was to post all the pictures we took of each other. There were so many good ones in there of me."

A vein in his temple jumps, but his eyes are soft when they meet mine. "I know, that's why I kept them for myself. All of my favorite photos of you are in that album." He places his hands on my waist. "The first picture that went in there is one I took of you in the cafeteria. You were laughing with Sloane about something, and the joy on your face stopped me dead in my tracks. We weren't even a thing then, but I knew I had to capture that moment. Freeze it in time. And I'm glad I did because now I can always remember you like that. "

"Remember me?" My brows fall together. "Baby, I'm right here, and I'm not going anywhere. You can see me smile whenever you like."

He stares at me for a moment, several different emotions flitting across his face before he gives my waist a squeeze and pulls back. "Right."

"Chris—"

I don't know what I'm going to say, but I don't get the chance to figure it out because his phone starts to ring. He pulls it out of his pocket, glances at the screen, and sighs as he brings it up to his ear.

"I've gotta take this."

And then he's gone, leaving me to finish getting dressed with a ball of dread weighing me down. It stays there, lodged inside my gut like a bullet, for the rest of the day. It's the only companion I have as I watch

Chris walk across the stage and receive his degree, surrounded by strangers because sitting alone was preferable to sitting with Reese and the DuPonts.

I would have thought the ball would have loosened once Chris and I got in his car and made the drive over to Mama's, but it doesn't. In fact, it felt like it was growing. Feeding off of the tense quiet in the car and the unfounded panic blooming in my chest.

By the time Chris parks on the road in front of my house, it's dark out and I'm ready to burst. I want to know what's going on with him, with us, and if it has anything to do with Trent. I don't even want to consider that, but it wouldn't be the first time Chris got in his head and let what happened come between us. I'm not exactly sure why the arrest would spook him, especially since my name was never mentioned and the charges are in another state, but I just have to be sure.

"Are you ever going to tell me what's going on with you?" I bite my lip to fight back the anxious tears that want to be set free now that the question is out there. We've been tiptoeing around this for days, but it's just now hitting me how much of a toll the wall he's erected between us with his silence has taken on me.

"Nothing is going on with me."

"If you don't want to talk about it, just say that, but don't lie to my face."

"Princess." He shifts in his seat and starts to reach for me but changes his mind at the last second. My heart free falls into my stomach, making a home beside the ball of dread. "I've just got a lot on my mind, okay?"

"Is it Trent?" I ask, unable to look at him. "Did the arrest make what he did to me more real?"

Of course, I still have the emotional scars. I'll always carry them with me, but they don't define me anymore. He knows that better than anyone else.

"What? No." This time he does touch me, and I'm filled with the most dizzying sense of relief as the tips of his fingers slip under my chin and tilt it up, so I'm looking at him. And when he speaks, there's an earnestness to his expression and an urgency to his words that has been painfully absent the last few days. "That's not it at all, princess. I'm glad that fucker is finally getting what's coming to him. People are about to find out exactly what kind of monster he is, and all the shit that's about to come down, is going to land on his head. Not yours. Not the other women he hurt. *His.* Don't you ever forget that."

I lean into his touch, wrapping my hand around his wrist to make sure he doesn't pull back. It feels desperate and maybe if it were anyone else, it would be borderline embarrassing, but it's not anyone. It's Chris. It's the man I love. The man I've trusted with every part of me, including the broken ones. I still don't know what's going on with him right now, but I'm willing to give him the time he needs to figure it out.

"Okay." I turn my head and plant a kiss on the inside of his palm. "I just thought…"

"I know," he says. "I'm sorry there was a single second where you felt that way. But nothing could ever change the way I feel about you, Mallory. You'll always be it for me."

All of my words get stuck in my throat, so I just nod to let him know I heard him. That I understand. He leans in close and gives me a soft, tender kiss on my forehead before letting me go. Then he reaches into the backseat and grabs my overnight bag, handing it to me silently. I take it from him and set it on my lap.

"Do you want to come in?" I shouldn't ask. I know he has to be somewhere, but I'm not ready to let him go just yet. "I'm sure Mama would like to congratulate you in person."

He grips the steering wheel tighter, looking out the window instead of at me. "I would love to, but I have to get going."

"Right." I force a smile and open my door. "Well, I'll see you later."

"Okay, princess."

It's not until two hours later, when I'm laying on my bed staring at the ceiling, that I realize neither of us said 'I love you.' Unbidden tears turn the glow-in-the-dark stickers Mama stuck up there when I was seven into a blurry mess, and I close my eyes against the surge of emotion. Fighting to quiet my instincts that keep screaming at me, telling me that something is wrong.

Mama has always told me to trust my instincts, to lean into those ripples of awareness and explore those thoughts lingering just under the surface of my consciousness. There have only been a handful of times when I haven't listened to her instructions, and every single one turned out disastrously.

Except for the kiss. I remind myself, sitting up and swinging my legs over the edge of the bed. A dangerous idea propelling me towards my closet where I search for a dress that will be suitable for the restaurant I heard Reese mention to Giselle's dad when we were standing outside the gym waiting for Chris to emerge from the sea of happy graduates.

I never heard of the place, but I can only assume that it's nice. The kind of place where the wrong clothes will get you turned away at the door. I'm almost ready to give up when, right at the back of my closet, I find the black cocktail dress Sloane got for me when she wanted me to come to a charity event with her and her mom. I toss it on the bed along with a pair of heels and then turn to the dresser to figure out what to do with my hair.

Mama's eyes stretch wide when I stride down the hallway, tucking my phone into the small black clutch I forgot I had. "Where are you going?"

"To Chris' graduation dinner. Can I drive your car?"

"Of course, baby, but are you sure you want to do that?"

I'm not sure. I'm not sure about anything except that something is wrong, and I need to know what. "Yes, Mama. Where are your keys?"

"They're hanging on the key ring by the door."

"Thank you."

I blow her a kiss and head out the door before I have the chance to change my mind. The drive to the restaurant is a quick one. Not because it's close, but because I sped the whole way. When I pull into the parking lot, I'm questioning all of my decisions, but the doubt doesn't stop me from walking in like I own the place. It doesn't stop me from saying yes to the hostess at the front door when she asks if I'm a part of the private party. Or from walking through the double doors that lead to the room Reese must have rented out for this special occasion.

I walk in like I belong there, expecting one or more of the people to turn and look at me. To ask why I'm there when I'm not family. But as the doors start to close behind me, no one looks at me.

Because they're all staring at Chris.

Watching his slow transition from standing to kneeling.

Kneeling. On one knee with an open ring box in his hands and his eyes on Giselle.

All the air in my lungs leaves me in a sudden, painful woosh. I can't make sense of the image in front of me. Of the smile on Giselle's face as she places her hand in Chris', her slim fingers trembling as he slides the ring on. Even from this distance, I can see it fits perfectly.

That it belongs on her just like RJ said she belongs with him.

The surprisingly large crowd of people in the room erupts into applause as Chris rises, a proud smile on his face as he hugs Giselle. She leans into him, the peaceful look I saw on her face when she hugged him after the funeral reappearing. When the hug ends, she rushes over to her mother and father and they make a show of marveling at a ring I'm sure they've already seen.

Reese moves over to Chris and slaps him on his shoulder, the same proud smile stretching his lips. He's saying something to him, probably telling him how happy he is that he finally decided to come back into the fold.

But Chris isn't listening, because he's looking at me. He mouths my name and something that looks like stop when he sees me backing away. I don't listen. I can't stay here, can't see him or talk to him after he's just undone everything we worked for. Broken every promise he made me. Unsealed every wound he helped heal.

In mere seconds, I'm back where I started, standing outside the restaurant where everything is untouched, but I am completely undone.

Unraveled by the same hands that claimed to want to put me back together.

"Mallory, wait!" I keep moving, half-walking, half-running to Mama's car. If I can just get there, if I can make it to the safety of the car then I won't have to face him. I won't have to face this. *"Please."*

I don't owe him anything, but the plea in his voice turns my feet into cement blocks. Chris' pants fill my ears as he rounds me, placing himself between me and the only way I have out of this storm he's created. He leaves a small bit of space between us, and those few feet feel like they say everything about the difference a few hours has made in our relationship, in my life. I can't stand it, can't stand him giving me distance I don't want, distance he doesn't deserve to have from the pain he's caused me, so I close it.

His scent hits me first. The familiar notes of leather and earth now tainted with her perfume, with the scent of a future that he'll have without me. I shove him in the chest with both of my hands. He barely budges, so I do it again.

And again.

"You asked her to marry you?" Tears stream down my face as I scream at him and beat at his chest, trying to create a hole beneath his sternum that matches the crater under mine. "Why would you do that? Why would you do that to us? To me?"

My voice cracks, all of my emotions spilling out of the split sylla-bles, and Chris is calm. Stoic, even. The way he said I was when we had our first kiss. The thought sets a fresh wave of tears free, and I step away from him because touching him—even in the most violent sense of the word—hurts.

"Breathe, Mallory." He adjusts his shirt, smoothing out the wrin-kles I caused while his eyes bounce between the restaurant and me. He's probably anxious to wrap up this little scene, to get back to his fiancé.

"Don't tell me to breathe. Answer my fucking question! Explain to me how this is happening right now when just hours ago you were telling me that I was it for you."

"You weren't supposed to be here." Finally, there's some flicker of emotion. It's brief, a small rearranging of the muscles in his face that lasts for half a second. "You weren't supposed to find out like that. I was going to explain—"

"That you're marrying her." The words leap off of my tongue. "That everything we did, *everything that brought us together*, was a waste of time, and even when you said it was real, it wasn't. Is that what you were going to explain to me? Well, you can keep your explanation because I don't want it."

The same tension I've been watching knot his muscles for days lines his shoulders as he shakes his head at me. "You wouldn't understand. You don't have any idea what it's like to have the future of an entire family dependent on you."

I want to scream, to throw something, to hit him again. Instead, I cross my arms over my chest, let my fingernails dig into the flesh, and glare at him. "Don't do that. Don't make this about some Johnson legacy bullshit. Your father has another son who's more than capable of getting married and fathering a new generation of Johnsons. Hell, he could probably do that with your new fiancé." A twinge of sadness goes through me when I say that word, but I push through it. "My point is, it doesn't have to be you, Chris. You spent the last couple of months telling me you didn't want it to be you."

His jaw clenches at the mention of his brother, and his nostrils flare with anger and something else I can't name as he lets out a humorless laugh. "RJ doesn't even know how to be a good brother. No one is going to trust him to be the head of this family when my dad is gone."

My jaw drops as I listen to him disparage his brother for the first time, and suddenly I know exactly what that unnamed expression was. The defiant way he lifts his chin confirms it. Ruthless ambition. I've never seen it on him before, but somehow it fits him better than everything else.

Better than his goofy smile.

Better than his soft and serious eyes.

Better than his heated gaze and earnest tone when he said he loved me.

The realization trickles through me, and I force myself to accept it.

To take note of his designer suit, rigid posture, and the air of sophistication swirling around him and let them serve as confirmation of a truth I'd hope would be impossible.

His brother and his father were right about him. They tried to tell me, to warn me that he was a product of their world and would come back to it. That nothing, but especially not me, would be enough to keep him from giving in to his urge to win. I don't know what flipped the switch, what made him go from denouncing the entire family to literally bending the knee, but I guess now it doesn't matter.

"So that's what this is about? You beating your brother?"

Chris shakes his head, disagreeing with my assessment, but every other part of his body screams yes. "You wouldn't understand, Mallory."

"You're right. I don't understand. I will never understand you making me fall in love with you, making me trust you, only for you to change your mind the second it looked like your brother might outrank you in the family hierarchy." I move around him to the driver's side door, intent on getting the hell out of here as soon as I finish saying what I need to say.

"I must have been fucking blind because not until this very moment did I realize this entire thing has been about being better than RJ. You just couldn't let him win. Even when you had me and a clear path to the life you claim to want for yourself, you just couldn't resist a chance to best him. To punish him for daring to pick up the toy you left on the shelf for four years while you were here faking defiance and playing at being human."

Chris is silent. His hands now tucked into his pockets as he watches me open the door. I never thought it would end this way for us. That he would be silent, emotionless as he watched me walk out of his life.

But then again, I never thought I would be walking out of his life.

I drop down into the driver's seat, and my hands shake as I start the engine. Chris finally moves. The sound of his footsteps echoing on the pavement as he walks over to the car and places his hand on the door. I glance up at him, hoping, praying, wishing he'll do or say something to change this.

"I'm sorry."

I turn away from him. My neck moving so suddenly it feels like I've been slapped. In a way, I guess I have. He waits, listening as I take unsteady breaths to hold in the sob dragging itself up my throat. Finally, when I can speak without my voice breaking, I turn back to him.

"You don't love her."

One tear escapes, turning me into a rain cloud, heavy and burdened with unspent grief. Chris watches it fall, whispering his reply.

"No. I only love you."

It should be comforting, but it makes it worse. It makes it so much worse because what he's saying is that our love doesn't matter. That it's not enough to keep him here, to make him give up the life he was born to have.

I start to reach for the door, to close him out, but he shuts it for me. We stare at each other through the glass, and I count the seconds in my head. I make it to ten before he taps the roof of the car and turns to walk away.

Ten seconds. That's how long he gives me before he moves on with his life, walking back to his future while I remain firmly in his past.

Once upon a time, I said the worst decisions I've ever made were sealed with a kiss, but I was wrong, it was sealed with a handshake. With a warm palm pressed against a clammy one. With words we pretended meant nothing when they meant everything. With an agreement entered into under false pretenses and with half truths.

I think I loved Chris then, even though I didn't know it or was too scared to admit it. But I'm admitting it now, to myself, when it's too late because the curtains have closed on this show. The lights are going down, and it's my last moment of playing this role. This version of me. It'll be written in the history books, etched into the stone of the grave marker above my heart, as my best role.

And only now, as I'm watching the curtains close around my lover while he takes his last bow, do I realize it's because I was never acting in the first place. It was all real for me. Every second of it. But for him it was all just a show.

An act.

And he's left me to pick up the pieces, to scoop the roses off the stage and snuff out the hope stored in their velvet petals with the heavy pages of the book that contains the story of us.

A tragedy.

Masquerading as a romance.

TOGETHER WITH THEIR FAMILIES

you are invited to

the wedding of

MS. GISELLE A. DUPONT

and

DR. CHRISTOPHER R. JOHNSON

SATURDAY 1ST AUGUST 2015

at two o'clock in the afternoon

BOSTON CITY CLUB
201A LAKESHORE BLVD. BOSTON

reception to follow

FOR MORE DETAILS VISIT

www.jlseegars.com

PART TWO: THE AFFAIR

The day he decided to kill me, I already knew what it was like to die. I had already experienced it once. Having the life leeched from my body, blood stolen from my veins, oxygen pulled from my lungs.

When he decided to walk back into my life, I was in the middle of my third resurrection, healing from the loss of my brother when I was still raw from losing him. It wasn't going well.

I guess the human heart can only stop so many times, can only take so much damage before it questions whether it's worth it to be revived.

Mal and Chris' story continues
November 2022

THE NEW HAVEN SERIES

ABOUT THE AUTHOR

J.L. Seegars is a dedicated smut peddler and lifelong nerd who's always had a love of words, storytelling and drama. When she isn't writing messy and emotionally complex characters like the ones she grew up around, she's watching reality TV, supporting her fellow authors by devouring their work or spending time with her husband and son.

ALSO BY J.L. SEEGARS

Restore Me: The New Haven Series (Book #1)

Again: A Marriage Redemption Novella

Revive Me Part Two: The New Haven Series (Book#2)

Printed in Great Britain
by Amazon

27829045R00242